THROUGH THY BEDROOM WINDOW
VOLUME ONE

Ferin Mezze

Through Thy Bedroom Window
Volume One

First published in Australia by FMBG-IPA Holdings Pty Ltd 2025

Copyright FMBG-IPA Holdings Pty Ltd © 2025
All Rights Reserved

 A catalogue record for this book is available from the National Library of Australia

ISBN: 978-1-7640313-0-1 (pbk)
ISBN: 978-1-7640313-1-8 (ebk)

Original cover artwork, *Boy at the Window*, by Richard Washbourn ©
Cover design by Stuart Flynn (Sunshine Design) 2025

Typesetting and design by Publicious Book Publishing
Published in collaboration with Publicious Book Publishing
www.publicious.com.au

Disclaimer: The actual persona of Chief Little Raven, General Rosecrans and Ulysses S. Grant, who have been long deceased, are characters portrayed as themselves in an alternative, fictional reality of which, trained eyes can see. Any other characters' resemblances to real persons, living or dead, or any events past or present are purely coincidental."

List of Twenty Four Titles in the Series

Contents

Contents

Foreword

Roughly around the age of fifteen or so, unable to sleep, I would lie awake some nights, gazing up at the ceiling and imagining intense battles against and between beings from other worlds. These battles took place in the skies above my house, my hometown, and a massive sporting arena. Instead of small, slow fighter craft, I envisioned the use of highly advanced battle suits. Man… they move fast.

Did you do something similar? Because during the mid-eighties, all the big sci-fi movies of the day conditioned us to the idea that yes, they were really out there. The Hubble Telescope took pictures of galaxies beyond count. The US government built underground facilities to hide 'those' secrets. Comparative religion had nothing to say about this burgeoning curiosity. We wanted to know more, and we could've handled the truth! Today, finding and meeting an intelligent extraterrestrial life form seems like an inevitable conclusion.

It may very well turn out that… they are already here. So many whistle-blowers now-a-days!

The first conceptual seeds of this project began to germinate midway through university. The ideas continued to flow, and inspiration came from every source: dreams, movies, television shows, books, and even those 'alternative' magazines with articles that seemed beyond belief. And yes, university proved challenging and soon became a struggle. Around the age of twenty-two I lost faith… in everything.

Both orthodox religion and classic physics appeared to be broken, where many things seem to be missing… incomplete. Disillusioned, dissatisfied, I cleared the slate and began a search for just one thing I could recognise as an absolute truth. And then, the nineties happened, which transformed my view of the world.

Interestingly, with the onset of the internet very little now remains concealed. Knowledge that was once hidden, or regarded as forbidden, has become freely available for all. And today, quantum physics is revealing a reality interwoven with layers of fields or waves, of consciousness and energy. It would seem the paradigms are shifting.

By the time I finally graduated in 2000, the entire structure of this project had formed. It would consist of twenty-four novelettes, each around 20,000 words, followed by a novel split into two halves due to its expected size. Each story is unique and independent in its setting, subject, and location. Many stories provide a piece of theology, connecting through similar themes and contributing to a greater reality. Twenty stories present the genesis of characters who will appear in the forthcoming novel. Collectively, these stories will lay the foundation for the novel, in which no further background will be provided.

In July 2018, all things told me that it was time. I was ready. It was now or never. I resigned my position and began to write. It would take five and a half years to complete the first draft of all twenty-four stories. Initially, the words flowed easily, but writing soon became arduous, akin to pulling string out through one ear. The easiest story literally wrote itself in two weeks, the most difficult, was a mental triathlon of four months. I needed to write all twenty-four stories first, to achieve continuity through the material, before returning to start to embark on the editing process.

The next step was finding a pathway to publication. Self-publishing seemed the road of least resistance, considering the structure of this series doesn't fit neatly into the conventional commercial format. I would like to thank Richard, who painted the cover art in oils, Laura's photography, Stuart who retouched the image to complete the illustration and title, Lesley's professional copy editing and Andy, who brought all the elements together to help publish this book. If you look closely, you will notice the texture of the oil painting. In the near future maybe, just maybe, I might be able to entice a traditional publisher to see the vision.

And so, after thirty years from inception and seven years of determined, persistent work, I present to you...

'Through Thy Bedroom Window'

...a work of the imagination. This is one of many meanings which can be bestowed upon the title and illustration, which describes the ability to see through into the beyond with the third eye of one's imagination, especially when we lie awake at night staring up at the ceiling.

So don't delay. Open thy window and delve into a world which combines and fuses spiritual fiction with science fiction, fantasy, action and adventure to produce what I shall describe as, and what I hope you will recognise as... a fourth dimensional experience.

The first edition of this book will be published in UK English, with units of measure determined by the location of each story. Hence, imperial units are used for stories set in the United States of America, and metric units for the rest of the world. There are plans for a second edition in US English, translation and there is also this website:

www.throughthybedroomwindow.com

Even though each story is independent, it is recommended to read them in the chronological order presented. For many stories in volume one, you can track the main character's progress using Google Maps. This can be done for *Lost Soul, Lost City, Resonance of the Bison, Alienation Games*, and *Lightning*. Just plug in the place names to view their locations, which should provide greater depth in context. For *Chickamauga Chill*, you can search for the Battle of Chickamauga on Wikipedia to find maps detailing the battle's three-day progress.

I hope you enjoy the adventure.

Lost Soul, Lost City

Lost Soul, Lost City

Chapter One

Out of the Wilderness

Dropping out of a daydream, Jaxon focuses his vision. Covered with a hood, he bows his head from the glaring sun. He looks down at the bare ground ahead, to watch one dust-crust-covered boot take the lead after the other. His mind had been placed on hold, on mute, whilst walking to a rhythmic beat on autopilot. He tries to recall the daydream and draws a blank. There is nothing but time lost.

The blackouts are a recent phenomenon, a rare skill he seems able to invoke with ease.

He wears well-worn hiking boots, laces loose, baggy green cargo pants which have turned brown from dust, tied in place by an old thin rope and with bulging pockets full of… stuff. He wears a sweat-damp singlet under a T-shirt, under an open flannelette, under a brown, long-sleeved, hooded jacket, ending just above the knee. Nothing has been washed in a month.

Over his left shoulder hangs a large, rope drawn knapsack carrying his gathered rations.

He looks ahead to see a thin dirt track. He turns to see a large farmhouse and barn down the end of a gentle slope to the right, and a forest rising over a ridge to the left.

"Where am I?" he whispers, in a dry, raspy voice.

Somewhat a little dazed, confused, he stops. He turns around slowly in a clockwise motion to look around. He does not recognise anything.

"How did I get here?" he mumbles.

Jaxon glances up at the sun. It is roughly midmorning.

"I can't remember anything since breakfast… three hours ago! Huh… must've spaced out!"

He resumes his slow walk up the thin dirt track.

"What's going on, Jaxon? You've been zoning out quite a bit lately. So bloody annoying! It's the third time this week. Could be a tumour! Might have to find a damn doctor. Wait... if it's a tumour... well, bloody fantastic!" he mutters.

Reaching the summit of a small hill he stops and turns around in the same motion to explore the view. Behind him to the southwest is a beautiful valley of apple farms with neatly measured orchard fields and clusters of homesteads and barns as the eye moves across the landscape from farm to farm. The valley is bordered on the northeast by a national forest, its carpet of trees blanketing a rising slope up onto a rough plateau extending far into the north. The forest and plateau are suddenly cut by a line of cliffs facing out towards the southeast.

Standing atop his lookout at the very low, southern end of this line of cliffs, Jaxon notices a silhouette, glimmering upon the distant horizon to the southeast. He cups his hands around his eyes. In the distance, through the glare of swirling heat, the sun's reflection blinks and shimmers amongst a cluster of tall needles pointing straight into the sky.

"Must be glass. Wow, it's... it's... a city. Massive!" he exclaims.

"No! Not a chance, not a chance I'm going down there," he grunts. "Not a city as big as that! Too many people, too many buildings and too much noise. And all those cars and their disgusting fumes clogging up the air," he snarls.

He drops his hands, looks up at the sky once more and turns on his right heel.

"It's such a beautiful sunny day, why would anyone want to leave the country?" he muses.

He walks down the hill. The path disappears between two orchards. He picks a few apples.

****

The following morning he is walking, blacked out on autopilot with that vacant look on his face. He suddenly comes to, regains composure and focuses his eyes. Ahead he sees a slow rising thin dirt track. He stops dead still.

"Damn, I zoned out again," he grunts. "What the… it's the same dirt track… and hill I saw yesterday. Man, what's happening to me? This is so strange!" he whispers. "Looks as though I didn't walk far enough away from this place."

He trudges once more to the lookout. He cups his hands around his eyes and re-examines the silhouette of the city. It's slow seductive wink reaches out through the waves of heat, beckoning, calling to him.

"Oh, no way. No, not going there. All those people, just too many people. Don't think I can handle being around so many strangers. Might get robbed, beaten or arrested and thrown in jail," he said to no one listening. "Right! I'll keep focused this time. I'll walk away, and keep walking until I am far, far away from this city," he growls.

With renewed determination, he turns, walks down the hill and heads off into the southwest. He keeps his mind firmly focused upon the task. He keeps walking further and further away from the city, until the sun finally sets and darkness creeps over the valley.

****

The following morning, he startles himself awake. Filled with doubt, wide eyed, he looks around in the darkness. The first dim rays of light shine through a small square stained-glass window behind his head. He is lying on his back in the corner of a small barn, having slept on the floor between a wooden rack of old tools and parts, and another filled with an array of mysterious dust-covered bottles, jars and canisters.

"Thank God, I didn't black out," he whispers.

Slowly, he climbs to his feet and stretches the stiffness out of his back and limbs. Having arrived in the middle of the night, he now looks around the barn. He is standing in a small tool and spare parts room. He quietly walks through the open doorway into the main open area of the barn.

It has a gravelled floor, long wooden-panelled walls and a very high angled ceiling, split in two halves and joined along a seam running the middle length of the roof. A modern looking tractor and machinery are neatly parked in a line against the far wall. Looking to the side wall on his right, a set of stairs lead up to a mezzanine level over the top of the tool room behind him, stacked with apple harvesting drums and equipment. His self-doubt quickly returns.

"I... I can't recall finding this place. How... how did I get here?" he mutters.

He squeezes through the large barn doors into a wide open courtyard. It's early. The sun has not yet broken the horizon. He hears some noise coming from the large, two-storey house across the courtyard facing the front of the barn. The kitchen sounds signal breakfast is ready. Jaxon's stomach churns at the thought of breakfast.

With a quick scan of the farm, he spots a chicken coop around the left side of the barn. From a large wooden drum, he grabs a handful of grain. He throws the grain across the floor to quieten the hens inside their coop and poaches a handful of eggs. He finds corn cobs in a storage bin and picks some more apples from a small orchard leading down a gentle slope to a water retaining dam. With fresh supplies in hand, he heads off down towards the dam and up the gentle slope on the opposite side and into the back field. He emerges out of and at the top of the back field and stands midway along a narrow ridge. Right in front of him, there is a thin dirt track leading up a small hill, to a lookout.

"NO WAY!" he exclaims.

Staggering in disbelief to the top of the hill, he slowly turns to look towards the southeast. In the cool dark blue of the pre-dawn, the city lights glare back at him, in their full might and terrifying splendour. He gasps at the sheer magnitude and size of the city. Recognition slowly rises in his mind.

"I think it's... yes... it's... New York City!" he gulps. "Of all the places, this would have to be the worst, by far."

Regaining his composure, he sits down and stares begrudgingly at the light show. He punctures two holes and sucks a raw egg dry. He polishes an apple with a somewhat half clean cloth and takes an oversized bite.

"Grrr... aaargh!" he suddenly growls. "What's going on?" he yells. "Did I black out again, during the night? How? Why? Why am I here? What's with that bloody city?"

He takes a second oversized bite and chews slowly in considered consternation.

"Something's happening when I zone out," he whispers. "Is this a sign? It must be! The hill, the city, three times in three days. Unmistakable! So, yes, most definitely a sign. And a sign with purpose, a message, a signal! Is someone or something calling me to that city? Maybe my 'search' will finally be over," he said and pauses to decide.

"Right! Only one way to find out. Ok... you win!" he yells in resignation. "Let's go have a look, shall we."

Chapter Two

Ooh, New York

Jaxon walks a few yards back along the path and veers off and down the southeast slope of the hill. He searches through the thick scrub on his left flank and finds an old overgrown bike trail. He carefully follows the twisting trail down the steep slope to the base of the hill. He looks up at the high cliffs which are suddenly ablaze by the light of the rising sun.

He stumbles out of the thick scrub and long grass and almost crashes into the six-foot wooden fence of an outer suburban house. He turns right and walks along the fence line of a few houses, until he steps out onto the dead end of a bitumen road. He crosses to the right-hand side, hiding beneath the shadow of a row of small trees and enters the suburb.

With an acute sense of direction, he quickly makes his way through the suburb, always aiming for the city. Along the tree-lined streets, only a very few of the large affluent houses have a light on, either in the bedroom or the kitchen, its resident rising early for the working day ahead. He moves silently from one shadow to the next.

Jaxon soon finds and enters the outer greens of a golf course. The course is empty except for the birds and doves eagerly scouring the perfectly manicured lawns for a worm or bug. The sun is rising fast. He picks up his pace, walking briskly, knowing that soon, there will be people. He walks through the course towards the clubhouse. Several staff cars are parked in the stone gravel car park. He walks out through the main gate as two cars turn in through the entrance, each driver glaring at him with disdain. He reads the large signboard at the entrance, 'Spook Rock Golf Course'.

Following the road away from the golf course, Jaxon soon intersects with a main arterial road. He turns into the arterial road and continues to head east. Before long, he enters the commercial area of a small township. In the centre of town, he discovers a very busy open market. It's a hive of activity, with vendors and buyers all vigorously negotiating their deals. He reads the large sign above the entrance into the main building, 'Spring Valley Market'. Ignoring the stares and strange looks, he decides to treat himself and buys a hot coffee from a vending van. He then skirts around the market and turns to head southward, out of town.

Passing the full-length glass panel of the last commercial shopfront, he notices his reflection and stops. He turns to face and inspect his appearance. Jaxon is quite tall, just short of six feet two inches in height. He has messy, unkempt, shoulder-length, light brown hair, hazel eyes with green and fiery golden flecks and fair, well-tanned skin. His face looks thin, gaunt, leathery and weathered from years of rough sleeping.

A long matted beard hangs from his jaw. His frame is lean, malnourished from an extended meagre diet, which hides what was a strong muscular structure. He does not smell of urine and alcohol like an inner-city rough sleeper, but more of a strong body odour mixed with wood, grass, hay and earthly smells. He is stunned by his appearance.

"Wow, you really look like… crap," he whispers.

He looks down, despondent, no longer able to look at himself any longer. He walks around the side of the building and sits down on the third, top step in front of a locked, steel side door. He sips his coffee and reflects upon his predicament in his mind.

Geez, I've been walking for a very long time now. Let's see! The year is 2025. That makes me… 37 years old. Wow, I feel so tired.

I left my old life about… seven years ago. I couldn't say for sure, where I'm going. I don't have a destination. I can't remember all the places I've been. I just keep walking, wherever my legs will take me.

I did have a life, long ago. Though now, that part of me is so buried, I can hardly remember it. There was comfort, laughter, enjoyment, friends and I knew the road ahead. I was young and all I need do, was to grab it all. I found something, it was my greatest discovery, but then… I lost it. I don't know how it happened, it's all a blur. But now, all I know is that I won't know what I'm searching for until it's found. I yearn for my search to be over.

I try not to think about my old life. Walking helps me forget. I clear my mind of all thoughts and focus just on the road. I'm alone, have been for a long time. I dwell in the long silences of my own mind. I hear the noise of the outside world but in here, the silence is my only comfort. The only thing of purity I know is the silence of my mind.

Haha… they say that's a kind of meditation, a kind of mindlessness, I guess. Well, I'm getting pretty good at it now. But this? This has never happened before, ever! How can I keep ending up at the same place? And why can't I remember?

Jaxon is suddenly overcome with despair. Bowing forward, he clasps both his hands around his head. A tear rolls down his right cheek, etching a path through the dust.

Even in death my failure will pursue me… aaargh… I just can't go on, I can't do this anymore. You know I failed You. Can You ever forgive me? I had everything before me, but what I wanted most of all, was to save my own soul. With this I would've had everything I ever dreamed of. And all I had to do was to make a pact with You, a promise to give You something, a personal sacrifice. Yes, it had to be more difficult than anything I had achieved before. But, this was not about religion, following rules, praying, worshipping in a holy place or anything like that. It was about being in direct contact with my own god. That was the prize. And I almost made it. I was so close. I only had a few months to go… and I broke my promise. I don't know how it happened, it just happened so fast. I always thought I was in control, and then… it was a moment of weakness. I lost it for only a matter of minutes, and then… it was all over… everything, everything was gone… FOREVER!

I was so close… so close. Now, I'll never know what it would've been like, to have kept my promise, to have completed my pact, to have direct contact with You. I can never forgive myself. My life is worthless. I'm too much of a coward to end it myself. Maybe I've just been hoping for someone else to do it for me, and then I'll know for sure if You are really there. And even now in my death, this seems an impossible thing, for me to see You. Maybe You don't exist and this has been the greatest joke of all.

But how can I live a life not knowing if You really do exist? Life is meaningless without that. I cannot accept such a fate. Am I to blindly accept what's written in the scriptures? Even after all that has been written, there's no real proof, and the world doesn't really believe there's a god. Seems something is really wrong here. People walking around without aim, without purpose, giving their lives to the pursuit of self gratification, dominion over others, wealth, power. What a folly it is without You. I need to know! I must know!

He snarls and crushes his empty coffee cup with deep enigmatic frustration.

But where are You? Where can I find You? How can I find You? Aaargh… Don't think about it anymore. Just keep walking… walk… walk…

Jaxon looks up at the sound of a car hooting through the nearby intersection and spots a train station sign. It was time to move. He climbs to his feet and walks down the street. Outside Spring Valley train station, he finds a map. The township is thirty-five miles almost directly north of New York City.

"Wow," he muses. "New York, hey. The last city I would ever want to visit. I wonder who wants me to go to New York City! Well, ok… so where to from here? Mmm… may as well go to the centre, I guess. How about Central Park… and then, let's see what happens."

Jaxon walks into the station. He grabs a note from his hidden money pocket and buys a one-way ticket to Hoboken. He steps into the second carriage of the next train and selects a secluded seat at the back right corner of the carriage. During the one-hour journey to Hoboken, the train fills and becomes more compressed with commuters at each successive stop. The standing commuters closest to him turn their backs to avoid his odour.

Arriving at Hoboken, the station is packed full of rushing commuters. He calmly looks for an escape and finds a way out to the river's edge. He stands against a handrail and looks up at the skyline of New York City across Hudson River. He tries hard not to panic.

Jaxon sees a nearby ferry terminal. He walks into the terminal, buys a ticket and boards the next ferry across the river. He hops off the ferry at Pier 78. He sees a tourist map of Manhattan and quickly plots a path through Hell's Kitchen to Central Park. He walks on.

Tall buildings, people, cars, trucks, noise. His senses are overwhelmed. Every person he passes offers a glance of disgust and disdain and moves to avoid him.

"Am I lost in a maze? Am I just a shadow in time?" he mutters. "I see the people I pass. I see them talk, the things that they do, the lives they lead. Do they not see me? Am I transparent, invisible? Keep moving! Just a passing image, captured only in the moment of a reflection."

Finally, he stands at the southern edge of the small lake in Central Park. He slowly turns in a clockwise motion to view the city skyline in all directions.

"Ok… Jaxon!" he ponders. "A city with a million people and a million places. Where do I go from here?" he mumbles. "No idea! May as well have a rest and wait for a while. Maybe someone will know I'm here."

****

Ambling around the park, a little bemused, he sees a nice lone, shady tree at the top of a gently sloping rise. He walks across the perfectly manicured lawn and sits down, leaning back against the trunk. He opens his knapsack. He drinks deeply from his water canister, finishes a raw egg, eats some bread and cheese bought from the market and chews on an apple, wondering what next. All he can do is wait. He feels fatigued. He rests his head back against the trunk, closes his eyes and slips into a light dose.

Jaxon suddenly raises his head and tilts it a little to the side. He listens, not so much with his ears but with his whole being. He pulls the hoody over his head, gathers his knapsack and stands up. He bows his head and opens his eyes. They are unfocused, blank. He has a stone-faced expression. He has not a single thought, his mind, blank. He senses something, only one thing… the direction he must walk.

He slowly walks to the top end of Central Park. Seeming to appear out of his mind, no one blocks his path. He turns into East 106th Street and walks to the end. He reaches the eastern edge of Manhattan Island facing Harlem River. He turns south and walks across the nearby Wards Island Bridge.

Using the footpaths through the sporting and athletic fields, he skirts around the southern tip of Randalls Island and walks across Hell Gate Bridge. He turns north and walks a few blocks through the narrow parkland that borders the western edge of East River. He stops.

The urge that has a hold of him subsides. He drops out of his blackout. He focuses his eyes and looks up. Standing at the southwestern corner, he sees a massive industrial complex in front of him, with a row of four huge chimney stacks rising into the sky from an immense building.

"Whoa!" he stutters. "What the...? Where am I?" he growls. "Did I just black out again?"

He turns to his left and sees the water's edge of East River just a few feet away. He looks across the river to see the tall buildings of Manhattan. There is a row of square-shaped commercial buildings behind him.

"Huh, still in New York, I see... northeast of Manhattan. Is this the place?" he mutters.

Jaxon walks a little further on, along the road that enters the complex. He sees a security box between an 'in and out' boom gate. He stops and reads the sign at the entrance, 'Con Edison Hydroelectric Power Station'. He sees the site is surrounded by a very high fence topped with barbed wire and several cameras, with one pointing directly at him.

Not wishing to attract any attention, Jaxon steps away from the front entrance. He walks back past a couple of buildings, perplexed. He stops and looks through the gap between two commercial buildings and sees a long row of high-rise residential apartment complexes beyond. Suddenly, he feels himself mysteriously drawn to them. He walks down 21st Avenue and enters the inner-city suburb of Ditmars Steinway, which runs along the southern length of the power station's industrial grounds.

Chapter Three

Enter the Ghetto

Wondering further and deeper into the back streets of Ditmars Steinway, Jaxon suddenly stops. His surroundings have completely changed and are nothing like the suburb through which he has just passed. He looks ahead at the strangeness of the sight before him. He is standing at the western cusp of a square, four-block precinct of old, high-rise, residential 'project' buildings. All the buildings are dark, quiet, graffitied and… abandoned.

This precinct is located at the far northeastern point of Ditmars Steinway and borders the southeastern edge of the power station's industrial park, a dumping ground of old rusting industrial machinery. He has never seen a place like this before. Suddenly, his senses seem heightened, sharper, on edge.

"What's this place?" he whispers. "Strange how quiet it is. It's a… ghetto!"

He senses danger. He feels no fear. He takes a step forward and crosses the invisible line.

He watches carefully. Neither light nor sound emanate from the first row of buildings on both sides. They are empty, derelict. Walking on, the buildings progressively become worse in appearance, showing major structural damage with no doors, gaping holes in walls and collapsed floors. Further on, a couple of buildings having completely collapsed leave nothing but hollow walls. All that remains of these once glorious ten-storey buildings are the one- and two-level high walls, barely able to stand over their foundations.

The street looks like a war zone, filled with burnt-out car shells, trash, rubbish and mounds of broken brick rubble, concrete and twisted steel from the decaying buildings. With such a hazardous barrier, the only way in is to walk. And in its decay, everything is stripped back to the colours of dark grey, brown and black, and the faded deep blues and purples in which many walls and doors were painted.

Standing in the central intersection of the ghetto, he sees the graves of four old concrete residential tower blocks surround him, one on each inner block corner. They look down at him with hollow doors and windows, and moan in agony with the occasional breeze.

There is no movement. The place is completely deserted, devoid of life, of anything living. Not a single sound can be heard, even from the outside city. It is dead still. He looks up at the late afternoon, grey and overcast sky. It does not look like any cloud he has ever seen, and yet resembles a perpetual, hazy smog blanket rolling in from the surrounding city.

"This silence, so strange, so complete," he mumbles.

Bemused, Jaxon turns around to double check that, yes, he is completely alone. No one has followed him. No one has stopped him. There is no sign of name, place or warning. With the growing gloom of dusk, a cold shiver shoots through his spine.

Suddenly, a small bird, a sparrow, flies in high over the top of his head. Following the sparrow with his eyes, he watches it land on the windowsill of a third-floor apartment, in the building behind him. It issues a few sharp tweets, which echo through the hollow floor. The sparrow disappears behind a wall in pursuit of a bug.

A moment later he hears a sharp ruffle, a half-screeched tweet in fright, a flap of feathers and then… silence.

"Oh my God, did something just kill that sparrow? A feral cat!" he exclaims. "And this macabre silence is restored. There's to be no joy here," he whispers. "This place… this place… is infused with the restlessness of death, lying in wait for its next victim. Looks like if you've found your way here… you've come to die. Is that my fate?" he ponders.

Jaxon decides to walk on, in the same direction he was going. The silence becomes even more pervasive, more foreboding. Yet, he finds that he is not bothered by the silence at all, feeling calm, at ease, even soothed by it. He senses eyes… eyes looking at him, watching him. He searches the shadows and cannot see who or where they are, yet knows they are there. He feels the prevailing sense of being hunted by a savage predator.

"Am I the bait, the prey, lured into a trap?" he mutters. "Not knowing if, and when death will strike. Is this the place that hope comes to die? Is this the place that souls, who have lost their way, their will to live, come to perish. Am I a lost soul? Maybe, probably!" he whispers.

He stops, looks up, haunted by his last thought. The shadow of darkness begins to creep across the sky. Suddenly, there is a soft pop, followed by a short, sharp whistle of air.

"Ouch!" he exclaims.

A sharp pain stings the back of his right shoulder. He reaches over with his left hand and pulls out a small dart. He looks at it stunned in disbelief. It has a one-inch needle, attached to a slender silver aluminium cartridge, with a plume of red feathers attached to its base.

"I've been shot with a... tranquiliser!" he exclaims. "Who?"

Jaxon quickly spins towards the direction from which the dart was shot. He stares into the darkness. Nothing, no one, silence. His sight begins to blur, quickly becoming lightheaded, dizzy. He sways and stumbles. He falls, landing heavily along his right side. He pushes himself back onto his knees, struggling to keep his balance. He collapses to the ground. He tries to move, only able to pull himself up against a pile of rubble, rolls onto his back and stares up into the sky. He battles to remain conscious for as long as possible. He finds breathing becoming more and more laboured. He loses focus, his sight now a blur. He senses the darkness closing in around his mind.

A shadow passes across his prone body. It's close, very close.

"Aargh," he sighs. "Death, at last!" he murmurs.

Unable to keep them open any longer, his eyes close, his head falls back, his body sags. Having lost all control, he lets go of his will to live and welcomes death.

I have no fear. At last, it's over. My search is over. I'll soon know for sure. Haha... I'll shout, "Are You there? Come on, show yourself... let me see You. I've been tormented for so long... all I want is to be free. Let me see You... PLEASE... SHOW YOURSELF!" Well, that's it then. All I see is darkness... I'm in darkness... I welcome the darkness... my mind is blank... its over... I have nothing more!

He loses consciousness and passes out.

****

Jaxon feels something. It's a growing sensation, a tickle… a thump… pain.

I think someone is hitting me. Yes, a slap… in the face. There… again!

A strong, sharp pain rips through the dark cloud of his mind, just behind the eyes. His head is pounding not only from the first, then second slap. His head wobbles side to side. He struggles against the atrophy, willing his muscles to respond. He tries to open his eyes and sees a blurred sliver of faint light. Sedated, his eyes fall closed.

Another slap… a little harder… ricochets through his skull.

He is grabbed by his jacket lapels and shaken. He groans, moans and tries to open his eyes. He sees a stronger light and fights to focus his blurred vision. He sees the shadowed, blurred shape of somebody standing over him, holding him up, reviving him.

"Gawd 'at you'?" he groans.

The drug begins to recede. He struggles to regain his senses, to clear the cloud of darkness from his mind, his muscles flimsy, yet to respond. He mumbles something unintelligible, his lips unable to form the words. With all the effort he can muster, he lets out a dull moan.

"Gawd… IS 'AT YOU'?" he asks.

As the cognitive prospect is realised, his heart suddenly leaps forward into action! Adrenaline is shot through his body. In that moment he regains his senses, his muscles obey and with extreme effort, he opens his eyes to see the 'Face of God'.

Eyes wide open, with acute concentration, his vision clears. He stares up at the figure before him. Time stops, for a moment. It seems like an eternity. Then suddenly, a realisation.

"You're, not… GAWD!" he growls.

He is overwhelmed, devastated by the revelation.

"Am I alive?" he mutters. "I'm still alive, aren't I? Still here in the real world. I didn't find death, did I? Argh… nooooo!" he groans.

He allows his eyes to close, his head to drop back and his body to slump.

How can this be? I thought it was over. I thought my torment was over. How can I go on? I can't go on. I won't go on!

"Leave me," he mumbles. "Just leave!"

Jaxon makes a face in a vain attempt to cry. He has nothing… dry… empty.

"Just let me die," he whispers.

Suddenly, he is yanked forcefully to his feet. His legs wobble loosely beneath him. He is held under the left arm by one person, and under the right arm by another. He makes no effort to gain control of his senses, refusing to open his eyes.

They drag him around behind the nearest side wall of one tower, shielding them from the view of the other three. They sit him upon an old oil drum with his back to the wall. He is offered something to drink from a small cup. He waves his feeble hand to refuse. They insist. He puckers his lips and takes one sip of the cough syrup... and then another.

A few long moments pass. The dark cloud in his mind quickly recedes. He can feel his muscles beginning to respond rapidly. He takes a third sip. It takes the antidote two minutes to nullify the effects of the tranquiliser. He rubs the last of the drowsiness from his eyes, face and throbbing head. Under the shadow of the wall above, his eyes focus, he stares at the two figures standing in front of him.

They are perfectly identical. Both are tall, six feet three inches, with pale grey blue skin, and no hair at all. They both wear a thin black turtleneck undershirt, hiding their neck to the jaw, straight cut black pants and black leather belt, over which is worn a black, long-sleeved trench coat to the ankle, buttoned twice above the waist. They both wear soft black leather gloves and black military style leather boots with rubber soles and no laces. They both wear a black, wide-brimmed hat which covers their bald heads and casts a darker shadow over their faces.

Jaxon's heart skips a beat. He gasps, loses his breath and coughs sporadically.

Beneath the brim of their hats, the front half of a thin silver metal disc, similar to a digital audio compact disc, protrudes out from both their foreheads. It is a clean protrusion, a precise line, no surgery, no scar. From the outer edge of the disc hangs seven sets of seven black balls, thread with a special reinforced optic fibre, that covers their entire face to the chin.

Regaining composure, he looks closer to discover that behind the beads, they have no eyes, nose or mouth, no face at all, just a blank, pale grey blue surface. Each bead seems to be made of a glass like material, filled with a thick swirling black liquid, or mist, from which a dull light and a very subtle vibration is emitted from their core. Each bead can generate a different, changeable colour; from red, orange, yellow, green, blue, purple to violet. A layered oval-shaped ripple structure is moulded into both sides of their head, with a small black rubber looking button at its centre, making their ears look like a highly sophisticated, light-frequency-resonance receiving dish.

"Whoa!" he exclaims. "You guys are… robots… androids."

Once he begins to recover from his initial shock, he does not feel fear of the frightful and intimidating appearance of his new companions. He is still alive after all. Now he feels intrigued. He senses their power, his mind wondering at their purpose, composing questions, knowing he is completely at their mercy. He simply waits… for a signal… for instruction.

"Are you the ones who have brought me here?" he asks.

Facing him, they study him, evaluate him. They do not speak. They read his every thought. Suddenly, they take a step back in unison. The one on his right, the lead, raises its right hand and indicates for him to follow. They turn and prepare to move to another location. The sun has begun to set, the shadows grow deeper, darker.

The lead, Jaxon and the second android, in a line, break their cover and walk into the central crossroad. They walk slowly at first and soon quicken their pace around several mounds of rubble, and then turn into and walk down the east-facing street. It is very still, silent. Even though they are taking steps, the two androids appear to glide across the ground.

"Are you the rulers… the lords of this wasteland?" he whispers. "Or do you have a Master?"

Both androids stop in unison. The lead turns and stares at Jaxon, its authority unmistakable. An invisible vibration enters his ears and splashes upon both eardrums. He hears the word 'silence' in a deep, mechanical voice. He slowly issues one nod in understanding. The lead turns, steps forward and walks on. He follows.

They quickly approach the halfway point of the block, move to the left-hand side and stop at the corner of a building. Just in front of them is a narrow laneway, turning left and heading into the centre of the block. They wait against the wall of a building. The dull lights inside the black beads of the lead android appear to be flickering and changing colour more frequently. The lead android seems to be conducting a scan of the area.

While they wait, Jaxon catches a glimpse around the corner into the laneway. Halfway down and on the opposite side of the lane stands a wide, one-and-a-half-storey wall. The floors above have long collapsed leaving a huge mound of debris inside the cavity of the building, which can be seen from the gaps on either side of the wall. In perpetual shadow, the wall had long turned black, stained by years of mould, rust, rot and decay.

Chapter Four

Afraid of the Dark?

The group wait for a long while. They are hidden beneath the shadow of the wall that towers high above them. The lead android has his back right up against the corner of the wall and does not look into the lane, yet seems to be waiting for a signal, a confirmation, the all-clear to cross out into the open. They take extreme care to make sure no one is watching.

The lead android completes its scan, satisfied, raises its right hand and signals to move forward. In single file, they all quickly turn left and enter the laneway. They cross to the other side and move swiftly to stand in front of the blackened wall.

The lead android raises its left hand and at waist height, in one motion, swipes across the centre of the hidden door, whilst at the same time, in five seconds, issues a code of thirty-two frequencies into the locking mechanism. The door unlocks and opens inward by a sliver along the right-hand seam, with the softest sound of released compressed air. The reinforced steel door is completely camouflaged and hidden within the outer wall.

The lead android pushes the door ajar, just enough to quickly and silently squeeze its body through. Jaxon follows closely. He steels a quick glance into the lane. There is no one... no one... to see him disappear. He passes through the doorway, with the second android right behind. From within, the lead android gently pushes the door closed, which locks instantly, automatically. They vanish from sight... in silence.

They stand still, motionless in a small chamber in complete darkness. The lead android conducts a second scan, waiting, listening, the dull light of its beads flickering. Jaxon's shallow breathing is the only sound that can be heard. The scan is complete. The lights of the beads switch off. Now, it's pitch black. Not a shred of light can be seen. So complete is the dark, a shiver ripples through Jaxon's body.

It is completely still, completely silent, cold but dry. Slowly he begins to adjust to the new conditions. The chamber is small. He only need sway a little to the left or the right and he brushes against one of the androids. After a full three minutes, his mind begins to wonder. The words 'listen, follow', rings through his ears, in that distinct metallic voice.

The lead android takes a step forward, purposefully using its rubber-soled boot to make the distinct sound of a step. A second step and a third is taken, as the android moves into the narrowing shoulder wide corridor ahead. Jaxon tentatively stretches out the right toe of his foot to test the ground in front of him. Satisfied he takes one step forward and a second.

The lead android takes another step. This time it has a different sound. It is the sound of the front of the foot landing first, followed by the heel. It's a step down a stair. A second and third step down the stair is taken, in a slow yet rhythmic manner. Once again, Jaxon extends his right toe, to feel the edge of the first stair. He tentatively takes the first step down. His body begins to wobble, uncontrollably. He stretches out both hands and touches the cold hard walls on both sides to steady himself. He continues. The second companion moves forward, silently, keeping a constant three steps behind him. They descend deeper into the stairwell.

The only thing he can use to navigate is the sound made by the lead android. He is forced to focus acutely upon his hearing. Progress is at a pace just enough for him to keep up. At first, he counts the steps. There are eight, then a turn to the left across a small landing and a further eight steps down, followed by another turn to the left. They descend a total of thirty flights of stairs, fifteen floors underground.

He is led through a long passage, where at the end, a flight of eight stairs leads upwards, with a turn to the right at the top, and again. Over the next hour the lead android takes him through a maze of passages and stairs, sometimes going up, sometimes going down, sometimes with a turn to the left and sometimes a turn to the right. There are no doors, just passages, stairs and the occasional small chamber with an open door on each wall.

Jaxon quickly grows quite accustomed to this mode of travel, now able to move swiftly in the darkness. By the familiar sounds of the lead android's walking motion, he knows what obstacle to expect, what change in direction has been taken, three steps in advance. He does not hear the presence of anything or anyone else. They march on.

Once again, he finds the darkness very soothing, comforting. He can remove all thought from his mind, of the future and the past, and focus only on the present moment and the very next sound in front of him. This soon becomes very intense, with no interference, no light.

"Are you guys trying to completely confuse me?" he whispers. "Feels like we've been doing a weird figure-of-eight loop for quite a while now. Well... I'm totally lost. There's no way I can find my way out of here," he mutters.

Of course, by now, he has completely lost all bearings of direction, where he's going or how to return to the surface. He has also lost all sense of time. The only thing he knows is that he is deep, deep underground, in a veritable maze. He trusts the androids know exactly where they are, this their domain, the darkness their defence, their weapon.

Fatigue and dehydration begin to set in. Jaxon starts to become very disorientated. His head starts to spin, his legs to wobble. Suddenly, a metal door closes behind them. He hears a motor engage and spin into motion above his head. The chamber begins to descend.

"Are we in a lift?" he asks. "We're in a lift!" he answers.

Looking up, swaying on his feet, he wonders to himself.

How deep are we? Who are they? Where from? What's down here? A base, a city? Hidden from prying eyes! Must have built this below the concrete foundations of the city above. How long ago? Huh... the ghetto up there is just an illusion, used to filter out any intrusion from the world above. No one is going to find me down here.

The lift suddenly stops. The metal door slides open. The trio turn and exit through the same door. In single file, they proceed down a long passage. At the end, they stand in front of a heavy steel door. No handle. The lead android pauses for a moment while it raises its left hand and issues a frequency code into the lock mechanism. The lock quietly releases and the door slowly swings open into the chamber beyond. No handle on the inside either.

The lead android steps forward and walks into a large, cubed chamber and steps to the right. Jaxon follows and stands next to the first android. The second android enters and steps to the left. The door silently closes and locks automatically. The chamber is illuminated by a single light bulb covered by a circular opaque glass fitting, high in the centre of the ceiling. Initially, the light appears quite blinding, forcing him to squint and raise his right forearm to protect his eyes, further accentuating his sense of disorientation.

His eyes adjust after a few moments, and he finds the light to be quite dull after all. He looks around. The chamber is completely bare. The floor is polished, charcoal grey concrete. The concrete walls and ceiling are finished in the same manner. There is a closed black, steel door in the centre of each wall, one on the left, one on the right and one straight ahead, all with a black, steel lever handle.

Both androids now stand one step back from him, one behind each shoulder. The door in front of him opens inward. A man steps through into the chamber and closes the door behind. He takes three steps forward and stops with both hands clasped behind his back. He takes a few long moments to inspect Jaxon's condition.

The middle-aged man is of medium height and robust build, with short cut, thinning black hair, combed back. He has a round plump face. He is wearing black, rimmed glasses and a black business suit with no tie and polished black, rubber-soled shoes. The top button of his white, collared shirt is open.

Chapter Five

Benjamin

"Hello, Mr Jaxon James. Welcome. My name is Benjamin."

"Hu… hello."

"Yes, well, I can see you are quite exhausted from your journey down here," he said quickly, pausing. "I think the immediate concern is for you to have a rest and some refreshments. The door on your left leads into a self-contained bed chamber with a bathroom."

"What is this place? Why am I here?" Jaxon asks.

Benjamin's short, sharp demeanour is very much like a managing director. He gives a distinct nod to both androids. They turn towards the right-hand wall, walk over and disappear behind the door as they close it behind them. Jaxon understands full well that there is no escape.

"I imagine you have lots of questions," he said quickly. "First you must rest and recover your strength. I will answer your questions a little later."

Extending his right arm with open palm, Benjamin beckons to the door on Jaxon's left.

"Shall we?"

Benjamin moves to the door and opens it. Leaving the door open, he leads the way and walks into the bed chamber. He stands inside and waits.

The charcoal grey polished concrete bedchamber is equivalent to a studio hotel room, just without the frills. The main room has a simple but sturdy queen size bed and dark oak headboard, with a small round table and pair of chairs in the far left corner. A pitcher of orange juice, deli sandwiches and a small fruit platter sit on a tray upon the table.

Through an open doorway on the right, is an en-suite bathroom with shower, basin, mirror and toilet. On the basin is another small tray with a razor, brush and gel, body wash, shampoo and conditioner, toothbrush and toothpaste, nail clippers, scissors and hair brush. A large black towel is hung over a rail. There is no radio, television or clock in the room.

Benjamin waits patiently until Jaxon walks through the doorway.

"Please make yourself comfortable," he began, business like. "As you can see, you have some refreshments. Please have a rest and clean yourself up. Have a shave and a shower. Discard all those rags in that bin over there. They will be incinerated. If you have any personal items you wish to keep, place them on that table. You will find a fresh set of clothes in the cupboard. Do you understand?"

"Uhm… Yes," Jaxon mutters.

"Very good."

Benjamin walks around Jaxon, careful not to touch him and back through the open door.

"I shall leave you to it, then," he said. "When you are ready, just pop over and knock on that door. You should know, there are no locked doors 'inside' this facility."

"Where am I to go?" Jaxon said flatly.

"I bid you good evening."

With a wry smile Benjamin promptly and silently closes the door.

After almost three hours of trekking in the dark, Jaxon fixates on the table. He lunges at the pitcher, grabs it, knocks over the cup and gulps down half. He slams the pitcher back on the table, takes a deep breath, reaches over, grabs a handful of sliced fruit and stuffs them into his mouth. A handful of sandwiches soon follows. Satiating his thirst and hunger his eyes suddenly grow heavy, his head wobbles. Completely exhausted he collapses face down onto the bed and passes out into a deep sleep.

A few hours pass. Jaxon slowly opens his eyes. He is lying in the exact position he collapsed in. He groans. Every muscle hurts. He rolls left onto his back and pulls himself up into a sitting position. He looks around the room and the mess he made of the food plater.

"Huh… it wasn't a dream. It's all real," he whispers.

He gets up, plonks in a chair and casually finishes the orange juice, fruit and sandwiches.

Jaxon walks through the doorway into the bathroom. He suddenly realises how pungent he smells. Standing in front of the basin mirror, he takes a long look at his reflection. He steps closer. His rough life is deeply etched around his eyes, nose and mouth.

"You look like absolute shit," he mumbles.

Returning to the small round table in the room, he empties all the contents of his pockets: A neat roll of notes, amounting to a couple of hundred dollars; waterproof matches; a compass on a leather string; a sports watch with no band, also on a leather string; a switchblade knife; a designer pen with his initials engraved, a gift upon graduation; an empty metal pocket flask; a well-used toothbrush; and some rubbish.

In the bathroom he removes his jacket, his flannelette, T-shirt, singlet, his boots and socks, his thick baggy pants and a pair of shorts worn underneath. He dumps all his clothing into the wide, plastic lined bin in the far corner. He stands in front of the mirror just in a pair of underpants, revealing his lean muscled body, covered in an array of sores and scratches.

Jaxon turns on the tap and washes his hands and face. He picks up the pair of scissors and begins to hack through his mattered beard. He collects the off cuts and throws them into the bin. He fills the basin with hot water and prepares to have a shave. Following the shave, he picks up the nail clippers, and trims both his fingernails and toenails over the bin. He cuts the frayed ends of his hair in a straight line as best he can. He drops his underpants into the bin and steps into a hot shower.

Jaxon opens the door to his quarters and steps out into the cubed chamber. He is dressed in a black, cotton, pullover, short-sleeved, double-layered top, overlapping the waist by two inches. There are no buttons or zips. From waist to ankles, he is wearing a black double-layered pair of straight-cut pants, with a thin cord for a belt and a pair of very comfortable slippers. Clean shaven and with his hair combed back and down just above the shoulder, he reveals a handsome mature, yet grim face.

Jaxon finds himself completely alone in the entrance chamber. He turns and approaches the locked, main entrance door. He takes a closer look at it. There is no visible lock, latch or hinge. He places his open right palm upon the surface and runs his hand from shoulder height down across his body to his left waist. The surface of the door is smooth, hard and cold.

At that moment the opposite door opens and Benjamin walks into the chamber.

"Yes, well, I see you are rested... and have cleaned yourself up," he said briskly. "I hope you are feeling much better?"

"Yes, I am. Thank you," Jaxon replies. "Interesting door! There's no lock or latch."

"Not that can be seen. The mechanisms are built within. Impossible to deduce its operation."

"Then how do you open and close the door?"

"The door is controlled by frequency. You need to emit the correct combination of frequencies to open the door and another combination to close the door."

"And how do you do that?"

"Ooh, not me. Our companions control that door."

"Ooh, right! Companions, you say! Those very sophisticated robots!" Jaxon said. "So, what are they, mind-droids?"

"Yes, something like that," Bejamin replies. "You probably deduced that they do not operate by sight, but by frequency. Did you notice those rows of beads hanging from the disc?" he asks. "Each bead can emit a frequency across a wide range and spectrum. Collectively, they can emit multiple frequencies at once, or in an arranged sequence. The frequencies rebound off any physical object, where the returning waves build a three-dimensional view of their surroundings," he pauses. "They can also detect brainwave emissions and read what you are thinking. Basically, they can detect anything which possesses a frequency, a vibration."

"That doesn't sound like human technology to me!"

"No, it does not," he agrees. "So, yes, they are not of this world."

Jaxon was about to ask the next most obvious question, when Benjamin quickly half turns, extends his right arm and open hand towards the far door.

"Shall we?"

Benjamin opens the door, walks through, turns and stops to wait for Jaxon. He closes the door behind them both. The room is a spacious rectangular chamber, with the same polished concrete decor. The chamber is lit by a row of soft, paired spotlights set into the ceiling.

Benjamin's very large desk occupies the left-hand side. A computer, phone, lamp, a small stack of closed files and the usual stationery, sit neatly across the top. A row of dark oak cupboards and drawers line the back wall behind the desk. An arrangement of three-by-three small monitors are affixed to the wall on their left, each displaying a camera view. Jaxon recognises the corridor outside the locked front door and the first entrance chamber.

The right-hand side of the room contains the square arrangement of a two-seater leather couch, two single-seat leather armchairs and a dark oak, square coffee table. A self-contained bar, bar fridge and small kitchenette, all finished in dark oak cabinetry, lines the back wall. A large television monitor is affixed to the wall on their right. A set of large, closed double doors is in the centre of the opposite wall.

"Please, make yourself comfortable."

With his right arm, Benjamin gestures for Jaxon to take a seat on the couch and moves on around towards the bar.

"Would you like a drink?"

Jaxon takes the left seat on the couch, stretches out his arms and legs and sits back. Benjamin stands at the bar behind him waiting for an order.

"How about something with a bit of kick, to calm my nerves. I'd like… a double bourbon over ice with a slice of lime," he replies.

"Excellent. I might have a fine old brandy, myself."

Benjamin grabs a crystal tumbler and a wide brandy glass and prepares both drinks.

"So… if those androids are not of this world, where do they come from? Who are you? What is this place? And why am I here?" Jaxon blurts impatiently.

"Of course, you have questions."

Benjamin walks around to the end of the couch, hands Jaxon his drink and sits in the closest one-seat armchair, with the television on the wall behind him. He raises his drink.

"Cheers."

Jaxon half raises his tumbler and they both take a soothing sip and sit back to relax.

"Yes, well, as you can see, I'm human. I'm also the administrator of this facility. Those androids and this facility were built by… how should I explain it… an intelligence, whose purpose… is to help humanity."

"You mean... an extraterrestrial intelligence?"

"Yes, that's correct."

"Wow, that's incredible!"

They sit in silence for a moment while Jaxon processes the enormity of the revelation.

"How do you know they are working... as you say... for the good of humanity?" Jaxon asks.

"Because... they operate under one very important rule... or more precisely... a principle," he began. "They are permitted to offer assistance but, they themselves cannot intervene directly in the affairs of mankind. So they have built this facility and now you are here," he pauses. "And, as you can judge from your experience, the measures that are in place, how far beneath ground we are, means that they do not wish to be known," he said and continues.

"You can think of this facility as a base of sorts. This place is so secret, not even your government is aware of it. We are located directly beneath that power station. As you can imagine, it emits all sorts of electromagnetic noise, making us virtually undetectable."

"I gather that ghetto up there, is just a cover, a smoke screen for this operation?"

"Exactly," Benjamin confirms. "The land is held in several companies, trusts and estates, with some long-term leases between them and some well-crafted disputes locking everything up in the courts, with environmental contamination, compensation and all that. Lots of boring paperwork," he explains. "The ghetto, however, serves one very important purpose... the means by which we can locate and draw out... someone just like you."

"Am I in danger?"

"That very much depends on you."

"Why am I here?" Jaxon persists.

"Yes, well..."

Benjamin takes a sip of his drink, savouring the soothing flavour. Jaxon does the same.

"We have been looking for someone... the right person you could say... for quite some time now. This person must have one very special... one very important quality... an immense, unshakable desire to believe in the existence of God. This desire must be so strong, that this person is willing to face death, to sacrifice his life, if need be... to find the answer... to find the truth."

"Right!"

"And you seem to be the very person we have been searching for."

"But how? How... do you know about this? I've never told anyone about what I'm doing, and why," Jaxon retorts angrily.

"I know this is a deeply personal matter for you. It will always be a very personal subject for anyone who seriously contemplates the question of God. It's the very nature of the question itself, is it not?"

"Yes, of course. It cannot be otherwise. So how do you know about me?"

"The androids! For months now, they go to the top of those empty apartment towers and scan the thoughts of millions of people in the region. We did locate a couple of candidates who possessed a strong conviction... or so we thought, but alas, their conviction didn't prove strong enough. And now, finally, we have found you."

"But how did I get here?" Jaxon probes.

"As I have explained, the androids can read a person's thoughts. They can also exert a little... influence, as well."

"The blackouts!"

Jaxon reflects deeply into his half-finished tumbler.

"The blackouts? That was you... or... should I say, them!" he concludes.

"Yes! The androids exert a little influence to point you in the right direction. The rest, is all you... and wallah... here you are."

"So, what now? Now that I'm here?" he asks. "I mean... well... all this and all the effort you've gone through. What happens now?"

"I'm pleased you don't linger upon the little things and cut straight to the point," Benjamin said leaning forward and whispers. "We are going to provide you with an opportunity... to give you what you want... what you have been searching for."

Jaxon looks harshly and mistrustingly at Benjamin. Deep emotions begin to well up.

"You have been wandering out there aimlessly... for what... seven years now! Like a lost goat. Do you really think you are going to find God this way? Were you really hoping for God to just go... 'Wham! Here I Am! Let's Rejoice!'?" he scoffs, raising his arms in a mock celebration. Sitting back, he continues. "It simply doesn't work like that. All you have done is run and hide, wondering aimlessly out there in the wilderness. But I guess you don't know any better, anyway. I mean… how would you know… how to truly go about the business of finding God… hey?"

Jaxon stares deep into his glass, struggling to grasp his emotions.

"No need to answer," he affirms. "In truth, there's no longer the means by which a man… or woman… can find a truth path to the realisation of God on this planet. So, if there's no longer a path, then how can 'you' find one, right?"

"In the Ancient Days, mystery schools and temples taught and trained disciples to take such paths to know God. But they have long since vanished. Today, there are societies and brotherhoods. However, they are a shadow of their former selves, and only really operate as a social network or businessman's club. True conviction in their ranks is very rare, as is the willingness to put that conviction to the test."

"In your case, there's one silver lining. In your renunciation of the world, you have availed yourself of all attachments. And without even realising it, you have managed to create the Causal Body in your aura."

"Causal Body! What's a Causal Body?" Jaxon asks.

"I'm afraid I don't have time to give you a lesson in theology. So, in the simplest of terms, you possess seven layers in your aura. Through renunciation, you break physical, emotional and mental attachments to the world, in favour of God. In doing so, you form, fuse and then dissolve the first three layers of the aura – the etheric, the astral emotional and the mental – to build the Causal Body. You have probably gone through dark, depressive periods of physiological turmoil in your wonderings and contemplation of God, right?"

"Yes. I guess you can say that."

"This is the process whereby, one layer of the aura forms and dissolves into the next, until you build and can utilise a fully formed Causal Body. Only a handful of seekers have managed to build a Causal Body. And this forms the reason as to why you are here."

"Right… ok!" Jaxon exclaims.

"With your conviction and your apparent desire to seek God through death, you have, unknowingly presented yourself as a candidate to us. In a way, you possess the perfect conditions for the person we have been looking for. Maybe… you were born for this task."

"Born for what? What's going to happen to me?"

"I think it will be better for me to show you, rather than trying to explain it. Think of it as something between a medical procedure and a tribal ritual. At its core, it's a 'Trial'… a trial which will force you to make use of your Causal Body and reveal your true nature. You couldn't pass this trial without it."

Benjamin finished his brandy, stood to collect Jaxon's empty tumbler and walked to the bar.

"I think it's time for you to return to your quarters and rest, now. All your clothing has been taken away for incineration. A meal and refreshments will be waiting for you. You will need to regain your strength."

"What if I don't wish to participate?"

Benjamin walked back around to stand in front of the coffee table. He looked up at the ceiling for a moment, raised his eyebrows and rocked his head from one side to the other, once.

"Yes, well… it's what you want, even if… your mind thinks it's not."

"I don't have a choice, do I?" Jaxon realises.

Benjamin confirms with a single nod and a wry smile.

"If I don't go through with this, I won't be getting out of here, will I?"

"It will be easier for you to simply comply. To resist will make it harder and reduce your chance of success. All is not what it seems and all will be revealed, but first, you must succeed in the trial. We NEED you… the planet needs you… all of humanity needs you… to succeed. There has never been a greater hour of need in our world than what there is right now. So, take some time to rest and when you are ready, I will call you."

Benjamin walks over to open the door back into the entrance chamber. Jaxon climbs to his feet and walks through, now mystified with what Benjamin means about a 'need'. He approaches the door of his bedchamber, grabs hold of the handle and looks back at Benjamin.

"Ok, I'll do what you ask of me. Call me when it's time."

Jaxon disappears into the bedchamber. Benjamin closes the door to his office.

Chapter Six

The Trial

Jaxon wakes from a long, restful sleep. He is lying on his back, dressed only in a pair of black boxer shorts and covered by a thin black blanket. He looks around the room in anticipation of what lies ahead. Growing restless, he leaps up and walks into the bathroom to have a hot shower. He dresses in a fresh set of the same style clothes. When ready, he moves towards the door and reaches out with his right hand. There is a quick double knock. He halts, pausing for a moment. He turns the handle and opens the door.

"Good morning!"

"Hello," Jaxon replies. "Although, I don't really know what time it is. I wouldn't know if it's morning, noon or night."

"I'm just being polite. Have you noticed… all clocks, watches and any reference to time have been removed. Once you lose track of time, you begin to disassociate from the normal fabric of reality. Time is no longer important and you loosen your psychological grip on being regulated by the clock. It's better you don't know the time."

"And why is that?"

"You look rested… and ready. Let me show you. Follow me, please."

Benjamin turns and leads the way back into his office. Jaxon follows.

"I have a question!" Jaxon announces.

Closing the door behind them both, Benjamin pauses to wait for its delivery.

"I've been somewhat perturbed when you say that you need me, that all of humanity needs me. So, I was wondering, why? Why do you need me and why now?"

"This is a very complex question," Benjamin began. "We don't have a lot of time to go through all the intricacies of explaining everything in detail right now. Furthermore, I neither wish to frighten you nor place you under undue pressure. What I will say is this," he pauses. "Basically, all of humanity has lost its way. Millions are trapped in the false beliefs of their dogmatic religious scriptures. Millions more have given up on God and spend their lives searching only for wealth and power."

"Essentially, everyone is looking for an externalisation of God and aren't prepared to change unless there is complete and undeniable proof. As soon as you identify with wealth, with power and forget about God, you are lost. Rare are those who fully commit to finding God deep within their own heart. There are many ways to do this, but of itself, it is the only way. Alas, this competition for wealth and power has brought our planet, our civilisation, to the edge of a cliff and as a result, a new threat has emerged. So, now we search for the right person who can help humanity in its greatest hour of need."

"Well… what's this threat you speak of?" Jaxon persists.

"At this point, this is all that I wish to explain. It would be premature to reveal any more to you. But first we have a task to complete. So, please, follow me and I will show you."

Benjamin turns, walks over and pulls the right-hand double door open. He waits for Jaxon to pass through and allows the door to swing closed behind them. There is a long wide corridor to the left, one to the right and one directly ahead, each barred by another set of double doors. Soft, paired spotlights in the ceiling run the length of each corridor. Benjamin leads the way down the right-hand passage. He pulls open the door. Jaxon walks through. The door swings closed behind them both.

The very large, square chamber, with a nine-foot ceiling, is divided in half by a three-foot-high, two-inch-thick partition. They both stand inside the middle far left wall of the chamber. On the floor in front of them is a seven-foot square, white-tiled area, with a drain in the centre. A two-inch concrete step encloses the tiled area, used to contain the outflow of water or any other liquid. Soft lights covered with a circular disc are positioned high, at regular intervals around the walls, only on the left half of the chamber.

On the other side of the partition, in the shadow, sits a raised armchair, like an old dentist's layback chair. The chair peers over the partition, facing the tiled area.

Benjamin beckons Jaxon to follow and leads him around to and through a low set of swing doors located at the far-right end of the partition. They approach the dentist's chair.

Suddenly, a large well-muscled man silently and with ease, pushes a large wooden contraption on wheels, through the same double doors. He raises the front wheels over the concrete step and then lifts the rear wheels over, and places the contraption in the centre of the tiled area, facing the dentist chair. He locks all four wheels in place with his foot.

The man is dressed in a full length, thick white medical gown, over a baggy, full length plastic top and pants, with slippers. He is wearing white gloves, head covering and a clear plastic shield, to protect his eyes, face and mouth. He is of medium height with a thick barrel chest and arms. The man stands at ease beside the strange contraption, with his hands clasped behind his back, in military style, waiting for the next command.

Stunned, Jaxon sees another man has been strapped back in an upright position, into the large, oval-shaped, vertically reclined wooden disc of the contraption. The disc reclines back at a thirty degree angle and is built upon a very sturdy steel A-frame with lockable wheels. The disc encircles the full length of his body, suspending him above the ground. The man is dressed in just a modest white loin cloth.

Jaxon studies the man. He is white, middle-aged and looks rather sick. He is very thin, severely anorexically thin, with a glazed look over his eyes. He has dark sunken eyes and deep lines in his face, from poor living and long suffering. He has scabs, sores and scars all over his body. Most noticeable are the track marks along both arms and ankles and around the side of his neck. All the signs indicate that he is a long-term hardcore heroin drug addict.

From what Jaxon can see, this man is well beyond recovery. He had long ago become totally consumed by his addiction, the driving force for his existence, with no willpower, no self-control and nothing to live for except the next hit. He has no hope of ever knowing a normal life again. His soul is truly lost.

The man is completely disorientated, totally out of it, not able to display any sense, feeling or recognition of himself or his surroundings. He is a living corpse. Jaxon was unsure how he felt about this person. Did he feel pity, sorrow, regret, anger? He did not know. He looked on, detached.

"Who is that man?" Jaxon asks.

"I don't have that information. Nor is it important."

"Is he from the ghetto above?"

"Yes, he is. That's the other purpose of the ghetto. It draws those who have lost their way in life, who have lost hope and given up, or those who society has thrown away. It's a place where these people have come to die. Didn't you feel that?"

"Ooh yes, I did. The ghetto is a very dark place. There's definitely an air of death hanging over it," he admits. "Is that what's about to happen to this man?"

"Well… yes."

"Wow… really?" Jaxon retorts exacerbated. "You've just been speaking about God and now, you're going to murder this man. That seems like a contradiction, don't you think?"

Benjamin raises his right hand, indicating for Jaxon to stop speaking.

"Firstly, by our calculations, this man will die within the next twelve to twenty-four hours. In his mind, he has already made and accepted the decision to die. In a way, taking his life would be an act of mercy. And his life can still serve one final, very important purpose."

"Secondly, we don't have a lot of time. We certainly don't have a decade to train you in the 'arts' and 'mysteries'. So, we must expedite things. We are forced to take the shortest path and aim for the greatest reward. And this comes with risk."

"Now, if you believe in God, you would also, by logical extension, believe in the existence of a soul. From our point of view, the principle of God cannot exist separately and exclusively from the principle of a soul. One cannot operate without the other, can they?"

"No, I guess not!" Jaxon replies.

"Is the soul eternal?"

"Yes, that's what we are led to believe."

"Then to propagate the idea we only live one life is ludicrous. So little consideration is given to the existence of the soul and the eternal nature of the soul's life. The questions should be: What happens when a person dies? Where does the soul go? What is the soul made of? How is the soul sustained out of the body? What is the reality of the soul out of the body?" he said. "You know, your own search to find God through death implies that you also want to find out if you can survive death itself, right?" he pauses. "Again, this brings us to the all-important question… of why we are here."

Benjamin turns and takes the last two steps forward to stand beside the dentist's chair and waves Jaxon to do the same. Jaxon suddenly notices a side table attached to the opposite side of the dentist's chair. Upon the table, atop a soft white cloth rests a small stainless-steel syringe with a long thin 100 ml glass canister. The canister is filled with a thick black liquid, reflecting the dull light with a dark silvery sheen, appearing to be like mercury, black mercury.

"So, this is what's going to happen," Benjamin explains. "You will take a seat in that chair. You will be injected with that serum. You will notice its effects after precisely one minute. The serum has two properties: first, you will acquire etheric sight; second, your Causal Body will become much more lucid, where you will find it easier to separate from and leave your physical body with greater freedom, whilst remaining completely conscious of the experience," he pauses. "Then it's all about the timing, which is also why it's necessary to use this method. At the same time, we will begin the sacrifice."

"How are you going to do that? How are you going to take his life?"

"My assistant will bleed him until he dies. The effect must coincide precisely with the serum. He cannot die too quickly, or too slowly."

"Ooh, right!" he exclaims.

Jaxon squirms and fidgets, feeling very uncomfortably about the whole procedure.

"He is already intoxicated. He won't feel any pain," Benjamin assures and continues. "As he approaches death, you will be able to see his dream body, his light body, his soul if you will, begin to separate from his physical body. Once he dies, his soul will open a doorway, a portal through the barrier, the veil of the *Physical Dimension*, and pass through. You are to follow. You will only have a few seconds," he pauses. "Do you understand?"

A moment of realisation enters Jaxon's mind.

"Y… yes, I do."

"Now listen to me!"

Benjamin turns and looks, sternly, directly at Jaxon, to gain his full attention.

"This is the most important thing. You must, at all times, keep focus on your strongest desire. Once you go through to the other side, you will encounter multiple planes, or layers of consciousness, each with their own set of forces. Do not lose sight of your strongest desire. Do not be distracted. If you do, you will become trapped by those forces and be lost to us, forever," he paused. "Do you understand?"

"Yes… yes, I do. Seek my strongest desire… at all times," he affirms.

"Right then, are you ready?"

Jaxon looks up, takes a long, deep breath and steels his nerves. He nods yes, apprehensively. Benjamin extends his right arm, with open palm, inviting Jaxon to be seated. He climbs into the chair and makes himself comfortable. The chair is in an upright position. His gaze fixates upon the addict. Benjamin tightens three straps, one around the chest, one around the waist and one over both thighs.

His mind is racing.

How did I get here? This is so surreal. Am I afraid? No! I'm not! Strongest desire, strongest desire. Ooh, my God… I hope you are up there, somewhere! Here we go…

"So, what's in the syringe?" Jaxon blurts out, nervously. "It looks like mercury."

"Yes, it does, doesn't it?" he replies. "But it's not. There's little point in telling you what it's made from. The formula is based on an ancient Egyptian alchemical recipe, which they used in their rituals. The original formula contained impurities and they administered it orally… they drank it. Today, we have the tools to remove those impurities and to strengthen its potency. And because of its high level of purity, we inject the serum directly into the blood stream to speed up the process."

"Are you ready?" he asks. "Remember, keep your complete attention on that man."

Jaxon makes a visible effort to relax and nods. He is ready!

Benjamin lifts a swab from the tray and cleans the inner left arm around the elbow. He threads an elastic torniquet around the arm and tightens it above the bicep. The veins pop. He carefully gathers the syringe in his right hand and with clean precision, inserts the needle. He releases the elastic band and slowly presses down on the plunger. He pulls the needle out and returns it to the tray. He quickly presses a sticky plaster over the tiny wound, removes the torniquet, stands, turns to his assistant and issues a hand signal.

The assistant steps forward and around to face the addict. He withdraws a short, razor-sharp blade from his right pocket. He grabs hold of the addict's right hand and bends it back to expose the wrist.

Within a few seconds, Jaxon feels the effect of the serum. His senses become intensely heightened. The lights, although soft, now become almost too bright. All the colours, vibrant, all the sounds, amplified. He hears his breathing, everyone's breathing, his heartbeat, everyone's heart beating. He can hear the blade, in one quick motion, cut deep through flesh, the blood splashes and gushes forward.

Benjamin clicks the stopwatch on his wrist. His assistant quickly gathers the addict's left hand, bends it back and cuts deeply through the wrist. He lets go, returns the knife to his pocket and moves back to his original position, standing at ease with hands behind his back. Red crimson blood spots are splattered across his white apron.

Jaxon is exposed to the full view. His eyes widen in shock. Blood flows down the bench under the addicts' legs and cascades over the edge to fall and splash upon the tiles. Two rivulets of blood begin to pool and stream towards the drain. He has never seen anyone die in front of his eyes before. He struggles to cope with the experience, his mind racing to reconcile. Everything is moving far to quickly, and yet, time seems to be slowing down.

It takes the addict a few moments to realise that something is wrong. He did not feel the cuts to his wrist. Intuitively, he raises his head and looks down at his hands and the sight of flowing blood. His eyes grow wide in terror, with the sudden shock realisation that they are his hands, his blood. He lets out a weak groan.

"What's going on?"

He tries to struggle. The straps hold him firmly in place. A wave of fear shoots adrenaline through his body. He is too weak to resist. It's already too late. He begins to feel dizzy, disorientated. His head falls back, his eyes roll, his breathing shallows as he begins to lose consciousness.

Jaxon watches the addict pass out, his mind racing to understand.

Is this a merciful death? He didn't feel pain, but he did feel fear knowing he was about to die. His suffering would last no more than a minute. Look, he's already gone. At least he will be free of his affliction. Maybe it is a merciful death, after all. What's happening now?

Benjamin quickly looks at his watch. Thirty seconds have just ticked over. Time is racing.

Jaxon's entire body is now under the complete effects of the serum. All his senses, having reached a crescendo of intensity, are now experiencing everything pass through into a state of translucence. He is beginning to see, hear and feel through and beyond the physical. His brain, his inner mind, is growing darker, as though all light is being drained or filtered out. Thinking is now a struggle, visualising anything no longer possible. His body now no longer able to feel, becoming numb, inanimate.

The physical realm is receding into darkness. Everything made of matter quickly appears to be overlaid with a new subtle, translucent grey-white-blue light. He feels the strange power of a presence. He does not know what it is, cannot identify it. With the fading light of his vision, he remembers to focus his attention upon the addict. He cannot stop his eyes from closing, yet he can still see... he can still see the addict within his mind's eye.

He can hear the addict's heartbeat, racing, skipping a beat, two beats and collapsing into cardiac arrest. There is no more blood. The addict's eyes are wide, open, vacant. With mouth agape, his last breath is pushed out by the weight of collapsing lungs. The addict's heart stops, he dies. It is quiet, dead still.

Benjamin steels a glance at his watch. The timer hits one minute. The silence is complete.

Jaxon's physical brain and body is completely encased within the shadow of a coma. Yet, he can still see. He can see everything in the chamber through the pineal gland of his mind's eye, when suddenly, his translucent white-blue light body, his Causal Body, an exact replica of his physical, separates and begins to slowly rise. Connected by a thin silver cord at the navel, he can see through the eyes of his Causal Body, think and feel at the soul level.

He focuses upon his dream-like vision. Suddenly, he sees something, his heart jumps, his physical body twitches. He sees a ball of light, small at first, but growing a little stronger, a little larger, with each passing moment. The light separates from and moves above the addict's body. The shape of the addict's thin body forms around the sphere. It is the light body of the addict, his soul, although somewhat dull and grey in brightness with a faint hint of red, and hazy around the edge.

The addict's light body hovers above the reclined bench, surveying the scene inside the chamber. The silver cord connected to the navel of his physical body disintegrates. He knows, lingering, wavering, peering through the empty shell of his physical body, seeing clearly the truth of a life wasted, a life lost.

Jaxon watches mesmerised, witnessing the emerging light body of another, seeing, realising, this to be the real energy and the real force behind life itself. The addict's light body turns and becomes aware of another presence. Both light bodies dance silently in the ether.

Focusing intently, he tries to read or feel the inner thoughts, motives and emotions of the addict's light body. Nothing is clear but confusion. He tries to connect, to communicate. He moves a little forward, extends his right arm and reaches out, to touch. The addict's light body half turns away and looks upwards, sensing that it's time to leave, being drawn by strong unseen forces.

The addict's light body decides that its ready to let go, straightens its body and tucks its arms in close. A gateway suddenly opens above its head, just below the ceiling. The portal is a perfect circle, roughly three feet in diameter. The rim of the circle is a smoothly raised bump or ripple, like that of a donut. The ripple is a stretch in the fabric of reality and emits flashes of colours and lights. The centre of the circle sinks deep into a dark hole. The portal acts like a magnet, drawing, pulling upon the addict's light body, with increasing increments of force.

At the last moment the addict's light body turns its head and looks directly at Jaxon.

Does he know? Does he know what's happening? Follow! I must follow. The door is open. Where am I going? To see... to seek... my God! Go, go, go now!

The addict's light body returns its gaze to the portal, relaxes its resistance and in an instant, is pulled through, into the portal, with a very subtle pop of a small bubble. He is gone. Jaxon panics for a moment, lurches forward in pursuit. In a split second, he swiftly glides across the chamber and dives in through the portal, pop and disappears. He can see the addict's light body just ahead as they move through the dark tunnel of the vortex. The portal behind closes.

Benjamin checks his watch. Two minutes. Three minutes. The ritual is complete.

He issues a hand signal to his assistant to begin the clean up. The assistant pulls out, unfolds and lays a body bag on the floor behind the reclined bench away from the blood. He binds the wounds on both wrists from a roll of plaster and unstraps the body from the bench. He gently places the lifeless body inside the bag and zips it up, ready for cremation. Using a long thin can, the assistant then sprays a solution over the entire recline bench and tiled floor area. The congealed blood dissolves immediately.

A hidden door to a cabinet in the nearby wall is opened. The assistant pulls out a hose with a shower like nozzle and hoses down the bench and floor. A special detergent is sprayed over everything and hosed down a second and third time. He uses a large white towel to dry every inch of the bench and floor. He then strips down to his boxer shorts, placing the towel and his kit into a second bag for incineration. Everything else is returned to its place.

Meanwhile, Benjamin tends to Jaxon's physical body. He lowers the incline of the top half of the chair, to a more comfortable position while Jaxon is in a comatose state. On the back wall he presses a small rectangular tile. Hissing hydraulics open a hidden door inwards, turning the wall panel to a ninety degree angle. He releases the wheel lock and pulls the chair into the small rectangular chamber and locks the wheels once more, close to the back wall.

The chamber resembles a hospital ward, climate controlled at 73 °F. Benjamin attaches heart monitoring sensors across Jaxon's chest. He places an assisted breathing mask over Jaxon's mouth and nose. He inserts an intravenous drip into Jaxon's right arm to prevent dehydration, places a pillow under his head and throws a thin blanket over his body. He checks the monitor to ensure all vital signs are reporting as stable.

On a small shelf, just above and behind Jaxon's head sits a metronome. Benjamin sets the weight to swing at one click per second. He gently pulls the arm to the right and let's go... click... click... click. He stands back to watch for two minutes. Satisfied, he turns, leaves the room and presses the tile on the wall. The door gently squeezes closed.

Chapter Seven

Into the Void

Both bodies of light travel through the dark tunnel. A small bright light appears and grows exponentially in size as they speed towards it. The large orb of light is almost upon them, and with a blinding flash, they are suddenly out, through the other side of the vortex.

Jaxon glances back down behind, as they rise into a clear, wide open void. They had burst through what he sees as a transparent sheet of swirling water over glass, now receding into the distance. Through the portal beneath the plane, he sees a circular, negative photographic imprint of the chamber they just left. The image fades away.

The void into which they float emits a deep crimson background light. All around them gigantic bubbles appear, float by and disappear into the mist. Each bubble displays images, played out in a dream-like fashion, of the desire of the trapped soul inside. He sees scenes of sexual fetishes, gluttony, vanity of the body, attachments to an object and addictions.

An empty bubble suddenly materializes out of the mist, floats towards, draws, catches and consumes them both in quick succession. From the addict's soul memory, a brief review of his life screens upon the inner surface of the bubble.

Jaxon witnesses a critical event during the addict's childhood, the breakdown of his parents' relationship, his father walking out the front door never to be seen again, leaving them to fend for themselves. With few options, his mother falls under the power of a violent, abusive stepfather. He leaves home aged sixteen to begin a life on the streets, working odd jobs here and there, and discovers the welcome escape of drugs. His deep scars lead to addiction, self-harm and eventually, to destruction.

The addict's troubled soul seems to reflect upon the tragic life just lived, unable to understand why, to see the lesson, to forgive his parents, to heal. He continues to crave the oblivion of heroin, becoming stuck and encased in his delusion. It is early. It will take time for him to see, to ask for help, to seek the light and dissolve the bubble.

Jaxon suddenly feels a sense of urgency. The surface of the bubble looks to be hardening. He realises he must leave, now or be trapped inside with the addict's torment.

Seek my strongest desire, seek my strongest desire... seek the light... find my God.

He looks out, beyond the inner surface and is suddenly ejected from the bubble. He looks back down, the bubble floats away and disappears into the mist. He is alone with his desire. He looks up and slowly begins to rise, swimming in a vast ocean of open space.

Soon, the background colour transforms to a deep orange hue. The bubbles continue to appear and float by. However, the screened images inside have changed. Now, they depict scenes of the emotional attachments and turmoils of the souls trapped within. He sees jealousy, envy, scornfulness, pity, resentment, impatience, deceitfulness and so many more. He knows that all these trapped souls need do, is renounce their faults and open their hearts to an ounce of love... to a love for God, to escape.

He continues to rise through the void. Before long, the surrounding colour transforms into a deep golden yellow. There are fewer bubbles appearing out of the mist to float past. The screened scenes have changed once more. They depict mental and psychological attachments, predominately of wealth and power, in all its forms, where the trapped soul was in service of the self, to the detriment of others and nature. The soul must let go to be free.

On all three levels, Jaxon noticed the occasional bubble pass by with a darker tint and hardened membrane, where he could not view the life scene of the soul inside. One such bubble suddenly appears and floats towards him. Curious, he decides to have a look and squeezes the top half of his body through the membrane.

The encased soul was a powerful head of state, having enjoyed an emperor-like status, with a lavish lifestyle and frequent military parades used to rule over the people with fear. The soul was struggling to realise that it had died, not willing to give up its attachment, not willing to recognise that there might be… more. The soul simply refuses to give up its need, its elation for dominion over others. Now, the soul is suffering, unable to break free from its illusion, because the influence of matter is so deeply engrossed through the fabric of its being.

Every soul I've seen has an available pathway of repentance to redemption. This doesn't seem like a place for an evil soul. So, what happens to a soul that has truly turned evil? What happens if a soul breaks this… their… silver cord? Where do they go?

He suddenly feels his body being drawn further into the bubble.

No! No… wait. Seek my deepest desire… seek my… seek my God!

He wilfully pushes himself out of the bubble. With relief, he watches it float away. Another bubble forms out of the mist and approaches him from behind. Before he can turn and react, he is captured and encased within its membrane.

He sees images displayed upon the inner surface. He recognises the scenes being played, all of them. They are from his own memory. He is in his own bubble, trapped, in the illusion of his own life. He feels the familiar sensation of anguish quickly overwhelm him.

Through the reflection, Jaxon can see that he has placed an immense amount of value in what he believed was true, that to avail himself to God he must completely reject the physical world out of remorse for his own failing. This remorse, this anguish, formed the foundation upon which he built his mental illusion, a loop from which he could not find an escape… the willingness to forgive his own humanity, his own weakness. Instead, he sought the forgiveness of God, as proof of His existence, an exacerbation which ultimately led him to death's door. Now, he can immediately see through his own vanity.

I'm sorry, so sorry that I wasted my life. I forgive myself… I forgive my weakness… I forgive the mistakes I made. I should've turned to a life of service, to seek my… to seek my God.

Suddenly, the bubble begins to dissolve. It disintegrates and vanishes into the mist, leaving him floating in the void, in his Causal Body of light.

Jaxon drifts. He feels a tension, drawing, pulling him upwards, slowly at first and then with greater increments of speed. He approaches a barrier, filled with light. He passes through. It is thick, not wet, not dry, with the consistency of condensed plasma. He exits through the other side and enters a void of green, blue, teal and purple blends of coloured lights.

He rises up and over a vast plateau upon which lies an expansive, semi-translucent city of light. The buildings are made of mental etheric matter and coloured in infinite shades of green, blue and teal. The sky and void above glows in a deep shade of indigo.

He has entered the *Etheric Dimension*, the *Dimension of Souls*.

He realises that he has just passed through the three lower planes of the *Etheric Dimension*, the cosmic equivalent of the three inner planes of the *Physical Dimension*. He understands that souls become polarised upon one of these three planes, in a state of purgatory, according to the presence and grade of an illusion, and must break through this illusion to progress.

Souls break through the barrier, the veil, from the planes below and are rising all around him. Collectively, all the souls intuitively float up and over the top of the city and move quickly in the same direction. He seems different, able to exert some conscious control over his body of light. He decides to follow and falls in line behind a long procession of souls.

He approaches the central hub of the city and sees a huge pyramid-structured temple appear before him. The temple glows with a bright white-blue light which radiates from its smooth, perfectly tiled cladding. The procession of souls enter and mingle momentarily in a large open square which leads to the great open doors of the pyramid. He waits patiently in line and soon follows the soul in front of him across the threshold into the pyramid.

He finds himself in a huge open chamber. It is massive. He stands upon a glowing white-blue marble ballroom floor. He looks up and slowly turns. From the ground to high above, there are tier upon tier, row upon row of open booths, like a Shakespearean theatre or opera house.

Once through the great door, the procession of souls begin to rise and disperse in all directions, each searching for their designated booth. He senses that everything now operates on a telepathic level. He follows one random soul and enters a booth on the fourth level right behind. Inside, the soul stands upon a raised dais before a tall sky-blue ethereal being who is completely covered in a full length gown and holds a white, stone-like tablet. The Being begins to commune with the soul.

Jaxon looks around the inner chamber. There are two more doors, one on the left and one on the right. Each door has a semicircular arch over the top. A plaque on the left door reads 'Hall of Learning', while the right reads 'Hall of Wisdom'. The communion between the Being and the soul reaches its conclusion, and for this soul, the door on the left opens. The soul passes through and the door closes softly. He deduces that this soul did not achieve its life purpose, resolve the necessary Karma and will be required to relearn the lesson.

He withdraws back into the main chamber and chooses to follow another soul into a booth on the fifth level. Following the communion with the Being, this soul is permitted entry into the Hall of Wisdom. He deduces that this soul successfully accomplished its life purpose, thereby raising its light-colour-vibration by one degree and graduates to the next lesson.

He backs out of the booth into the main chamber. He decides to leave the temple and returns to the square, floating high above the massing group of souls below. He rises high above the pyramid and looks out across the city in all directions. The Etheric City is astounding.

Jaxon suddenly makes sense of what is happening. The city and its population of cosmic ethereal beings all work towards one purpose, to evaluate, process and train returning souls from their incarnation in a physical life on Earth. The whole city is responsible for managing the evolution of souls for the entire planet, numbering obviously, in the billions.

He looks down and far below. Through the translucence of etheric matter, he notices a very faint outline. He focuses and follows the outline. It's a circle, a huge circle. He gasps with sudden familiarity. The clarity of the full structure pops out at him.

It's Earth... planet Earth. I'm on the other side of the barrier, the veil, just beyond the inner orbit, in the same space... but not in the same space... in a different mode of space. Wow, its just like a dream, an etheric experience inside... no, outside the physical brain.

He decides to explore some of the Etheric City. He floats down and through the laneways that separate the buildings. There are no cars, bikes or buses. He stops and approaches a wall. He pushes his hand through, slowly and withdraws it. He pushes his whole body through into the living space of a home. It is empty. Luckily, the occupants are away, busy at work. He feels nervous and backs out through the wall. He can focus his vision to see through walls. He watches an ethereal being who, in turn, notices and stares back until he moves on.

Everything is made of the same, green-blue-teal etheric matter, matter of the mind. He does not possess the skill or understand how this is accomplished.

There appears to be no day or night, or any reference to time. Here, time operates completely differently to Earth. It seems eternal, unbound, unmeasured, yet there is process, order, functionality throughout the city. So, maybe there is something akin to cosmic time.

He looks up to notice a spark of light in the distance, rise high above the city and disappear behind a tiny flash. Curious, he floats up to the same vicinity. There is nothing, only the vast empty shell of purple etheric space. He looks down. The city glows far below.

He suddenly realises that the Etheric Dimension, is an in-between dimension, a dimension between two others, the Physical Dimension far below and something more… high above. He looks up, tries to peer through the mist and remembers his deepest desire.

Seek my God. Where's my God. I must know the truth. Seek my…

He chants this, over and over, turning it into a mantra, again, stronger, again. Louder, again.

A light appears above his head and shines brightly down over his Causal Body. His entire body appears as a bright spark from afar. A thin gateway, a portal opens. He looks up into the tube of light and within the flash of a split second, he is pulled through. The gateway closes.

He travels with immense speed through a tunnel of intense white light. He breaks through and is expelled out the other side. Far into the distance on both sides, he sees a wide arching expanse or bridge of intense colours. The bridge consists of forty-five degree angled strips of colours, slowly moving down on both his left and right and rolling in under itself, continuously, endlessly. He senses that the colours themselves are conscious, or rather, raw consciousness.

He decides to cross and literally steps forward onto the bridge. The first colour he touches, is a deep, rich red. He gasps. His Causal Body instantly changes to the same colour. He is filled with the raw sensation, raw vibration of cosmic willpower through love, God's love. He lingers for a while assimilating the experience. He steps onto yellow, and is now completely overwhelmed with inspiration and perseverance to evolve back towards perfection. Green embodies him in harmony and purity. Blue is the radiance of pure wisdom, and indigo, pure devotion. Progress is slow and laboured as he works his way across the bridge and each new colour experience. Finally, he makes it to the other side.

He stands in front of a thick black cloud. The cloud is a wall in all directions. The rainbow bridge of colours disappears into this black mass, or rather, looking back, it emerges out of it. The black mass slowly swirls and bubbles in front of him, and appears wet, like boiling tar.

Jaxon reaches out with his right hand and touches the black mass. There is no sensation at all. He pushes his hand into the black mass and withdraws it. The black mass coats his right hand, taking a while to dissipate and for his hand to return to its normal luminosity.

He feels no pain, heat or cold, wet or dry. He felt that the black mass has density, weight, his hand heavy while immersed. He knows he has little choice but to enter.

He steels his nerve, focuses on his mantra and steps through, into the wall. The rainbow bridge and all light, even from his own body disappears. He is completely immersed in the blackness. The mass is heavy, pressing in on him from all sides. He can barely move, only able to wriggle his shoulders, hands and feet, trying to swim forward. Somehow, he feels he is floating upwards, his body lighter in density. He knows he is rising, slowly, being regurgitated up and out from the bowels of this mass.

He continues to focus on his mantra, repeats it continuously, whilst maintaining his wriggle. The weight of the mass is beginning to sap his energy, his strength. Intuitively, he knows there is a surface… hopes there is a surface. Exhausted, he stops to rest for a while and enters a docile state, not quite awake, not quite asleep. At long last, a rupturing bubble spews him out onto the surface of the black mass. He floats on his back.

Slowly he regains composure. He floats up, off the surface of the mass into an upright position and waits for the last of the attached black material to dissipate and fall away. His Causal Body quickly returns to its normal luminance.

He peers around to find he stands in a vast empty, deep purple void. He looks down to see the subtle purple hue reflect upon the black swirling mass. He floats up, away from the boiling ocean, and continues to rise to an immense height, until he can no longer see anything below.

Wow, what was that black stuff? Ooh, hang on, I get it, I understand. God must manifest the base components of what is used to sustain Creation. That black mass must be... the first matter, the primordial materium. The rainbow bridge is the primordial light-colour-frequency of conscious force and energy. They merge to provide life, form and expression to the dimensions below. All we need now are the sparks of... wait, what's that?

High above, in the distance, he sees what emerges as a huge bubble emitting a light from within. He moves up towards the light. It grows, larger and larger. It is immense. He slows his approach, unsure if it's safe to continue. He stops.

The bubble is equivalent in size to a small, slightly squashed moon. It looks like an enormous single cell organism, with an outer, double membrane enclosing the body, the light cell. He sees that the entire organism sits atop a massive sphere, making an indentation in like manner to a small pebble sitting upon a balloon. He stands beneath the cell inside the sphere.

The organism emits a low and very deep vibrational sound, permeating down around the outer surface of the sphere. The organism is alive. It displays the very slow motion of breathing in and then exhaling, and occasionally wobbles like jelly. It seems to contain an immense amount of power and energy. Metallic colours flash across the surface of the cell.

He hears... no feels, a deep distant roll of thunder high above and beyond the organism. He feels a second roll of thunder at a slightly different pitch. At the point where the primary wave intersects the secondary wave, a sharp distinct crack of sound is produced.

Suddenly, a massive beam of light force from high above streams down and hits the top of the organism. The beam lasts for about ten seconds. The organism completely absorbs the light conscious energy and grows larger within its membrane. The immense cell vibrates and wobbles. Shortly thereafter, waves of intense light-colour-energy of all colours, roll down the outer surface of the sphere.

Something catches his mind's eye. He moves closer towards to the inner surface of the sphere. He sees billions and billions of very thin strands of fibre, which protrude out from the middle waistline of the organism and collectively, forms the illusory outer surface of the sphere. The cell continually transmits the light-colour-energy down each and every fibre.

Suddenly, a flash of light appears far behind his left shoulder. The flash subsides. Something is moving with lightning speed towards him. He turns to face and see what it is. A figure, growing in size, in clarity, approaches. He gasps.

Illuminated by white light from within, a figure rides, glides, upon a large horse… a winged horse… its wings stretched out wide on both sides. They ride up to him. The horse rears up on its hind legs, kicks out with both front legs, neighs, snorts and flaps its wings vigorously twice, then settles into a quiet, attentive stance. The horse glares at him.

The figure is clad in white illuminated plates of armour and wears a helmet with a thin extension down the bridge of the nose. In the right hand, a long white spear is held, with a long thin, pointed arrowhead at the end. A large white shield is attached to the left forearm. The figure glares at him through two glowing white orbs for eyes. The nose, cheeks, ears, mouth and chin appear plain and perfectly proportioned. He cannot tell if they are two entities or joined as one. He is certain though that he stands before an archetypal warrior archangel.

A slow, deep voice speaks, seemingly from all angles at once, telepathically into his mind.

"You have travelled a long way in your search. This is the furthest you can go."

"Is that God?"

"That which you see, is a Supernal Creator Being, a Cosmic Monad, a creator of souls, if you like. You have seen the Supernal receive the divine force, which in turn is channelled to sustain all the life connected to this Supernal."

"*That which you seek exists in the next dimensional realm, which both encompasses and pervades through the All. It is the realm of emptiness, filled only with the mind of God. It is not possible for you to stand before God. You will not be able to withstand and survive the experience. Your... body... will simply, disintegrate.*"

"*This is truly amazing, beyond my imagination.*"

"*Your greatest desire has brought you here. What you have witnessed is the highest truth permitted to you for your understanding. You have lived without attachment, yet apart from your world. When you return, you can no longer continue to do so. This would be considered a rejection of Creation.*"

"*Your world is at a crossroads, on the brink of destruction. Many messengers have been sent, yet through all their divisions, humanity has strayed from the path once more. Know thy enemy, they do not!*"

"*Your world can no longer determine its own fate, its own future, for its own benefit. Your world is in free fall. As such, your fate will be determined by others and in so doing, your freedom and your divinity will be lost.*"

"*Know that this is 'not' the plan... the Divine plan for your world. So, now, the time has arrived to implement an intervention... through you... Jaxon!*"

"*You will be provided with the power to defend your world and repair that which is broken. And 'only' in DEFENCE, are you permitted to use this power. And in so doing, you must always remain upon the Path of the Righteous. Do you understand?*"

"*Y... Yes, I do!*"

"*Do you!? So, who is the enemy?*"

"*If you and I are the Light, then it's the Darkness, and anything which creates Darkness in others!*" he replies.

"*Yes, correct! Although... you do not yet realise the full extent of your answer. Humanity sustains a world of Darkness. It feeds upon your suffering and misery and exerts an influence to also help bring your world to the brink.*"

"*So, Jaxon... it's time to decide. We will give you the power to defend your world. Do you wish to accept this burden, for a burden it will be?*"

"*Yes... of course! Is it not my purpose?*" he replies instantly.

The archangel lowers the spear and points the tip at his chest. A bolt of light fires out from the spear and crosses the void between them in an instant. The bolt of light hits Jaxon square upon his breast plate. He recoils back, his Causal Body momentarily flashes brightly with the light, as the energy, the power, is quickly absorbed and assimilated.

"Return and defend your world. You have the eyes to see, the ears to hear and the knowledge to know all things. Trust in yourself at the darkest hour."

The archangel raises the spear. The horse knows, rears up, throws out its wings and flaps them with might. They turn, fly and disappear in a flash of distant light.

Jaxon remains alone in the vast void. There is nowhere to go. He knows it's time to return. He looks down. Suddenly, he hears something... a click... another click... and another. He is drawn by the sound and simply allows his Causal Body to fall, pulled by the silver cord with increasing speed, back towards his physical body.

Chapter Eight

Awake, at Last!

Jaxon's eyes spring open wide. In one motion he pushes himself up, into a sitting position with arms straight, behind and supporting him. He throws his head back and takes a huge gulp of air, feeling, sensing, that he has just resurfaced inside his physical body. He stares blankly at the ceiling, disorientated, as yet unable to know or remember where he is. A silent alarm announces that he is awake.

Emerging from deep sleep he lets out a gruff groan, now able to hear his own voice.

"Aaaarrrgh!" he gasps.

His breathing settles. His eyes quickly focus on the soft spotlights in the ceiling. He lies back. He looks down at the oxygen mask over his mouth and nose. With his right hand he gently pulls the mask up, over his head and lets it fall away. He notices the intravenous needle, pipe and bag. He leans over to look at the dentist's chair, now a hospital bed. He lies back. He feels weak, weak in the arms, body and legs. His memory begins to recall the pieces.

The door in front of him quietly opens inwards and turns ninety degrees. Benjamin stands in the doorway and briskly walks into the chamber.

"Jaxon, you are awake! Welcome back. Wait, relax, relax!"

Benjamin walks up and places his hand on Jaxon's shoulder to calm him. He raises the bed into a sitting position. He inspects the vital signs on the monitor, steady and normal.

"Whoa, my head... is spinning, I can't... get a handle on things. Where am I?"

"Just relax. It will take a while for all your senses to return. Here, drink this."

Benjamin grabs a nutrient rich can out of the cooler box under the bed, opens it and pops a straw through the hole, before placing it in Jaxon's hands. He quickly removes the intravenous needle and binds the wound with a plaster and removes all the sensors.

"Yes, well, it will take a little while for you to re-orientate yourself. Just try to focus on your breathing while you drink that," he pauses. "Physically, everything seems normal."

Benjamin quickly moves around to the left side of the bed. He stops the metronome and from a small hidden cupboard in the wall, he withdraws a small portable cylindrical ophthalmic imaging device.

"Now, please relax. This will only take... a few... short... seconds."

He places the device close to and over Jaxon's open left eyeball, bends forward and looks through the scope, to inspect the optic nerve and retina.

"Argh, excellent, excellent!"

Benjamin stands and returns the device to the cupboard. He walks back to look down at Jaxon with a thin smile. He nods, pleased, satisfied and relieved.

"What... what's happening?" Jaxon whispers.

"You have survived an intense ordeal and passed. The trial has been a complete success."

"Ooh, right!"

"Don't worry, it will all make sense very soon. Come on, let me help you up."

Benjamin throws back the thin blanket and lifts the armrest. He gently grabs Jaxon's ankles and slowly moves them over the left edge of the chair. He holds Jaxon's left elbow and underarm and pulls him into a standing position. He lets go.

Jaxon wobbles but quickly regains his balance. He steps forward with his left and then his right foot. He walks towards and through the open doorway. He sees the partition, the tiled floor and the double doors on the far wall. Suddenly, with a flood, he remembers everything. He wobbles and holds onto the doorframe to steady himself.

"I'm the first and only person to survive, aren't I?"

"Yes!"

"And what happened to... the others?"

"Yes, well, they haven't been so fortunate," he said. "Invariably, they either never return, trapped on the other side or, if able to make it back, they wake up damaged, mad, insane and without the light. All we can do is offer a quick, merciful end."

Jaxon stands in silence for a moment. He stares at the tiled floor and nods in acceptance.

"How long was I out for?"

"I think you should try and answer that yourself."

He looks up and stares through the ceiling. He allows his mind to connect with physical time.

"Pretty much bang on… five days," he whispers.

"Precisely! You are no longer the same person. You have changed. It will take some time for you to understand these changes, and what they mean. So, be patient."

Jaxon steps forward to stand in the middle of the right-hand partition of the chamber.

"What happens now?"

"Are you hungry? Let's go to the mess hall, shall we. And then I can show you around the rest of this facility."

Benjamin leads the way past the waist-high swinging doors, through the double doors and down the corridor. They turn right at the main intersection.

"I remember you, now. You're Benjamin Burgess, born on, holy cow, the 4th of July, in 1972. Rather patriotic of you. You're fifty-three years of age. You were recruited on the premise of saving your country, to be the administrator, by those… who… built… this…"

Jaxon slows to a standstill. He looks up, peering far ahead. Benjamin turns to watch.

"By those who wish to help."

"We're in trouble!" he exclaims. "The planet… is in trouble!"

"Yes, it is!"

A few long moments pass in silence. Realisation sweeps over Jaxon's face.

"There's more… than… one. There are others… from…," he gasps. "We're being invaded! And this facility… this facility is a…"

"Yes, yes, it is! Welcome… to your new home."

Benjamin smiles, turns and pushes the double doors open.

Jaxon brings his gaze down and stares through the open doorway.

I can see. I am awake.

Resonance of the Bison

Resonance of the Bison

1

A deep rumble rolled across the prairie, over the cusp and down the hill towards town. Reaching the first cottage, the vibration shot up through the stumps, across the floorboards and into the legs of the cot. Startled, Zachariah's eyes sprang open. He felt it through his arms, legs, spine, before he heard it. He sat bolt upright and tilted his head for a moment. He knew exactly what that sound was.

He leapt to his feet and grabbed his thick deer skin jacket from the hook behind the closed door. He slipped it on, the tassels under the arms and around the hem at the waist, whipped violently back and forth in the rush. From the side table he grabbed a long-sheathed hunting knife and tucked it in behind the belt of his leather pants, also tasselled down the outer length of each leg. He grabbed his knapsack and hurriedly thread the leather strap around his left shoulder, slammed his beaver hat over his head and reached for his musket leaning up against the wall in the corner. He always left his boots on.

He strode out from the back room, crossed the front room in three long strides and pulled the cottage door wide open. He jumped over the three steps to the bare ground and ran around the back. Stopping dead in his tracks, he stared out at the grassed hills. It was late in the afternoon. The blood drained, turning his face a ghostly white in shock.

A dark shadow had already burst over the ridge and was quickly rolling down the top half of the hills in a long wavey ripple, as far as the eye could see, both to the north and the south. Easily a million horn of buffalo, American Bison, running shoulder to shoulder, row after row, were bearing down upon the town in full stampede. The herd so enormous, he had never seen anything like it before.

A bubble in the centre pushed forward ahead of the line. A huge white bull, standing taller than a full-grown man and twice the size of any other bull, led the charge out in front. The white bull bore down directly for Zachariah.

He dropped the knapsack and ran forward a dozen paces whilst loading the musket with power and ball as he ran. The white bull crossed into range closing in fast. He stood in a balanced side-on position, raised his rifle and took aim. He drew in a slow even breath and at the end of the exhale... he fired.

The lead ball hit the white bull at the base of the neck, between the bison's left collar and shoulder bones. The ball pierced through the heart, went straight through the entire length of the bull and out through its rump. Without losing a step, completely unfazed, unhindered, the bull continued the charge at full gallop.

Zachariah was stunned. He had no time to think. He felt a pang of panic. He raised the barrel and reloaded frantically. He set the fuse cap and looked up in readiness for the next shot. The rumbling of the charge across the ground was deafening. The white bull raised its snout and roared. The long bellow echoed across the plain. He was mesmerised. It was too late.

The white bull dipped its head and hit Zachariah with the full force of its charge. The right horn speared straight through the middle of his chest and out through his back. The bull raised its head, easily lifting him off the ground. The bull leapt up and crashed in through the back wall of the cottage, crushing his body against the splintering beams of wood.

Many of the townsmen had also appeared in a long line to fire their muskets upon the herd, alas, to no avail. They were all struck down. The herd of bison smashed into the town with the full force of its might. Bison crashed through doors, windows and walls of every single building, in a fury of destruction.

The men who tried to fight were quickly gored and torn to pieces. Those who ran along a patio, through a lane or street were hit, knocked down and trampled beneath 2,000 pounds a beast. The women who tried to run for cover in a vain attempt to escape were also crushed. The children, hiding in closets, chests, the attic, a basement, all died beneath the weight of every collapsing building. The carnage, so complete that every single man, woman and child perished, every building levelled. As the sun set, the herd dispersed and vanished, having purged this newly arrived pestilence from their plains.

****

Drenched in feverishly hot sweat, Zachariah opened his eyes wide and sprang bolt upright to gasp for air. He threw off his blanket over the nearly dead coals of the campfire as he grabbed at his chest with both hands, his eyes frantic, the images fresh in his vision. He inhaled a second gulp, realising he was still alive. There was no pain, no hole pierced through his chest. There were no bison, in the quiet dark.

"A dream. It was a dream!" he muttered.

He looked down at the corner of his blanket as it began to smoulder and smoke. He reached forward, yanked the blanket back and stamped the burning fibres out in the dirt. He looked up into the sky. By the stars he measured two hours till dawn. He quietly crouched forward to rekindle the fire. Watching the flames flicker helped to shake the dream from his mind.

"Gawd, damn it!" he whispered. "Third time I've had the same dream… in as many months! What's going on?" he pondered.

He sat a billy of water on the fire and prepared his tin mug with sweetened black tea. Soon, he poured the steaming water into the mug, stirred and took a sip. His nerves began to settle, beneath the half moon on 25th July 1860.

To loosen his creaking bones, Zachariah rose to his feet, stretched his back and walked a short distance to the edge of the small flat-topped ridge. Between sips, he gazed out over the iridescent grassed plain below. A small, dark clump of bison were nestled in a gully between two hills to avoid the night's chill. He was standing at the foothills of the Rocky Mountains in far western Kansas, as they merge eastward into the rolling hills of the mid-central plains.

Turning around, he looked back over the camp. A small band of young hunters are all still asleep, two near the small campfire and three preferring to sleep under their wagons. The four wagons are tied together in a semi-circle around the camp, with the horses corralled within the arch by rope. He always preferred to camp on high ground with steep sides, and dig a pit for a small cooking fire, than be trapped in a gully. He rubbed the ache from his temples.

"I'm already too old for this business," he mumbled. "It's becoming harder to keep these young folk from getting themselves killed. The night watch fell asleep, again."

He sipped the black tea in contemplation. As guide, he led the band of hunters into the area to begin a three-day buffalo hunt, without being threatened by the Arapaho. He knew they had travelled southeast into the open plains of their summer hunting grounds.

Zachariah's imposing figure stands at a height of six foot three. He is broad shouldered, strong and evenly muscled. He is light and agile on his feet despite his size. His once dark-brown hair has now turned into a shaggy grey mop, which he tries to keep neat and tidy under his beaver hat. He sports a thick robust grey beard that hides his thick neck. He has tanned olive, leathery skin, with deep lined wrinkles around his squinting black eyes, large round nose and wide mouth with thin lips, which display the angled scars of two deep, parallel cuts.

He always wears two cotton shirts under his tasselled, deer leather jacket, along with tasselled, deer skin trousers, a thick leather belt and boots. He carries a Henry rifle and one, long-barrelled, six-shot, Colt revolver on his right hip. He sheathes a long, sharp hunting knife on his left hip, a smaller one hidden in his left boot and several pouches tied to his belt.

Having lived in the wilderness for thirty years now, he understood the importance of being clean. He bathes regularly and thoroughly checks his body for fleas, ticks and other biting bugs. His cotton clothes are washed regularly, sometimes dipped into a large pot of hot boiling water. The leathers are routinely wiped over with a wet cloth, brushed down with a small soft brush and wiped again. Once a year the leathers are treated and waterproofed with neatsfoot oil. These and many other traits have kept disease and ill health at bay.

As soon as the first light broke the horizon, illuminating the deep purple sky, the band of hunters woke and stirred, like a pack of rattlesnakes, each waking the other. They rose as a collective, stretched, rolled up their rough bedding and walked over to the campfire. With their billy steaming, they filled their mugs with either black tea or coffee, and a breakfast of corn bread, salted bacon and boiled eggs was already waiting.

Zachariah sat upon his rock watching the hustle and bustle and excited chit-chat of the expeditioners, whilst sipping a fresh mug of tea. His kit was already packed. Each of the five young hunters looked like a complete dishevelled mess after just three days of trekking.

He rose to his feet and poured the cooling water from his billy into two water skins. He tied them to the back of his saddle, resting them atop the rear rump of his horse. He turned and instructed the men to clean up and ready themselves for the hunt.

When the sun had cleared the horizon by a foot, Zachariah led the troop of hunters out of the camp. They rode gently down the northern slope from the summit they were camped upon and turned northeast to canter along the ridge of a row of low-lying hills. The small herd of buffalo that sheltered in the gully, below to their right, had moved out to join the larger herd in the open plain to the east. They rode around the tip of the gully and into the open prairie.

Out in the middle of the plain a large herd of bison was grazing and moving slowly into the warmth of the rising sun. It was still. Downwind, the hunters formed a line, rifles drawn, their barrels casually pointing into the clear blue sky. Zachariah issued a distinctive whistle, a cry from an eagle, to let them loose. He remained behind, out of the line of fire and watched.

The hunters charged at full gallop. Startled, the bison broke. The men spread out along the southeast flank of the herd, firing at will. They pushed the main herd in a wide left turning arch across the plain, as it began to splinter with buffalo scattering in all directions.

Zachariah turned north and meandered along the western edge of the plain, expecting to meet up with the hunters once they rode full circle. He cantered just inside a long row of pine, fir and spruce trees, when a bull stepped out twenty-five yards in front of him. The bull was blowing hard, frothing at the mouth and snout. The bull looked all but spent.

His horse, well versed, slowed to stand still. His loaded rifle was ready, the butt resting upon his right thigh. He raised the rifle and took aim at the buffalo's heart. The air was dead still. Remaining calm, quiet, he drew in a breath. Time slowed. At that moment he… hesitated. The floating dust, suspended in mid-air, paralysed. He felt haunted, overcome with a surreal sensation. Something was wrong. This did not feel right… at all.

Suddenly, Zachariah was gripped by an overwhelming sensation of sadness, of immense loss. Was it pity? Did he feel sorry for the buffalo? He was uncertain. Yet, he could not bring himself to pull the trigger... and... shortly thereafter, he lifted the barrel. Somehow, he knew he could not shoot the buffalo. The exhausted bull turned and disappeared among the trees.

He walked his horse on and stood beneath the shadow of a huge pine tree, deep in thought. The troop of young hunters soon appeared, riding out of the plain from the northeast. Their horses were gassed, breathing hard and wet with sweat.

"That's enough for today," he said. "Go get the wagons and strip every carcass of skin, horn, and tongue," he commanded. "That's what you're here for, right?"

He watched the men work, leaving almost two hundred exposed, red corpses to rot in the sun. His heart wrenched at the sight, even for someone so experienced. He found himself shocked, appalled and dismayed at the wasteful destruction.

He was a mountain man and had managed to avoid the buffalo hunt until now. He needed the money and out of necessity, enlisted to guide this expedition. All other avenues of income had dried up and the mountain men were fast becoming a dying breed.

By nightfall, the camp was boisterous and jubilant. The hunters drank a bottle of whisky between them to celebrate the bountiful harvest well into the night. Zachariah did not take part. He moved away to sit on his rock, sullen and forlorn. Something was wrong. Something was very wrong. He could not put his finger on it. He did not understand why, why did he feel this way? Yet, he knew deep within his bones. He slept uneasily through the night.

The hunters rode out for the second day and followed the herd far to the north. When found they simply charged the buffalo. Zachariah did not give the call and left the field of carnage to flank the southern rim of the plain looking for fresh Indian sign.

Suddenly, a severely wounded cow, shot through the shoulder, staggered across his path. Out of breath, the cow stopped and stared at him, seemingly pleading for a mercy. He aimed his rifle for the kill shot. Once again, an overwhelming sadness swept through him. He could not bring himself to kill the buffalo. He lowered the rifle and rode to a nearby stream.

He dismounted and knelt beside the stream. He washed his hands and face and then dipped his whole head into the chilled water. He held his head submerged for a few moments, before sitting up and swishing the water over his back with a flick of his head.

"What's the matter with me?" he muttered. "I... I... can't do it. No... it's... it's wrong. I know it in my bones. But... but... why?" he whispered.

He sat beside the stream for almost an hour, before mounting up. He rode back out onto the plain and followed the line of dead bison, until he found the wagons, and the men, busily processing each carcass. He could not watch. A tear swelled up and rolled down his left cheek, and then another swelled and rolled down his right. He looked away and quickly kicked his horse into a brisk canter towards the nearest tree line, a mile away.

By the time he dismounted behind the trunk of a large pine, the tears were streaming down his face. He fell to the ground, leaned back against the trunk and wept uncontrollably. No matter how hard he tried to stop, he simply could not stem the flow. Finally, the sobbing subsided on the hour, and he regained some composure. The only other time he had ever felt such distress, such anguish, was following the death of his wife, some fifteen years ago. Ironically, it felt like the same thing.

He rode back into camp at sundown.

"What's wrong old man? Lost your edge?" the youngest hunter commented jovially.

Bemused by their elation, he returned a disapproving scowl.

The celebrations continued once more through the night. With hot mug in hand, he moved away and sat stoic upon his rock, staring out over the ridge and across the plain, earning him a few uneasy glares. They knew something was wrong.

"They know not what they are doing!" he whispered prophetically.

Unable to bear further witness, Zachariah silently gathered his things and left the camp in the middle of the night. In the morning, feeling vulnerable, the hunters immediately broke camp and hastily made tracks for home.

Zachariah Yanasie was born into the large Jewish community of Charleston, South Carolina on 7th May 1815. His Jewish, Judaic father Jeremiah Yanasie, met, instantly fell in love with and married his tough, robust and highly spirited, Irish Protestant mother, Fiadh, in Charleston. The union was virtually a scandal in both the Jewish and Irish communities.

However, Jeremiah's strict adherence to his Judaic religious practices, unexpectedly, merged rather comfortably with Fiadh's strict Christian Protestantism. They viewed each other's dedication as being next to godliness.

Thus, Zachariah, his elder brother Elijah and his younger sister Lydia, were all given biblical names. They were all heavily schooled in both Judaism, including the Kabbalah, and the biblical version of the Christian Protestant faith. Fiadh taught them to read using religious texts. Only Elijah received a formal education afforded by the family. Zachariah and Lydia began work at an early age, both around the house and within the community. The work Zachariah found in Charlestown was long, tough and paid meagre wages.

The moment Zachariah had saved enough to buy a musket, hunting knife, leathers and kit, he professed his intent to go west and try his hand on the plains or in the mountains. Exhibiting the same wild spirit as his mother, Jeremiah knew Charlestown was not the place for his son and bought Zachariah his first horse. Jeremiah bade him good luck and farewell when Zachariah promptly left Charlestown in the spring of 1831, just before his sixteenth birthday.

From South Carolina, Zachariah travelled west through the northern parts of Georgia and Alabama, working from plantation to plantation. He instantly discovered a profound distaste for the treatment of African slaves and quickly moved on. He rode northwest into

Arkansas and Oklahoma. He spent the summer, autumn and winter helping ranchers and settlers build and establish their farms upon their newly acquired lands.

On hearing news that the Rocky Mountain Fur Company were looking for trappers, he rode northwest into Kansas and west through what would become Colorado, as soon as winter broke, in the spring of 1832. He signed up with the Rocky Mountain Fur Company and found his way into the Rocky Mountains to begin his life as a mountain man.

He learnt his trade and how to survive in the wilderness quickly, under the wily guidance of James (Jim) Felix Bridger who, with his associates, had purchased the company two years earlier. He traversed the mountains and nearby plains working for Jim through to 1834, becoming very proficient at hunting beaver and deer, until the company dissolved. He went out on his own and would push further and further into the new frontier.

Zachariah was soon introduced to the Flathead and Shoshone native tribes and began to learn how to speak their languages. The first time he encountered a war party of Arapaho, with whom the Flathead and Shoshone occasionally fought, they pursued him out of the lower hills of the Eastern Central Rocky Mountains, onto a large wide open grassy plain.

To escape, he dumped and burned all his hides and belongings, and stripped himself and his small-statured, white-and-apricot patched appaloosa mare to the flesh. He completely covered himself and his horse in buffalo dung, and then slowly and calmly walked into and immersed himself among a massive herd of buffalo for the next two days. Their tracks were soon lost, untraceable, among the mass of buffalo.

The Arapaho war party returned to their chief, Little Raven, to report the story of a young white hunter who had turned into a 'heneecee', a buffalo bull and disappeared. Little Raven pondered upon this deeply and saw it as providence.

Over the next few years, when he began to explore the northern territories of Dakota and Montana, Zachariah used the same tactic to avoid war parties of the Ojibwa and the Crow. In the southern states of New Mexico and Texas he evaded capture by the Apache, Comanche and Kiowa. He did not carry anything of value he was not prepared to burn.

Word of his renown spread, and he quickly earned the respectful connotation of 'little white bull', in the native Arapaho language. This was an honour considering the white buffalo bull was held as the highest revered spiritual animal within their culture.

Chief Little Raven sued for peace with the Comanche, Kiowa and surrounding tribes in 1840. With fewer war parties on patrol, Zachariah found he was able to traverse the mountains and plains a little more freely. He no longer needed to cover himself in buffalo dung.

At the same time the fur trade virtually collapsed overnight, both from over-exploitation of wildlife and the drop in demand for beaver and deer pelts. Bored and needing to escape the winter of 1841, he left the mountains and milled around the trading posts dotted further east of the Rockies along the trails of the mid-western plains.

Arapaho trading parties would regularly appear and trade hides for food and European goods. He met and befriended them and quickly began to learn their language. When winter thawed into spring and with nothing better to do, he asked and was permitted to join them and travelled with the party to their northern tribal lands, near the southern border of what would become known as Wyoming.

On the way, sharing a peace pipe around the campfire and laughing jovially, the Arapaho shared their revered tale about 'little white bull'. Zachariah cried with laughter as well, revealing how he managed to lead their war parties around and around in circles, and in so doing, acknowledged that he was in fact, the little white bull. The Arapaho sat in shock.

As soon as they arrived at their main tribal camp, he was immediately summoned to meet Chief Little Raven. He graciously and respectfully introduced himself as Zachariah Yanasie. On hearing his family name, Chief Little Raven, turned and looked at his fellow elders a little stunned and perplexed.

"Providence… indeed, this is providence!" he told them. "And the little white bull, is not so little after all," he said. "Too late to change your name, your spirit is legend now."

He laughed merrily and called for a feast and dance that night to celebrate. He invited Zachariah to stay and teach him about the ways of the European settlers. He was given his own teepee on the edge of the encampment close to the nearby river.

Zachariah quickly settled into a routine. At first light he would rekindle his campfire, boil a billy of water and prepare a hot mug of sweetened black tea with breakfast. He would walk a mile upstream to check his traps for trout, strip and bathe in a shallow secluded nook in the river, and return to camp with his catch, to the delight of the children. He would then assist with the running of the camp, helping to solve problems with a white man's solution. Roughly every three months he would ride to the nearest trading post to restock his supplies.

Chief Little Raven's second daughter, Litonya, which means hummingbird, took an interest in him. At a very discreet distance, she followed him upstream one morning and watched him bathe. With years of experience, he caught on rather quickly that he was being followed and with his sharp eye, spotted her almost instantly. The following morning, he disappeared and caught her by surprise as she tried to find him. He introduced himself and explained that she need not hide. She was shy and he went about his business as usual.

Litonya was of medium height with slim shoulders and round hips. She had a gentle face to match her curious manner, with large brown eyes, delicate nose and thin lips. She wore her straight long dark-brown hair behind the shoulders and dressed in the softest deer leathers adorned with all the usual tribal markings, tassels, beads and lacings.

They began to spend more and more time together during the summer, invoking much gossip. She helped him master their language, taught him their ways, customs and mythology. When out foraging, she explained the properties of plants and herbs and how to use them for medicine. In return, he talked about his heritage, where he was from and the mythology of his people, although she did not quite conceptualise what a Bible was.

With the onset of autumn, Chief Little Raven invited Zachariah to a powwow. After breakfast, they rode out of camp and Little Raven led the way to a sacred gorge in a deep, semicircular ravine, surrounded by a barrier of tall pines. A small stream fell over the edge, down into the gorge. High atop a cliff, a naturally formed rectangular rock bench, a few feet from the edge, faced westward overlooking the gorge and out through the open entrance to the horizon. The view and beauty of the gorge was breathtaking.

Sitting beside Chief Little Raven upon the rock bench, Zachariah was asked to explain everything he understood about the ways and customs of the Europeans. He spoke for a couple of hours explaining the different nations, from whence they came, how they lived, how they built their towns and cities, about their laws and methods of governance, and their history, including their many wars and how they were fought and won.

When Chief Little Raven had heard enough for the time being, he motioned for Zachariah to stop. They both sat silently for a long period of time staring out at the horizon. In deep contemplation, Chief Little Raven understood that his people were no match against the Europeans and that the world around him was about to change. His thoughts slowly turned to ones of survival. They finally stirred and returned to the tribe once the sun began to set.

On their second visit, the morning after the first snow, Zachariah completed his dissertation. They both sat for a long while before Chief Little Raven, spoke in a slow, deep, well considered tone. He seemed saddened.

"I have heard everything about the people from across the seas," he began, "And I have given the matter of the Europeans much thought," he said. "Your people do not live as we do. Your people live in a way where they consider themselves separate to… and apart from nature, the Great Mother. Whereas… we consider ourselves to be an intrinsic part of her," he paused. "If you believe yourself separate, you will not be able to connect with nature and experience her spirit in the way that we do."

"Experience the spirit of nature? I'm not sure what you mean!" Zachariah exclaimed.

"Strangely, I feel compelled to explain our sacred ways to you."

Chief Little Raven paused and slowly drew in a deep breath. He motioned for Zachariah to do the same. They continued to breathe, slowly, in unison for almost two minutes.

"Look at the distant line in the horizon, where the sky meets the Earth," he began. "Don't look directly at the line, look through it, past it, until you are seeing the beyond from within your mind, from your mind's eye," he paused.

"Once you are in this space, let go of yourself, lose the sense of self, and be free of the self. When you are able to truly accomplish this, then try and attune, try to feel the 'Great Spirit', the Great Mother… and connect, become one with her, feel her presence all around you," he paused.

Chief Little Raven stole a glance at Zachariah to see how he was faring.

"You will know… you will know when it happens… you will feel it," he stated. "Practise! You will need to practise until it feels and becomes natural to you. You can practise anywhere – by the river, on the plains, in a forest or on a mountain."

"But why… why should I do this?" he asked.

"It's of the greatest importance. You must understand that you are not separate from nature… that… you are connected to her. In fact, everything in nature is connected and contained within the Great Mother. When you feel it, you will understand why."

"Ok… ok! I will practise as much as I can."

"Good. Good!" he replied. "Once you can attune and connect with the Great Mother, she will always be there to help you."

"What… what do you mean! How so?" he asked, mystified.

"When you are attuned and connected with the Great Mother, you can ask her a question for advice or to show you the way. With a true heart, keep a strong focus on the question in your mind and project it out into space, into the 'Great Spirit'. It must be simple, concise and worthy of her attention… and after a while, let it go and then wait," he paused.

"When she is ready, the Great Mother will reply. And you will know the answer when you hear it... when you see it. It will be unmistakable. It will fit the question," he stated. "If you are lucky enough, the experience will change you... and then... you will understand the why."

"Wow," he gasped.

For the remainder of the afternoon, they sat together in silence.

All through winter Zachariah practised and practised and practised. He just could not seem to break through. In the meantime, he had fallen in love with Litonya and she with him. Chief Little Raven gave permission for them to marry, which they did when winter broke and the snows began to melt. The whole tribe joined in the celebration.

Three days after their marriage, Chief Little Raven asked Zachariah to join him on their third visit to the sacred gorge. He explained the problem of the Settlers' encroachment into their territory and asked for advice. Zachariah warned against armed conflict, demonstrating that the Arapaho were simply outnumbered and outgunned. He also warned that the Settlers and the US Government would want to take more and more, and the best the Chief could do would be to make peace and buy as much time as he could and find a way to survive.

Chief Little Raven fell silent peering out into the distance. Zachariah did the same.

For a few long moments he forgot himself. Suddenly, he saw it. Around the pine trees, the birds, the grass and even the rock, he saw the faint outline of an energy field. He slowly raised his hand and saw the outline of the energy field around his hand, wrist and arm. He closed his eyes and sensed the subtle hum of energy around and through his body, elevating him to a higher state. He connected with the Great Mother, and within that moment, felt the vast consciousness of all the life around him.

He had just found, grasped and touched the Universal Energy Field.

"I can see it! I can feel it!" he whispered.

At that moment, the field disappeared and his vision returned to normal. Chief Little Raven looked across at him with a broad smile. He slapped Zachariah on the back of the shoulder.

"Well done, my friend. You have seen the Great Mother."

Zachariah was filled with an immense sense of contentment. He also felt deeply at peace, something he had never felt before. He was happy, truly happy for the first time in his life.

Litonya fell pregnant during midsummer of his fourth year living with the tribe. He felt blessed and their love for each other bloomed through autumn and into winter. He looked after her and provided all that she needed and imagined becoming a father.

However, as the ice beside the river began to thaw, she slipped and fell awkwardly. Litonya haemorrhaged and went into labour early. Zachariah's wife and premature son both died that day, just before the spring of 1845. His peace and contentment were shattered.

Zachariah was distraught and struck down with immense grief. He wept and wailed in his teepee for the first few nights. He milled around the camp for three months looking sullen and forlorn, not knowing what to do with himself. The camp, the river, the grass all held the memory of her, which only added to his deep sorrow and depression.

With a heavy heart, Chief Little Raven summoned Zachariah to the sacred gorge.

"Little White Bull!" he began. "The tribe has suffered a terrible loss. Yet for you, the loss has been the most severe. You see our little hummingbird in everything, don't you? This only deepens and prolongs your sorrow, your grief," he said. "You have lost your way, your purpose. To save you from yourself, it's time you return to your own people."

Zachariah, looking down into the gorge below, nodded his head in understanding.

"Our lands are being encroached upon from the east and the south. I fear it's only a matter of time before there will be conflict between the tribes and the Europeans, as we try to defend our territories. As you say, it will be futile. They continue to arrive in greater and greater numbers and bring with them machines and weapons we cannot even dream of."

"If there is war... and they find you with us... their treatment of you will be particularly harsh and brutal. So, it's best that you go... go... and return to your people."

Zachariah saw the wisdom and agreed that this would be for the best.

"Yes, you are right!" he replied. "I will say farewell and ride out at first light."

"But know this!" Chief Little Raven warned. "You are no longer the same man. You have changed. You have seen the Great Mother," he said. "When you return to your people, you will see them differently. You will become... like... a ghost to them... an outcast, if you like, among your own kind."

"Why? What do you mean?" he asked, a little confused.

"Your people consider themselves separate from nature, that nature is something to be dominated, subjugated. The lands of the Europeans are themselves out of balance, including the way they see and use this thing called money."

"Their whole society, from their rulers down to the everyday man, is infested with a sense of selfishness... and... they are only truly considerate towards themselves. You can see this in the way that they fight and war and compete amongst each other for new territories."

"We have a name for this," he went on. "It's a sickness we call... Wetiko. In the past, some of our own tribes have been struck by this sickness. And even now, many of our people help the Europeans exploit these lands so they can be paid in your currency."

"Wetiko? I have never heard of it. What does it mean?"

"When a person sees himself as being separate from nature, and nature as an object, he then becomes selfish... and... in this state, he is at the greatest risk of being consumed by Wetiko," he explained. "Wetiko is like a force which enters into your mind. It changes you and makes you do things you never otherwise thought you could," he paused.

"Wetiko is like a disease. It can spread and infect everyone around you, until the whole community... the whole society is consumed by it. And once a society is consumed by Wetiko, that society behaves in a way which is harmful to the natural world, to themselves and towards the Great Mother," he said and continued.

"If no one can recognise and stop Wetiko, and if the fundamental laws of nature are broken... then even the Great Mother is weakened and can no longer resist being touched by and contaminated with Wetiko," he professed, "I need not explain what will happen if the Great Mother becomes sick with Wetiko."

"You make this sound like wickedness... like evil," Zachariah said.

"That is its outward expression, its causal effect, if you will," he paused.

"You see wickedness and evil as the act of ungodly men... and not as a thing of substance. As such, you do not consider from where Wetiko originates," he said. "Wetiko is like the essence, the sound of darkness, of entropy, of death, of destruction. It has only one goal, to draw and capture everyone within its trap, so that it can feed upon and consume everything."

With a stern face, Chief Little Raven turned to look at Zachariah.

"You will see. When you return to your people, you will see. And when you see the Wetiko, you must resist... or else risk being consumed yourself."

"I will do my best to stay true to what you have taught me," he promised.

Satisfied, the Chief nodded in acknowledgement. They both fell silent and meditated into the horizon until sundown.

That night the Arapaho had a feast and a dance to bid farewell to Little White Bull. They all wished him good spirit and good fortune on his travels. Zachariah was heartbroken, apprehensive and excited all at once. He rose early and rode out of camp at first light.

4

Riding eastward, Zachariah returned to the trading posts along the trails of western Kansas. He immediately hired himself out as a guide for the continuous stream of new settlers. He led wagon trains around the southern tip of the Rocky Mountains into Northern Texas, southwest through the Santa Fe Trail to the future territory of New Mexico, and west into the territory of future Utah, helping to ease tensions with the native tribes along the way.

The Mexico-American war broke out over the disputed territories of Texas and Southern California in May 1846. He enlisted to assist the topographical engineers of the US Army to complete their scouting and mapping works through these territories, and the future territory of Arizona, until the conclusion of the war in February 1848. Eluding Wetiko, he did not engage in any direct combat between the Mexican and American forces, preferring to avoid the west coast and remain close to the southern Rocky Mountains.

He did find the transition back to 'modern civilisation' extremely difficult. He kept mostly to himself and survived comfortably on his commissions. Chief Little Raven was right. He seemed unable to make any meaningful long-term contacts or friendships after leaving the Arapaho. In one way or another, in varying degrees, he saw the Wetiko sickness in all the settlers and cavalrymen. He saw it in the way they spoke, their views on things, how they regarded the land and behaved towards each other. The women, in general, were less consumed... but, the men... so quickly and easily provoked into aggression and violence.

GOLD! Discovered in Northern California in January 1848, sparked a boom. Zachariah led thousands of settlers through the California Trail and into the goldfields. In his eyes, the Wetiko was never more apparent, never more visible than watching the miners toil, day after day, knee deep in the mud to find the precious metal. And then to see them spend their hard-won bounty on liquor, women of ill repute and gambling. Madness!

He watched men cheat a less wily fellow out of his claim, rob him and even murder him for the luminous metal. The local native population were completely decimated and driven out of the region. He could not bring himself to partake of the insanity, promptly leaving the goldfields, to continue as a trail guide for the newly arriving prospectors and settlers. By 1855 the gold had all but dried up and the rush was over as quickly as it had begun, as was Zachariah's work as a trail guide.

The Panama Railway opened far to the south in Central America, linking the Atlantic with the Pacific Ocean, the eastern states with California. Passengers and goods could travel by steamship to one side, ride the train across and board a second steamship in comfort.

Catering to the huge influx of migrants into Northern California and San Francisco, many agricultural farms and ranches sprang up during the gold rush. Once the rush ended, Zachariah found work helping to establish a new cattle ranch east of San Francisco, close to a row of three small lakes, just below the western slopes of the Yosemite Ranges.

He managed the grassing and feeding of a small herd of cattle through the inter-mountain rangelands surrounding the ranch. In the spring, the cattle would graze the lower elevation foliage. He would move the herd to forage at higher elevation pastures during the summer months. The ranch hands would forage for, harvest, gather and store foliage during the summer and autumn for winter feeding, once he brought the herd back down from the slopes.

The greatest dangers were wolf packs, grizzly and black bears. He would often scout ahead looking for their sign, before moving the cattle. He would avoid any known range of a grizzly bear and try to scare them away if one approached too close to the herd. He would throw over a grizzly pelt, make himself appear huge and ring a loud cow bell to confuse the bear. Only on the rarest of occasions would he have to shoot one dead. He kept the herd close together in open areas and avoided thick wooded brush, cliffs, ravines and caves.

Everything was tracking nice and comfortably for the first two seasons of 1856 and 1857.

Zachariah travelled to San Francisco… once. He was astounded by the growth and expansion of the new, modern city. He had not set foot in a large town or city since leaving Charlestown so many years ago. The noise... the hustle and bustle... quickly became overwhelming and all too much for him. The people... so many people... all engrossed in their own daily lives, seemed completely foreign and distant to him. He hardly managed to sleep a wink at night, due to the cacophony of unusual sounds he heard in the streets surrounding the boarding house. He left and returned to the ranch after two days, much to his relief.

Keeping mostly to himself, he lived a simple, clean and structured life. He was organised and very good at looking after the cattle. He did not drink or socialise with the other ranch hands and cowboys and never spoke of his story. During the summer months he would often bed down further out into the wilderness, away from the main camp. Many of the other ranchers, rough ex-miners from the gold rush, grew suspicious and sceptical of him. Watching him work in the wilds, they soon guessed that he may have lived with the native Indians, which drew out their animosity towards him.

Approaching fifty-three years of age, he still held a strong, calm, experienced and imposing figure and a sharp wit. He was a dead shot with the rifle and quicker than the eye with the blade. He had the measure of each and every rancher, who all knew better than to seek a direct confrontation. As time passed through 1858 and 1859, he found himself more and more an outcast among his peers. He knew his time was up and took leave of ranching and his fellow ranchers as winter set in that year.

Having heard that buffalo hunting expeditions were looking for experienced guides, Zachariah took the slow road south and then east into New Mexico. He traversed the southern tip of the Rocky Mountains into Northern Texas, aiming to return to the Midwest by spring. It would not be long before he found himself leading his first expedition and would soon learn what a European American buffalo hunt was to entail.

5

Under the guidance of the halfmoon, Zachariah, with reins in hand walked his horse quietly, silently, away from the camp of sleeping hunters, on the low-lying ridge. After a mile, he mounted and rode northwest, seeking the sanctuary and respite of the Rocky Mountains.

The most prevalent display of Wetiko... the sickness... that he had ever seen, during the bloody killing frenzy of the hunters as they massacred the buffalo with a collective and particularly enthusiastic zeal, was still very fresh in his mind. It was no longer a hunt. It was the complete destruction of the entire herd. Shocked, disgusted and very troubled... even at himself... he was filled with a deep aching sorrow.

"How can they do this?" he muttered. "My own people. My own kind."

"I can no longer bear to be around them anymore," he growled. "What am I to do now?"

He stopped and looked up into the sky. The sun was just about to breach the horizon and bring in a new day. He considered his options. He could not go south, back into the new territories of Texas and New Mexico. California was on the other side of the Rockies.

"I guess it's north then," he grumbled.

Dejected and uncertain of his future, Zachariah rode a slow trek northwest until he hit the Rocky Mountains. His horse was a ten-year-old chestnut mare, with white-tipped hooves and a small white diamond patch upon her forehead. He then turned northward and rode parallel with and along the eastern slopes of the mountain range.

The calm, relaxed ease of being immersed in the wilderness quickly returned and lifted his spirits. He lived comfortably from the land and savoured the solitude. In the early hours of darkness before morning on the fifth day, he was haunted by a dream and sat bolt upright.

"What the hell!" he exclaimed.

Drenched in sweat, sitting wide-eyed, staring into the blackness of the night, the image of his death and the destruction of the whole town, were fresh in the vision of his mind.

"That... that buffalo dream... again!" he stammered. "What... what's going on?"

He flung his blanket off to the side, rose to his feet and then knelt to rekindle the campfire.

"Every few weeks... I have the same dream. Why? Why am I having these dreams? What's happening to me?" he pondered.

He placed the water-filled billy over the flame, his troubled mind unable to reconcile.

The dream would recur four weeks later as Zachariah found his way to what would be called Steamboat Lake. With food abundant and the scenery magical, he milled around exploring the lake for a couple of weeks, on what he thought was a wonderful holiday camp.

When the summer heat began to wane into autumn, he left Northern Colorado, on a north-westerly trajectory. He crossed the arid, desert-like plains of Southern Wyoming to reach the western slopes of Independent Mountain, Lizard Head Peak, Roberts Mountain and Wolverine Peak. He followed the mountain range on the same trajectory.

He rode past Fremont Lake, Willow Lake and stopped at New Fork Lakes. He noticed a small river flow out of a narrow valley and feed into the two lakes. Curious, he decided to follow New Fork River and turned north into a narrow ravine between Double Top Mountain on the right and Dome Peak on the left. He passed a row of half a dozen tall, black rock, boulder-stacked formations on his right and entered a beautiful, lush valley. The long north-south valley was dissected, virtually in half, like a 'T' intersection, by the western end of Palmer Canyon, a narrow, straight ravine which pointed a fraction below true east.

A long flat-topped cliff face, with several rounded outcrops of rock, ran the length of the northern wall of Palmer Canyon. Centuries of fallen rock, sand and dust, had piled up along the base of the cliff. A gently inclining slope of thick vegetation and pines ran along the southern side of the canyon. Reynolds Creek diverged from New Fork River and flowed down Palmer Canyon.

He saw the valley blocked to the north by mountains. Feeling as tired as the setting sun, he did not wish to camp on low ground in the valley. At the T-intersection he dismounted. With reins in hand, he led his mare a little north, to the right and behind the first round, jagged outcrop of rock. He found a path and climbed up onto the plateau, behind the cliffs.

He carefully walked east along the bare plateau, away from the edge and soon found a large pond of still water, in a wide open depression in the rock. He tested a drop of water on the tip of his tongue and immediately spat it out. There was a wall of rock running along the northern edge of the depression. He set up camp against the rock wall, lit a small cooking fire, ate a meagre evening meal and then reclined comfortably against a smooth rock.

Drenched in sweat, his eyes sprang open. He sat bolt upright, visibly shaken by the dream. The first light reflected beneath heavy, low-lying cloud. A gust of wind rolled across the plateau and over the top of the rock wall. The sudden chill sparked a shiver down his spine. It began to rain, a heavy downpour lasting only a few minutes before the clouds blew across the valley and around the mountain to the west. He leapt to his feet and busily broke camp to shake the vision from his mind.

Winter was not far away. He needed to find a sheltered location, with time enough to build a small cabin. With the reins loose, he walked closer to the edge of the plateau to survey the canyon and adjacent valley. Under the morning sun, the canyon glistened. He was suddenly struck by the immense beauty below him. He stepped a little closer. Every drop on leaf and needle sparkled in the light. Buffalo and deer grazed in an open pasture, the birds happy, relaxed and in a playful mood. The whole canyon was filled with a deep sense of peace, which seemed magical, even mystical, to behold.

Alas, the canyon and valley were too narrow. He would be trapped once the snow arrived.

Zachariah turned and stepped forward with his right foot. The loose sand and gravel slipped under the full weight of his left foot, which was yanked back from beneath his body. He fell heavily onto his left knee. His ankles tilted over the edge, and he slid across the gravel down a steep embankment on his stomach. The reins were instantly snatched from his grasp.

As he slid, he kicked out with both feet while grasping wildly at the loose rock passing beneath him, only to dislodge a cascade of small stones, which tumbled down with him. He slid five, six, seven yards down the steep embankment, until his feet found purchase on a narrow ledge and halted his fall. Panting heavily, he hugged the embankment. The loose stones tumbled over the cliff's edge to clatter upon the pile of rubble below. The resounding echo broke the magic, sending startled birds screeching into flight and scattering the deer.

Severely scratched along his front, he remained dead still. He rolled his eyes down and looked under his right shoulder. He stood on a ledge only two feet in width. With extreme care, he rolled onto his back. He peered over the edge, down the cliff and quickly looked straight back up and caught his nerve and breath. He kicked the loose stone around each boot over the edge, to secure his footing. He tilted his head sideways and looked up.

Three yards above his head, he watched the sand trickle away and an elongated oval-shaped rock slowly dislodge and roll, across its middle, down the embankment. The rolling rock began to pick up pace. It hit a tiny bump and bounced out into the air. It floated above his head for a moment and then dropped. He watched the rock fall across the front of his nose, down the front of his chest and belly and land heavily across its mid-point, upon the ledge, directly between his feet. The rock instantly split open in half. Each side fell back, in a half spinning wobble and slowed to a stop.

In stunned disbelief, Zachariah looked down at the split rock. The bright crimson red of a stone flickered back up at him under the sunlight. He stared at the dark red stone mesmerised, realisation slow to dawn. A gem! He saw a gem, a large uncut ruby, embedded in the centre of the right-hand half of rock.

Gathering a little courage, he used his arms to carefully push the top part of his body forward and bent over at the hip making sure to keep his buttocks firmly against the embankment. He reached down with his right hand. His fingers tips crawled over the rock, until he managed to grab a hold of it and quickly stood back up and leaned back against the safety of the embankment. He turned the rock over in his hand looking closely at the embedded gem.

He gently tapped the outer casing of the half rock against the jagged edges of the embankment, until a piece of rock split off. And then another and another. Little by little, the rock fell away revealing only the ruby. The disc-shaped ruby was flat along one side, with a shallow rounded dome over the other. The surface of the gem was smooth with a few dimples embedded across the dome. The ruby fit comfortably into his palm, allowing him to close and just touch his thumb to fingers, when grasping the whole gem in one hand.

Zachariah was astounded at his good fortune. He had survived the slide and found the largest ruby he had ever seen. His predicament quickly returned to mind. He dropped the ruby into his top left jacket pocket and fastened the button. He turned around onto his belly once more and looked up. Searching for diverts and handholds in the rock, he began the slow arduous climb back to the top of the embankment.

Panting heavily, muscles aching, he finally rolled over the lip onto his back.

"Ooh man… thank God for that!" he exclaimed.

He slowly rose to his feet. He stood back from the edge and looked down at the canyon with relief. He glanced around to make sure he was completely alone. He withdrew the ruby from his pocket and inspected it closely. He rolled it around in his hand and raised it to the sun. The central bubble of the ruby seemed flawless to the naked eye. Elated, he knew its value and returned the ruby to his pocket and again, fastened the button.

He backed away from the cliff and turned. His chestnut mare had drifted a dozen yards back towards their previous camp. He approached her calmly and greeted her affectionately. He gathered the reins and led her down from the plateau and back to the T-intersection. He mounted and rode south, back out through the entrance of the valley.

Zachariah continued northwest and quickly found the lush wetlands along the banks of Green River. He followed the river north and entered a wide open valley between a range of mountains on the eastern side, consisting of Kendall and Saltlick Mountain and the distant snow-topped mountains of Tosi and Triangle Peaks farther to the west.

The wide valley floor consisted of thickly grassed open pastures, teaming with wildlife and a massive herd of buffalo, stretching far into the north as far as the eye can see. Thick forests of pine, fir, spruce and aspen trees blanketed the gently rising slopes, beneath the bare rock mountain peaks on both sides.

He rode to the crest of a small hill below Saltlick Mountain and stopped. He was able to gain a wide view of the valley as it spanned out into the west and far into the north. The panoramic view of the untouched wilderness was spectacular, the wildlife abundant. He knew he could wait out the winter here. The river, the pastures, the forests would provide food aplenty. Now he just needed to find somewhere to shelter.

Looking down into the gentle ravine below, he noticed a creek that flowed downhill into Green River from a high gap, a pass between the northern slope of Saltlick Mountain and the southern slope of Gypsum Mountain, further to the northeast. Inexplicably, he felt drawn to the pass and to explore what was on the other side.

He rode down the northern slope of the ridge towards the creek. The lightly grassed slope, on both sides of the creek was littered with small to medium-sized rock and loose stone. He merely allowed his mare to find her own footing and pathway up to and through the pass.

Just inside the pass he found the creek to be the union of a northerly and a southerly junction, with a large semicircular basin forming in the open space between them. The southern creek simply descended around the circular base of Saltlick Mountain's northern slope.

The southern fork of Gypsum Mountain, a long sharp ridge, in the shape of an upside-down crescent moon, descended from peak to pass, forming a sheer wall of rock encircling the north to western portion of the basin. The northern junction of the creek descended side by side along the base of this wall. A small twin-peaked hill rose in the centre of the basin.

He decided to take the northern junction and followed the creek to its source. The creek led him along a steadily rising semicircular arc, starting northward, turning northeast and then east. The trail rose along the body and opened out onto a widening snakehead-shaped plateau, bordered on the left by the yellow-white rock walls of Gypsum Mountain and looked out over the open basin to the right. The creek ended or, rather, began from a small lake near the lower southeastern edge of the plateau.

From the small lake a trail, or goat track, ran south southeast along a gently rising, barren yellow-white dusty slope, along the front of a wall of rock. The wall was a descending ridge from north to south, topped by a row of six tall rough boulder heads. The trail cut a pass through the lower southern tip of the wall and a clumped tail of jagged rock, and then dipped beyond the pass and disappeared behind the wall of rock.

The air, still and quiet, began to chill in the late afternoon. The cliffs protected the plateau from the winds. Heavy, dark grey clouds drifted in slowly over the basin. He dismounted beside the lake, crouched and scooped a hand cup of water to test with his tongue. The water was ice cold, a little salty, mineralised and unpleasant. He stood and inspected the rugged beauty of the plateau and decided to make camp here for the night.

Just at that moment, flakes of snow began to gently drift down from above, magically filling the air with tiny white specks. He looked up, closed his eyes and allowed the soft touch of the snow to fall and melt upon his cheeks. He felt the peace he so longed for begin to return.

6

Suddenly, an immense, deep roar, sounded out far behind him, followed by an angry grunt, snort and forceful blowing of air. It was a bellow louder than what he had ever heard before, and immediately shot a cold shiver through his spine. He was struck with that familiar feeling, recalled the visions and knew exactly what that sound was.

Zachariah's mare, instantly spooked, reared up in fright. He fought with the reins. As the horse came back down, he pulled hard on the reins, reached for and gripped the butt of his rifle. The rifle caught momentarily, the hammer tip hooked on a leather strap. Yanked forward, stumbling, he managed to pull the rifle free, just as the mare turned, skittered and bolted back down the trail, snatching the reins from his grip.

He heard the grinding scrape of a large hoof along the gravel. Another grunt and blow of air. A second, even louder bellow rang out. Regaining his balance, correcting his grip of the rifle at waist level, he turned to the sound of thundering hooves he knew were bearing down upon him and loaded a cartridge into the chamber.

His eyes twitched as he searched for the beast. At first, through the falling snow, he could only see a very large white-grey blur moving across the front of the yellow-white cliff face. The beast, returning from a forage, appeared through the pass in the rock wall and on seeing the intruder violating its sanctuary, bellowed its outrage and now charged down the goat track. The thundering hooves grew louder and louder, the double echo reverberating off the nearby cliffs, fused with the clatter of splayed stones as the charge gained momentum.

His eyes worked to focus and refocus. He saw the outline of the beast, then its head, the huge grey, black-tipped horns, its black snout and the steam of its breath. He stood stunned, appalled and mesmerised. A huge, shaggy white buffalo bull, twice the size of a full-grown man, materialised out of the ghostly mirage and bore down upon him. He gasped at its sheer size and only just managed to hold his nerve, knowing he had but one shot.

The white bull had already crossed more than half the 150-yard distance between them. He drew in a deep breath to steady his nerve, raised the rifle in a side-on stance and took aim down the long barrel at the buffalo's heart. Sixty yards… fifty yards!

His eardrums were busting with the reverberation, his vision completely consumed by the sight of the huge bull. Forty yards! Holding the barrel straight and steady, he slowly let his breath out and with acute focus, gently pressed down on the trigger. The hammer slammed, with a click and… nothing.

With instant shock, he quickly turned the rifle and looked at the hammer. It was bent and missed the flush cap of the cartridge. He looked back up at the relentless bull. Thirty yards!

He let his arms drop straight down, holding the rifle loosely across his front, below the waist. Out of time… he now resigned himself to his inevitable fate. Twenty yards!

No Fear. He felt no fear at all. He had always felt lucky he had never been mauled by a grizzly bear, bitten by a snake or broken a bone. He looked up at the heavy sky hanging over the huge bull, and thought to himself…

Thank you, thank you Great Mother for the most amazing adventure!

He cleared his mind and let go. Ten yards!

At the very last moment the huge white bull pulled up hard… and stopped, dead still, right in front of Zachariah. The bull's head dipped a little forward, its eyes now stared directly into his at the same height. The bull's horns encompassed his shoulders. The bull's long flat forehead and snout ran down the front of his torso, its warm breath blowing across the top of his thighs. In stunned silence, he blankly stared back at the bull.

An eternity of ten seconds slowly ticked by. The bull raised its snout and breathed in his scent, in one long breath from his belly to his chest. The bull nudged the buttoned pocket on his left breast with the tip of its snout, once and then twice. He noticed something, felt something. He raised his right hand, unbuttoned the pocket, grabbed the ruby and pulled it out. He held his hand up in front of both their eyes and opened his fingers.

Subtly, almost undetectably, the ruby was vibrating and emitting a very low humming sound. They both stared at the ruby. The bull bounced its snout up and down twice, seemly placated by and enjoying the vibrational sound of the ruby. Suddenly, the bull raised its head, extended its tongue and gave him one long lick, along the side of his neck and over his left cheek. Standing still, in shock, he winced and staggered back one step.

The bull raised its horns over Zachariah's head, turned to its right and trotted a few yards down beside the small lake. The bull lowered its head and ripped at a tuft of grass and while chewing slowly, watched him intently.

Completely at a loss as to what just happened, he watched the bull pass by and begin to graze beside the lake. He looked back down at the ruby in his hand, the vibration and hum slowly diminishing the further the bull walked away. He looked up and turned around. He was completely alone, with the rifle and ruby and only the Great Mother as witness.

He dropped the ruby back into his pocket and fixed the button. He stepped back one, then two steps and continued to back away from the bull and the lake. Once fifty yards clear, he turned and briskly followed the creek back down the slope of the curved plateau.

His mind was shattered, numb, in the growing darkness of dusk. He could not put a logical line of thought together. The only thing he could think of, which was more instinctive than anything else, was his horse… to find his horse. He had to hurry before nightfall.

Panting, he soon made it back to the fork in the creek, just inside the pass. The tracks he found along the soft bank of the creek showed that his horse had turned and continued to bolt up along the southern junction around the base of Saltlick Mountain. She had not gone back out into the valley filled with buffalo. He followed easily at a steady, yet brisk trot over the rough, rocky terrain. With the onset of nightfall, the rising moon barely managed to illuminate the way through the thick cloud, slowing his progress to a mere stroll.

Zachariah followed the creek to its source, a tiny dried-up dam, on the southeastern side of Saltlick Mountain. The dam was bordered by a jagged rocky slope on its northern bank, an arid stone and sand basin on its southern flank, and a stepped rock wall ahead. Exhausted and frothing at the mouth, his horse stood in the middle of the dry dam, with nowhere to go.

He approached her slowly whilst making soothing and calming noises until he was able to gather the loose reins. He rubbed the nervous tension out of her neck, putting her at ease.

Exhausted physically and emotionally, he decided to stay where he was for the night. He had no wood for a fire, very little water and merely wrapped himself in a blanket and huddled in a nook of rock for shelter. The cold woke him in the middle of the night. Snow was falling gently. His muscles and bones ached and creaked as he rose to his feet. He was restless and tried to slap the cold out of his arms and thighs, in vain. He decided the only way was to walk the cold out of his legs.

He threw his blanket over his horse, untethered her and walked slowly in front, following the creek back down around the base of Saltlick Mountain. He stopped several times to rub the neck, shoulders and legs of his mare, to make sure she did not seize up or become impacted by the biting cold. The mountainous landscape began to turn white.

He led the way through the pass and into the wide open valley and finally reached the bank of Green River, just as first light illuminated the heavy clouds in the east. He watered his mare and let her graze. He immediately caught a trout and lit a cooking fire to cook it for breakfast and boiled enough water to refill his water skins.

The fast-rising sun lifted the heavy cloud and melted the thin layer of snow leaving the valley wet, damp and glistening beneath the light. Lying back against a tree to rest following breakfast, it all felt and looked like a dream.

"Wait, wait!" he grunted.

Snapping out of his daydream, he sat up and looked up at the sullen sky.

"What happened? What the hell happened… yesterday?" he growled.

The memory of the previous day instantly returned. He stared blankly across the river and replayed the encounter with the great white buffalo in his mind. He removed his hat and rubbed his eyes and temples, racking his brain trying to reconcile how such a thing was possible and what it meant.

"What happened? What happened?" he repeated. "The buffalo... charged. The rifle... misfired. I was ready to die... made my peace, and... he stopped. He stopped right before me. He didn't kill me. In fact, he let me go!" he pondered. "How? Why? Why did he let me go?"

He peered through the water of the river deep in thought. Almost on autopilot he drew the ruby out of his pocket and lifted it three inches from his eyes, in the open palm of his hand. He inspected every minute spec of the gem and could not see anything out of the ordinary.

"Was this... was this... some kind of spiritual experience?" he whispered. "I guess it was. Otherwise, what else could I call it?"

Between index finger and thumb, he held the ruby up to the light and peered through the gem.

"Chief Little Raven did say I could commune with the Great Mother and ask for her wisdom. Well, let's try that then," he said.

He enclosed the ruby in his grasp, closed his eyes and looked up towards the sky.

"Great Mother...Great Mother... I need your help," he began. "What happened with the white buffalo? Why did it stop? Was it because of the ruby? Why did it vibrate?"

He repeated the questions twice more and opened his eyes.

"I guess I'll just have to wait now," he whispered.

He returned the ruby back to his pocket and fastened the button. He broke camp, mounted his horse and rode north between the river and the left edge of a long open pasture.

"What is the Great Mother, anyway?" he dwelled.

He thought back, for the first time in many a year, to his religious upbringing.

Well... the Great Mother must be like... a field... of consciousness... the universal field of consciousness for all living things. No, wait, it's... it's the universal conscious energy field of life itself. That makes sense... right? Yes, yes... The Great Mother is the all-consuming, all-immersive, living, breathing energy field of life and the collective consciousness of all living things on Earth! Then how does it work?

Feeling elated by his deduction, he did not realise that he rode within twenty-five yards of a small group of buffalo, which had separated from the main herd and was milling around close to the riverbank. The ruby began to vibrate, very subtly at first. Every head in the small herd lifted and peered at the approaching horseman. They were not afraid. Instead, they were drawn and began to walk towards him. He soon felt the vibration against his chest, looked down, touched the ruby and then looked up again, to notice that he was being quickly surrounded by the small herd. They were walking in unison with him in an oval formation.

Suddenly, at that very moment, a word popped into his mind's eye… 'RESONANCE'!

He spoke the word out loud and then, simply allowed his mind to ponder its meaning.

"Is that the answer? Yes, it must be. Thank you, thank you, Great Mother," he whispered.

The small herd followed him for half a mile. He felt it necessary to break from the herd and nudged his horse into a brisk canter until they all peeled off. He continued to ride north out of the valley and into an open prairie. He made camp on an open ledge, a little below the summit of a gently sloping hill and looked up at the stars.

"Resonance! Resonance? What am I to make of this word 'resonance'?" he muttered. "Where do I begin?"

He reclined back against a smooth rock and sipped his hot brew of sweetened black tea.

"So, through the Great Mother, we are all connected. All things living are sustained by her, sustained by the same conscious energies of life. And all that lives adds to her vast diversity and makes her strong. Nothing can live separate from the Great Mother," he whispered.

"Yet, this resonance, how does this resonance fit into the picture?" he paused. "Does it have something to do with my spirit animal? Yes, maybe. It is plain to see my spirit animal is the buffalo. So, does this mean my spirit can resonate with the spirit of the buffalo? Yes, yes, of course. And this ruby…"

He pulled out the ruby and rolled it around in the palm of his hand under the moonlight.

"…is it attuned to resonate with my spirit and the spirit of the buffalo as well? Yes, yes, it must. When the buffalo and I are close, the ruby will pick up on and detect our resonance and vibrate. It, it seems to… amplify our resonance and strengthen our bond," he paused. "Wow… how is such a thing possible? I guess only God knows the answer to that."

He returned the ruby and sipped once more from his mug.

"Well, that's the best that I can do," he mused. "So... now that I have this... resonance... what I am to do with it?" he paused. "The only thing I can think of is to... help the buffalo. Yet, they are so... 'ab... und... ant'! Ooh... wait!"

In that moment, he foresaw the future clearly in his mind.

The Europeans! They do not live connected to the Great Mother. They are consumed by the sickness, the Wetiko of greed, wealth and power. They will hunt the buffalo to the very last. And once they are gone, the Great Mother will become weaker. She will no longer be able to protect us from the growing influence, the growing power of... Wetiko. And if the force of Wetiko becomes unbalanced, it will harm our world, the Great Mother will be infected by it.

A tear of realisation rolled down his right cheek. He looked out across the peaceful prairie.

"Will all this be destroyed? Will the New World break our connection to the Great Mother... forever?" he mused. "I must help the buffalo. But how?"

Not sure whether he felt joyous or disturbed, he finally drifted off to sleep. The first light hit him flush on the right side of his face. He sprang awake and leapt to his feet. He walked around the camp to stretch his legs, which helped to bring his mind back to Earth. He felt alive with new purpose, yet a little lost and unsure. He crouched to rekindle the campfire.

"What am I to do? Great white buffalo! Big red ruby!" he muttered. "I understand, how it works... this resonance thing. Save the buffalo? How is one little old mountain man going to save the buffalo?" he pondered. "I guess the Great Mother will show me, right!"

A gust of wind suddenly wiped up and swirled around his feet, as though in confirmation.

Contrary to common sense, he felt compelled to continue riding north. He intersected Green River once more, since it had turned east heading towards its source of Green River Lakes. He passed the immense rock barriers of Osborne Mountain and Three Waters Mountain far to the right. Three days it took to carefully cross a barren rocky wasteland where, upon reaching the other side, he found himself standing before the southern fringe of the Shoshone Mountains. Autumn had now turned into the start of winter.

****

In the years that followed, no report had ever surfaced of anyone seeing, encountering or hunting a great white buffalo, standing twice the height of a man, in the valley surrounding Saltlick and Gypsum Mountains.

Zachariah soon found he no longer suffered from his nightmarish dream.

7

Snow fell steadily from morning all through the day and was already one foot thick upon the ground. The cold bit deep. He had shot a brown bear a few days earlier for a winter pelt. He laid his blanket across the shoulder, back and rump of his mare, over which he laid every deer skin he had, all affixed beneath the saddle. Finding a permanent shelter was paramount.

Zachariah traversed northwest along the southern slopes of the Shoshone Mountains. He explored every ravine, too sheer; every pass, blocked; every slope, impenetrable, as he passed by both Ramshorn Peaks. He found a narrow, strong flowing stream, South Fork Shoshone River, being squeezed out through two very high, sheer walls of rock. He could see that the northern pass was long, straight and just wide enough to ride through. He knew that his luck was in – at least he hoped that it was – and wondered from whence the water flowed.

He rode through the two-mile-long pass and discovered a long narrow north-south valley. The valley opened out into an open narrow pasture beside the river, which ran for three miles of its five-mile length. The open pasture merged into thick forested slopes, which rose to the foot of the sheer rock mountain walls on both sides of the valley. The Shoshone Plateau above the east wall, looked down into the valley. The river and pass into the valley from the north were literally impenetrable, due to the twenty miles of the toughest, narrowest, mountain terrain around and beyond Hardluck Mountain.

He instantly fell in love with the isolation and seclusion of the hidden valley. There were no buffalo, no Indian signs and the wild game was sparse.

High on an eastern slope of the valley, he found a cave in the centre of a thirty-yard long rock wall which rose to four yards at the highest point. This rock wall was pinched at both ends and marked the juncture where the gentle slope below ended, and the steep rising side of a mountain began.

With rifle in hand, he stooped through the triangular shoulder high entrance. It was vacant. He found that the cave opened out into a sixteen-feet deep and seven-foot high, roughly domed cavern, with a couple of low, narrow pointed recesses ending at the back.

He quickly felled a few small trees and mixed grass with mud to build a small, windproof stable, facing the entrance of the cave, for his mare. He waited out the winter, whilst exploring every inch of the valley on fine weather days. The snows thawed and the southern pass out of the valley reopened as the spring of 1861 blossomed.

Zachariah wanted to make this valley his new home. He soon encountered the Shoshone, who were surprised when greeted in the Arapaho tongue. They were more than elated to share a pipe with the legendary Little White Bull. He asked permission to reside in and care for the valley, which was happily granted. He was relieved to be allowed to live in peace.

Just after midsummer a small band of Shoshone ventured into the valley and spoke with Zachariah. They informed him that the Europeans had split into two tribes and gone to war against each other, over whether or not the southern tribe had the right to continue enslaving the black-skinned man, who was from a distant land called Africa.

He was both intrigued and conflicted, debating on whether to remain in the mountains and sit it out, or to re-enlist and participate. He knew full well that the act of war was the most destructive display of Wetiko. Yet was hiding from a problem in fear also Wetiko? And would not the abolishment of slavery remove a form of Wetiko altogether? The concept of Wetiko was certainly a complex one.

He left his paradise and rode to Fort Laramie, where he re-enlisted with the United States Union Army. The Confederates seceded the territories of southern New Mexico and Arizona. He was immediately deployed to Fort Craig in New Mexico, under the command of Colonel Edward Canby.

He was too old to participate in direct combat, so his greatest value was his knowledge of the terrain. His role was one of intelligence: to train, organise and supervise the troop of scouts and trackers for the small Union Army, to report on the enemy, and advise on logistics. His strategies involved pairing scouts to work and support each other, using bird calls as a method of coded communication in the field, and how to set a false trial to evade capture. The scouts watched and protected the flanks of the army when on the march and whilst engaged in battle.

The Confederate Army of New Mexico under the command of Henry Hopkins Sibley, advanced northward out of Fort Bliss in El Paso Texas, in February 1862 and marched to Fort Thorn in Mesilla, New Mexico. Their objective was to capture Santa Fe, the east Rockies, the Colorado Gold Mines and on to Fort Laramie to cut the Oregon Trail.

Sibley enticed Canby out of Fort Craig at the Battle of Valverde Ford. The Union forces were repelled and returned to the protection of their fort. Sibley lost more horses than men. He could not lay siege with so few supplies. Instead, with the majority of his army on foot, Sibley's column travelled slowly further north. This allowed the Union scouting parties to remove stock and grain from Sibley's path from Albuquerque and Santa Fe prior to his arrival. Sibley engaged and defeated a Union advance party out of Fort Union further north, under the command of Colonel John Slough, at the Battle of Glorieta Pass.

Meanwhile, Zachariah's scouts identified a weakness in the exposed and lagging wagon train of the Confederate Army and played a pivotal role in helping the 1st Colorado Infantry under Major M. Chivington to destroy their entire supply train. Sibley was forced to retreat back to Albuquerque. Outnumbered and with few supplies, Sibley promptly left Albuquerque after a couple of brief skirmishes. His rear guard lost Fort Thorn and Mesilla. Sibley was forced to retreat to Franklin and then all the way back to San Antonio. The Union Army secured Arizona, New Mexico and West Texas by the end of July.

By the end of 1862, Zachariah found himself reassigned to the Army of (West) Tennessee, under the command of Major General Ulysses S. Grant. He was a natural at the art of intelligence gathering. Once again, he was placed in charge of training and organising the army's network of scouts and trackers, which proved far superior, faster moving and more evasive, than those of the Confederates.

The Army of Tennessee lay siege to Vicksburg, which surrendered on 4th July 1863. Then, under General William Tecumseh Sherman, the army opened a supply line to the besieged city of Chattanooga, following the defeat of General Rosecrans at Chickamauga and helped repel the Confederate Army from Missionary Ridge. The subsequent defeat of Braxton Bragg's Confederate Army opened the door to the Deep South.

Sherman's Army of Tennessee then marched on to relieve the city of Knoxville in the fall of 1863 and cut the railroad which linked the Confederacy from east to west. Early in 1864, the army captured Meridian, Mississippi and destroyed most of the city and its railroad infrastructure. This marked the beginning of the tactic of 'total war' upon the southern states.

Through the summer of 1864 Sherman invaded Georgia to sack the city of Atlanta by September, before marching to the sea. To Zachariah's horror, in the act of total war, the army destroyed everything in its path: farms, crops, mills, railroads and factories. The destruction was so complete the southern states lost the capacity to continue the war.

The final march into Carolina saw the defeat of the Confederate Army under the command of General Joseph E. Johnstone at Bentonville. This effectively ended the war in April 1865, giving General Robert E. Lee little choice but to surrender his forces. Shortly thereafter, the Army of Tennessee was disbanded in August and Zachariah returned to Fort Laramie by the end of 1865, only to find the plains of the Midwest in complete turmoil.

He learnt that Deer Creek Station, Sage Creek Station and Platte Creek Station had all been attacked earlier in the year. Many wagon trains travelling through the area had also fallen under attack. The Sioux, Cheyenne and Arapaho had joined forces against the continued incursions into their territories by settlers, hunters and miners, breaching the treaty of 1851. The US Kansas Cavalry were sent out to build new forts to counter the raids along the Bozeman Trail and to engage the Indians along Powder River and the Black Hills. This resulted in the Battle of Tongue River and the destruction of Black Bear's Arapaho village.

Needing quality scouts, Zachariah accepted the post of being one of a handful of chief guides and trainers operating out of Fort Laramie.

From the new year of 1866, he trained cavalrymen in the ways of Indian scouting and tracking, and the Pawnee scouts who sided with the US Army in the ways of the US Cavalry.

In June 1866, he assisted with translation when a group of Powder River chiefs travelled to Fort Laramie to negotiate a new treaty. At the same time, Colonel Henry B. Carrington travelled up the Bozeman Trail with the 2nd Battalion to Fort Reno and then established Fort Phil Kearny at Piney Creek and Fort C. F. Smith a further ninety-one miles north, deep into Powder Creek territory. This sparked Chief Red Cloud's war of 1866–68 to contest the establishment of these forts. All three forts would be abandoned by late 1868, after a US Army investigation ruled in accordance with the newly formed Fort Laramie Treaty.

Attacks upon the plains continued into 1869. Zachariah continually encouraged the chiefs to attend peace talks with the newly arrived peace commissioner at Fort Laramie. He tried to persuade the chiefs to agree to peaceful terms. He well understood from his experience of the civil war that the Native Indian Nations simply did not have the numbers or capacity to wage war, with the same level of destructive powder as the US Army.

The Union Pacific Railroad joining east to west was completed, flooding Wyoming and surrounding western territories with new settlers. The pressure of territorial encroachment forced the plains Indians to maintain their attacks on isolated pockets of farmers, ranchers, miners and hunters. In response, the US Cavalry strengthened its presence by establishing the new forts of Bridger and Stambaugh by year's end.

Raids continued on both sides. Indian villages were attacked. Ranchers had their cattle stolen. The Indian Nations became more and more dependent on food rations from the US Government, as they were pushed into smaller and smaller reservations.

By midsummer 1871, Zachariah saw that the situation was all but hopeless for the Indian Nations. He had also lost patience and become disillusioned with the US Cavalry, which seemed unable to enforce any ideal solution for either side and, at times, made things worse.

****

The dinner bell rang out, which immediately insighted a chaotic stampede for the mess hall at Fort Laramie. Zachariah strolled into the mess hall a little late, collected a bowl filled with beef and vegetable stew, grabbed a knob of bread and sat at the head of the scout's table.

A new, young, fresh-faced trainee scout squeezed into a space in the middle of the long table on the left. He was from Cleveland, Ohio and filled with chatty enthusiasm.

"Just got into Fort Laramie this morning," he announced. "Rode the Union Pacific to get here. And my God… you should see what the railway is freighting back east?" he said.

He paused while the muttering died down until he held everyone's attention.

"Hundreds, thousands of buffalo hides… and bones… especially buffalo skulls. They're piled high, as high as a windmill," he said. "The further west you travel, the more you see along the railway. Just pile upon pile of skulls. I've never seen anything like it before," he professed. "How many buffalo are out there? It's a wonder there're any left."

A rugged middle-aged scout with thick black hair stared across the table at the young trainee.

"The southern plains are completely bare. There're still large numbers further out in the northwestern plains," he reported.

The news gutted Zachariah. Realisation slapped him on the face that he had forgotten about the buffalo. He had been enlisted in the service of the US Army for ten years and had not considered how ten years of hunting would decimate the buffalo herd.

"Well, judging by what I've seen, the buffalo are done for. There's nothing that'll stop the slaughter…" he continued. "…until there's not one single buffalo left… until they're all wiped out," the young trainee concluded.

"Surely the government will stop this madness in time," Zachariah grunted.

"Nuh! Not going to happen," he replied.

"How do you mean?"

"Once all the buffalo are gone, the plains Indians will lose their source of food. It'll stop them from being so nomadic and force them to farm the land like we do," he explained. "It'll end all conflict and subjugate the natives."

"Just like we did to the Confederates. How have I been so blind," he muttered. "To wipe out the buffalo, would be an unthinkable catastrophe... that could never be reversed."

"Why? What's so important about the buffalo anyway?" he mused.

Zachariah looked the young trainee directly in the eye, with a very stern expression.

"The buffalo... the buffalo are part of the Great Mother. To lose the buffalo would weaken the Great Mother," he said.

"The what!?" he asked, confused.

"The Great Mother... the Great Mother is the collective conscious life force of all living things. To lose the buffalo would weaken this force," he repeated.

Everyone around the table turned to look at him intently, with surprise and bemusement.

"If we wipe out the buffalo, they'll no longer exist. The buffalo will become silent, absent, their resonance forever removed from the collective conscience... from the Great Mother."

Zachariah stared deeply into his mug of sweetened black tea. He saw it clearly in his mind.

"This would weaken the collective field. The more we destroy, the weaker the field becomes... and the easier it'll be for the sickness of Wetiko, the darkness, to set in... and permeate through an unbalanced field... towards destruction," he professed.

"What? What's he talking about?" the trainee replied. "Does anyone know what he's talking about?" he said louder.

Surprised, confused and trying to save face, he laughed at and mocked Zachariah, who suddenly stood up. Everyone stared at him.

"I know... I know what I must do," he whispered.

He looked down at the new trainee and at all the faces around the table.

"I must become like Chief Little Raven, a guardian and try to save something for the future."

"I think he's gone completely bonkers!" the trainee yelled accusingly.

"If I tried to explain... you wouldn't understand. You don't have the capacity to know the Great Mother and I don't have the time," he said flatly. "In fact, I don't have much time left at all."

"The Great Mother? What's that... some kind of Indian thing?" he smirked.

"Well fellas, reckon I've something more important to do than run around the countryside playing cowboys and Indians with you guys. It's time to take my leave. Farewell and good luck," he announced.

With everyone watching intently, Zachariah finished his tea and slammed the mug down hard upon the table, startling the trainee. He turned and walked out of the mess hall.

"Crazy old man!" he muttered. "What's got into that old buzzard anyways?"

Zachariah handed in his commission with the United States Army and collected his final wages from the paymaster. He quickly packed his meagre belongings and rode out of Fort Laramie for Kansas City. He had some business to take care of and supplies to gather. In return for his services to the United States Army he secured a land grant for a remote valley in the Shoshone Mountains, indicating his intention to start a ranch.

His old chestnut mare was now well into her twenties and slowing down. With the military wages saved, he purchased a young, chocolate-and-white spotted mare from a horse breeding farm, and two pack mules to carry tools and supplies. He also purchased a new lever action rifle, a six-shot revolver, plenty of ammunition and a small case of dynamite sticks.

He rode out of Kansas City near summer's end of 1871.

8

Zachariah used the well-established trail and rode into Denver mid-autumn and stayed as winter settled in. He visited many of his old hunting grounds and was saddened by how drastic things had changed in only a decade. The Arapaho and buffalo were gone. The open plains were transforming into farmland. The west was no longer wild.

As soon as the snows began to melt, he departed Denver in late February 1872, heading directly north into Wyoming. He finally arrived at the southern pass of his hidden valley in the Shoshone Mountains five weeks later, on the first day of April.

Unbeknown to Zachariah, the Yellowstone National Park had been established one month prior, on 1st March 1872, by the US Congress and ratified by President Ulysses S. Grant.

Yellowstone was created to protect the wildlife and game from wanton destruction. However, no staffing or funding was provided until 1884, when Congress ordered the United States Army to take over the park and enforce the law. The eastern boundary of Yellowstone was essentially almost next door to Zachariah's hidden valley.

He surveyed the eastern slopes of the valley for a location to build a cabin. He preferred the warmth of the afternoon sun, rather than the morning sun on the western side. He found a gentle grassed slope, with a panoramic view over the largest, central portion of open pasture. The gentle slope backed up against the steep rising side of a mountain covered with a thick forest of pine, which would protect him from avalanche and rock fall.

At the juncture between pasture and forest he suddenly rediscovered the entrance to his old cave, in the middle of a wall of rock. He carefully ventured inside. This time the cave smelled damp, heavy and musky like wet fur. He saw the tracks of a large male grizzly bear in the thin muddied sand on the floor. He knew the bear had emerged to forage for food and would not be willing to share the valley with anyone. He tracked the bear into the woods a further two miles north, shot him dead and took his thick fur hide.

Zachariah decided to build his log cabin right in front of the cave entrance. He knew the cave would offer greater protection during a blizzard and the ability to store tools, wood, water and extra provisions to survive a harsh winter. He cleaned out the cave as best he could and immediately began to compile his stock of resources inside.

He levelled the ground around the front of the cave entrance and marked the foundation for a cabin. He cut down select trees from the nearby woods and used his two mules to drag the logs up the gentle slope to the building sight. He laid the foundation and built the floor, walls and high pointed roof. He filled the gaps between the logs with a mixture of grass and clay, and completed the oversized, one room cabin by mid-June.

During the summer, he added a front porch, stone fireplace and chimney, and an enclosed outhouse, a latrine on the northern side of the cabin. He fashioned a table, two chairs and bed bunk. On the southern side of the cabin, he built a small smoking hut for trout and meat, and three small stables, one each for his retired and new mare, and one for the two mules.

The new bearskin was used to cover a narrow open doorway cut through the middle of the back wall, which led into a ten-foot long, enclosed corridor to the entrance of the cave. The cave was fitted out with water barrels, tool bench, shelves and large bins to store fodder for the horses. He decorated the cabin with skins and ornaments from the wilderness.

Throughout the autumn, Zachariah hunted and foraged to build his storehouse of food for the coming winter. He fished the nearby lakes and rivers beyond his valley, for as much trout as he could carry and smoked them in his smoking hut. He did the same with deer to make jerky, collected and dried wild fruits, berries and herbs. He gathered wild honey in small wooden tubs. From the plentiful supply of ripe brown acorns, he boiled out the tannins and ground them into flour to make bread, just as the native Indians did.

Winter soon arrived with heavy snowfall and ice. Once again, both the narrow southern and northern passes into the valley were frozen shut. He did not mind being completely cut off from the outside world. He found a certain kind of peace in his isolation.

Luckily, the winter was not severe. The snow and ice thawed through to the end of February. He survived the winter comfortably with one-quarter of his stores remaining. He now had a fair idea of what was needed to survive through winter. The valley bloomed and sprung forth into new life. Yet, there were no buffalo.

He was now ready to build a herd of bison. He sat on the porch and pulled the ruby out from his top left pocket and held it up to the sky. The central dome was flawless. During his ten-year service with the US Cavalry, the ruby was wrapped in cotton and secretly sewn into a leather pocket inside and under the left armpit of his jacket, positioned a little above and behind his left nipple, and never saw the light of day.

On his new mare, he rode out of the southern pass and travelled northwest in search of buffalo. He soon found a small herd and watched from a distance. His target was the younger animals and he spotted several foraging on the fringes. He dismounted, tied the reins to a branch and slowly walked out into the open, down wind. Once within thirty yards, the ruby began to vibrate, drawing the bison to its resonance. They followed him back to his horse. He mounted and slowly walked the first two cows and a young bull back to his valley and set them free on the first open pasture.

On most days through spring, he returned with one or two bison and soon amassed a herd of forty cows and two bulls. He built a log barricade at the top end of the southern pass to prevent the herd from escaping. He found more caves in the southeastern corner of the valley, and through the summer into fall, filled them with as much fodder as he could gather.

He used all his stores to keep himself, his horses and the bison alive through winter. He found the carcasses of three cows mauled by a wolf pack. He hunted the pack down and shot four of them, before they were forced to leave the valley through the difficult northern pass.

As soon as the southern pass was open, Zachariah extended his range further west and northwest to find and capture more buffalo. He did cross paths with the killing field of a hunting party where, he was able to corral several lost and stray calves and lead them back to his valley under the light of a full moon. Once the new animals were released into the protected pasture, he would go back and carefully cover and confuse his tracks on the approach to home. From a lookout, he would sit guard over the southern pass for hours following each excursion.

On one trek he spotted a small group of goats milling around the mid-slope of a mountain. He deduced they had escaped and run away from a wagon train. He rigged a rope pen around some trees and patiently corralled them into the enclosure on foot, and captured all eight animals. Returning to the valley, he built them a small, covered compound. The goats quickly adjusted to a comfortable life of being let out in the morning and returning to a warm shelter at night of their own accord. Now he had milk, butter and cheese.

By spring end of 1874, he added a further thirty head of buffalo to the herd. By the summer of 1875 the herd reached a total of 100 buffalo, where the odd death was matched by new births. It became hard work to gather enough foliage for the winter. He knew he was approaching the optimal number of buffalo that the valley could comfortably sustain.

With the onset of autumn, a travelling party of Shoshone Indians entered the southern pass, made their way around the log barrier, and were surprised to find a herd of buffalo in the valley. They soon found Zachariah gathering and drying some tall grasses for fodder beneath the afternoon sun. Little White Bull greeted them in Arapaho and invited them to join in the evening meal, which they gratefully accepted.

Sitting around a large campfire, he shared a feast of smoked trout and deer meats, dried fruits and acorn flour bread, goat's milk and cheese. They were impressed. In return, the Shoshone brought out the long pipe and smoked their favourite blend.

While the pipe was shared, the leader of the Shoshone party dispensed all his news. Every Nation had lost vast tracts of their homelands and been forced into reservations, from which it was nearly impossible to generate enough food to live a comfortable life. The buffalo herds had all but vanished from the plains by the relentless destruction of the hunters, turning the mood sombre.

For the first time, he told the story of his encounter with the Great White Bull, to the amazement of the Shoshone, and with open palm, proceeded to display the ruby. He said he had been gifted a task by the Great Mother, to save and protect the last of the buffalo. The Shoshone nodded their understanding in reverence. His legend quietly grew among the Shoshone, where he was never threatened by them for the rest of his days.

9

The first chilled wind of winter blew in from the mountains to the north, when a shot rang out and echoed through the valley. Zachariah sat bolt upright in his bunk, awoken from his late afternoon nap. Was it a dream, he wondered. A second shot rang out. He could hear shouts, a whistle and a joyous... hoorah. He leapt out of the cot, grabbed his rifle and bolted out through the door of his cabin, as the third shot rang out.

Upon the open pasture below his cabin, the small herd of buffalo was scattering northward in fright. From his left, four hunters had entered the southern pass and followed the creek into the valley. Two precious buffalo lay dead, as the men rode in towards their carcasses.

He ran a short distance down the hill to his left and stood behind the first tree of the light wood that skirted the southeastern slope from his cabin. The four men were all mounted and roughly 150 yards below and to the left of his position. They rode along the opposite, western bank of the narrow river.

"STOP!" he screamed.

His voice carried across the valley and bounced off the high mountain walls.

"Stop what you are doing," he repeated.

Surprised and spooked, the four men immediately stopped their hollering and turned to look up the slope in his direction, trying to spot him among the trees.

"Says who?" the biggest man replied.

"This is private land... and... you are trespassing," he yelled.

He remained concealed behind the tree. The barrel of the rifle pointed upwards at the ready.

"I have a land grant issued by the United States Army," he continued. "So, it would be best... if you would turn around and... leave this here, valley," he yelled.

"Well… there are buffalo here. Do you have a grant over buffalo?" he bellowed back.

"They are my buffalo, under my protection," he yelled louder.

"I believe I have the right to hunt them buffalo and take their fur and horn."

The big man, their leader, turned sideways to the other hunters and issued instructions.

"Jenson, get up there through that wood and flush him out. Kyle, go round left and see if you can get a fix on him," he whispered.

"Rightio, Dillon!" Jenson spat.

The thick tobacco bile landed on a rock.

"These here buffalo are privately owned and not to be harmed," Zachariah yelled.

He knew the longer he kept talking the easier it would be for them to get a fix on him.

"By who?" Dillon prodded.

"I own these here buffalo. And they are under my protection," he replied. "As I said… it be best if you turn around and went on your way," he yelled once more.

Kyle, the smallest of the group was of olive skin and sandy-blonde hair. Jenson, skinny, of medium height, had a fair complexion and short black hair. Dillon, older and displaying a heavier build than his younger brother Dusty, were both tall with a light tan and chocolate-coloured hair. They all wore leathers, boots, long-sleeved cotton shirts, scarves around their necks and wide-brimmed hats of various colours.

"And who might you be… if you don't mind my asking?" Dillon pressed.

He and his younger brother crossed the shallow water and slowly rode up the slope towards the voice, at walking pace. Kyle had quickly ridden across the open ground of the slope below and in front of the cabin and up around on Zachariah's northern flank. He spotted his target leaning back against the tree, raised his rifle and took aim. Zachariah took the bait.

"My name is…"

Kyle's mare took a small half step and shifted her weight from one rear leg to the other, at the very moment he pulled the trigger. The shot hit the tree a few inches beside Zachariah's left ear. Horrified at missing, he feverishly worked the lever action of his rifle to reload.

Zachariah stepped one pace forward and turned towards Kyle. While leaning his left shoulder into the tree, he quickly brought the barrel down and took aim. He moved with purpose and slowed it all down at the point of shooting. He drew a quick, short breath, exhaled and pulled the trigger.

The shot hit Kyle directly upon the bridge of his nose, snapped his head back and killed him instantly. His rifle fell to the ground. His horse turned and began to trot down the slope. Kyle's left foot caught in the stirrup as his body slumped forward, fell and was dragged across the ground. His horse kicked back at him until he finally rolled free.

Approaching through the trees from the southern flank, Jenson had a clear view of Zachariah's back as he fired the shot at Kyle. With the horse in a canter, Jenson raised his rifle and took aim at Zachariah's head. Filled with adrenalin and panting with both excitement and trepidation, he pulled the trigger in haste. Shooting at an armed man was not like shooting at buffalo. The shot hit the tree high above Zachariah's head.

Zachariah raised the barrel into the air to efficiently reverse his stance, while reloading at the same time. He stood side-on to face Jenson, using the tree to shield the right side of his body, making himself a slim target. He brought the barrel down, took aim and held the shot for a full second and… fired.

Jenson's head and upper body was moving far too erratically for a guaranteed hit. Instead, he aimed for a different part of the body, knowing from his experience in the US Cavalry that such a wound would invariably, always end in death… and if he missed… he most certainly would graze the top flank and skittle the horse.

The bullet hit Jenson through the right hip just below the belt line, shattering his pelvic bone and nicking an artery. He instantly screamed out in pure agony, dropped his rifle and fell to the ground. Startled, his horse turned and scampered back into the wood. Jenson rolled onto his back, groaning. He tried to stem the blood in vain and would not rise to his feet again.

On spotting Zachariah, Dillon and Dusty stood upright in their saddles and charged him from the creek below. They fired their rifles intermittently, reloaded and fired again. Their aim was weak, hopeful at best. Shots hit the tree and the ground around his feet.

Dillon and Dusty were ninety yards down the slope and closing fast. Zachariah broke from his cover and made a zig-zag dash across the twenty-five yards of ground for the safety of his cabin. Shots hit the ground on both sides of his legs and whizzed past his ears. His sixty-year-old legs moved as quickly as they could. He burst through the cabin door with his assailants only thirty yards behind.

Zachariah turned and prepared to slam the door shut just as Dusty took aim at his heart and fired. The bullet hit Zachariah an inch above his left nipple and knocked him onto his back, flinging his rifle aside. A sharp ping rang out through the valley. He instinctively rolled to his left, out of sight of the doorway.

Stinging with pain, Zachariah grabbed at his chest. No blood. He felt a crumple in his top left pocket, his treasured ruby now shattered into a dozen shards. The bullet had hit the ruby, ricocheted and grazed the front of his left shoulder. With no time to ponder his good fortune, he scrambled on his belly and pushed with hands and legs through the bear skin curtain and into the corridor beyond.

Dusty dismounted and ran to one side of the open cabin door. Quickly and gingerly, he took a quick look inside and withdrew his head. He did not see a body. He took a second peak.

"He's gone." Dusty exclaimed.

"What do you mean?" Dillon replied.

"The body! It's gone! There's no body!" Dusty yelled, frantic.

"He can't just… disappear, can he? Go in, 'n' have a look." Dillon jeered.

Dusty appeared in the doorway with rifle extended at the waist. Dillon dismounted and walked briskly towards the cabin.

Dusty stepped inside and inspected the one open room. There were no cupboards, shelves, trap door or attic. The bunk was only three inches off the floor. The walls all covered with skins. He was dumbfounded, turning around to face the cabin door, then full circle, to look back inside once more. Dillon was now only four yards from the one step up to the porch.

Right at that moment a stick of dynamite, cut and alight with a five-second fuse, rolled out from under the bear skin along the floor and stopped two feet in front of Dusty. He looked down at the stick, stuck in stunned silent disbelief, as he watched the fuse burn home.

The explosion ripped, lifted and slammed Dusty violently through the wall behind him, killing him instantly. The whole of the cabin's front wall, as well as the front half of both the left and right walls and the roof, blew out in a cloud of flame and shattered timber.

Dillon was knocked back and off his feet by the force of the blast. His face and body lacerated by a multitude of flying splinters. Every horse scattered in terror. Zachariah had time enough to dive face down, behind a water barrel. He clamped his hands over his ears and held his breath through the blast. The water barrel burst and flooded the cave floor. Everything around the front entrance of the cave was destroyed.

One... two... three... minutes passed, before Dillon, with ears ringing, managed to raise himself into a sitting position and view the damage. He could not see his younger brother, but knew he was dead. Most of the back wall and a small portion of the side walls and floor was all that remained of the cabin. A gaping black hole exposed the entrance into the cave.

"Clever man!" Dillon spat. "Building your cabin in front of a cave! But... now... I know where you're at."

Blood rolled down over the snarl of his top lip. He wiped at it with the cuff of his left hand. Painfully, he rose to his feet, steadied himself and looked around the ground for his rifle. He found it and picked it up. He checked the breach and loaded the weapon. Looking at the cave entrance with single-minded determination, he took one step forward.

THWACK!

Out from the looming darkness and drifting smoke, the largest buffalo bull appeared and hit Dillon side-on with the full force of its charge.

His rib cage crumpled. His neck snapped left. The hardest portion of the bull's forehead, above brow, hit Dillon just under his armpit. The bull lifted and carried his body a further fifteen yards across the ground, before dumping and trampling him, until the bull was completely satisfied he no longer posed a threat. As calm returned, the bull left the mutilated body and trotted off into the darkness down the slope.

Completely frozen still, Zachariah watched from the shadows, just inside the cave entrance. He did not dare show himself or make a single sound, until the buffalo bull had left. When clear he emerged from the cave to survey what was left of his home. The smokehouse, outhouse, stables and goat barn all suffered minor damage. His animals were skittish but ok.

After dusk, Zachariah stacked much of the shattered wood and built a large bonfire. He gathered all four bodies, arranged them in a line and covered them with tattered deer skins. He collected all their weapons, ammunition, knives and any item of value and placed them upon the bench in the cave. He walked down the slope and gathered their horses, milling around the bank of the river, unsaddled and tethered them to a stable rail.

He cleaned up as much as he could around the shattered cabin and cleared the path leading to and around the entrance of the cave. He burned everything that was damaged beyond repair and contaminated beyond safe consumption. He salvaged what he could to fashion a cot along the inside north wall of the cave. When exhaustion overtook, he collapsed into a disturbed sleep.

Following breakfast, he sat on a stump in front of the cave contemplating what to do. Winter had arrived. There was no time to rebuild the log cabin. The cave would be home for now. He reached into his top left pocket and gathered the crumbs of his shattered ruby. He opened the palm of his hand. The breeze blew away the dust leaving a handful of splintered shards.

"What happened last night?" he muttered. "That bull... how did it...? I don't know! Maybe, it's just our resonance. I protect them, they protect me, I guess," he said.

"These damn hunters, they'll just keep coming!" he whispered. "How do I stop them... how do I stop them from finding this valley?"

Staring at the row of dead bodies, he was suddenly struck by a perplexing idea. He stood and threw the shards out across the grassy slope.

Using the two pack mules, he pulled the remaining timbers out from what was left of the cabin and transported them to the entrance of the southern pass into the valley. Here he built four funeral pyres. He stripped all four bodies naked and wrapped them in skins.

He placed each body in the central hollow of each pyre together with their rolled-up clothes, boots and saddle. He stripped the dead buffalo the hunters had killed of meat and arranged their skulls and bones around the base of each pyre. At dusk he lit the pyres ablaze and issued the final rites as best as he could remember them.

The following day, over the ashes and bones, he erected several rock pillars and wooden poles to mark the burial site. He adorned them with native Indian signs, beaded necklaces, crow and eagle's feathers, wooden wind chimes and a couple of scary rattles. Finally, he was satisfied the newly created sacred burial sight appeared authentic and ominous.

The hunter's four horses were branded. He could not gift them to the Shoshone, which would only raise suspicion. He could not shoot them either. Tethered together in single file and under the cover of darkness, he rode them out of his valley. After a couple of days riding only through the night, he released them near a group of wild horses on the far northeastern slopes of the Shoshone Mountains, over 100 miles from his valley... and returned home.

****

A party of Shoshone visited the valley a few days later and were themselves spooked at first sight of the new burial ground. Zachariah explained what had happened and its purpose. The Shoshone were amused and more than happy to add their own authentic tribute to the hunter's burial, in the form of old discarded clothing and ornaments, and an addition of both animal and human remains that were found upon the plains of Wyoming.

The illusion of a diseased and cursed burial ground was so complete, no hunter would dare enter the pass into the valley for a very, very long time.

He erected a protective barrier across the cave entrance as the first snows fell. Winter was very difficult to endure without the cabin. He ran out of food stores and fodder midway through and was forced to shoot several buffalo and a couple of goats to survive. He greeted spring with immense relief and found he had lost a third of his herd through starvation.

Zachariah rebuilt the cabin through the spring and summer of 1876. He managed to track down and capture enough young buffalo to replenish his herd to 100 head, the optimal number for the valley. No longer needing to leave the valley he simply allowed his herd of buffalo and goats to grow organically.

10

From 1877 onwards Zachariah's herd never grew beyond 120 buffalo. Life too, became a regular, pleasant cycle to manage in his later years. During spring and summer the herd would basically look after themselves. The only work required was to accumulate enough dried grass and fodder to make it through winter.

As the snows melted in 1883, a group of Shoshone travelled into the valley and asked Zachariah for some buffalo to feed their starving people. The year marked the complete destruction of the North American buffalo herds on both the northern and southern plains. The once abundant herds were now reduced to roughly only 300 bison remaining in the wild. The Shoshone people, pushed into reservations had very little means by which they could sustain themselves all year round. He selected five bison to slaughter and donated ten more they could use to start their own herd within their reservation.

In the spring of 1884, the Shoshone returned to ask for a further five buffalo. Regrettably, the attempt to create a herd of their own was unsuccessful. Hunger proved too powerful a driving force. The Shoshone also informed Zachariah that the United States Army had been called in to protect and manage the twenty-five or so buffalo left in Yellowstone National Park. He felt his calling to save the bison was now vindicated.

During midsummer of 1890, a company of eighty cavalrymen from the Yellowstone barracks overcame their superstition of the burial ground, entered the southern pass and rode into the valley. To their surprise and amazement they found the peaceful, strong and healthy herd of buffalo grazing upon the open pasture. On finding and speaking with Zachariah, they learnt of his amazing work to protect the herd from the outside world.

Now too old, frail and weary to continue the work, he decided to donate his herd to the Yellowstone National Park. He asked the company of soldiers to muster and relocate the herd into the protection of the park. By autumn, the bolstered Yellowstone herd numbered over 200 head of buffalo. An eerie quiet emptiness befell the valley.

Meanwhile, the intuitive foresight of a handful of private citizens took it upon themselves to gather a few buffalo and raise their own private herds. These small pockets of privately owned buffalo were pivotal in saving and restoring a sustainable population of bison, an American icon, from permanent extinction.

Zachariah was well satisfied that his work was now complete. He hoped in his heart that enough had been done to restore something of a balance to the Great Mother in the new world of America, and that she may continue to find ways to speak to its many peoples.

As the winter eased and the snows began to melt in early March 1891, the Shoshone worked their way through the southern pass and entered the valley. Once more, they arrived to ask Little White Bull for some more buffalo, to help feed their hungry children. Instead, they found the valley bare of bison.

Concerned, the Shoshone approached the cabin and shouted for Little White Bull to show himself. Their only reply... silence. They entered the ghostly interior of the cabin. A fine dust had covered the floor. It was empty. They tentatively made their way through the buffalo skin curtain into the cave.

Upon the bed cot, lay the frozen body of Zachariah Little White Bull Yanasie. His eyes remained half open, peering into the distance, with a hint of a contented smile across his lips. He had died a couple of days earlier, no longer possessing the strength to withstand the cold, two months short of reaching seventy-six years.

A solemn countenance befell the group of Shoshone as they debated what to do with his body. Finally, they all agreed.

Wrapped in a thick buffalo hide, the Shoshone carried his body to the cursed burial ground at the entrance of the southern pass. They built a massive pyre of logs in the centre of the shrine and laid him atop its pinnacle. They set the pyre alight and wished Little White

Bull a safe journey back to the Great Mother. The burial ground now became sacred to the Shoshone.

As the pyre burned, a huge mass of ice on both sides of the valley gave way, causing a massive double avalanche into the northern portion of the valley. The sound reminded the Shoshone of an immense herd of buffalo migrating across the Great Plains, a sound now bequeathed to the wind.

The Rose

The Rose

The Rose

Ellantine, in her pyjamas, raced into the kitchen announcing her arrival with a shrill giggle-scream. This meant a game of chase was afoot after rudely awakening her older sister and brother. Her mother, Arissa, standing at the kitchen sink gazing out through the window at the magnificence of the pre-dawn twilight spreading across the clear purple sky, leapt momentarily out of her skin.

Her little body dashed through the kitchen, pushed the fly screen door open and continued out into the backyard. Arissa half turned to her left to watch Lauren, the eldest at ten and Jerard, who was eight, appear and run through the kitchen. They both threatened vile retribution, as they pushed through the same door in hot pursuit of their wild little five-year-old sister. Their mother shook her head smiling and returned to the task of preparing breakfast while watching them through the window. They all ran towards their favourite toy.

The backyard was wide, expansive and enclosed in a shoulder-high, black-painted, flat-topped, wrought-iron fence. A row of small trees and shrubs surrounded the outer fence, which then made way into the fields and orchards that stretched eastward across the gently rising slope of a small hill behind the farm. The ridge across the hill shared its boundary with a vast, deep forest. The farm was located fifty miles northwest of Ottawa.

In the centre of the backyard sat an ancient pickup truck, where its axles were permanently bolted to four thickly cut tree stumps. The engine, tyres and all the electrical wiring had been removed. The truck was painted in all manner of bright and vibrant colours, and fitted with a windscreen, wind-up side windows and a rear window. The cabin was laid out with a very comfortable bench seat, a large steering wheel, working gear shift, a restored dash and a radio permanently tuned to a children's channel.

The rear open tray was fitted with a thick rubber mat and a few waterproof cushions so the children could lay back and look up at the sky. Using their vivid imaginations, many adventures had been undertaken driving through wild lands, encountering and defeating all manner of foe and obstacles in their path.

Going unnoticed, three dozen or so vibrant birds of all varieties were perched in the trees and upon the fence surrounding the yard. They all hopped, skipped and scurried from branch to branch, chirping and singing their morning song in a strange unison.

The farm seemed truly alive this morning.

The sky exploded in a rich tapestry of light and colour as the sun pierced the horizon. Ellantine reached up, pulled on the lever handle, and opened the passenger door. All the birds leapt into the air all at once. Arissa watched mesmerised and momentarily held her breath. Her daughter stopped dead still, let go of the handle, and stared into the cabin. She took a step back, as her sister and brother caught up behind her and instantly mimicked her response.

Ellantine turned and raced back towards the house. Arissa stopped what she was doing and watched her daughter push through the screen door, appear before her and pull on her apron.

"Mama, Mama… there's a strange old man sleeping in the truck," she yelled. "Mama, mama, a strange old man is in the truck."

Arissa reached down and grabbed her hand.

"Ok, ok! Let's go have a look," she replied. "Olivier, GET UP!" she yelled at her husband.

Ellantine turned and pulled her mother through the screen door and out into the backyard. Arissa followed, feeling nervous and apprehensive. They reached the truck where she corralled the children behind her before peering through the open door.

She first saw his worn boots, then legs, torso, shoulders and head. Yes, there was indeed a strange-looking old man sound asleep across the bench seat of the truck. He was small in stature and looked like a wanderer, a vagabond. He had crept into the cabin sometime through the night. He did not look threatening, which eased her mind a little.

The old man was snoring softly, making a slight whistle sound when exhaling. He was dressed in old, dusty clothes which were made of tough material, maybe linen or calico, and covered in a dark green, knee-length jacket folded across his chest. He had faded rusty-orange hair sprinkled with grey, which was neither too messy nor all that tidy. His beard of the same colour was long enough to hide his neck.

Astonishingly, he did not smell that bad at all. She detected the rich aroma of wild grasses and flowers, of woodland trees and the earth itself, wafting through the cabin, which she strangely found quite pleasant. She wondered why the dogs didn't make a racket when they usually detect an intruder, and intuitively felt there was something unusual about this fellow. She gently pushed the passenger door closed without clicking the latch.

"Shh... shh... let's not wake the old man, ok," she whispered. "Let's go back inside and have breakfast. Come on, let's go."

Arissa turned and quickly ushered the children back into the kitchen. She sat them down at the kitchen table and gave each a small bowl of cereal and milk. She pushed the lever down on the toaster and began to fry some bacon, eggs, tomatoes and bananas she had prepared.

Olivier Franck walked into the kitchen, dressed in his farming overalls ready for the day's work. He was tall, just over six foot, lean and strong. Being French Canadian, he had fair skin, light-brown wavy hair and a well-manicured moustache. He was mostly quiet, sometimes aloof, consuming himself with his inner thoughts and did not express a lot of emotion. Yet, he was deeply loyal, dependable and always there for Arissa and the children.

He yawned and stretched, as the children wasted no time letting him know there was a strange man sleeping in their truck. On hearing the alarming news, he became instantly attentive readying himself to confront the intruder.

"Olivier, please stay here and watch over the children," she said sternly.

Arissa returned to the stovetop, reduced the heat and began to plate up. She spread butter and apricot jam on a thick slice of toast, poured a glass of orange juice and placed everything upon a tray. With tray in hand, she turned back to face her husband.

"He looks like a harmless old wanderer living in the forest. I've made him a nice hot breakfast. If we show a little kindness, I'm sure he'll be on his way before too long," she counselled.

"Fix yourself some toast and clean up when you've all finished. Then go and get ready for school, ok!" she instructed the children.

Olivier nodded and pushed the screen door open for Arissa. He then moved to the window and watched her carry the tray across the backyard towards the truck. She placed the tray on the truck's bonnet, gently pulled open the passenger door and peered inside.

"Good morning," she whispered.

Arissa spoke in a pleasant soft tone, loud enough to awaken but not startle him. The old man mumbled and slowly opened his squinty eyes. He raised his head and looked down over his legs and feet to see Arissa bending forward in the passenger's doorway. She offered him a warm smile.

Arissa Gyawachia Franck was a native Iroquois Canadian. She was of medium height, with full round hips, strong thighs and legs and slender shoulders. She displayed the reddish-brown skin of her people and had rich, strong black hair braided in two plaits down her back. She had a round gentle face which easily displayed her nurturing nature through her large dark-brown fearless eyes. She was dressed in a plain long-sleeved cotton top, printed full-length skirt and soft leather moccasins.

"Don't be alarmed, I've made you some breakfast," she said hospitably.

The old man looked around the cabin of the truck, as though he was not sure where he was. After a full minute he pushed himself up into a sitting position behind the steering wheel and looked out across the backyard and at the house. Nothing was familiar. It did not matter. He had not used his eyes but his intuitive instinct to find his way here. All his senses informed him that he was in the right place. Olivier gave a wave through the kitchen window. He turned and calmly smiled back at Arissa.

"Why, thank you. You need not have troubled yourself," he replied in a deep gruff voice.

"Oh, it's not a bother at all."

Arissa placed the tray on the passenger's side of the bench seat beside the old man. He looked down at breakfast upon the tray and a wide toothy grin quickly appeared on his face.

"Well, this is a treat. I'm not usually afforded such kindness. I'm honoured by your generosity," he said.

She handed him the plate, which he placed in his lap and took hold of the knife and fork. Delicately, he began to eat his breakfast.

He took the time to savour each and every mouthful and thoroughly enjoyed the experience. He finished off the toast and washed it all down with the orange juice. Satisfied, he returned the empty dishes upon the tray. In the meantime, Arissa mulled around and leant back against the bonnet. She waved Olivier away.

The old man opened the driver's door and stepped out of the truck. Arissa turned. He placed the tray on top of the bonnet. He reached into the cabin under the steering wheel and pulled out a large knapsack, which clanged and clattered with the objects inside. He then grabbed his black waist-high, wooden walking stick, with intricate carvings from tip to handle.

"Thank you very much for breakfast. I've not had such a fine meal in quite a while," he said. "Most of the time, residents such as yourself, politely, and sometimes aggressively, make it very clear they wish me to move on and leave."

"Really! Why, that's just awful," she replied. "How long have you been living this way, in the wilderness... with the Great Mother?" she asked.

The old man looked at Arissa and offered her a wry, all-knowing, smile.

"Well, it seems like forever," he replied. "I was born into this life. My mother taught me everything I needed to know... about the land, and... many things that would amaze you. I live as she did, before me. There's only a handful of us left."

The old man stared out towards the forest.

"Unfortunately, I have no children. I have no one to teach, to pass on the things I know. And all the knowledge we hold... will soon be lost... to a different kind of life," he said.

"What do you mean?" she asked. "Who are you... and where do you come from?"

He turned back to look at Arissa with a mischievous grin.

"What am I, is more the question," he replied. "I'm not sure there's a word in your language that can describe what I am. Gardener? Guardian? Druid? Hmm, no, no."

"All I can say is that I'm of the wild... the wilderness," he revealed. "It's my home you see. Yet, over time, I've noticed there to be less and less wilderness left. My ability to move freely has become more and more restricted. Everywhere I go, I trespass on someone's private property. I can no longer move as freely as I once did. Alas, that's the way things seem to be nowadays," he said.

"Well, you're welcome to pass through here any time you wish. I would be delighted to make you another breakfast. In fact, if you would like to stay, I'd be honoured to make you a wonderful dinner," she offered.

"Ooh, no, no. There's so little time, and I must keep moving," he replied.

"So little time?" she queried. "What… are you not well?"

The old man ignored the question.

"You are kind, generous and have a good heart. I feel… I know that about you," he paused. "In fact, in return, I would like to give you something… a small gift."

"Oh really," she said, delightfully surprised.

The old man crouched down and rummaged deep inside his knapsack and pulled out a small bundle of cloth. He held out the bundle and gently placed it in her open, cupped hands.

She carefully peeled back the folds of the bundle to reveal two small identical cuttings. She studied them curiously. The cuttings were both three inches long and about as thick as a small tree branch. The cross section of the cuttings was in the shape of a five-pointed star, without being quite perfectly symmetrical.

"How strange," she mused. "What are they?"

"They're two cuttings from a very special plant… a rose tree, or as I prefer to say, a tree of roses," he replied. "You must plant the cuttings together in the most peaceful, or rather sacred place in your garden… a place close to your heart," he paused.

"You must love this tree. For if you do, I assure you, the tree will reward you with great and plentiful joy," he said.

"Well, I don't know what to say. Thank you very much."

Arissa returned the folds and gently placed the bundle into the pocket of her skirt.

At that moment Ellantine ran out from the kitchen, grabbed a hand hold of her mother's skirt and looked up at the old man. He crouched down onto one knee and offered a warm smile.

"Hello there," he said. "Well, if it isn't our little wildling!"

"My name is Ellantine."

The old man held out his right hand. Ellantine held out hers and grabbed hold of the top middle of his index finger and they shook hands.

"My name is Guillaume. I'm very pleased to meet you."

Ellantine let go and the old man stood up. He swung the knapsack over his left shoulder and grabbed hold of his walking stick in the right.

"Farewell ladies, it was a pleasure to meet you both. May the Great Spirit protect you."

"Goodbye," Ellantine said.

He turned and walked towards the gate in the middle of the back fence.

"Don't forget…" he yelled over his shoulder, "…give it lots of love. The tree… lots of love… and you will see."

The old man opened, passed through and closed the gate behind him. Arissa watched him walk into the orchard and disappear among the trees leading up to the hill and the forest beyond. High above, the three dozen birds reassembled and followed in a loose formation.

Arissa collected the tray and walked back into the kitchen. Ellantine followed. She placed the tray next to the sink and stared out the window at the truck, feeling quite perplexed. She turned to face Olivier as he approached.

"What a strange man," she commented. "He's the strangest person I've ever met. At no time did I feel threatened. Rather, I felt a kind of warmth around him. So very strange."

"What did he give you?"

"A pair of cuttings. Look."

Arissa withdrew and opened the bundle to show Olivier.

"He said it's… a tree of roses, and to plant it in the most sacred place I can think of and… to give it lots… lots of love."

"Well, that sounds ominous, doesn't it?"

Olivier looked out the kitchen window in the wake of the old man. Arissa looked down at her daughter.

"He was quite taken with Ellantine, as though… he knew of her."

"Maybe it was Ellantine he wanted to see."

"Yes, well, maybe!"

"I think he is up to something."

"What do you mean?"

"I think he meant to give us those two cuttings," he said suspiciously.

"Maybe these cuttings are really for her."

"Do you really think this meeting was by chance?"

"I don't know," she replied. "Anyway, I must get the children off to school."

Arissa wrapped the cuttings and placed them into a small drawer of odds and ends and trinkets at the end of the bench. She began to clean up after breakfast.

The farm was quite large and roughly divided into four sections. The apple, pear and orange orchards extended back directly behind the main house to the boundary across the ridge. Along the southern border of the orchards, three long greenhouses grew a variety of vegetables. Further south were fields of corn and barley.

A long barn extended northward from the main house in front of the orchards. The barn was split in two. The first half housed tools and machinery and the kennels for the three working sheep dogs. A large henhouse was built inside the second half, which was also used to pen the fifty or so head of sheep at night from the weather and predators. The sheep grazed the empty, resting corn and barley fields to the north, and were allowed to wander through the orchards from time to time. Every two to three years, the corn and barley fields would swap with the grazing fields.

It was the middle of September, with just one week remaining in the summer of 1995.

****

The following morning Arissa enacted the same routine. She finally sat alone once the children left for school, Olivier for the barn and the kitchen was once again clean following the mayhem of breakfast. She wondered about the strange old man and decided he reminded her of a wizard from one of her daughter's fairy tales.

"What am I to do with those two cuttings?" she whispered. "Plant them, I guess. But where?" she wondered. "He said… in the most sacred place I could think of. Well, the place I love the most is my private little garden. And now that I think of it, I know just the spot."

Arissa rose to her feet and carefully withdrew the small bundle from the drawer and walked out to the first, closest greenhouse. She stood in the middle of a long potting work bench. She placed the bundle atop the bench, opened the folds and carefully inspected the two cuttings.

"Wow, they're so dry. I wonder if they will grow," she whispered. "They don't look like a cutting at all… more like… something between a seed pod and a root. I've never seen anything quite like these before. I wonder where he got them from. And how does he know if they will grow. I guess we'll find out soon enough."

Arissa grabbed a shallow knife and carefully cut three incisions into the base of both cuttings, to break the outer layer. She placed the pierced ends of both cuttings into a liquid solution of water dissolved with a high amount of hydroponic nutrients. She allowed the cuttings to soak for about three hours to soften their ends.

The cuttings were then planted into a small pot, filled with a high nitrate and phosphorus organic fertiliser, and watered with the same solution. The pot was covered with a large glass dome with a circular adjustable vent at the top. Arissa placed a thermometer beside the pot inside the glass cover and adjusted the vent to achieve 23 °C within the dome. She now waited for the cuttings to germinate, checking on them regularly.

Nothing happened for three days. She grew rather anxious that the cuttings would not germinate. However, on the morning of the fourth day, Arissa entered the greenhouse after breakfast and found that both cuttings had geminated and sprung forth one strong green stem each. She was ecstatic and clapped her hands with glee.

Over the next couple of days, Arissa nurtured the cuttings with regular dowsing of water and made sure the temperature within the glass dome remained constant. Both cuttings grew fast. The main stem, for each cutting, shot straight up. No further shoots would sprout from the stems themselves. Two leaves appeared at the top of both, which exploded outwards to form the first division of branches.

By the first week both cuttings had reached a height of ten centimetres. She re-potted them together in one large knee-high pot and placed them in a warm, sun-drenched corner of the greenhouse. The roots of both cuttings merged and became intertwined. She followed the instruction and ensured both cuttings would grow side by side, as one tree.

By the end of autumn, the growth of each trunk matched the other and surpassed a metre in height. Further growth slowed with the imminent arrival of winter, and the tree remained in the greenhouse to protect it from chill wind and frost. Once winter began to thaw the following March, the rose tree had just about outgrown its pot.

On the first day of April, Arissa decided it was time to find a permanent home for her tree of roses. Upon completion of her morning duties, she stepped out of the kitchen, turned right and walked along a small stone-paved path that led to the southern side of the house. She opened a small wooden gate in a tall, weathered archway, entered her garden and closed the gate behind. The garden was quite large, enclosed within a shoulder-high wooden fence with only the one entrance.

A stone-paved path led from the entrance to a two-foot-deep circular pond in the centre. An old carved sandstone bird bath wired to a wooden block, sat in the middle of the pond. The pond was filled with water lilies and some begonia and philodendron, but no fish as the pond would freeze during winter.

The pond was surrounded by five feet of stone paving, where three wooden benches carved from fallen tree trunks were placed at even intervals around the circumference. Native shrubs, wildflowers and herbs were planted in the deep garden beds that ran along the south and western fence line, and along the wall of the house, which formed the northern boundary of the garden. The eastern fence line was bare. A lush lawn filled the open spaces.

Looking around her oasis, Arissa confirmed what she already knew would be the best place to plant the rose tree; in the centre of the bare, east-facing fence, between the entrance and the southeast corner of the garden. Pleased with her decision, she sat back against one of the benches to plan what needed to be done next. Before long, she stood and got to work.

She retrieved a shovel from the barn and began to dig a large round hole one metre inside the fence line. Olivier arrived to help, and together they dug a wide, two-metre-deep hole. Then with wheelbarrow in hand they went around the orchard collecting an array of fallen fruit from the ground. They collected decaying corn and barley stalks, clippings, cut grass, dried leaves, sheep droppings and anything organic, which was all dumped into the hole, filling the first metre. She opened a large bag of rich organic black soil and mixed this with some compost and mulch and filled the next half metre of the pit.

Olivier wheeled out the pot from the greenhouse to the garden using a trolley. He carefully pushed the pot over onto its side next to the hole. He dug around the inner edge of the pot to loosen the soil. He pulled the pot away and rolled the base of the tree into the pit. Arissa filled the surrounding space with the last of the soil mix, patted everything down and watered the newly planted tree thoroughly. They sat back upon a bench admiring how beautiful the rose tree looked in its new home.

With temperatures warming, the rose tree shot up and outwards. Both stems grew to a height of two metres and thickened to the size of a man's forearm, without touching. At the crown of each stem, a total of five branches grew out at the first division. From these branches a mass of shoots built a thick-domed canopy over the base and overhung the fence, reaching a further metre in height.

By the end of autumn, the growth of the tree stabilised at a height of four metres and a diameter of three metres from one side of the canopy to the other. Both Arissa and Olivier were amazed at the size of the tree which, as yet, had not bloomed a single flower. Standing on a stepladder, she carefully pruned the outer branches in line with what she felt the tree wanted to achieve... a thick full bloom in spring. Winter arrived and the tree went into hibernation.

As spring broke through the winter chill well into March, a cacophony of new shoots sprang forth, throughout the canopy. Arissa maintained regular and moderate fertilisation and watering. Five large rosebuds formed on straight stems in May. Excitement grew as she watched the buds grow. On the 4th of June, the first rose bloomed into full colour.

Arissa and all the family stood with mouths agape in awe upon seeing the first rose.

The rose was as big as cupping both open hands together. The outer petals were a pale pink at the base fading to white round, curved tips. As the layers progressed to the centre, the petals displayed more and more of a stronger pink in colour, whereupon reaching the centre, the petals bloomed in a full, rich and vibrant fuchsia pink.

Arissa cut the long stem and placed it in a long thin vase upon the kitchen table for everyone to admire. The rose emitted a subtle yet rather pleasant aroma. All four remaining buds bloomed within the next two days and were quickly added to the vase for display.

A couple of weeks later with the onset of summer, no new buds formed. Arissa sat upon the bench in her garden basking in the warmth of the midmorning sun looking at and inspecting the now enormous, barren rose tree.

"I wonder if there's more to this tree than meets the eye," she whispered. "What did that old man... Guillaume say... give it lots of love and you will see. I wonder what he meant. A few massive flowers are amazing... but... is that it? He made it sound like there was more. Am I missing something?" she pondered.

To avoid the rising heat, she went inside to prepare sandwiches and fruit juice for lunch.

The children were soon home for the summer holidays. Arissa and Olivier kept them busy by sharing the endless array of chores that needed to be completed around the farm. The reward for their hard work was a trip to the mall in Ottawa to see a movie and for a little shopping. They visited the local rural show and took day trips and picnics to nearby nature reserves and favourite old camping grounds that were once the domain of the Iroquois, as well as attending the local indigenous Green Corn Festival.

September arrived, as did the new school year. Lauren was twelve, Jerard ten and Ellantine had now turned seven years old and was about to begin her second year in primary school.

Ellantine's first year was rather turbulent. Her wild nature got her into all sorts of trouble with her fellow classmates and teachers. Once again it had only taken three days before she was sent home for yelling and screaming and being overly disobedient in class. Having sent Ellantine to her room, Arissa and Olivier sat in the kitchen perplexed.

"What are we going to do about Ellantine?" she asked. "The school year has only just begun. She won't last long in this school, if we can't think of a way to calm her temper."

"I'm not sure," he replied. "We can't home school her. We're not qualified. Nor do we have the time," he paused. "And we can't afford a tutor, not for the whole school year."

"Yes, I agree. That would be expensive and unfair on the other children."

"Maybe we should go and see our doctor about this," he suggested.

"She doesn't have ADHD," Arissa quickly retorted, "and I don't want her medicated either. I think that would be counterproductive. I think she likes her freedom and can't settle down when cooped up in a classroom full of other children."

"What about stronger discipline… or maybe… a reward system," he offered.

"You know very well how strong her spirit is. If we try more discipline she will rebel. If we try to break her spirit, she will turn against us. A reward system won't last long… not for a seven-year-old."

"Then I'm all out of ideas. I don't know what to do," he confessed.

"I don't know either. I don't know what we can do if no school will take her," she replied. "This is just the worst situation for Ellantine."

Tears began to form as Arissa felt herself becoming upset with no solution in sight. She walked out of the kitchen into the backyard, her mind swimming. She instinctively sought a place of comfort and solitude, and without thinking followed the stone path into her garden. She flopped down onto the grass exasperated and rolled onto her back to look up at the sky. The canopy of the rose tree cast a shadow overhead.

She stared up at the branches beneath the canopy and after a few minutes, she began to relax. Inexplicably she felt at ease and let go of her worry about Ellantine. She closed her eyes and drifted off into a light afternoon doze.

Arissa woke up with a start and sat bolt upright. She stared ahead, seeing a clear distinct image in her mind. She knew exactly what the solution ought to be for Ellantine's predicament. The image in her mind was that of a puppy, a short-haired Border Collie. She raced out of her garden and found Olivier in the barn.

"Olivier!" she yelled. "I have the answer! I know what to do about Ellantine."

"Ooh, really."

"We get her a puppy!"

"A puppy?"

"Yes," she affirmed. "Don't you see? Ellantine has too much energy… much more than other children. She has a vivid imagination and is far more curious about everything," she paused. "So, let's get her a puppy. It will be her responsibility to look after it, train it and to exercise it. This will burn all that pent-up energy and give her something to focus on. You've seen how she loves all the animals. It's perfect."

"Right... ok... I see what you mean," he pondered. "I think you might have something here."

"It must be a short-haired Border Collie. We must find one as soon as we can."

"Why a Border Collie?"

"Because I think it will be the best fit for her personality. And the image was in my vision when I woke up under the rose tree," she explained.

The very moment she said these words, Arissa half turned and stared out through the barn door. She wondered about receiving the image of the Border Collie under the rose tree.

"Is everything all right?"

She turned back to look at Olivier with a strange, distant expression.

"Yes... yes of course," she replied. "Can you call around and see if we can find a Border Collie puppy. We need to get one as soon as possible."

She smiled warmly, turned and walked out of the barn for the kitchen.

On Saturday morning, Olivier and Arissa, together with Ellantine, drove to a sheep farm in a nearby valley northeast of Ottawa. They found a female Border Collie who had been mated with an Australian Kelpie and given birth to six pups. Already eight weeks old, four had been sold leaving only two left.

They followed the owner into the barn and stood before a nice warm kennel. Olivier gently guided Ellantine to the front of the cage. Brimming with anticipation, her eyes fixated upon the mother and the two remaining pups snuggled between the folds of an old blanket.

"Here is our special surprise for you, Ellantine. We're going to buy you a new puppy dog."

"What... a new puppy! Ooh, Papa!" she exclaimed.

Her eyes wide, her face glowed flush with excitement as she could barely contain herself from jumping up and down. Olivier knelt and placed his hands around her shoulders.

"Now, if we get you this puppy, it will be yours to keep, but only on these conditions," he said. "You and you alone will feed your puppy. You and only you must train, exercise and look after your puppy. No one else. Is that agreed?"

"Yes, yes. She will be mine and only mine, and I will love her forever," she replied.

"Ok… let's have a look at them."

The owner opened the kennel door. He grabbed hold of the two unclaimed pups, who yelped in protest at being awoken and carefully placed them into her hands. Olivier encouraged her.

"Ok, Ellantine, have a look and choose the one you like."

She carefully looked over each pup. She quickly settled upon the smallest of the two.

"This one!" she said. "She's the cutest one of all."

The farm owner retrieved both pups from Ellantine. He returned the last unclaimed pup to the kennel and carefully wrapped the one she chose in a nice, warm puppy blanket. He returned the bundle to her grasp and said her pup was the smallest one of the entire litter. She immediately kissed her puppy on the tip of her snout.

"I'm going to call her Holly," she announced proudly.

Olivier gave them both a hug.

"Holly, hey! I like it. What made you think of that?"

"Well, Papa, this feels like Christmas! And it rhymes with Collie," she replied joyfully.

"We can't argue with that now, can we?"

Olivier paid the farm owner and were delighted to return home with a new bundle of joy. Holly had short black fur and white tips on her snout and tail. She had a white stripe around all four paws and a white, diamond-shaped patch upon her chest.

$$3$$

For the remainder of the weekend Ellantine was completely consumed with her new puppy. She played with, fed and took Holly out onto the lawn at regular intervals. She made a small warm cot on the floor next to her bed. She set up a small kennel in the backyard, a little to the left of the kitchen door, where Holly was to stay outside during the day. She made some toys for Holly to play with and found an old book on how to train your dog. Ellantine was happy and content when she went off to school on Monday morning.

Once the children left and the kitchen tidy, Arissa decided to have a break and walked around to her garden. Beneath the warm morning sun, she sat on a bench facing the rose tree. Throughout the whole weekend just past, she had been thinking about how she intuitively discovered the solution to Ellantine's misbehaviour. Something about the tree had been gnawing at her ever since.

Arissa stood up and walked over to the rose tree. She reached out with her right hand and touched the trunk with the tips of her fingers. The trunk felt as it should, a rough wooden bark texture. She laid the flat of her whole hand upon the trunk, with her fingers facing upward. She looked up into the canopy of branches. Nothing seemed odd or out of place.

"There's something about this tree... I know it," she whispered. "I know it deep in my stomach. Why? Why did he give me the cuttings? What for?"

She withdrew her hand and stepped back one foot from the tree. She slowly traced her gaze from the canopy through the branches and down the trunk as it disappeared into the earth.

"Mmm... I don't know, I just don't know what it is," she said.

She then turned around to walk back to the bench. At that moment, she stopped and stood still with her back to the tree, for a few long moments. She slowly turned her head and looked behind her at the two-trunked rose tree with the gap in the middle.

"It's strange..." she pondered, "how those two cuttings have grown together and left that gap between their trunks."

Suddenly, instinctively, without really thinking, Arissa turned, tucked in her skirt and sat down upon the ground. She carefully nestled her spine between the gap and leant back against the two trunks. Once comfortable, she allowed her head to slowly drift back against the tree.

At the very moment her head touched both trunks, Arissa felt all the worry and stress she was carrying, suddenly drain away. The sensation was subtle but unmistakable. The tension in her body just seemed to melt away, into the earth.

She was overcome by a deep and overwhelming sense of calm tranquillity. Her heart rate and breathing slowed substantially. She felt herself become grounded in the earth, and in doing so, she sensed a growing immersion with the tree. She emptied her mind of all thought and basked in natural, blissful unity with the tree and entered into a transient state.

Time did not exist... or at the least... seemed not to pass.

After a while, Arissa lifted her head from the wood and leant forward to separate her spine from the trunk. She regained awareness of herself and her surroundings once more. She quickly leapt to her feet and raced into the barn where Olivier was working.

"Olivier, Olivier!" she called out.

Running through the barn door, she spotted him opening the kennels, where he intended to unleash the dogs upon the herd of sheep to move them into the next field on the rotation.

"Where have you been?" he scolded. "It's been an hour since the kids went to school."

"I've been in my garden," she replied slowing to a walk. "I've worked it out!"

"Worked out what?" he replied, a little annoyed.

"The rose tree... the rose tree. I've worked out what it does," she proclaimed.

"The rose tree! What do you mean?"

Arissa walked right up and grabbed Olivier's left hand with her right.

"Come with me, I'll show you."

She led him out of the barn. He closed the barn doors and pushed the bolt home to prevent the dogs from escaping and running amuck. He followed to her garden.

"The rose tree… I've worked out what it can do."

Entering the garden, they soon stood a few feet in front of the rose tree.

"It was here that I found the answer to Ellantine's problem. I felt that the rose tree had something to do with it. I couldn't figure it out… until… I sat down there under the tree, with my back against the trunk," she paused. "It felt like I was grounded in the earth… and… that I became immersed with, united with, the tree. I felt its energy."

Pondering Arissa's claim, Olivier looked at the tree, perplexed. She saw doubt in his eyes.

"Look, you try it then."

With her hands, Arissa guided Olivier to be seated with his back against the trunk. He followed her directions and when ready, allowed his head to fall back and touch both trunks.

Nothing! A few moments elapsed and nothing happened. Olivier did not detect any sensations at all. After three minutes he climbed back to his feet.

"I didn't feel anything," he reported.

"Well, that's strange. It worked for me," she countered. "Let me show you."

She tucked in her skirt and sat before the tree once more. She leant her back against the tree and as soon as her head touched the wood, she entered easily, seamlessly, into the transient state almost instantly.

After a short while she felt her right arm being gently pulled. Her head separated from the tree, and she quickly regained normal awareness.

"Arissa… Arissa!" he called.

"What… what are you doing? I'm right here," she replied.

Olivier held her arm in his, as he pulled her away from the tree.

"I've been calling you for two minutes now and waving my hands in front of your face. You didn't respond or acknowledge me. You were completely out of it," he stated.

"Ok, yes, yes. You see. The tree! I was with the tree."

She paused for a moment to consider what she had just said.

"That's it. That's how I would describe it. I was communing with the rose tree."

"Well, it didn't work for me," he retorted. "And this is rather too strange for me. I'm not sure I like this idea at all."

Olivier began to stand up. He still had hold of her right arm, wanting to help her to her feet. Arissa reversed the grip and grabbed his arm in turn with a firm hold.

"This is a good thing," she said in a gentle voice. "In fact, it's a great thing. I'm not sure why it didn't work for you. But don't be afraid, Olivier," she said reassuringly. "You will see… you will see. This is something we must look after and nurture."

"Is this what you want?" he asked.

"Yes, it is. Remember… this was given to us… as a gift," she assured him.

"Ok then," he replied. "Be sure never to speak of this to anyone else… even the kids. For if you do, I'm not sure they will understand. I mean, I don't really understand. And I wouldn't want anyone to think that you were a little… crazy… alright!"

"Yes… I can do that," she agreed with a smile.

"Very well!"

Olivier helped pull Arissa to her feet.

"I'm happy for you to have this thing. And whatever it is, you will need time to figure out what it is and how it works. However, for now, let's get back to work. We have a farm to run," he said.

The next day, with the afternoon free following lunch, Arissa returned to her garden.

Instead of jumping straight into the deep end, this time she slowed everything down. She sat in front of the tree without touching the trunk. She slowed her breathing and concentrated on relaxing every muscle in her body. When completely calm, she eased her back onto the tree and laid her head back. She immediately became immersed yet, having slowed down the transition, she managed to maintain some instinctive cognitive ability.

Arissa focused on her eyes and worked to regain her vision, instead of allowing herself to be completely immersed in a blind state of emotional bliss. With a short struggle of will, she managed to regain the use of her eyes and could see the view of the garden in front of her, which was overlaid with the sensory stimuli that was flooding her mind.

In her transient state, she quickly recognised that she was between two worlds.

She pulled away to release herself from the tree for a few minutes, before returning to practise entering that state once again. She managed gained some control whilst under the influence of the tree.

After a few minutes of looking at the shrubs and wildflowers in her garden and the canopy of the rose tree while immersed, Arissa noticed something different. She could see a light blue green energy field surrounding all the plants, by no more than an inch.

Tiny globules, like little white balls inside a darkened membrane, would appear in rhythmic waves in the surrounding atmosphere, all moving in a random squiggly manner. They would either disappear or be absorbed by nearby plants, after only a few short seconds.

The word 'orgone' appeared in Arissa's mind.

"Ah, so they do have a name for those little spots... orgone, hey," she whispered. "The energy field of the plants is absorbing the orgone... wow," she mused.

Two birds landed and drank from the bird bath. Arissa noticed they too were surrounded by an energy field. She slowly raised her right arm and saw the field around her hand. She waved her hand up and down to see how the energy field flowed and operated with the movement of her arm.

"This might be what the Chinese people call Chi and what the Indian people call Prana," she muttered. "Amazing!"

"It's an energy... but... it moves like a liquid. So, it must have substance... a substance that we can't normally see. What can I call it... something organic... something a bit modern... something a bit more scientific," she paused. "Ooh, I know... 'bioplasma', although I might've read that somewhere," she confessed to herself.

She put her hand down and continued to look around her garden.

"This must be a universal thing. It surrounds everything," she whispered. "It permeates through everything... and everything seems connected to it."

Arissa withdrew a little from her immersion and returned to her inner mind to gain more of a sense of what this energy field was. When immersed, she used the tree as a medium to feel and merge with this energy. She sensed the energy field was also pure consciousness, not the consciousness of the individual plant or animal... but... the consciousness of the collective whole. Everything was connected to and sustained by this collective consciousness.

Upon that realisation, Arissa leant forward to disconnect from the rose tree and returned to her normal awakened state. She stood up, turned and stared at the tree in amazed awe. It took her a few long moments to process this realisation, and once understood, her entire perspective changed.

****

Over the next couple of weeks, Arissa developed something of a routine, a process. She would only spend one hour a day after lunch communing with the rose tree, except on weekends. She did not want to overdo it and become overly attached to the experience. Nor did she wish to give the children an inkling of what was happening.

On the Monday of the third week, Arissa sat before her rose tree to prepare for the day's immersion. She slowed her breathing and cleared her mind. She stared straight ahead at a random point in space in her garden. She did not focus on that point, instead, with defocused eyes, she looked through that point into the beyond and entered the space of her mind. At that moment, when ready, she leant back against the rose tree and lost her sense of self.

Once her perspective was attuned to understanding the interconnectedness of nature and the intuitive, instinctive sensation of merging with the collective consciousness, Arissa began to feel very comfortable with the experience. She allowed herself the opportunity to explore.

Sensing direction became very vague. There did not seem to be an up, down, left or right. The experience of space was a vastly different sensation. It felt like she had entered a plane parallel to that of the physical world. Within the field, the plane, she could easily pick up on and detect anything living. She was able to feel the presence of the living plants close to her in her garden. She was able to focus on one and then the other, and tell what type of plant it was, what it felt, how healthy it was and its age, purely by its vibration within the field.

Arissa felt the presence of some insects within the soil. She was able to follow her sensing of the form to its source beneath the earth and work out what type of creature it was: an ant, spider, cockroach or beetle, to name a few. She also felt a couple of birds nearby in the bird bath. She turned her attention to them and again was able to feel the inner nature of each bird.

Arissa quickly recognised that every plant, insect and animal had a slightly different feeling or sensation. Each creature had its own signature vibration – its own unique resonance within the field – for all of the creatures of that type. Conversely, all the creatures of the same species were connected by their signature resonance, their unique morphic resonant frequency.

She realised this mechanism allowed a creature in one location to learn a new behaviour from the same species in a different location who had adapted their behaviour to an environmental change. She began to appreciate anew the intelligence behind all of existence.

As soon as she discovered this phenomenon, Arissa separated from the tree and dropped out of her immersion. She leapt to her feet and ran off in search of Olivier. She found him napping against a tree in the orchard, under the warm afternoon sun, surrounded by sheep. She sat down and gave him a gentle kiss upon the cheek. He smiled and opened his eyes. She laid back against him and explained her new discoveries while he listened.

"When I commune with the tree of roses, I can merge with the universal energy field and connect with the collective consciousness of all life. Within the field I can detect the unique morphic resonance of each species of plant, insect or animal that holds a kind of collective memory from which the whole can learn to adapt and survive."

"It sounds like your universal energy field possesses the principle of sympathetic resonance," he replied. "This is where, if you strike a tuning fork, a second nearby tuning fork will vibrate at the same frequency and produce the same sound. And since all things living possess mass, an electric current and the energy of life, each species will have its own unique electromagnetic code. So, what you are witnessing might be a kind of harmonic communication, where the source of new information will resonate it across the fundamental frequency specific to all members of the same species."

"Ooh, you know exactly what I'm thinking, don't you?" she said jokingly.

They both laughed. Arissa kissed and gave Olivier a nice warm hug, before rising to her feet and walking back into the house. Feeling a little worn out, she laid down to rest for a while before tending to the evening meal.

****

Arissa continued to commune with the tree, always able to discover a new pearl of wisdom on the workings of nature. September quickly moved into October and the temperature dropped. Soon it was too cold to sit out in the garden comfortably and the workings of the rose tree slowed into hibernation, preventing immersion. Just like the year before, Arissa pruned back the tree just before the onset of winter.

4

The new year arrived. Winter finally thawed with the arrival of spring in March. As soon as the temperature began to warm, life returned to the rose tree where a mass of new shoots sprang forth throughout the canopy. Arissa gave the tree plenty of loving attention. She loosened the soil around the base, added some fresh organic fertiliser and carefully removed aphids and caterpillars she found in the branches. A half dozen rosebuds appeared in April. She was delighted.

With the children back at school, she resumed communion with the tree.

Arissa's skill and vision developed even further. Becoming very familiar and comfortable with the process of immersion, she soon found that she was able to continue seeing the energy field around plants and animals, whilst being away from the rose tree.

She would walk through the orchard, focus on an apple tree and see its resonance. She could do the same when looking at a bird that stood still long enough. Insects were easy if she could draw close enough. Walking around looking at the energy field of all the plants and animals on the farm, she discovered that things were not as well as they seemed.

When inspecting a bee, she found the insect's field to be rather weak. The bee was not healthy at all. Olivier and Arissa were well aware that bee populations were suffering and in decline around the world. Mainstream scientific research already alluded to the collective impact that multiple toxic pesticides and fungicides were having on the health of bees.

Olivier did not spray across the farm during pollination. However, he did a minimum amount of spraying as the first fruit began to germinate and once more a month prior to harvest. On seeing the poor condition of the bee's resonance, the issue suddenly hit home for Arissa.

She told Olivier what she saw.

During the week to follow, Arissa used her newfound ability to analyse all the plants, insects and animals on the farm. Since the bees were an introduced species, she found they had limited sources of food other than just the flowering of fruit trees in spring. They needed a greater array of wildflowers and weeds to sustain them all year round.

Currently, the flowers and weeds were being eaten and cleared from the ground by their sheep. She convinced Olivier to stop allowing the sheep to forage in the orchards, to stop using pesticides and fungicides and find alternative natural processes, at all costs.

Arissa quickly understood that they needed to invite nature back onto the farm by introducing more organic methods.

She began to realise that by introducing and allowing wildflowers and weeds to grow along the ground floor of the orchards, the population of both, bees, wasps and other predatory insects would flourish and keep in check other insect populations.

Being a relatively small family run farm, Olivier devised a new strategy on how to handle the occurrence of mildew through the orchards. All their trees were now adult fruit-bearing trees. He would stop spraying pesticides and fungicides during the budding period of the fruit and instructed the farm hands to regularly inspect all the fruit trees.

As soon as a tree was found to have mildew, the affected branches would be cut and burned, where only that tree would be targeted with a spray and covered with a fine net to keep the birds and the bees away from the quarantined tree. The target rate of five per cent infection was set using this strategy over the next two years, with a revision if the infection rate was found to be higher.

Arissa found that healthy populations of several good ant species was also beneficial for their orchards. Ants eat the eggs of other insects and are themselves a food source for birds and lizards. Their tunnels aerate the soil allowing water and nutrients to flow freely to the roots.

Olivier ensured that all the fruit trees were properly pruned so that no tree touched another. Arissa formulated an organic tanglefoot wax herself, using beeswax as the primary ingredient, which was applied to burlap bands wrapped around close to the top of each trunk, to prevent the ants from cultivating herds of aphids in the foliage.

Olivier reconfigured the watering system to irrigate the orchards with sprinklers below the canopy, helping to keep the fruit dry and not washing away the tanglefoot wax.

Arissa analysed the layout of the farm. The current trees in the orchard were a little over half way through their twenty-year life span. To help with better water retention, she devised a plan of replanting the orchard in the future along tiers in line with the gentle contours of the farm, instead of rectangular fields. The top edge of each tier would be at soil level to slow the dispersion of water down the hill, with regular drainage points to prevent water from standing too long within each tier.

Using the greenhouse, Arissa grew and planted all manner of medium-sized, native flower-bearing trees throughout the spare spaces of the farm, keeping land strips designated as fire breaks clear. Again, no tree touched the other and each was also ringed with her tanglefoot wax and burlap wrap. She planted more tall native pines and other woodland trees familiar to the surrounding wilderness around the boundary of the farm.

No pesticide or fungicide was permitted to be used inside their greenhouses. The glass shutters were opened early in the morning to allow bees and other insects access to pollinate the fruits and vegetables being grown. The shutters were closed as the sun began to dip late in the afternoon, to prevent moths from gaining entry. Unwanted insects found upon the plants were gathered using a small, specially fitted, handheld vacuum. The resulting insect mulch was emptied onto a purpose-built tray behind each greenhouse and fed to the birds.

Arissa also noticed that the health and quality of their corn and barley crop was quite poor. She attributed this to the deteriorating quality of the soil and an increase in its acidity. She embarked on a programme of acquiring a variety of materials to replenish the soil.

Over the next few months, several tonnes of manure, wood chip and pulp from felled trees were acquired, together with rotting fruit and plant material from her own and neighbouring farms. She added a few tonnes of organic dark-brown earth. All this material was dumped in the resting fields and mulched, together with some added lime.

A backhoe spread the mulch out across the entire field which was then tilled into the earth with a deep plough. The following season, the growing and resting fields were rotated, and the same process repeated for the worn-out fields. The soil soon returned to a rich and nourishing quality, high in carbon, nitrates and phosphorus.

The resting fields would now be sowed with deep root grasses that grow very quickly. Arissa ensured the grazing sheep never stripped the soil of plant coverage and acquired surplus hay from a nearby wheat farm. She never used antibiotics or hormones on her animals.

Flowing down from the hills, a small stream cut through the back left corner of the farm. Olivier had long ago tapped into the creek, siphoning water to fill a reservoir at the lowest left end of the property which was then used for irrigation during the dryer months. Arissa installed a separate pipe to siphon fresh water from the creek through a filtration system and into large sealed ceramic vessels stored in the dark, cool basement of the barn. This purified water was only used for the family's drinking water.

Six huge roses blossomed late in May. Arissa and the family were amazed at their size and colouring. The roses were infused with a beautifully rich arousing aroma, a scent which was difficult to draw away from. No one managed to truly describe its likeness.

Whilst Arissa applied her energies to the corrective activities of reorganising the farm, for the first time, the rose tree launched a second round of rosebuds late in June. This time, over a dozen roses bloomed throughout the month of August.

The children begged Arissa to enter the roses into a competition. However, she forbade them from taking and showing the roses to anyone outside the farm. She explained that people would invade their house, their garden and take cuttings from the tree. She warned that if something bad were to happen to the rose tree, that something bad would surely befall them all. Arissa obtained firm assurance from everyone that the rose tree was to remain a family secret, never to be broken.

****

The winter hibernation arrived, and once again, new life sprang forth in March. Arissa busied herself reviewing the energy fields of all the farm's inhabitants. She continued to find ways of refining methods, processes and structures around the farm, managing to achieve ever greater degrees of balance.

The farm produced most of the fruit and vegetables consumed by the family. The health of Olivier, the children and Arissa improved as the nutritional quality of the produce improved. She observed everyone's energy field radiating like a blossom. The farm flourished.

The rose tree mirrored the healthy condition of the farm by casting a dozen new rosebuds at the start of the season and then continued to produce a half dozen new rosebuds every four to five weeks. At least one giant rose was continuously on show, in full bloom, from late spring and all through summer. The flowers generated a shared joy among the family.

At summer's end, Arissa sat in her garden and reflected on how the rose tree had brought the farm and her family to this point, and how the spirit of the farm was now attuned to the spirit of the tree. Everything was now in perfect harmony.

One Friday, late in September, Ellantine was unexpectedly sent home early from school. She was embroiled in a vicious fight with two boys she caught throwing stones at several crows perched atop the fence line in one corner of the sports field during the lunch break.

The deputy principal drove and dropped her off at the farm gate. Ellantine threw her bag down inside the front door and went in search of Holly and her mother. She looked through the house. Neither could be found. She walked through the kitchen and out into the backyard. It was quiet and sparse. No one. Even the birds seemed unusually quiet.

Intuitively, she walked around to her mother's garden. She peered over the wooden gate. Holly was stretched out on the paving beside the pond, basking in the warmth of the afternoon sun. Holly opened her eyes to look at Ellantine. She did not move or make a single sound. This was surprising, strange and very much out of character.

Ellantine leant forward and looked to her left. She saw her mother sitting up against the rose tree. Arissa did not acknowledge her presence. In fact, Arissa did not quite seem herself. She was staring straight ahead and appeared to be in a hypnotic state. Ellantine thought better than to disturb her mother and withdrew back to the kitchen. She opened the fridge and made a snack from some leftovers.

Ten minutes later, Holly raced through the doggy door into the kitchen to greet Ellantine excitedly. Arissa hadn't realised she was home and walked over to the barn to help Olivier with the afternoon chores. Ellantine grabbed an old chewed-up tennis ball from the backyard and ran into the orchard with Holly in hot pursuit.

The following morning Arissa prepared breakfast and called everyone to the table when ready. Olivier, Lauren and Jerard all quickly appeared. Ellantine was missing. Arissa called again… no reply. She went to investigate Ellantine's room. She opened the door to find the bedroom empty. The bathroom… also vacant. She returned to the kitchen perplexed and decided to check the backyard. She knew if she found Holly, she would find Ellantine.

No one. Silence. Strangely, Holly was nowhere to be seen either. Suddenly, Arissa felt uneasy, disturbed. She walked briskly around to her garden and looked over the gate. Holly was lying down upon the paving with her head between her paws. Arissa shot a look towards the rose tree and her heart skipped a beat. She caught her breath and gasped.

Sure enough, Ellantine was sitting with her head and back against the twin trunks. She was staring blankly, straight ahead into invisible space. Arissa was stunned with immediate concern. She quietly opened the gate and entered the garden. She sat down on a bench and kept watch over Ellantine. She knew not to disturb and break the hypnotic immersion. She chose instead, to wait until her daughter dropped out by her own inclination.

About seven minutes passed by before Ellantine leant forward from the tree and stood up to see Arissa watching her. Arissa reached out with her left hand and beckoned to Ellantine.

"Good morning. Here, take my hand," she said in a gentle tone.

Ellantine stepped forward. Slowly, she reached out with her right arm and grabbed hold of her mother's outstretched hand. Bending forward, Arissa drew her closer and ran her hands around the top and back of Ellantine's head, reassuring herself that everything was alright. With the thumb side of her index finger, she pushed Ellantine's chin up and looked into her eyes.

"Are you ok?" she asked.

Ellantine stared back with her usual unflinching wild intensity.

"I'm fine," she answered flatly.

"You know that… tree… is a very special rose tree?"

"I know," she replied matter-of-factly.

Arissa let go of Ellantine and leant back.

"I wasn't sure if I could tell you about this rose tree. I felt you might be… too young to understand how it works… what it can do," she explained. "I didn't want you to sit with the tree, until you had… grown up a little more. I wasn't sure if it would be safe for you to sit with the tree, when you're just nine years old."

"That's ok, Mama," she replied.

"Are you really… ok?"

"Yes! I'm fine," she assured her.

"What happened?"

Ellantine used a few long moments to consider the question. A broad smile appeared upon her tiny face. She looked up at Arissa, and with her child's logic she simply said, "I spoke with the Great Spirit."

Sitting straight up, Arissa was astounded at the reply.

"I see," she said.

Ellantine took one pace back. After a few moments of further consideration, Arissa continued.

"I don't want you sitting with the tree again until you're older, and until I think you're ready. Do you understand?"

"Ok then," she replied.

"And don't speak of this with your sister or your brother. They're very much like your father, and I suspect, the tree won't work for them either," she said.

Ellantine turned and raced out of the garden. Holly leapt to her feet in hot pursuit. She ran into the kitchen to join the others for breakfast. Arissa lingered deep in thought.

"How did that old man know?"

Deep in the back of her mind she knew, as did the old man, that Ellantine would be naturally gifted at communing with the tree. She felt there to be an element of fate, of destiny at play. If so, then a higher purpose there would be. She allayed her fears by allowing herself to trust in the Great Mother and the natural order of things. By the time Arissa reached the kitchen table, she was at ease and smiled and teased the children remorselessly.

Arissa would never discover Ellantine sitting with the tree again. Nor would she ever ask if Ellantine disobeyed and had sat with the tree once more. As time passed by, however, Arissa became suspicious that her daughter secretly communed with the tree from time to time. Maybe she was with the tree during the night or before dawn when everyone was still asleep, or during school holidays when she found herself the only one home. As Ellantine began to grow up, Arissa noticed subtle changes taking place in her nature.

Although still wild in spirit, Ellantine developed a sense of knowingness, of grounded connectedness. She became abundantly more compassionate, nurturing and empathetic towards all things living. She no longer spoke out abruptly or lashed out at others unless they were intentionally harming a creature. She would never hesitate to defend the world of nature. Subsequently, she had no interest in toys, material objects or money, beyond their intrinsic value and regarded people who displayed such attachments as being stupid.

She seemed to know exactly what a plant, insect or animal was feeling, thinking and doing. If a creature was in distress, she would instinctively know how to make it feel better. If she was feeling unhappy, she would go into the orchard or nearby hills and be completely revived upon her return. She found solace in nature and nature found solace in her.

Arissa and Ellantine developed a strong unbreakable bond. Arissa explained what the universal energy field was and how the many changes made around the farm would benefit all its inhabitants, especially the health of the family. Ellantine did not reveal that she too, could see the universal energy field with ease.

On many occasions they would find themselves leaning against a fence watching the sunset without speaking and then point out the presence of a rare bird. They would complement each other's insight into its behaviour and why the bird was doing what it was doing. When walking through the orchard together in winter, they would identify which creature the tracks in the snow belonged to and predicted the location of its home.

Arissa no longer roused upon or restricted Ellantine's freedom. Her elder sister and brother did not seem to fare as well. They incurred Arissa's displeasure purposefully and deemed this either as an immense comedy or the drama of eternal rebellion. Ellantine remained rather aloof to such silly games. They quietly knew she was Arissa's favourite. Yet they dare not make it a point of conjecture and risk invoking the wrath of Ellantine's furious temper.

Ellantine carried out her duties on the farm expertly and without complaint. In fact, she loved farm work far more than schoolwork. Her favourite task was to call Holly and herd the sheep into the barn for the night. She spent vast amounts of time with Holly. From a pup, she trained Holly to know and understand a full array of whistles and hand signals, more so than just a sheep dog. Holly always walked by Ellantine's side and had never been placed on a leash. They were inseparable.

Ellantine moved seamlessly from elementary school into secondary school. Growing bigger, stronger, she would take Holly for long forays deep into the wilderness beyond the hill behind the farm, during weekends and the summer holidays. Naturally, they would not forage as far from the farm during winter.

During the summer holidays of her final two years of secondary school, Ellantine and Holly would both camp out in the wildness for one, two and then three days and nights at a time. At first, Olivier and Arissa were very concerned about this development. Ellantine assured them she was fine, that she knew where to find food and water if needed, and that there was never, ever the slightest possibility that she would get lost and be unable to find her way home. She said that she knew her way around a forest better than a shopping mall.

Upon one return from the wilderness, a pair of owls perched in a tree outside Ellantine's bedroom window and hooted their mating song for three consecutive nights. On another occasion, a small herd of wild deer led by an enormous stag followed her home and fed upon the lush weeds and wildflowers in the orchard. On a third occasion, Ellantine returned home exhibiting an array of scratches and bruises on her body. Much to Arissa's chagrin, she explained how she befriended a grizzly to help free her from being trapped beneath a fallen tree branch. This was the only time she ever hinted about her adventures in the wilderness.

Several boys displayed an interest in Ellantine during their final year of high school. Those who were more interested in their own sporting status and vain prowess, in material things and wealth, were treated rather harshly. One young man did try hard to express his affection for her. She saw right through his veneer: that he was dishonourable and wanted to earn the reputation of being the one to 'break her in'. She rebuffed him in no uncertain terms.

Out of spite, he followed Ellantine out of the grounds when school ended and confronted her. He pushed her to the ground and threatened her. She was immediately enraged.

"WAIT! Look... there!" she shouted.

He stopped and turned, not knowing what he was looking at. Leaning back against her extended left arm, she calmly raised her right hand and casually pointed at a crow sitting on a fence with her half-extended index finger. With slow breath, she altered her vision to view the universal energy field, and within the field, honed in on the unique signature of the crow.

She did not issue a mental command. That's not how it works. The animal kingdom does not possess the same degree of mind as the human kingdom.

From the core of her body, her solar plexus, with natural intuitive ease she projected outward the resonance of her current emotional state – fear, anger – towards the target creature. Within a 100m radius, every crow suddenly felt threatened, and were enticed by the required response of wild rage. In unison, a half dozen crows turned to look at the source of their disturbance and immediately flew in to attack the threat.

Bemused and frightened at being attacked, scratched and pecked around the face and neck, he quickly ran off. The crows gave chase for a short distance and began to dissipate into the sky and trees as she ceased the resonance, with the threat subsiding.

Ellantine was more relieved than pleased to have completed her diploma and that high school would soon become a distant memory. Initially, she thought that this would be the end of her required education. She spent the next twelve months working on the farm, and continuing with her forays into the wilderness throughout the summer.

However, Olivier knew better. He encouraged Ellantine to continue with further studies if she wanted to make something more of herself than just a farm hand. He explained the need to understand the scientific process, how to gather and build evidence to prove a case, how to develop critical and process thinking to solve problems and, of course, understanding how the modern world operates. No one would consider her affiliation with nature as a qualification.

Ellantine knew she was not cut out for university. She simply did not have the patience to study for another four years. Instead, she gained admission into a two-year diploma in an agricultural course at a local college in Ottawa. She completed the course whilst maintaining her workload at the farm and, in the process, earned a reputation for not holding back on her views about any farming practice which proved harmful to the environment.

She met a nice young fellow studying the same course and engaged in a short romance. He had a similar background, growing up on a farm in a nearby valley. He was only just a fraction taller and possessed a very strong physique. Initially, things went well and they shared a lot in common. However, Ellantine soon realised his ambition was to progress along the path of industrial scale farming. He said that he respected nature and the environment, yet industrial scale farming was the only way to meet the growing needs of the future. She could not see herself living on an industrialised farm and promptly ended the relationship.

During college, she found little time to trek into the wilderness and would venture out for no more than half a day or so. Holly began to show signs of her age and was more than happy to remain within the boundaries of the farm, preferring to bask in the warmth of the sun upon a nice smooth paving stone. Growing old, she could no longer help bring in the sheep and began to suffer epileptic seizures. Holly died the year after Ellantine completed her college diploma, at the age of fourteen years.

Naturally, Ellantine was distraught with grief. She carried Holly's body into the wilderness and buried her in front of a small grotto they found which became their sacred home away from home, during their adventures together. A natural underground spring rose to the surface within the nearby cave, which was part of an extensive subterranean network.

Ellantine felt rather lost without Holly and became somewhat absent minded. The quality of her farm work dropped quite noticeably. For the first time, she sensed there to be little or no direction in her life and she really did not know what she wanted to do.

In comparison, her older sister Lauren completed a master's in economics and business management and moved to Toronto to enter the corporate world. Her brother Jerard was no academic and planned to take over the farm from Olivier. He too completed a diploma in agriculture and Olivier taught Jerard everything he knew, grooming his son for succession.

Lauren and Jerard never showed any real curiosity in the rose tree other than an appreciation for its aesthetic beauty. They simply did not possess the acumen to become aware of the rose tree's true sacredness or of the experiences shared by Arissa and Ellantine.

Arissa always maintained a consistent communion with the rose tree. Whilst the farm maintained its healthy state of harmony and balance, the rose tree bloomed a continuous stream of flowers, year after year. As the children grew up, Arissa developed a formidable understanding of the intelligent interconnected mind of nature.

She would gain an intimate appreciation of how nature built one level of evolving form upon another, increasing further and further the complexity and diversity of all living things. How one tier of creation would become the foundation and sustenance upon which the next tier was built. In her mind she could picture how it all weaved and fit together.

The mind of the mineral world simply consists of the consciousness of like and dislike, expressing the law of attraction and repulsion through the force of its physical properties. When like substances attract into a mass, its consciousness becomes composed of its combined particles, producing the pattern of that which has been formed.

The mind of crystals, a mineral acting like a plant, will grow 'en masse' under favourable conditions and by design provide the foundation for both the plant and animal kingdoms to complement each other.

The mind of the plant world utilises the power of crystalline fragments combined with silicious materials to build the structures of very simplified plant forms, giving rise to the actions and reactions of protoplasmatic cells. The simplest plants grow by distinguishing and processing nutrition and can reproduce and adapt to their environment. More evolved complex forms comprise a nervous system and the ability to carry out an act or process of thought, to cooperate with their environments and the laws of nature.

The intelligence of a plant is held within the memory of its cells passed on in its seed when reproducing and within the function of its outer sensory organs which can distinguish feeling, knowing the difference between pleasure and pain, direction and sources of nutrition, water and light. Plants possess sufficient 'mind' to serve their needs and adapt to a changing environment.

The mind of the animal world also utilises the power of crystalline structures present in the formation of both bacteria and Monera, a single cell form of protozoa animal life, able to absorb oxygen and food through a form of digestion. Protozoa consist entirely of stomach and lung and reproduce by growing larger and dividing themselves in two. Amoeba are a single cell with internal parts such as a nucleus, an expanding and contracting stomach cavity, extended limbs or fingers and an external membrane. Amoeboids form the foundation of animal life, where types of cells resemble a collective variety of independent amoeba cells, possessing enough group mind to coordinate the activity of their specific office within the organism.

The complexity of organisms has grown from infusoria to sponges, polyps, starfish and urchins. Then onto annulosa, jointed creatures and insects with well-formed external skeletal and nervous systems, culminating in the first appearance of a primitive internalised central brain. The mollusc was followed by the first vertebrates, with the appearance of the internal skeleton and spinal column. Fish were followed by reptiles, birds and then mammals, finally leading to the primate, each level demonstrating a higher degree and quality of manifested intelligence but still living instinctively, clothed in skin or fur, reacting and adapting to the environment day by day, knowing only that they 'ARE' alive.

The emerging mind of the human world possessed a new element of intelligence, the element of self consciousness, allowing man to say about himself, 'I think, therefore I am'; recognising the ability to think separately, apart from his thoughts and senses.[i]

Each kingdom merges into and becomes linked to the others, from the lowest to the highest degree of manifestation. And yet… it is ALL imbued within the universal energy field, built with intelligence and connected through the resonating force of consciousness, to fulfil the unrelenting desire for the universal mind to seek expression through creation.

Arissa suddenly understood that, when communing with the rose tree, she was suspending the 'I', the identity of self and simply becoming the 'AM' with nature when merging with the resonance of a particular life form. She knew she was now a 'mystic of nature', the very same thing as the wanderer, who had given her those cuttings so many years ago.

Elated with her new revelation, Arissa leant forward from the tree to exit communion, and was slightly startled to see Ellantine, quietly sitting back against the furthest bench, watching.

"Ellantine!" she gasped. "Don't you know how creepy you're being? Don't you have something better to do, some work maybe?"

"No, not really," she replied in a depressed, unenthusiastic manner.

"What's wrong Ellantine? You look miserable."

"I don't know. I feel lost, maybe a bit lonely. I miss Holly," she confessed. "It's been over a year now."

Arissa climbed to her feet, walked over to a nearby bench and sat down.

"Funnily enough, I've been thinking about you a lot lately," she began. "The problem is you haven't been able replace Holly with something new to grow into," she paused. "You do know about the rose tree and what it can do, don't you?"

Staring at the rose tree, Arissa turned to see the display of an unflinching, blank expression.

"Yes, of course you do!' she said. "I think it's time we work out a way for you to have a rose tree of your own. Would that be something you would like?"

"Yes, yes, I'd love to have my own tree," Ellantine replied happily.

"Ok, good! Do you think you're ready for your own tree?"

"Yes, of course. Why wouldn't I be?" she pondered.

"Well, I don't think you're ready, my dear. You don't seem to know what you really want to do with your life. How do you know that having your own tree will answer this question. How do you know that you won't regret having your own tree down the track?"

"Umm, well, I guess I can't really be sure about that," she replied.

"There you go, see. You have doubt, where there shouldn't be. So, it's settled then."

"Settled! What's settled?" she replied bemused.

"You won't know what you want unless you go and see what's out there," Arissa said and paused. "I'm sending you on a vacation, a trip around the world. Take a year… take two if you like. Go and explore. Work in as many places as you can. And when you're ready, return home and let me know if, and when, you're sure you want a rose tree of your own."

Shocked, surprised, Ellantine sat stunned for a few long moments until it registered. She suddenly sprang to her feet and gave her mother a huge warm hug.

6

At twenty-two years of age, Ellantine had grown into a striking and uniquely beautiful woman. Her features depicted a graceful balance between both her French and Iroquois heritage, neither of which overpowered the other. She was taller than her mother at five foot nine with a slightly lighter skin tone. She was lean, agile and possessed a very self-assured strength and confidence. She had rich, straight black hair that was cut just below the shoulder, where it could be braided, wrapped in a bun or allowed to fly freely. The most striking thing about Ellantine was the intensity of her presence, bolstered by the health and strength of her energy and her attunement with nature.

Arissa made the preliminary arrangements. She purchased an open round the world airline ticket, a new mobile phone with global roaming, pre-programmed with every emergency phone number imaginable, a translation device consisting of one hundred languages, a small travel-size laptop computer, the necessary travel and health insurance, and two debit card accounts, one Visa and one American Express, each with US$10,000 and a daily spend limit.

Fully kitted out with hiker's backpack and heavy-duty waterproof gear, Ellantine flew to New York City in late September, the autumn of 2012 and spent her first week there. Although interesting, the city was too big and she wanted to move on and explore more of the US.

By train, she headed southwest through Philadelphia, Washington, into Virginia and crossed the Midwest through Kentucky, Tennessee, Arkansas, Oklahoma, Texas, New Mexico, Arizona and spent Christmas in Las Vegas. She didn't gamble but watched many who did.

After celebrating the new year of 2013 in Los Angeles, she then flew to Mexico City and travelled south by train until she reached the mountains of Peru. Possessing an Iroquois complexion allowed her to blend in and mix comfortably with the peoples of South America.

Feeling drawn, she found her way into Brazil and lived for eight months with a native tribe on the edge of the Amazon Forest. Immersed in nature, her spirit flourished, earning the love and reverence of the tribe. And she loved them all in return. During one full moon, she was seen sitting quietly beside the water's edge of a small grove, gently caressing the ear of a rare ocelot. Responding to the resonance of love and affection, the wild cat purred loudly with delight. When time whispered for the need to leave, the entire tribe was deeply grieved. She travelled through Bolivia, Chile into Argentina and spent the rest of the year in Buenos Aires.

The new year of 2014 began with a flight to Cape Town. With bandana, sunglasses and now looking the seasoned traveller, she used trains, buses, vans and trucks to trek northward through South Africa, Botswana, Zambia, Tanzania and into Kenya where she spent three months working on a plantation just south of Nairobi. The African continent was vastly different. Its people had a deep affinity with the land but suffered from its inherent savagery.

One evening three men wanted to have their way with her and were deterred by the sudden appearance of a very aggressive, hissing black mamba, responding viciously to the impending sensation of being violently molested. She immediately left Nairobi the following morning.

She flew to Cairo and made her way around the Mediterranean and into southern Europe via Turkey and Greece. She travelled through Italy, southern France and into eastern Spain, where she spent the next seven months working on a horse stud farm inland of Valencia. This was a luxurious change of pace where she demonstrated quite a unique touch with the horses.

During the summer of 2015, she travelled into the UK, across to the Netherlands and then went on to explore the forests and wilderness of Norway, Sweden and Finland. Just before the onset of winter, she left Europe and flew to Mumbai, India. She spent two months travelling through India and ended the year in Kathmandu, near the southern edge of the Himalayan Mountains.

After a little mountaineering to kick off 2016, she travelled down through Southeast Asia, Bangladesh, Myanmar and into Thailand. She found some work in a beautiful coastal tourist village for a couple of months and spent time visiting the nearby tropical rainforests. She soon moved on through Malaysia and from Singapore flew down to Perth, Australia.

Ellantine boarded the Indian Pacific Train across the Nullarbor Desert into Adelaide and then onto Sydney, a nice restful three-day journey. She worked her way up the east coast picking fruit and vegetables from farm to farm over the next few months, until she reached the Whitsunday Islands and spent Christmas and New Year visiting the coral reefs off the coast of North Queensland.

Basking in the morning sun on a pristine beach on New Year's Day of 2017, alone by herself, thoughts of home suddenly entered her mind, for the first time in a long time. She felt tired, worn out, the urge to continue had finally, completely vanished. She knew it was time.

She flew out of Sydney for LA, with a connection through to San Francisco and landed in Ottawa on 27th February, exactly two months before her twenty-seventh birthday. She was warmly greeted by Olivier and Arissa at the airport, who drove her back home to the farm. She had been away for four and a half years.

The following morning Arissa and Ellantine sat in the kitchen together.

"I'm so happy you're back home. I missed you terribly."

"I'm very happy to be back," she replied gratefully. "I went for a walk through the orchard and into the back hills earlier this morning. And I feel a lot better already. It brought back a lot of memories."

"Of course, this is your home."

"You know, for the first time this morning, I felt the balance you've achieved here on the farm. I haven't experienced this anywhere else. I felt revived and re-energised almost immediately. This is where I belong, where I'm the happiest. You have truly made the farm a very special place," she commended.

"Thank you, my dear. That really means a lot to me," she replied and paused, as they sat quietly for a few moments. "So, how was your trip? I knew where you were when you kept in touch, but what did you discover on your travels?"

"Well, you know how much I love nature, I tried to connect with the Great Mother everywhere I went. The biggest thing which struck me was how fast the natural world is dwindling, not just here or there, but in every corner of the world," she said. "It breaks my heart to even think that one day, there might be nothing left of the natural world at all. It's such a tragedy."

"I know, I've felt the same," Arissa agreed. "It's truly beyond comprehension that such a thing could actually happen."

"I've seen what industrial farming does, it completely strips nature from the land. All that's left is the soil and the sun. The crops are then fertilised with chemicals and sprayed with pesticides, herbicides and fungicides. Everything is poisoned. It makes no sense," she paused. "Modern farming doesn't seem to know how to make friends with the insect world. They're just seen as pests and destroyed."

"Scientists are producing these genetically modified crops. I see the energy field of these plants, and something is not quite right. I can't quite put my finger on it. It's like a bug, an anomaly, has been inserted into the energy field of the organism, which seems to cause a malfunction, or a confusion. It's as though the original template of the species has been altered and no longer fits its physical form properly."

"Yes, I've seen this as well."

"I fell in love with all the places where I found pure pristine nature: in Brazil, Africa, Northern Europe, South East Asia and Australia. I felt at peace, connected, grounded, just like I do here, at home. These places are magical, filled with the sheer diverse beauty of life, demonstrating the inspiring power of nature."

"The more humanity pushes back against nature, the more we are losing our connection with its energy," she said and paused. "You can see this in all the big cities. People are losing the normal vibrancy in their energy fields, which has become less colourful, filled more with greyness and an unhealthy resonance, especially through their unnatural, unbalanced diet. People are losing their knowledge of the earth and the earth is losing its vitality."

"And then, there is the problem of pollution which exacerbates this situation even more," she stated. "Pollution is everywhere: in the air, across the land and in every ocean, strangling what little of nature we have left. I could only stay in a city for no more than a week or so before I began to feel drained and strangely sick. I had to leave."

"And then there are those who pollute their own bodies, especially addicted drug users. Their energy field is so deteriorated, that it barely exists at all, which then progresses into the complete deterioration of their physical body. It's like their whole metaphysical system is imploding, collapsing and consuming itself, just like a black hole. And everyone around them can sense this decay. I felt quite disturbed seeing people in this situation."

"Yes, having the ability to see these things does make it a burden sometimes, doesn't it?" Arissa revealed. "When you see such things... you want to help... or to tell that person what they are doing... but you can't because you know they won't believe you... or listen to you at all. And so, you become dispassionate... a situation which brings me great sorrow."

"Yes, me too. I tried to help some people but was rebuked, pretty much every time."

"Why do you think that is?"

"Well, I think most people simply have no connection with nature in the first place and don't regard it with the reverence that it deserves. Otherwise, things might be different," she said and paused. "Consider the universal energy field... basically, not one person I met who didn't grow up in a forest, was aware that all things possess an energy field, that this energy field is connected to a collective whole. And without this connection, this knowledge, people are far more prone to harming themselves and nature, and now, we find ourselves standing upon the precipice where nature is on the brink of complete collapse."

"Well, that's rather dire, but true, so true."

They sat there for a few long moments pondering the enormity of the problem.

"You were right, you know!" Ellantine stated.

"Really! How so?"

"I needed to see the world, to experience the world," she said. "Thank you... from the bottom of my heart... for sending me on my way. It was exactly what I needed."

"Well, I'm glad. You were miserable, moping around the farm," she recalled. "And so, did it do the trick? Did you work out what you needed to? Have you worked out what you want to do with your life?"

"Yes, I think so. I know this is where I belong. This is where I feel at my best, connected and closest to nature."

"So, would you like to help your brother Jerard run the farm?"

"Yes, I would be very happy to help Jerard," she confirmed.

"Well… Jerard has been running the farm for three years now. Your father and I are too old to carry out all the work. He's in charge now. You will have to work under his direction, ok!" she said and paused. "But don't worry, we've trained him in everything that we've learnt and applied over the years. This might also give you time to focus on other things, if you know what I mean. And Jerard will be here to look after the farm if you need time away."

"Yes, of course. I understand," she said with a mischievous smile. "If I discover something new, I'm sure I can persuade Jerard to see the benefit."

"I'm sure you will," she said, with a thin smile in return. "Is there anything else upon which you have reached a conclusion?"

"Yes! I'm ready!"

"Ready? For what?"

"Ooh, you know!" she smirked. "A rose… a rose tree of my own."

"Ooh, right! I almost forgot," Arissa teased.

"Oh no you didn't," she countered and paused for a long moment. "I'm going to replicate what you have done here on the farm and expand, amplify and extend it out to help nature survive and recover across the world."

"In that case, you will need your own rose tree for that," she affirmed and paused. "You know that the rose tree will become a part of you… a part of your very existence. You don't necessarily become attached to it like an object… but… it's like you share a part of each other's consciousness. Are you ready for that?"

"Yes, of course. I'm quite familiar with how the rose tree works. I can hear nature speak… if that alleviates your concern," she said.

Ellantine only alluded to the extent of her development. Arissa never fully realised the depth of her daughter's ability to commune with and influence all manner of creatures.

"Ok, then. It's time for you to have your own tree," she said, finally satisfied.

"Awesome! Wonderful!" Ellatine replied elated. "So… how do we make a new tree?"

"I'm not sure. I imagine we would take a cutting from the tree… but… from where?" she pondered. "I can't see any portion of the tree which looks like the cuttings I started with. The original cuttings were about three inches long, with a cross section in the shape of a five-pointed star. Strange, I know, when I think about it now."

"Yes, that is a rather strange cutting. Well... the rose tree is no ordinary plant. Maybe... we should just ask the tree... and see if it will provide us with an answer," she suggested.

"Yes, that's a great idea. I'll sit with the tree tomorrow. I'll ask how to obtain a cutting... or how the tree reproduces itself. I have a feeling the rose tree will know the answer."

"I'm sure it will," Ellantine replied encouragingly.

$$\boxed{7}$$

The following afternoon Arissa sat with the rose tree and entered communion. In her mind she formulated a simple question and projected it out into the consciousness of the tree.

'How does the tree of roses reproduce itself?'

She waited… and waited… for quite a while.

'How do I obtain a cutting for a new tree?'

Arissa's vision was normally a blended array of pastel colours, just out of focus and filled with a collection of layered consciousness, resonances and mind. Suddenly, her vision turned black, white, back to black and then white again… strobing one instant after another… and then returned to normal.

Feeling the sensation of a tear, a wound, deep within her own chest, she leant forward, aghast with wide eyes and gulped at the air. She clutched at her chest with her right hand and caught her breath. She struggled to stand up. When she managed to find her feet, she stumbled to a bench and sat down. She took deep breaths to recover from the experience.

Once she regained some composure, Arissa made her way into the kitchen. Her face was white as ash.

"Mother! What happened?" Ellantine gasped.

Arissa pulled out a chair and sat down at the table, holding her head in her left hand.

"I… I'm not sure," she replied. "The tree… I was with the tree," she stuttered. "I asked the tree how to reproduce itself… just like we talked about," she paused, staring ahead with a vacant expression. "My vision! It went black, white, black, several times! It felt like… something inside me was torn out… that something inside me… DIED!"

Arissa looked at her daughter fearing the worst.

"I… I think something is wrong with the tree," she said, distraught.

"Ok, calm down, calm down. It's not going anywhere in a hurry."

Ellantine promptly put the kettle on. Within a few moments she prepared and handed her mother a hot cup of herbal tea.

"Here, drink this. It should settle your nerves a bit. I'll go and have a look at the rose tree."

Ellantine walked out, around the house and into the garden to inspect the tree. She soon returned.

"Everything looks normal. The tree looks fine," she reported.

"Did you sit with the tree?"

"No, I didn't," she replied. "If something has gone wrong… maybe we should let it be for a while. Let's try again tomorrow once you settle down and get some rest," she advised.

"Ok, ok. That sounds like a good idea."

Feeling drained, Arissa went to her room and slept through most of the day.

The following morning, they both entered the garden. Ellantine sat quietly on a bench and watched Arissa take her position against the tree. She leant back to begin communion.

Nothing! Nothing happened.

Arissa simply remained in her normal wakeful state. She tried two, then three times to initiate the transition. Nothing happened. She could not induce communion with the tree. She stood up, stepped away and turned to look at the tree.

"Nothing is happening," she announced. "The rose tree is unresponsive. I'm not sure what's happening. Can the tree be blocking me?"

"I don't think so. That wouldn't be consistent considering the long relationship you've shared with the tree. It wouldn't block you just because you asked a question."

"Yes! That would be rather unreasonable, I guess," she agreed. "Maybe there is something wrong with the tree then!"

"Unfortunately, I think you might be right. We'll just have to wait and see what happens."

"Yes, I guess, that's all we can do."

The following day the rose tree seemed to have withered. The new green shoots suddenly began to wilt and fade. As each day passed, both Arissa and Ellantine, with a growing sense of foreboding grief, watched the rose tree wane and shrink, its life force drained from its very core. After a week, merely a skeleton remained. The rose tree… died.

At the same time, during the course of the week, a small wooden protrusion grew, in the middle of the first branching of limbs, one atop each trunk. Both emerald-green protrusions steadily grew to three inches, before the outer circular shape matured and hardened into a dark auburn, five-pointed star-shaped stem.

Arissa and Ellantine stood side by side in grief looking at the dead tree. They noticed the vibrant stems growing yet were too distraught to pay them much attention. Suddenly, realisation dawned, and they looked at each other in bewilderment. Arissa ran to fetch a pair of pruning shears. She quickly returned to cut both stems as close to the base of each trunk as possible and placed them into a soft white hand towel.

"The tree... the tree died to bring forth two new cuttings," Arissa said.

From the depths of her grief, she found a little elation. Tears welled up as she stared longingly at the remaining shell of her own tree. Ellantine gave her a long warm hug.

"I'm so sorry, Mama. I didn't know that this would happen."

"Well, we know now, don't we. We know how the tree replicates itself," she replied. "I guess it makes sense. The tree knew... my work is done... and yours is just...," she sniffed. "A new cycle begins. It makes perfect sense," she smiled tearfully.

They turned and walked arm in arm back into the kitchen. Later that morning, Arissa walked over to her workbench in the greenhouse and placed the two cuttings in a safe, warm location beneath the protection of a glass-topped dome. She felt it too early to plant the cuttings, instead opting to allow more time so they could dry and harden further.

****

On the morning of Thursday 27th April 2017, Arissa invited Ellantine into the garden just after breakfast and sat beside her upon a bench.

"My dear Ellantine," she began. "Today is a very special day, we can all agree. It's your birthday," she said with a broad smile.

She gave her daughter a kiss on the cheek and a long warm hug. From the pocket of her jumper, she then brought out a soft white folded cloth and opened it.

"As a gift from the bottom of my heart, I would like to give you this... the two cuttings from the rose tree," she said.

Arissa gently placed the cloth into Ellantine's open hands and closed her fingers around the bundle.

"They belong to you now."

"Thank you very much," she replied. "I know how hard it's been to lose the rose tree. That wasn't what I wanted."

"I know, I know. It wasn't what I expected either," she said letting go of Ellantine's hands. "It's alright, though. I had my time with the tree and I'm an old woman now. It's the natural process. What becomes old must be renewed once more," she said and paused. "I couldn't be more pleased now that you have the new cuttings. There's no one more suitable. And I'm absolutely sure you will do your very best with the new rose tree."

"Thank you, Mother. Yes, I will... I'll do the best I can," she promised.

"Now, since you have Iroquois blood, do you remember what your Iroquois name is?"

"Umm, no, not really..." she confessed.

"Shortly after you were born, I took you over to the council and presented you to our tribal chief. He sat down upon an old fallen tree trunk, with eyes closed, facing the sky. He waited for the right name to appear. After deliberating for a long time, he suddenly opened his eyes and said, 'From this moment forward your Iroquois name will be... Tekonwenaharake.' Everyone in the council gasped... and then... slowly, they all nodded in agreement."

"Wow... that sounds amazing. What does it mean?"

"It means... the whispering wind," she explained. "I didn't want to tell you this when you were younger. I thought it a little superficial, just an old Indian custom. However, as I've watched you grow and become the woman you are... now I think that the old chief could not have given you a better, more befitting name."

"Well, I like it," she stated. "I think it's perfect."

Arissa sat back against the bench looking once more at the dead rose tree.

"You know... I was up most of the night thinking last night. It occurred to me that I might not have much time left either. And, when I thought of that... I remembered someone else had said the very same thing. It took a while to remember who it was," she paused. "It was that old wanderer who gave me the original cuttings."

"That old man sleeping in the truck... when I was... five, wasn't it?"

"Yes, that's him. You remembered!" she said surprised.

"Yes, I do remember him."

"Let's see. What did he say?" Arissa paused to remember. "He said... he had no children, no one to teach and that he didn't have much time left."

A realisation suddenly dawned on Arissa. She sat bolt upright upon the bench.

"He appeared out of nowhere and gave me those cuttings," she paused. "It wasn't by accident at all. He chose me, us, this farm. And now the rose tree has passed on to you. This can't possibly be a coincidence," she said.

"Maybe the tree of roses chose you. Guillaume was just the postman."

"Yes, maybe. Over the years I've learnt some amazing things about nature, just as that old vagabond predicted," she chuckled. "You know the mind of the plant is stored in the memory of its cells, right. And you saw what the tree did, it was like... it drew its life force, its memory and placed it inside its seed... those new cuttings," she said and continued.

"Wow. This didn't occur to me before. How did I not see this?" she pondered. "The mind of the rose tree might possess a continuous continuity, a history. I didn't even think to look for this," she paused. "When you commune with the new rose tree... if you look for it... you might find that it has stored its entire history somewhere deep within its being."

"Yes, ok, I will. This tree might hold a few more secrets yet," she commented.

They both sat in silence for a long while looking at the skeleton of the dead rose tree.

"What are you going to do with the dead tree?" Ellantine asked.

"Well, there's quite a bit of rose wood there. I guess we can ask a carpenter to make a few things out of it. How would you like a new trinket box?"

"That would be nice," she replied.

"Ok, done! I'll ask Jerard if he can dig the tree out for us. Right, let's go and see what everyone else is doing. It's your birthday you know."

A couple of days later Jerard dug up the dead tree and the wood went to a local carpenter to craft a few useful, ornamental items. The garden appeared empty without the tree. Ellantine sat upon one bench looking around the garden, wondering where to plant the new rose tree. She didn't want to plant her tree in the same spot as her mother's. That ground was sacred and it didn't feel right. Yet, no other position in the garden seemed right either. She walked all around the farm and even went into the hills, only to return unhappy and frustrated. She could not find a place for the new tree and decided to put the quest aside for the time being.

Jerard took care of all the hard labour around the farm. Olivier, though very much an old man now, was as stubborn as always and could not help himself. Late one afternoon in June, he tried to move a bale of hay for the sheep and suffered a severe stroke. Caught short of breath, he could not call out, and died strewn across the floor of the barn, beside the broken bale.

The whole family was devastated. Hundreds of people from the local district arrived at the funeral to pay their respects. Olivier was very much loved and admired throughout the whole community. His body was cremated and the ashes given to Arissa. In time, on her own, she took those ashes out onto the farm and released them across the fields and floor of the orchards, weeping as she said goodbye to her beloved Olivier.

Arissa withdrew more into herself. Having lost both her rose tree and Olivier in a few short months, she became depressed and suddenly aged tremendously overnight. She was a ghost of her former self, being less and less interested in life and the living. Jerard and Ellantine tried everything to cheer her up, to no avail. Nothing seemed to work.

The summer soon passed into autumn and winter arrived with a cold ferocity. Arissa didn't venture outside at all, feeling the cold more so than any other year gone by. No matter how hard she tried, she just could not get warm enough. Sure enough, pneumonia struck and Arissa died in her sleep one night late in November. Ellantine discovered her lifeless body the next morning and commented to Jerard that it was a broken heart that killed their mother.

Arissa was cremated in the old Iroquois tradition. Her wrapped body was taken to a local reservation and placed upon a small wood pyre within a sacred grove. A large number of tribal folk turned out for the ceremony. The great chief said a few words, and everyone sang a song as the fire was lit to invoke the Great Mother to take back the spirit of Arissa.

It was a bright afternoon with a clear blue sky. The bitingly cold wind lashed at the top layer of fallen snow, creating waves and swirls of mist across the ground. As the fire burned, Arissa's ashes were carried high into the trees of the surrounding forest.

8

Christmas, New Year and the rest of winter were rather bleak for both Jerard and Ellantine. Slowly, their grief began to dissolve as they filtered through Olivier and Arissa's personal belongings and only kept the most sentimental of items. However, they could not decide on what to do with their parent's main bedroom, study and en suite bathroom. As spring broke through to thaw the cold, Ellantine decided that after more than thirty years, the house needed a complete makeover. Jerard agreed without hesitation as they began to look into the future.

The house was completely remodelled. Olivier and Arissa's main bedroom, the lounge and the kitchen were all completely gutted and renovated into a new open plan, shared living space. The main bedroom became a huge rumpus room as an extension of the lounge. The kitchen was extended, refitted and modernised.

What were previously the children's bedrooms were refurbished into Ellantine's section of the house. This consisted of a main bedroom, study and en suite bathroom, laundry, a spare room for guests and a small entertainment area. In similar fashion, a new section was built on the other side of the house for Jerard. In essence, two dwellings were built, one on either side of the common space. The renovation and extensions were completed over six months.

Ellantine decided to remodel the garden, which was on her side of the house, as well. The pond in the centre of the garden was rebuilt against the outer wall of the house in a long U-shape, where the top of the U was against the wall. The paving was reset around the water feature. Two benches were positioned, one along each length of the U, and a third at the tip of the curve. The birdbath was placed in the centre of the water feature. New wildflowers and native shrubs were planted along the inside of the three lengths of the fence line.

After extensive deliberation, Ellantine decided that the only place for her new rose tree was in the middle of her garden, which was now free and bare, and would become its centrepiece. Following Arissa's specific instructions, she deepened and prepared the open pit in the centre of her garden and filled it with the same compost composition.

Ellantine germinated the two cuttings in the greenhouse midspring and re-potted the new saplings during autumn, to protect them through the approaching winter. It was not until the following April that she finally planted her new, one metre rose trees, side by side, in the centre of her garden. The two stems were aligned east to west.

Jerard met and fell in love with Sophie, while discovering they virtually shared an identical heritage. Sophie had an Iroquois father and an English mother, and grew up in the northern suburbs of Ottawa. They met at the wedding of a mutual friend a few months earlier and before long, also married in May, one month after Ellantine planted her rose tree.

Sophie gave birth to her and Jerard's son on 5th February 2019. They gave him the name Oliver, in memory of Jerard's father. He was strong, healthy and very boisterous for a newborn baby and grew very quickly on the farm.

Following Oliver's birth, the rose tree threw out its first bud in April, which bloomed a couple of weeks later into a massive rose, with the same colouring as its parent. Ellantine, Jerard and Sophie were smitten with awe at the sheer size and beauty of the rose. Sophie was gently sat down, and the family secret of the rose tree was explained to her. That was the one and only flower which bloomed that year.

With everything that life had recently thrown at her, Ellantine had not yet sat with her new rose tree. She gave the sapling all the love and attention she could. However, she didn't feel ready to commune with the tree. She wasn't afraid. She simply knew that once she did immerse herself, she would become psychologically 'coupled' with the tree. As such, she wasn't ready to fully commit to a union and to any new challenge that may present itself. She needed a little more time.

Life on the farm settled into a harmonious groove. Ellantine helped Jerard run the farm. Sophie looked after Oliver and the kitchen. Sophie gave birth to their second child on 10th March 2021, a daughter. After much thought, she was bestowed with the name

Arielle. She was also strong, healthy and grew quickly upon the farm. Once again, the rose tree threw out only one bloom for that year.

Before long, it was the morning of Ellantine's thirty-first birthday. Everything on the farm was running smoothly and in good order. The family was happy and in harmony. Following breakfast, she left the kitchen and walked around to her garden. She sat quietly on the first bench and looked up, inspecting her rose tree. The twin trunks stood three metres tall beneath a wide expansive canopy. The tree looked strong and vibrant.

"I think it's time," she whispered.

She drew in a slow deep breath, stood up and took several steps towards the rose tree. Suddenly, out of nowhere, three white doves flew down and perched themselves in the top branches of the tree. They chirped excitedly a few times and fell silent to watch.

Stunned, Ellantine stopped dead still.

"Three white doves!" she gasped. "What does this mean? A coincidence?"

She stood there for a few long moments pondering upon the possibility. Soon, she simply smiled and allowed herself to be completely at ease. A long forgotten joy began to well up deep inside of her.

She walked up and stood on the north-facing side of the tree. She sat down with her spine facing south, resting comfortably against both trunks. She drew a shallow breath, peered forward with steady vision, and leant her head back. The moment her head touched, the three white doves leapt into the air and flew high into the sky.

---

[i] A concise adaptation from: *The Secret Doctrine of the Rosicrucians: A Lost Classic by Magus Incognito.* William Walker Atkinson, Clint Marsh (ed.). 2012. Weiser Books, pp 71–95.

Alienation Games

Alienation Games

Alienation Games

New Moon

I look down at my feet. I can't see them. I look inward, at my body. I can't see my body either. I can feel my body, yet it's completely translucent, invisible.

I'm standing in a pure white space on the ground. Surrounding me is a forest of broadleaf woodland trees, including aspen, birch, elm and oak. The visible roots, trunks, branches, twigs and leaves are all coloured black. All the remaining spaces in between, where the sky would normally shine through, are coloured white. The whole scene is set within a two-dimensional black and white space with, however, the sensation of three-dimensional depth.

I turn to look all around me. The small white space I stand upon is bound on all sides by the thick knots and twisting roots of the surrounding trees. Being on the ground there are very few white spaces amongst the roots, thick trunks and first outcrop of branches.

Something moves in the corner of my eye. I turn quickly to see what it is. I look for it, try to face it. I can only see black merging into black, with a few small, intermingled spaces of white. I stand still in likeness with the forest. It's so quiet.

Slowly, upon a low, thick branch a few feet away, a shape moves out from the blackness across the front of a white space. I can see it now.

The figure has a childlike body, with small, yet oversized hands and feet, covered with bumpy leathery skin. Each hand has three long fingers and a thumb, all ending with a long, pointed nail. Each foot has a long-curved arch, with three fat front toes and a hind toe, all ending with a sharp, pointed claw. The round face gives away a pointed snout and a wide grinning mouth, with sharp, uneven, pointed teeth. It has long, pointed ears, with a crooked downward kink halfway along their lengths and a strong medium-length tail. Its eyes are curved and slit backwards, in an evil, menacing red-orange, glowing glare. The creature looks like something between a small monkey and a gremlin, but more closely resembles... an Imp.

The Imp grins, giggles, leans forward towards me, and looks at me intently. It makes me feel very uncomfortable and maybe I'm in danger. The Imp crouches as though it's preparing to jump at me. I move as far away from it as I can, to the opposite edge of the white zone I'm standing in, without touching the black border. Instinctively, I feel I shouldn't touch anything black. I look behind in search of another white patch.

I see another white shape nearby, just as the Imp leaps at me, with all its nails and claws outstretched. Startled and without thinking, I immediately hop over to the next white space.

I land safely. I didn't touch anything in shadow. The Imp lands on a tree root behind me. It just barely missed touching me. I look back, its grin continues to menace me. I feel frantic. Its preparing to jump at me again. I just know it. I search for another white patch.

There are so few white spaces across the ground, separated by wide expanses of tree root and trunk. I preempt the Imp and vault over to the next open space. The Imp quickly follows, lands and digs its claws into the side of a tree trunk.

Now I know the Imp is going to continue to follow me. I search for an escape. I look up and see more white patches. Remaining on the ground is limited, difficult. The Imp looks ready to jump again, enjoying the chase by pitching a harrowing and annoying giggle.

I quickly plan a series of three jumps, enabling me to reach the first fork in a nearby tree. I leap to the first white space and land on my left foot. With all my strength I bound to the next space on the ground beneath the target tree. I land and in one motion I push with both feet and arms and jump with all my strength. To my surprise, I float up swiftly with relative ease. The overexertion was unnecessary in this place. I land firmly within the open space of a fork between two thick branches of an oak tree.

I don't look behind me. I spot another clear space a short jump up to the next fork in the branches. Reaching as high as I can into the tree seems like a great idea. I leap up and forward across to my left towards the higher space.

The Imp, more nimble and far more practised at the art than I, springs from the tree trunk. It bounds from one tree root to the next across the *ground and runs up the tree trunk below me in a seamless motion, pushing from one leg and then the other, reaching forward with one clawed hand over the other. The Imp grips and swings up under the left-hand branch of the first fork as I land within the space between. As I leap for the higher space, the Imp reaches out and tags me on the back heel of my left foot.*

****

Theo, twisting, turning and kicking out in his king-size bed, suddenly sprang up into a sitting position with eyes flung wide open. Propped up against his arms, he screamed out loud.

"Aaarrrgh!"

Staring at the ceiling for a few moments, he quickly realised what was happening.

"A dream!" he yelled. "It's a dream… a nightmare."

Feeling disorientated, he looked down at his sweating body. A few moments later, there was a light knock on the bedroom door. It was Theo's slightly agitated and concerned long-time friend and flatmate Axel.

"Theo! Theo? Are you all right?" he asked from behind the closed door.

"Yes, yes! I'm fine. Just a bad dream, is all it was."

Theo looked across at the digital clock atop the nightstand.

"Well, that ruined my sleep-in, didn't it?" he whispered.

It was 4:35 am, on Sunday 29th January 2006.

"What did you say? Are… are you sure?"

"Just go back to bed!" Theo snapped back loudly, aggressively… surprising even himself.

"Ooh, ok! Wake up on the wrong side of the bed, did we?" he retorted.

Now feeling flustered and perturbed himself, Axel casually walked back to his own room.

Theo swung his legs over the side of the bed and rubbed his eyes with his fingers. He had a slight headache, and discovered that he was in the foulest of moods. He turned on the bedside lamp, squinted and looked away with a snarl. He stood up and walked into the en suite bathroom of the master bedroom. In the shadowy darkness, he looked at his thin, gaunt face in the mirror. The dark shadows in his eyes made him look like a ghoul. He decided to wash away the sweat and remnants of the dream in a nice hot shower.

Themor (*Th-ee-more*) Mortusson was five days short of his twenty-second birthday. He was a relatively lean, six foot one inch tall, with light-brown hair that grew out to a more golden-sandy brown. He had light grey-blue eyes and the typical light-tan-yellow complexion of a young Swede. He sported a well-manicured four-day beard, which ran along the jaw line, around his chin and thin mouth, with narrow sideburns and bare cheek bones.

With shower complete, Theo dressed in a pair of thick, dark-blue jeans, woollen socks, a thermal T-shirt under a long-sleeved, patterned collar shirt, covered with a thick cream-coloured woollen jumper. Being winter, it was still very cold outside in Stockholm.

He knew Myra, his loving and adoring younger sister by three and a quarter years, would drop in with breakfast as was her custom, and demand to know what the plan was for the day ahead. He made his way down to the kitchen to brew a hot cup of coffee.

Having completed a business degree in economics, banking, finance and investment through Stockholm University the year before, Theo had now entered the ranks of the young professional. He found employment inside a small investment and loans bank located within the central business district of the city.

Theo leased a small, yet comfortable two-level, two-bedroom loft apartment, with his best friend Axel Blomqvist. Both bedrooms, en suite and second bathroom were in the building's roof. A narrow stair led down to the open plan kitchen, dining and lounge.

Axel essentially followed Theo out of high school, through university and along the same career path, into employment with a retail commercial bank, located only one city block from Theo.

Their building was located along Bondegatan Street, just north of Vitabergsparken Park, in an area called Katarina-Sofia. This was next door to the alternate indie district of Södermalm, all positioned upon a large inland island just a little south of Stockholm's city centre.

Myra continued to live with their parents, Arvid and Jo-Anna Mortusson, in the wealthy, upper middle-class family home in the exclusive area of Östermalm, a relatively short distance from Theo. The large lavish four-storey apartment, with the additional rooftop attic and basement car park, comprised one unit of a large four-apartment building complex.

Arvid was a loving, very strict, patriarchal father, instilling in his two children a strong work ethic throughout their schooling years. He demanded and expected high performance and warned that he would not support tardiness. Naturally, both Theo and Myra grew into very active high achievers and kept their father pleased.

With coffee in hand, Theo walked from the kitchen to the lounge and sat down to contemplate the day ahead. He twitched and turned and could not find a comfortable position. He rose to his feet, returned to the kitchen and opened the fridge. He didn't know what he wanted, closed the fridge and returned to the couch. He picked up the remote and turned on the television. He flicked to a new channel every two minutes. There was nothing of interest this early and he decided to turn the television off, now feeling ever so aggravated.

He paced up and down, fidgeted and was consumed by his dark mood until, at last, the doorbell rang. He bolted for the intercom.

"Myra!?" he asked, almost yelled expectantly.

"Theo! Good morning," she responded joyously. "You're up already?" she quizzed, noting with surprise his almost instant answer to her pressing the button.

"Yep! Been awake for ages. Couldn't sleep!" he reported.

He buzzed Myra in, opened the front door and left it ajar three inches. He returned to the kitchen to prepare a fresh pot of coffee while awaiting her arrival via the lift to the top level.

The sound of boots ringing out across the floorboards in the hallway preceded Myra's appearance. She nudged past the door into the apartment and back-heeled it shut with an echoing bang. Her zest and enthusiasm made her quite a noisy person, by design of course, to divert all attention towards her presence. Among the older boys of Theo's peers, she soon learnt to be the daring and fearless life of the party.

She unwound her scarf and threw it over the hook beside the door, quickly followed by her long, charcoal-grey, thick winter designer jacket. She sat down on a carved, high back, wooden chair beside the door, removed her black leather gloves, unzipped her black leather boots and slipped her feet into a pair of warm woollen slippers reserved solely for her use. Having placed her bountiful bundle momentarily on the floor, she picked up the printed hessian bag, stood and walked over towards the kitchen island bench.

Watching, Theo's heart suddenly skipped a beat. He caught his breath. Being his sister, he had never really paid Myra a great deal of attention, considering her more of a persistent nuisance, than anything else. However, for no particular reason, he was inexplicably instantly smitten, besotted by her beauty.

Myra was also quite tall and lean, just two inches shorter than Theo. She was dressed in thick black corduroy jeans and a cream-coloured form fitting woollen jumper. Her complexion was very similar to Theo's, except for her rich, long, golden, wavy hair which extended down to the middle of her back. Her figure was quickly maturing into that of a very capable, energetic and confident young woman.

"Theo! How are you?" she greeted with a warm smile. "Whoa! It's nice and fresh outside. There's a blue sky, so it'll be a glorious day today."

She heaved the bag onto the island counter. Leaning back against the kitchen cabinetry on the other side, Theo glared back at her, somewhat stunned, speechless.

"Good morning, Myra." Axel announced.

Smiling jovially, he stood at the base of the staircase, dressed in thick navy-blue jeans, white-collared, long-sleeved shirt and a red, white and blue striped woollen jumper. He was one inch shorter than Myra. He possessed a pale pink complexion with typical strawberry blonde hair, blue eyes and a robust, chubby build in body. Loving his food, he greeted Myra's Sunday morning visit with eager anticipation.

"What delightful delicacies have you brought us this fine morning?" he asked.

Distracted from his perplexing perversion, Theo glanced over at Axel.

"Well, since it's going to be such a beautiful winter's day, I brought you guys something special," she revealed excitedly.

Axel approached the bench. Theo was still distracted.

"I have some Danish pastries, one blueberry muffin for each of us and some elven bread."

Myra drew each item from the hamper as announced and laid them out on display.

"Elven bread?"

"Carrot cake!" she corrected with a giggle. "It so looks like elven bread, right? And... I also brought this..." she teased and paused.

Drawing out the moment, Myra slowly drew a square container from the bag, placed it on the countertop and pulled open the lid, revealing the most tantalising delight of all.

"One poached egg benedict for each of us."

Myra looked up at her brother searching for his approval.

"Ooh, my God! You've outdone yourself this time," Axel howled, bedazzled.

Still silent and somewhat stunned, Theo returned his glare to Myra, his mind confused.

"Are you all right?" she asked.

Myra instinctively felt a little uncomfortable with the way Theo was looking at her.

"THEO!" Axel called out loudly.

He noticed the unusual, pale expression upon Theo's face.

"THEMORE! WAKE UP!" he yelled.

Theo suddenly snapped out of it and realised he had been staring at Myra. He looked down at the bountiful breakfast on display.

"Wow… this is… fantastic," he said, with a blank expression.

"Are… are you ok?" she asked concerned. "You look like you've seen a ghost."

"Hmm… what?" he replied groggily, seemingly still a little confused.

Theo was just about to move around from behind the island bench when he realised he had a very hard erection. With a sudden expression of embarrassed surprise, he froze in shock.

"Um… um… I… I… have to pee," he stammered.

Thinking the only thing he could use to escape, with hands protecting his groin and feigning a full bladder, he immediately dashed across the kitchen and ran up the stairs and into his en suite bathroom. Myra and Axel watched bewildered.

Theo stared at the pale face reflected in the mirror.

"What just happened?" he muttered. "My sister? NO! It can't be possible. This has never happened before. What's going on?" he paused peering down into the sink. "Lust! I was filled with hunger… a hunger for lust," he realised.

He stood back and looked down at his crotch. He was still hard.

"Theo! Are you alright?" he heard Myra calling from below.

"Yes, yes. I'll be down in a minute," he yelled in reply.

"What am I going to do?" he whispered. "I could be stuck here for ages."

He realised there was only one thing he could do. He quickly dropped his pants, sat down upon the toilet seat and knocked one out! It was all over in sixty seconds. He flushed, washed his hands and face, and composed himself before casually walking back down the stairs.

"Phew! That's better," he sighed, returning to his usual confident demeanour. "I almost peed myself," he said with a wry smile.

"Are you sure you're ok?" Myra asked suspiciously.

"I hope so. Although, it's been a very strange morning."

"Yes, it has been," Axel suddenly chimed in. "Did you have a bad dream this morning? You yelled out and woke me up. And you were rather antsy when I checked on you."

"Umm, yes! I don't know if it was a nightmare, or what, but... it was the strangest dream I've ever had," he recalled.

"Well, I'm famished," Myra interrupted. "Let's eat!"

After briskly collecting plates, cutlery, orange juice and coffee, to each one's taste, they all moved to the dining table to eat breakfast. Axel listened to Myra's detailed account of her week just past and a little family gossip, while Theo, distant in thought, reflected upon the vision and sequence of the strange dream in his mind.

The day was glorious. Theo, Myra and Axel decided to go ice skating under the clear blue sky to work off breakfast. They cycled across the bridge to a temporary, open-air rink in Kungsträdgården, on the southern edge of the city centre. They literally bumped into a group of friends, a pair of guys and gals, while traversing the ice rink. Once worn out, everyone agreed to lunch and ordered their preferred 'fika', a coffee with a deli sandwich and a cinnamon bun, at a nearby café. As the afternoon rolled on, excitement grew and conversation solidified around a plan for dinner at a café in Södermalm, and then maybe on to a bar or club later through the evening.

Everyone arrived at the café bang on time by seven, refreshed and dressed in their most splendid and trendy nightwear. Theo quickly caught on that Astrid, a second-year university student, was sneaking regular glances at him. Once his attention focused on her, he immediately sensed her hunger, her desire and her growing lust for him. Milking his growing influence, Theo paid Astrid more and more attention as the evening progressed.

Following dinner, the group moved to a nearby bar for warm-up drinks. Alcohol added fuel and fire into the mix. With vodka courage, Astrid became emboldened, while Theo's passion was set alight with bourbon. They were soon looking deeply into each other's eyes and soul and losing affinity with the group and their surroundings. They touched hands, elbows and hips continuously as the crowd grew, twisting and churning, like a swirling storm.

Suddenly, without thinking and out of character, Theo kissed Astrid longingly and nipped lightly at her bottom lip. She looked up at him trembling excitedly. Everyone else in the group looked at them a little stunned, with half smiles of uncertainty, each grappling with whether they should applaud or object.

The bar suddenly became too noisy, too claustrophobic and unbearable.

Through a hazy mist, Astrid and Theo followed behind the others into a nightclub. A couple of shots evaporated reason, where they separated from the group and lost themselves in each other's arms somewhere on the dance floor. It was hot, steamy and crowded. Astrid could bear it no longer. She invited Theo back to her place which, luckily, was only a few blocks away. They escaped the heat of the club, stepping out into a lane only to be slapped by the gasping winter night's air.

They walked briskly down the narrow lane arm in arm. Wobbling on his feet, Theo's cheeks blushed red in the frigid cold which pierced his blindness and stabbed him with a moment of clarity. He had been involved in two short-term romantic relationships during university and had never engaged in a one-night stand. Such a thing would be out of character and was very much against his personal moral code. He did not quite understand what was happening and why. How did he manage to lose control, so quickly, so easily? Instinctively, he knew this was a mistake.

They soon reached the front entrance to Astrid's apartment building, Theo turned to face her. He kissed her gently while holding both her hands in his. He stopped still for a moment.

"Astrid, I… I… can't go upstairs," he stumbled. "I've only just met you. I… I… don't know anything about you. Maybe…"

She stared at him in shock.

"Maybe… I can give you my number and we can get to know each…"

Enraged, she punched him right on the left cheek, turned and slammed the door shut behind her. He reeled back stunned by the sting. He walked on and trudged through the cold lonely streets back to his apartment in self-pity.

****

Sporting a bruised cheek, hell followed Theo through the working week ahead. He found himself overcome with desire for money and wealth and for things he could not afford. He used this newfound motivation to drive his focus towards maximising his bonus commission. His proposed trades were deemed too high risk by his superiors and rebuked.

On the loans front, several customers found difficulty repaying their loans. Theo ruthlessly proposed they foreclose, and their properties seized. His alarmed superiors rejected his recommendation, preferring to renegotiate the terms of the loan over a longer period and allowing interest-only loan repayments, to ease the burden. Theo was reprimanded and lectured, more than once, concerning the bank's values and principles.

By the time Theo arrived at his parents' house for a dinner party to celebrate his twenty-second year on Friday evening, he was still in a brooding mood. Everything proceeded smoothly through dinner and the happy birthday and cake ceremony, until Theo was drinking cognac with his father in the lounge.

Theo inexplicably announced that he intended to buy a high-performance sports car. Arvid almost chocked, turned and told Theo he was mad, pointing out he had no driving experience at all and such a decision would only end in disaster. Arvid suggested Theo consider buying something less powerful for his first motor car. Theo rebuked his father vehemently. The ensuing argument ended with Theo storming out of the house. He knew his father was right, yet refused to admit defeat, all the same. The whole family was stunned, having never witnessed such a performance in all their time together. The night ended with Arvid and Jo-Anna wondering if Theo was in some kind of trouble.

The weather turned through the middle of the night. Axel awoke to a loud clap of thunder. A storm approached. It was a little after 4 am. He decided a hot chocolate would help settle his nerves. He trudged down to the kitchen, switched on the rangehood light and spun around.

"Holy shit!!!" he gasped.

Axel wobbled at the knee and brought his hand to his heart as he suddenly spotted Theo who, in the glow of the light, he could see sitting on the couch in the darkness. Theo held a hot cup of chocolate in his hand and stared back at him with dark sunken eyes.

"What the hell are you doing... sitting there in the dark?" he barked.

"Just thinking... and... listening to the thunder," he replied glumly. "It's kind of soothing in a way, isn't it?"

"I guess so!"

Axel recovered from his fright. He turned back around to find the kettle, the top drawer, the cupboard and began to prepare his own hot chocolate.

"Thinking? About what?" he enquired.

"Well, I feel I haven't been myself lately."

"Yes, I've noticed. You've been super grumpy and moody all week."

"It seems like... all of a sudden... I'm filled with this insatiable desire for... sex, money and expensive things... which have never concerned me before. It's like I have this longing, this hunger, this lust for all these things," he said and paused. "And I don't know why. Strangely, I'm not even sure, I really want these things at all. Anyway, it's all a bit confusing."

After a few moments Axel sat down beside Theo, sipping his hot chocolate.

"How long has this been going on?"

"All week! Ever since I had that dream," he recalled.

"Ooh, right, your so-called nightmare," he sipped. "What're you going to do?"

"I have no idea."

They sat in silence for a long while.

"You know... we've been going to the Lutheran Church, like, forever. One time, I remember the pastor saying that if you're feeling confused about something, are in doubt or if your morality is in question, that the best thing one might consider doing is becoming abstinent."

"Abstinence!"

Theo looked across at Axel with a stark expression, who curled his bottom lip and nodded.

"Uh huh! You know... to keep a lid on those... urges of yours."

Waxing Crescent

I open my eyes to see my shadowy feet, standing upon the black apex of a tree trunk between two enormous branches. My body is a translucent shade of dark grey. I look up and around at the surrounding branches and the canopy above me.

I hear a giggle behind. I turn around. On the next branch above, the Imp is sitting back on its haunches, with its hands resting upon its knees, looking down at me... grinning... with a broad toothy smile. I curl my lip in a grimace and glare back up at the Imp. Why am I here? What am I supposed to do? I swing around while looking up into the higher canopy.

Then I remember. Last time I was here, the Imp tagged me on the heel. I return my gaze back towards the Imp once more. Am I supposed to tag the Imp in return? The smile slowly drifts from the Imp's face, to be replaced with an expression of concern. Yes, that's what I have to do. Tag the Imp!

I suddenly leap in the Imp's direction, surprising the Imp and even myself at how effortless it seems. The Imp squeals in fright and leaps to the branch on its left, just in time to avoid my swiping outstretched hand. I land on the black branch, twist to my left on the ball of my heel and leap forward from the opposite foot. I look all around me while in mid-flight, preparing myself for a continuous hard chase.

The Imp squeals once more and leaps across to another branch. I land where the Imp had been and spring forward quickly, again, from the same leg in quick succession. The Imp begins to bound from branch to branch. I follow in hot pursuit.

The Imp tries to go low, towards the ground. I keep on the lower inside track, trying to cut off its descent and force it to remain in the branches. Adjusting to the style of movement and the terrain, I manage to pick up speed and gain a small amount of ground on the Imp.

Across a wide gap to an adjacent branch, I see and anticipate the Imp's next move. I hold the lower ground cutting off its escape. The Imp takes the jump to avoid my pursuit and leaps diagonally across my left side. At the same time, I leap forward and upwards, to intercept. I stretch out with my left arm as far as I can reach. My hand and fingers are fully extended. The Imp's right heel is only just dragging behind the rest of its body, with arms and tail raised high in readiness for landing. As the Imp reaches the apex of the arc and dips, mid-flight through the leap, I just manage to touch and tag the Imp's back heel.

The Imp squeals and lands on the target branch and turns to watch me... furious. As soon as I touch the Imp, my body, in mid-flight, instantly loses its grey shadow and turns clear and translucent once more. I bring my arms in, raise my knees and look for a landing. A large white space opens before me, high above the Imp's branch. I land in the clear space, wobble and manage to keep my balance. I stand and stare back down at the angry Imp.

****

Theo's eyes suddenly sprang open. He immediately sat up in bed, covered in a layer of sweat.

"Whoa!" he exclaimed.

He stared wide-eyed past the wall in front of him, the dream very much in the forefront of his vision. The dream receded from his mind as he turned to look at the nightstand. The clock displayed 5:20 am, on this day, Sunday 18th February 2007.

"This looks like a theme," he remarked, regarding the time.

Theo leapt out of bed and dashed into the bathroom. He switched on the light and stared into the mirror. His face appeared normal and full of colour. The dark patches around his eyes were gone. He felt great... lighter... unencumbered. That unsatiated longing and hunger which constantly plagued him, vanished. He felt energetic, enthusiastic and genuinely happy.

"It worked!" he exclaimed, in a high-pitched whisper. "Took a while, but it worked," he said and paused. "I can't wait to tell Axel."

He jumped into a hot shower.

Theo did embarked upon a programme of abstinence. He forbade himself to act on any impulse of desire, whether it be for sex, wealth and money, or for material objects out of reach and out of character. He would only consider a choice if it passed his test of sound mind. He managed to successfully maintain his abstinence and resulting strict moral code for a little more than a year, through the preceding spring, summer and autumn... until now.

Luckily, or rather unluckily, Theo had already celebrated his twenty-third birthday dinner. This was a massive test for his perseverance and persistence. His parents were happy to note the positive change in his attitude. Jo-Anna was impressed with his polite gratitude. Arvid was relieved the sports car idea had long been scrapped. Myra remained sceptical of his sincerity where she usually found him such a dour soul to be around. Everyone seemed pleased that he had made the effort to turn things around and exonerate himself.

Dressed sharply in his best casuals, Theo dashed down the stairs into the kitchen. He made coffee and grilled ham and cheese croissants for the two of them. To his pleasant surprise, Axel noticed the change in Theo's countenance immediately and was quickly briefed about the dream. They soon left the apartment together and headed over to fetch Myra. Theo decided that it would be wonderful to embark on a jolly, posh, cultural day touring the city's art galleries. He knew Myra would just love being the centrepiece.

Slowly and steadily, Theo progressively found through his abstinence of harmful choices, that he no longer possessed an attraction towards lustful acts of self-gratification. He was forced to discern the difference and let many a thing go. He managed to tame the need to satisfy his immediate physical urges which no longer had any sway over his behaviour.

In the process, he found he had grown in patience and independently developed his own power of will, earning a degree of inner peace and wisdom. Upon quiet reflection in the months to follow, Theo felt he had broken attachment to the desire for all things of a physical nature. Through moderation, he had introduced a little balance across his life.

During the working week that followed and beyond, Theo's performance at the bank shot through the roof. His analysis and recommendations were sound and approved by his superiors. He searched for and presented best case scenarios and solutions for his customers. He gained immense satisfaction by providing great service and received compliments and commendations from both his customers and fellow peers alike.

When spring bloomed forth in March, Theo began to experience a strange new sensation. He noticed it when he casually focused his attention upon his immediate superior nearby. He was able to pick up on and detect the core physical desire and subsequent emotional state that drove the motivation and behaviour of his superior.

His body seemed able to detect and register a sensation which would instantly manifest in the likeness of an idea in his mind, although an idea not his own. It felt like he was able to detect the core emotional resonance of his target's physical desire.

Theo scanned his fellow work colleagues and managers. He quickly discovered who fancied who and which colleague possessed a desirous ambition towards another. This instantly revealed another dimension to office politics. He kept this discovery strictly to himself.

When eating out with friends and associates at cafes and restaurants, he was able to determine who had the hots for whom and assess who was engaged in a secret romantic relationship. The sensation was rather pronounced when Theo met someone who found him rather attractive. He instinctively implemented an immediate rule to never act upon and take advantage of such an opportunity. He needed time to reconcile his newfound ability.

If a person's motivation was not sexual, Theo could also sense if a person's dominant driving ambition was the desire for money and material gain. Some desires such as owning one's home were noble, while others, such as a sports car were self-indulgent.

Theo could only read a person if their base desire was physical in nature. Thus, he could scan the overwhelming majority of people, but not everyone. On regular occasions, he found himself unable to read a person, deducing their ideals were probably of a higher morality.

He found a lot of very devoted religious people could not be scanned. Happily married people who were truly in love and satisfied were unreadable. A larger proportion of retired elderly people could not be read where, overall, they had managed to accomplish their life's goals and were also happy and content.

As the months ticked by, Theo's experience and analysis of reading people grew. He could clearly see how people focused upon and planned their lives around the attainment of a physical desire and, in many instances, became entrapped by that very ideal. He noticed that the stronger the attachment, the harder it was to break free and the deeper that person became entrapped, to the point where that person and the people around them began to suffer.

Strangely and yet luckily, Theo could not read his parents, nor Myra or Axel. Maybe they each, in their own way, were motivated by and lived according to a more noble value.

It became all too apparent that it was in Theo's best interest to avoid and stay clear of anyone he could read. During such instances he would only engage in a brief, plutonic encounter, such as completing a transaction at work. He absolutely had no inclination of becoming embroiled in another person's personal trauma of desires.

Theo clearly understood the importance of maintaining his self-imposed abstinence. He knew instinctively that whatever was happening to him had not yet run its course and was by no means over. Thus, he stood himself apart, and in doing so Theo began the first stage of his separation, his alienation, from society.

First Quarter

I awake to find myself where I last left... standing upon a white space, roughly in the middle tier of the tree canopy. I'm already familiar with my surroundings. I look ahead in front of me. The Imp is sitting patiently upon the black branch glaring straight back at me... with a broad toothy grin.

I don't wait... I know what to do. I turn and leap for a nearby white space. In the middle of the canopy there are numerous small white spaces scattered between the thinner branches, all a short distance from each other. I run, stepping from one foot to the other, moving swiftly through the tree.

The Imp giggles loudly, taking delight in the chase, as it leaps forward. The Imp manages to keep up with ease, gains a little and seemingly relishes in running me down. This place is practically weightless. I don't appear to be tiring. The chase goes on... and on... and on.

I don't know what to do... other than to run. How do I escape? How do I make it stop? I run... and run... and run... in a wide circle. The Imp is in close pursuit, giggling heartily.

Suddenly... it all seems futile. I slow a little, perplexed on how ridiculous this game is.

At that very moment I feel a firm slap on the back of my left elbow.

****

"Faaarrrk this game of TAG!" Theo yells out loudly the moment his eyes sprang open.

He was awake instantly, staring up at the ceiling, lying in a thin veil of sweat. He lay there for a long while, the dream clear and fresh in his mind. He cringed and scowled and twisted his top lip in anger and once more, found himself in the foulest of tempers.

He heard the pitter-patter of Axel's slippers upon the polished wooden floor approaching down the hallway.

"I'm fine, Axel!" he yelled.

Axel stopped dead still before he had a chance to knock.

"Just a bad dream! You don't have to check up on me every time I have a bad dream, you know. Go back to bed!" he yelled gruffly.

Axel turned around and tip-toed back to his sanctuary.

"Ooh no, woke up on the wrong side of the bed… again!" he mumbled.

He slid into his bedroom and quietly closed the door, with a click. A foreboding shiver crept across his shoulders as he suspected Theo just entered into another monstrously bad mood.

Theo looked over at the clock on the nightstand. It read 4:45am in the morning of Thursday the 7th of February 2008. Theo groaned in knowing frustration. He felt awful, even worse than the last time. Begrudgingly, he climbed out of bed and walked into the bathroom, bypassed the mirror and went straight into a hot shower.

"I knew this wasn't over yet," he whispered softly

Leaning his forehead against the tiled wall with closed eyes, he simply allowed the hot water to cascade around and down his head, shoulders and back, his body absorbing the warmth.

"What's going on? Why is this happening to me?" he pondered. "Lucky, my twenty-fourth birthday bash is already over."

Once dressed and in a dark, dour and sombre mood, Theo quietly slipped out of the door and into the cold dark, predawn fog before Axel dared to make an appearance. He was not of a mind to bear Axel's early morning happiness and enthusiasm.

On the long, lonely walk to work, Theo was drawn to an unusual boutique café. Walking to the back, he hid himself within the dark confines of an old oak-timbered booth, thankfully with padded seat. He ordered breakfast and a hot black coffee, which he didn't normally like. He was compelled by a strange urge to try one. He only reluctantly departed the café an hour later, when there were barely enough minutes left to make it to work on time. He felt secure and a little more at ease in this morose solemn surrounding, which instantly became a habitual morning ritual.

Work was tedious that day and the days to follow. He immediately felt bored and could not focus on any one task for long. He relished and encouraged interruptions. His performance and level of service dropped drastically, noticeably. Many tasks and projects remained due and outstanding and would take an unacceptable amount of time to complete. By the time a couple of 'how are things going' meetings were held, Theo had exhausted all excuses. His superior was forced to issue his first warning. With pride dented, Theo's dark demeanour deepened even further.

For Theo, when consulting with his more wealthy, affluent and powerful clients, he felt himself being overcome by an overwhelming sense of jealousy and envy. This was something that had never really bothered him before. It wasn't the material wealth itself but the freedom and lifestyle the wealthy enjoyed that he craved. Theo began to take interest in a particular fantasy. Oh, to be free of the necessity of having to work was something he could covet. Little did he realise that wealth was encumbered with its own level of responsibilities.

On the last Saturday of April, Myra and Axel thought it a great idea to invite Theo out for dinner to cheer him up. They decided to try some interesting and different healthy food options at a brand new trendy vegetarian bar in Södermalm.

Since Theo had withdrawn into a more solitary existence, both Myra and Axel found themselves compelled to explore newfound friendships. Now in her last year of university, Myra brought along her new boyfriend, Mikkel, who was tall, well built and four years older. Axel, on the other hand, arrived with his new girlfriend, Gabrielle, who was quite petite, shy and possessed the same complexion to match his.

Looking ghoulish, Theo greeted everyone with as much pleasantness as he could muster. He dispensed quickly with the small talk during the first round of drinks at the bar, before their waiter escorted them to their table. He discovered Mikkel was an architect and already a junior partner with his family run firm, whereas Gabrielle was a student at the same university as Myra. In fact, Myra had strategically introduced her to Axel in a bar three weeks earlier.

On the way to their table, Mikkel's hands were rather active. He held Myra's hand whilst walking, touched her on the elbow when speaking softly to her and caressed her shoulder gently, when helping her into her seat. Being with such a gentleman made Myra feel adored. Watching closely, Theo felt scepticism and loathing build.

Gabrielle, already holding her third drink, courtesy of Axel, was becoming a little more boisterous, playful and suggestive. However, when Axel touched her tenderly, she feigned the pretence of being a little coy, not wishing to be seen showing too much affection in public. Theo grew ever so suspicious.

Working through entrée into the main course, Mikkel continuously touched Myra's hand, arm and elbow. They sampled each other's food and delighted in the other's splendid choice. Gabrielle did not wish to share her food with Axel, yet the steady serving of drinks caused her cheeks to flush red and her eyes to roll merrily. Theo refrained from drinking, very aware of his own frailties. He had built an appreciative tolerance for the bitterness of black coffee.

Suddenly, Theo was struck with a powerful pang of jealously, which quickly morphed into envy towards Myra and Axel. He did not desire intimacy. Rather, realisation dawned that he was all alone and did not have anyone to share his life with. Beneath the surface he questioned the veracity of his abstinence.

Mikkel had his hand casually resting upon Myra's arm whilst he whispered something mischievous into her ear. She giggled with mirth. Theo could take it no longer.

"Stop touching her," Theo barked gruffly.

"What?" Mikkel replied, surprised.

"Theo!" Myra exclaimed. "That's rather rude of you," she retorted. "Apologise, this minute," she said firmly.

"Stop TOUCHING her!" he repeated, louder.

With gaunt face and scary dark-shadowed eyes, Theo glared at Mikkel aggressively.

"What's got into you?" Myra exclaimed.

Mikkel withdrew his hand, unsure, debating in his mind whether to withdraw or... fight.

"What's wrong with you, Theo? You've been nothing but a depressed, miserable bore over the past couple of months," she proclaimed angrily.

Stunned and alcohol blocked, preventing any substantial reaction, Axel and Gabrielle simply sat back and watched the fireworks.

"Nothing is wrong with me," he growled.

"Well, what is it then?" she pressed on. "Are you unhappy that I'm in a relationship... with Mikkel... with someone other than you?"

"Don't be ridiculous," he scoffed.

"Are you worried I might be having sex... actually having sex... with someone else," Myra continued, turning spiteful. "Are you jealous... envious... that I have a boyfriend, that you can't even make a friend, let alone find a girlfriend?" she spat angrily.

"Bang whoever you want Myra. See if I care. Just don't bring 'em to dinner," he countered.

Mikkel's eyes widened. He pulled back, refraining from interjecting in what seemed, a family feud. The patrons at the surrounding tables fell quiet to watch the show.

"Why, what's wrong with Mikkel? Is he not good enough for you... for your high and mighty moral code?"

"Well, I'm absolutely certain that you guys haven't even done it yet, but as soon as he nails you, he'll dump you like a tonne of bricks and move on," he said... what he read.

"What!" Myra exclaimed, shocked.

Axel dumbstruck, saw the anger triggered in Mikkel's face.

"Whoa!" Axel, piped in. "That was uncalled for."

"I don't wish to see you hurt. But don't call me when he does," he continued indignantly.

"I think we should all stop... and... calm down," Axel said attempting to intervene.

"Shut up, stupid," Theo said, turning on Axel. "Have you shagged her yet?"

"We only just met!" Axel replied defensively. "Wow, you really are jealous."

"Well, it won't happen," he pressed, ignoring Axel's jibe. "She'll only stay while you pay, for those drinks... and everything else. As soon as you stop, she'll drop you like a sack of potatoes," Theo confessed his vision of Gabrielle.

She laughed in a resigned drunken stupor, too inebriated to say otherwise.

"Actually, she has no physical attraction for you at all," he said.

Axel sat stunned, in a wide-eyed, heartfelt silence.

Myra promptly stood up, grabbed her half-full glass and threw the red wine into Theo's face.

Silence befell the restaurant.

Having splashed him square in the face, the warm red liquid dripped down across the front of his shirt and into his lap. He sat for a long moment and nodded in acknowledgement. He grabbed his serviette, wiped his face and stood up. Everyone watched in silence. He withdrew a couple of large notes from his wallet and dropped them on the table. He pushed his chair in, turned and walked out of the restaurant.

Theo wondered aimlessly through some of the back streets, taking the long walk home, whilst feeling very dejected.

What happened? Am I really jealous, envious? I don't know… maybe. Did my pride get in the way? Probably! I don't think I should have said those things. I… I just couldn't help it.

A wave of sadness, sorrow and guilt crept over Theo. On approach to the front entrance of his building, he changed his mind and instead walked into the park two blocks to the south. He found and slumped down upon a bench to contemplate the events of the evening and the prior two months. A few tears welled up and fell down his cheeks. Finding no resolution, he soon dozed off into a restless sleep.

The sorrow and guilt persisted, even seemingly amplified, over the next two weeks. Myra and Axel refused to speak to Theo. His premonitions proved true. Myra resisted Mikkel's sexual advances for longer than he could bear and he broke up with her. Axel reduced financing Gabrielle's social outings and her affection for him evaporated in similar proportion.

When Theo's heart could no longer bear the weight of his burden, it was time to visit the one person he could rely upon. Late one Friday evening in mid-May, he found himself reclining in an armchair sharing a cognac with his father Arvid. Theo recounted all that he had experienced over the past couple of months… with one exception… that of his dreams.

"Do you think you're having some sort of mental breakdown?" Arvid suggested. "Do you think you need to see a psychologist… for professional help?"

"I've thought about that," he replied. "If it was a psychological issue, I would've had the problem since childhood. No, this feels different. My experiences seem far more intense than merely a psychological issue. This feels… paranormal… spiritual even, in nature."

"Ooh, right, something like… you're being tested… a conundrum of the soul."

"Yes, yes, precisely."

"Well, I'm not sure why this is happening to you. Maybe it's just your way of growing up," Arvid pondered. "All I can tell you from my experience is this... there is this thing called the ego. When you have wealth and flaunt it, people will tend to say, 'you have a big ego' and things like that. The ego possesses both good and bad qualities. The bad qualities are the flaws of the ego and if followed, they will consume you and lead you into trouble. Sounds as though you might be going through something like this now," he paused.

"As you know, when your mother and I grew more and more wealthy, we always resisted such urges and managed to keep our feet on the ground."

"How did you do that?"

"We never had any ambitions which were beyond our means to achieve. We just took one step at a time. In your case, you want something impossible in your life, right now! So... it would be better for you to renounce the things which you know to be unobtainable. In other words, you should renounce anything which you recognise as a flaw in your ego."

"If you experience something which creates a negative emotion within you, then renounce the thing which is its cause. I know this sounds very simplified. It does take time to practise, but you must try, and try again. In time, you will see," he counselled.

"The next thing your mother and I always did was to remain humble and always thankful for the things we had," he continued. "Humility and thankfulness help to keep you grounded. They stop you wanting and wishing for things which cannot be yours. And hopefully, if you can do these things, you might be able to break through the flaws of your ego and alleviate these feelings of sorrow and guilt you are having. After all, if you don't indulge in the ego, you have nothing to feel sorry or guilty about, right?" he reasoned.

"So, strive for these things, keep positive and hopeful, and with a bit of luck, all this will pass before too much longer," he said with a broad smile. "Now, how about you take your sister and Axel out for lunch this weekend and make up."

Theo left his parents' house feeling a little lighter and happier. At the very least, by sharing his burden a small weight had been lifted. He felt steady, reassured and that he now had some direction to follow.

Waxing Gibbous

My eyes spring open. I know where I am. I didn't need to look down at my body. I know it's clouded in shadow. I look around, searching. Argh, there's… the Imp, sitting on a nearby branch with a wide toothy grin.

I don't think or hesitate. With a determined snarl, I just leap towards the Imp, who squeals, in surprise at the immediacy of my pursuit. The chase is on.

Once again, I stay on the inner lower side of the Imp, preventing it from descending towards the thicker branches below. If the Imp tries to go down, it will cross my line and I'll be within reach of a tag. The Imp can only go up.

The Imp moves quickly. I'm possessed by an extremely focused, single-minded determination. As the elevation rises, the Imp looks like it's finding it more difficult to gain purchase on the thinner branches and leaves.

The Imp pauses in doubt as it reaches the furthest outer bulge of the middle tier of the canopy and finds a wide expanse of white out in front, before being able to reach the edge of the next tree's branches. In that moment of indecision, I surge upwards and tag the Imp's back left elbow. The Imp bellows in a cacophony of angry squeals. I land in a clear white space higher up in the treetop canopy.

****

Theo's eyes burst open.

"YEAH! I got you back you motherf…," he yelled tapering off.

He pumped his right fist into the air and sat bolt upright in bed. He stopped himself and briefly looked over at the clock.

"Of course, it's ten past five in the morning," he muttered. "And the day is…?" he checked his watch. "It's Monday 26th January 2009."

He laid back down in bed staring up at the ceiling, feeling somewhat relieved and elated.

"Thank God!" he exclaimed "Am I… am I… back to normal?"

He sensed that his gaunt brooding disposition had lifted.

"Holy crap! Work! I'd better get in there and fix everything, pronto."

Theo leapt out of bed, showered and dressed in a flash. He yelled a quick good morning as Axel opened his bedroom door in a sleepy stupor. Theo ran out the door with coffee in hand, picked up breakfast to go, and bypassed the dark dingy café he had become accustomed to.

The global financial crisis peaked late in 2008 and hit worldwide financial sectors and economies hard. Arriving at work bang on seven, he passed through the security protocols and let himself into his office to begin the day's work. He had a mountain to work through.

Theo organised all his outstanding tasks and projects in order of priority and responded to and cleared all his emails. He forbade his clients from selling stocks and properties and incurring massive loses. He trimmed the fat and diversified as much capital into gold to balance each portfolio, and set his clients up for a two-year holding pattern, where passive incomes earned would cover the interest payments. His clients would make no money, but incur no losses either, during this recovery phase. He managed to have everything back on track within a fortnight, to the relieved jubilance of his superiors and fellow colleagues.

His twenty-fifth birthday fell on a Tuesday. This time Theo decided to treat Jo-Anna, Arvid, Myra and Axel out to a stately three-course lunch to celebrate, on the Sunday prior. Pleasantly surprised, everyone was happy Theo had returned to his usual buoyant self. Speaking once dessert was served, he apologised for his miserable behaviour.

During the many months that followed Theo's talk with Arvid, he did indeed take up his father's advice and strove with determination to renounce anything which would cause in him a negative emotion. As difficult as it was, he practised humility and thankfulness for the things that he had and looked forward to the next day with hope.

Thus, he did not formulate any great plan for the future or allow any ambition beyond his current scope to derail his thoughts and motivation. He no longer experienced jealousy or envy of any client or associate with whom he made contact. At last, he finally found himself free from the impact of these negative afflictions, having broken attachment to all things of an emotional nature and thereby further strengthened his willpower.

Over the next few weeks leading into the next few months, Theo's ability to read people had evolved. As well as being able to detect a person's core physical desire, he could now detect a person's core emotional state, especially if it were negative. He could sense if a person was predominantly jealous, envious, prideful, angry or hateful, and whether that person was consumed by sorrow, shame or guilt. Although less common, he managed to find people who exhibited well-grounded, good emotional states, such as truthfulness, empathy, compassion and the capacity for forgiveness.

He was able to read his parents, Jo-Anna and Arvid, now both retired. They were satisfied and content with what they had achieved and the level of wealth they had attained. He saw that they knew they had little time left, had gained immense joy from seeing their children grow up and savoured as much quality time as they could when together as a family.

Myra, on the other hand, was more of an idealist. Physical relationships were not a means to an end. Nor was the attainment of wealth. All she truly wished for was to find ways to nurture the environment and the natural world. Axel was quite straightforward. He was far more adventurous, preferring to focus on life experiences, and wanted to travel and see as much of the world as he could.

Theo began to learn a lot about his fellow humans. In so many cases, he could clearly see the link where a person's unobtainable and unfulfilled desire festered into a driving and forceful negative emotion which, in many cases, led to destructive behaviour. In the worst of cases, a person was driven to impose their desires onto others, through coercion or physical intimidation, causing trauma within the person being afflicted. Theo found that a great many instances of addiction, particularly drug related, were a result of unrecognised, untreated and unhealed emotional trauma where, in most instances, the cause of the affliction was external.

Theo read a great many emotional attachments among his work colleagues, clients and their acquaintances, on a daily basis. He developed the tactical nous to stay clear and disassociate himself from becoming embroiled in another person's emotional drama, dilemma or trauma. He became increasingly more reclusive and found it more difficult to make new friends. In fact, he no longer bothered, thereby standing himself further apart from his peers. Theo consolidated upon the second juncture of his separation, his alienation, from society.

In his solace, Theo found a similar demeanour amongst particularly devout religious people. He found it easier to converse with a pastor or a nun, as they did not possess the emotional hang-ups of most people, until of course, they attempted to bring Theo into the doctrine of their particular denomination. Theo knew that although the faith of the devout was very strong, it was more often than not also blind.

When questioned on matters of key importance, Theo could see that, like himself, the devout did not really know with absolute certainty that what they preached and believed in, was the absolute truth. Without any experience of the 'phenomenal' themselves, doubt was always going to be the persistent nemesis of the religious.

And what was the 'phenomenal' basis of his experience? His mind was now consumed. From time to time, Theo found himself sitting in the back pew of an empty church, wondering in quiet contemplation, trying to fathom, reconcile, some basis of understanding.

"What is happening to me?" he whispered, whilst looking high up into the arches of the ceiling above. "I can read, I can see… their true nature. Can anyone else do this? I'm pretty sure this isn't normal," he said pausing for a moment. "How is such a thing even possible?"

Theo had never been overly religious or spiritual. Typical of his youthfulness, he had not given any serious contemplation to the question of God, or of a higher power, until now.

"Is this a religious… or spiritual experience… of some kind?" he pondered. "If so, then, there must be a higher… a greater power. There would have to be a higher conscious thinking being, for this to be possible," he reasoned. "Then… why me? I'm nobody! I'm not important at all," he mused. "There must be a reason, a purpose to all this, surely."

Theo continued to ponder these questions for some time.

"Well, I'm stumped. I've no idea where to find any answers," he admitted to himself. "I don't think I even know anyone who can actually help me," he whispered, in reflection.

Nope, no one.

He knew no one who might possess the credentials to ask for help. He was alone. Theo brought his gaze down and looked around the church, at all the artwork and holy statues, and resigned himself to his solitary plight.

"Well, 'He' was all alone in the end. So, I'll just have to tough it out for now, I guess."

Theo sighed, steeling his resolve. He stood up, turned and walked out of the church. Standing upon the top stair outside, he glanced up at the partially cloudy sky.

"Is this thing over, yet?" he mused. "Hardly! The last dream didn't feel like an ending. And I have no answers… to any of my questions. So no, this is far from being over," he concluded.

He took the long stroll back to his apartment. In the meantime, he thought it prudent to maintain a strong vigilance upon his abstinence and renunciation.

Full Moon

I look around. Of course, I know where I am. Perched upon a thin branch, the Imp looks across at me with a renewed grimace on its face. I stand still for a moment. The Imp doesn't appear to be in a hurry. It watches and waits... waiting... for me to make the first move.

I look down at the large thick branches, trunk and roots far below. I look around and up at the thinning twigs and leaves. I know the Imp experiences more difficulty the higher we go. The thinning black twigs and leaves and the widening, more numerous white gaps, provide little space for the Imp to manoeuvre. I decide to go as high as I can.

I leap upwards. The Imp immediately follows, revelling once more in the chase. I bound from one clear space to another, circling around the outer central core of the tree and spiral towards the top, highest point, of the canopy. I stand upon the last, highest space bound within the border of thin branches. I pause, unsure of what to do next.

Can I leap out into the open white void of the sky and be free of the tree? I don't know. The Imp struggles and is almost upon me. Being so high, I quickly look around at the view. Over the top of a smaller, nearby tree, I can see a clearing... a clear white circular clearing. The grove of trees is arranged in a wide arcing circle around an open field. It looks beautiful, mesmerising, inviting. It's obvious. I must reach the clearing so that the Imp can't...

TAG! I took too long. The moment I sight the clearing and work out what to do, the Imp knew there wasn't much time. Just as I change direction towards the clearing and prepare to leap forward, the Imp reached out and touched me on the right hand.

****

"NOOOOO!" Theo yelled, instantly awake. "AAARRRGH!" he grimaced.

He lay in bed for a few moments, sweating, staring at the ceiling, gritting his teeth in sheer frustration, wondering what this meant. Axel, also rudely awoken, refrained from checking on Theo. He knew and wondered about the very same thing.

Yes, it felt like he did indeed, wake up on the wrong side of the bed. Theo found himself to be in the blackest of moods with a thumping headache. This time he didn't feel it through his body but rather, it seemed centred very much around his head… his mind, clouded.

"FAAARRRK," he growled angrily under his breath.

He threw back the covers, sat up, swung his legs over the side of the bed and looked over at the bedside clock with seething hatred.

"Yes, I know the time already!"

In confirmation, the clock reported 4:55 am, on the morning of Sunday 14th February 2010. Fortunately, Theo's transition had missed his twenty-sixth birthday celebration.

On the way to the shower, Theo hit and cracked the mirror with the soft underside of his clenched left fist.

"That's bad luck, isn't it?" he mused without care.

He dropped his boxer shorts and stepped into the shower. First, he turned the hot water. It was quickly hot… too hot… and within seconds, Theo scalded himself. He didn't mind a little pain at all. He turned the cold water… just a little. When finished and dry, he felt black, and dressed… accordingly, all in black… much to Axel's perplexed chagrin.

It had snowed throughout the entire week prior. Today however, cleared into a bright blue-sky day. Myra, who no longer brought breakfast on the weekends, suddenly showed up unexpectedly at eight. She glared at Theo's morbid appearance a little aghast.

Having been cooped up all week and with hamper in hand, she used the delightful treats as an enticement to beg them to go skiing with her. They were all accomplished skiers since an early age. Axel said yes instantly. Theo groaned, rolled his eyes, was unable to resist the persistent pleading and reluctantly agreed.

Ready and appropriately decked out in ski gear within the hour, they climbed into a taxi for the short, ten-minute drive to the Hammarbybacken skiing park, a little southeast of Katarina-Sofia. Naturally, it was already crowded on this bright and glorious Sunday.

Theo remained quiet and reserved during the taxi ride, preferring to stare out of the back seat window, whilst brooding at the passing world. Already agitated, he felt a sense of aggression build at the sight of so many noisy children already on the slopes. The thought of having to wait in line for the chairlift all day long, surrounded by kids, was particularly irritating.

On his first run down an intermediate slope, Theo was consumed with a nasty impulsive thought. He 'accidently' lightly clipped the back of a small boy's ski, who was going slowly and trying to centre his balance. The trip was enough to send him spilling forward onto his belly and face first into the snow. Theo smirked menacingly behind his goggles and visor. Now he was having some fun.

Theo repeated his tactic twice more on the next run. On the third run, a young lad having lost control and in trouble, was hurtling towards Theo. Feigning blindness, he strategically positioned himself in the boy's path and landed his right shoulder directly upon the boy's sternum, knocking him flat onto his back.

"Watch where you're going!" Theo protested gruffly at the stunned boy.

He turned to meander gently down the slope, with a satisfied smile beneath his visor.

"Theo!" Axel called out. "Do you want to race me down the slalom slope? Let's see how good you are, hey?" he taunted.

"Ok, you're on."

Theo instantly bagged the red line of flags, leaving Axel with the blue line. At the starting gate, the timing clock counted down, three… two… one… they both sprang forward. Down the slope they raced, keeping pace with each other, swerving in and out around each flag.

They passed halfway, the race neck and neck.

Theo suddenly felt the dark bite of stigma if he were to lose. He couldn't bear the thought, the disgrace. He wasn't about to let that happen. Approaching the finish, Axel swung out wide around the second last flag and crossed into the red lane. Theo swerved out wide as Axel approached. They came together and touched. Theo bent his knee forward into Axel's thigh, causing his legs to buckle. Theo skied onward, as Axel tumbled forward over his own legs. He crashed heavily and came to rest dazed in a heap of snow.

Swooping through the finish line, Theo raised his arms with inglorious victory. When he regained composure, Axel stood up and checked to see that he wasn't seriously hurt.

"What the hell was that, Theo? You knocked Axel over." Myra exclaimed. "You could've injured him severely. What do you think you're doing?" she scolded harshly.

Theo looked back at her blankly, surprise, stunned.

"Well! What do you have to say?"

"It was a race... and... I won!"

"No, you didn't. You cheated!" she refuted loudly.

Axel appeared by her side, bruised and battered, to listen.

"Actually, you lost! In fact, you disqualified yourself," she stated angrily. "You should be ashamed of yourself."

Theo simply shrugged his shoulders and slid downhill casually. Myra turned to Axel.

"Are you all right?"

"Yeah! I'm fine."

They both watched Theo ski away.

"I don't know what gets into him sometimes," she pondered.

"He had another bad dream this morning. I don't know what's happening to him, but I think he's about to go through another bad patch again," he warned. "Maybe we should just give him some space for a while."

Myra's scolding festered in Theo's mind and intensified into nasty and vengeful thoughts, over the next hour or so. He felt an overwhelming sensation of meanness when he saw Myra skiing down one side of a gentle slope.

Impulsively, without thinking and without checking himself he skied at high speed directly for Myra. With a gasp of fright, she suddenly saw him racing towards her. At the last second Theo swerved and turned sharply, spraying her with a wide wall of snow. Myra staggered, slipped and fell, twisting her right ankle with a squeal of pain as she tumbled in the snow.

Axel, only a little further up the slope, saw the whole thing. Theo circled around to a stop with a smirk across his lips. Myra pushed herself into a sitting position and held her right leg in agony. She glared at Theo. He didn't move to help her. He simply stared at her, pitifully.

Axel skied up to intercept Theo.

"What the hell do you think you're doing?" he interjected angrily. "You knocked Myra off her feet and caused her to sprain her ankle. What are you thinking, man?" he pressed. "Why would you hurt your sister like this?"

Theo simply stared back at Axel blankly.

"Well?"

"Well, what?" Theo countered gruffly. "You guys left me to myself over an hour ago."

"That's because we felt you needed some space. Clearly... for some reason... you're not yourself today, are you?"

"What do you mean?" He exclaimed.

"I saw you knock over those kids. You knocked me down and now your sister. Wake up on the wrong side of the bed this morning, did we? Got the short end of the mean stick, have we? Why don't you tell us what's really going on?"

A vile defensive pressure immediately built up inside Theo's mind.

"What's really going on... is that I'm sick of you trying to be 'ME'... and having eyes for my sister!" he blurted out spitefully.

Axel and Myra both stared at Theo, gobsmacked.

"That... that's... not true," Axel replied, in a shallow voice.

Myra struggled to her feet and stood upon her one good leg.

"How could you say such a thing?" she practically screamed.

In that instant, a moment of clarity cleared inside Theo's mind. Suddenly, he knew he had crossed a line. He turned away from Axel and looked down at the snow-covered slope. He suddenly realised the destructive state of mind he was currently experiencing.

"Yes, you're right," he said in a muffled voice. "I think you'd better give me some space, after all. I probably won't be any fun for a while until I figure this out."

He tucked his ski poles under his arms and slid down the slope. Theo left the park and disappeared for the rest of the day.

Work became a veritable nightmare for Theo. Try as he might, he simply couldn't put aside the constant barrage of mean and nasty thoughts he was having. He found it very tiring and wearisome to continuously resist the impulse to backbite, manipulate, undermine or victimise both his fellow colleagues and superiors. He found that he sported a healthy contempt for all his clients, to the point that it was almost impossible to withhold laughing and mocking them, especially when a client made a rather ridiculous request. He felt his newfound arrogance was quickly reaching a dangerously unprecedented level of exhibition.

Being self-conscious of these symptoms, Theo found that upon reflection, he had become consumed with an underlying hatred for people, society and all things mankind. His mind was constantly filled with nasty, angry and destructive thoughts and the impulse to do awful things to other people. He knew this wasn't normal at all and yet, he didn't know how to find its countering resolution either. It was a relentless torment.

By Friday, the end of the working week, and at wits end, Theo sought solace and solitude in the only place he knew he might find it... the back pew of the church he visited from time to time. He sat alone, in the semi-darkness of dusk. Thankfully, he had the entire empty church to himself. There was no one around upon whom he could foster a nasty thought. Sitting forward, he clasped his head, along with his withered mind, in his hands and emitted a long deep sigh.

He closed his eyes to rest his mind, now vacant of thought.

After a few long moments, he felt a light touch on his left shoulder. Startled, he looked up at the church pastor, dressed in a simple full-length black cassock, with white priest's collar. He was tall, thin, middle-aged with fair skin and short kept, very dark brown hair and eyes.

"Are you alright?" the pastor asked gently.

"Ye... yes, I'm fine," Theo replied, hesitantly.

"You seem... distressed. I thought it best to at least... check on you."

"Well, that's very kind of you."

Theo was just on the cusp of saying goodnight when the pastor interjected.

"You do look troubled, though. May I sit?"

The pastor gestured at the spare space beside Theo and sat down upon the bench before he could muster a protest.

"Friday nights are always the quietest and I have nothing planned."

"Umm... sure," Theo groaned resignedly.

"So, tell me. What's troubling you?" the pastor persisted. "No pressure, no judgement here."

Reluctantly, Theo began slowly. However, once the gate opened, his discourse became a flood. He revealed everything he had gone through over the past week, how he felt and admitted he had no idea how to deal with his affliction. As was customary, he refrained from confessing the repeating dream sequence.

"Do you believe in God, or at least, a higher power?"

"That's been on my mind. I've given it a lot of thought lately," he acknowledged.

"Ok, well… simply speaking, there are two sides to every person, the higher side and the lower side. Right now, it would appear you are experiencing the full force of your lower self," the pastor began.

"From my experience, there is only one way to resolve such a problem," he said with a momentary pause. "You need to take a leap of faith and place your full belief in something higher than yourself… a higher power, or God. Define it how you like."

"The important thing is that, once you do this… and I mean, with real committed sincerity… your point of focus, your point of reference, shifts… from the self to that higher power or God. And in so doing, you leave the self behind," he explained and paused. "In other words, you place the higher principle before oneself and over time you will subdue the lower self completely. Do you understand?"

"I think so," Theo replied, hesitantly.

"When you think about something, just put God… or the higher principle first… before your own self, your lower self. Think about it for a while. You'll soon get the hang of it," the pastor said confidently. "In time, you'll see. You'll become selfless," he mused with mirth and continued.

"I'm sure you realise that all negative emotion, unchecked, will transition into hatred. This is extremely dangerous because it has the power to completely consume a person. As you well know, the remedy for hatred is love. And the best way to cultivate love for our fellow man is through compassion. All religions teach this," the pastor pointed out. 'So, practise compassion and selflessness, and before long, this affliction will no longer find a home in you," he said with a beaming smile.

Waning Gibbous

My eyes open staring straight at the Imp. My mind fills with driving determination. The Imp looks back at me with a fading smirk. For the first time, a worried look spreads across the Imp's jowl and a quiver of doubt runs through its spine.

I stand where I last recall, upon the last thin branch bordering the highest enclosed clear space. The Imp sits close on a nearby twig. I drop down a body length, making sure the Imp remains above me, around head height. The Imp watches me intently. As soon as I land, I leap forward at the Imp. Squealing, the Imp darts backwards, behind its current position.

I move to guard the lower ground, preventing the Imp from escaping down the tree. I drive the Imp towards the outer edge of the canopy, where it stops and turns to face me. I have cornered the Imp who has nowhere to go without being intercepted.

The Imp looks back behind itself once more. There is a wide expanse of open space to reach the edge of the next somewhat smaller tree. Seeing little option, the Imp leaps up and out into the breach. It reaches out and only just manages to grab an outstretched branch. With a two-step run-up, I leap after the Imp, covering the expanse and easily landing high within the canopy of the next tree.

The Imp sprints down for the trunk. There is no way I shall regress. I strive hard at the Imp, intercept and block its escape. I drive forward at the Imp, reaching out to the left and right, pushing the Imp across and to the furthest opposite edge of the tree.

Approaching and landing upon the last twig, the Imp suddenly realises there is no further tree to jump to. All the Imp can see is the open clear expanse of the circular field ahead. The Imp squeals in panic and turns, knowing the only remaining option is to move back across the outer perimeter of the canopy. I have the Imp boxed in.

I watch the placement of the Imp's feet. The Imp stands still, twitches, suddenly jerks right, trying to bait me into moving first. I hold firm, patiently, edging closer, ready.

With eyes frantic, the Imp leaps from its right foot, facing downwards to its left. I leap forward to my right to intercept. The Imp lands on the next lower twig and bounces outwards from its left foot in one single motion. The Imp pulls its limbs in closer like a mid-air hug. I land and push off from the last enclosed space with the front toes of my right foot, desperate, with outstretched arm as far as I can reach.

The Imp floats out across in front of me. I didn't even consider my landing. I have only one, clear, single-minded intention. I swing my right hand far out in front of me, just as the Imp reaches the zenith of its arc and begins to dip and drop away. I slap the Imp's left hip with the tips of my fingers, spinning its body in mid-air. The Imp squeals in anguish and distress, throws out its arms, legs and tail to recalibrate its balance and lands far below in a tumble. I'm overwhelmed with joyous relief the moment I manage to tag the Imp.

No longer in shadow, but clear and translucent, I relax my body. I look not where I am to land. In fact, I realise that I have not yet landed at all. I look to see that I'm floating out towards the middle of the open circular clearing. As I'm drifting, I twist to look back. The Imp stares at me in dismay, its smile gone. I'm completely out of reach.

I slow to rest in a sitting position upon the precise centre of the circular clearing. I gaze joyously at the vista of the surrounding grove.

****

Theo's eyes sprang open. He stares at the ceiling holding his breath for a few seconds, gauging his mood. His mind seemed clear. His mind IS clear. He felt great.

"I tagged the Imp. It's over! I tagged the Imp back… I landed in the clearing… I'm out of reach… The Imp can't touch me. It's over, it's over!" he exclaimed.

With overwhelming realisation, he sat bolt upright.

"I bet its 5 am."

He quickly spun round to stare at the display. Indeed, the clock reported precisely 5 am on the dot, this Thursday the 3rd of February 2011.

"WHAAAAHOOOOO!" Theo exclaimed with unmitigated joy. "And it's my birthday!"

Being awoken, Axel opened his door and tentatively walked halfway down the hallway.

"Are you alright, Theo?" he called out.

Theo threw the covers back, leapt out of bed, dashed across the room and flung his bedroom door open. He ran the few paces up to a very surprised Axel, gripped him in a huge, but firm bear hug and only let go after smacking a huge wet kiss on his right cheek. Axel issued a feeble protest.

"Are... are you alright?"

"Yes, yes. Never better. Absolutely fantastic, in fact!" Theo asserted loudly, emphatically.

"I have to admit, you are the strangest person I've ever known," Axel declared.

"I know! I've been a proper shit lately, haven't I? But I think it's over. It's all over now. I got the final tag and I'm out of reach," he alluded happily.

"Tag! What do you mean, tag?" Axel enquired bemused.

"Oh, Um... never mind. I'll explain it to you one day," he said dismissively. "But, today, it's my birthday! How about we take the day off and I take both you and Myra out for lunch? What do you say to that?"

Axel knew Theo would not take 'no' for an answer and so nodded in acceptance.

Theo called Myra and woke her up. He used all his natural charm to convince her to skip work and allow him to take her out for lunch. She offered moderate resistance yet accepted. Then he soon rang the office and took advantage of his birthday privileges. He quickly reorganised his calendar.

After speaking with the pastor, he had indeed learnt to practise compassion and selflessness. Theo had managed to resist all destructive urges and incurred very little, if any damage at all, to his client base and professional reputation. He held it together long enough to have broken attachment to all things of a mental nature. His willpower now had dominion over the physical, emotional and mental elements of his nature.

By mid-morning, Myra, Axel and Theo stepped aboard the S/S Stockholm, to enjoy an archipelago boat cruise served with lunch. It was a calm, splendid day with splotches of thick fluffy clouds, drifting slowly across the sky. They traversed the waterways around the islands to the east of Stockholm, becoming rather merry after a few glasses of champagne and wine.

They sat down around their designated table in time for the entrée to be served. Before they began, Myra, feeling very fluid, made a trivial comment.

"Did you know, Theo, that this year, your twenty-seventh birthday lands on the exact same day as the Chinese New Year?" she stated with a giggle. "How auspicious is that?"

"The what?" he replied unamused.

Theo was far more interested in the delightful arrangement that was on his plate.

"You know... the Lunar New Year... dummy," she said rolling her eyes. "According to the cycles of the moon, it's the first new moon which falls between 21st January and 20th February," she explained with mirth. "I think... it's like... the first complete half cycle of the moon, leading into the first new moon of the year."

"Oh!" he replied nonchalantly. "The first new moon, hey."

One... two... three... seconds ticked by.

"Ooh... right!" he repeated sitting up straight.

He stopped, looked straight at and then through Myra, with an expression of wonderment and realisation. Understanding suddenly dawned in his mind. He burst out laughing, almost hysterically. Myra and Axel looked at each other a little perplexed.

"Wow! That can't be just a coincidence... can it?" he muttered.

Lunch was a smash hit. So was dinner with his parents, Jo-Anna and Arvid later that evening.

****

Over the next few months, Theo grew to realise his ability to focus upon and read a person was now fully developed. He could detect a person's dominant desire, the core emotional resonance this created within that person and their subsequent preeminent psychological disposition. However, Theo could not read a person's thoughts directly.

His ability allowed him to gain an accurate sense of that person's true inner nature, their true level of spiritual development...

represented by the reverberation of their core resonance, the frequency of their core vibration.

With this ability, Theo was able to evaluate a person along one of two poles or axis.

If a person's core was consumed with a negative emotional state, he could measure and place their resonance along the axis of darkness, depending on the degree or severity of their consummation. Occasionally, he found a person whose heart was filled with hatred and darkness, and watched them consume, vampirise, the emotional energy of others. He could clearly see the correlation between desire, emotion and state of mind.

On the other hand, if a person's core was filled with a positive emotional state, he could measure and place their resonance along the axis of light. If a person's heart was filled with love, they would share their light amongst others. Fortunately, Theo found the vast majority of people he read did love someone, or had someone love them, and so determined that most people aspired to possess a good nature.

On sensing, seeing and experiencing this phenomenon, Theo found himself standing even further apart from his peers and the people around him. He became cemented upon the third stage of his separation... his alienation... from society. He found no one like himself.

Conversely though, Theo found that his newly acquired faith in something higher than himself... of principle or being... grew even stronger. He just knew there had to be something more... something hidden... something above... that provided the basis for, the power behind, his experiences.

He lay back in bed one night, late, in darkness, wide awake and wondering, once again.

"How did this happen?" he mumbled. "I don't understand how this happened! And why? Why me?" he contemplated.

"Who would know the answer to such a question?" he pondered. "I'm not sure the pastor can explain this one. So, *who*? Who would know the answer to my questions?"

He imagined such a person, many a person and in the end no one and finally fell asleep.

Last Quarter

Theo's practice of abstinence, renunciation, selfless compassion and being free of the Imp, inexplicably led him to develop an overwhelming sense of love for humanity and society. He also felt a genuine joy and happiness with his own existence. His consistent buoyancy and enthusiasm were infectious.

Theo's service and performance at work was exceptional. Where needed, he helped his clients, colleagues, friends and even family, providing sound, concise advice and instruction. He demonstrated a natural flare to articulate a well-constructed warning to prevent a person from making a catastrophic mistake and how to turn a negative situation into a positive one.

As the cold thawed into spring, Theo soon realised that he was forever changed. Through the newfound experiences his ability afforded, he had passed through a paradigm shift. He truly felt, saw and experienced a higher reality in motion. He believed without question that something higher truly did exist. Yet, he was unable to determine or define what this alternate reality looked like. He simply knew something WAS there.

A longing began to germinate deep within his own being to devote himself to a divine cause. He began to question the higher purpose of his position of employment, his job, his role within the bank. Could he achieve a higher purpose as an investment and loans trader and advisor? He questioned what he really wanted out of life. He had been with the bank for over seven years now. Was banking what he really wanted to do for the rest of his life?

As this longing progressed and took hold with no solution in sight, Theo soon found himself in a rut. He quickly spiralled into a deep depression. Psychologically, he entered a crisis of conscience and felt that he needed to step away. He needed time to think. Over the years he had accrued a great deal of annual leave. With summer one month away, Theo applied for an immediate leave of absence. He decided to pack some gear and head for the mountains.

Theo drove north out of Stockholm. He skipped from one mountain lodge to another, from one retreat to another. The first four weeks shot by briskly. His dark depression showed no signs of dissipating. He extended his leave indefinitely. By the end of the second month, he found his way to Fjällnäs, a high and relatively remote small mountain community retreat on the east bank of the long and narrow Lake Malmagen, eight hours northwest of Stockholm and close to the border with Norway.

Here, he found an abundance of solitude. During midsummer, he embarked on long extensive solitary hikes along the bank of the lake and into the surrounding mountains. By the water's edge or perched high on a rock looking across a valley, he would sit by himself for hours, thinking and reflecting upon all things of great importance.

Before long, he arrived at two conclusions.

Firstly, he was no longer suited for a life and career in banking. In his mind, he finally made the decision to resign his role at the bank. He immediately felt a small weight lift and a little lighter in disposition. The prevailing question now was, what the heck was he going to do with himself? Not short of funds, he was happy to savour his freedom for the time being.

Secondly, he no longer felt comfortable in a highly populated environment. When immersed in a crowd and surrounded by a lot of people, he was inundated with a barrage of foreign desirous and emotional stimuli. This became so overwhelming and confusing at times that he could not generate a single thought or feeling of his own. He had to leave Stockholm for a place of peace, quiet and respite within which to reside. Maybe, he should take a page from Axel's book and travel the world before deciding.

At last, he felt his dark disposition begin to turn.

Arriving home near the end of August, he awoke the next morning to a bright and glorious Sunday summer sunrise. He felt elated and refreshed. Not knowing quite how or why, his dark disposition of future dread had completely lifted and was gone. Myra soon arrived to help Axel welcome Theo's return with a delightful bundle for breakfast.

He was happy to see them both yet, with a little sadness, announced that their reunion would be short-lived.

On Monday 29th August, Theo entered his bank at 10 am and officially resigned, effective immediately. He cleared his desk, placing the few remaining personal items into a shoulder bag he brought along. With little fanfare, he wished his colleagues farewell, good fortune and walked out of the building. He stood outside, noting how rather quiet it was. He breathed in deeply, and out, savouring the moment of being free and unencumbered of commitment.

He bought a large takeaway coffee from a nearby café and decided a nice long relaxing stroll was in order. He did not realise how enjoyable the city was on a Monday. With no task, goal or design in mind, he meandered southward from the city centre and crossed a bridge onto the small island of the Riksplan. He made himself comfortable on a bench in the open park between the Helgeandsholmen and the Medeltidsmuseet exhibition centre, to bask in the warmth of the summer sun. He chuckled happily. He watched the odd passer-by and amused himself by reading a resonance at random. He was in no hurry after all.

Fifteen minutes drifted by, as did a half dozen people of no particular interest. An elderly gentleman appeared from the museum and exhibition building and walked slowly down the wide pathway towards Theo. Interestingly, he looked eccentric, dressed smartly in an older style, grey, brown tweed suit without a tie, polished black shoes and a bone-handled walking stick with a black stem. He had long lost the hair on his head and sported a five-day old silver-white manicured beard. He was shortish, reaching five foot seven inches tall, a little robust without being overweight, with fair skin and clear blue eyes.

Strangely, the elderly man wore a silk-looking, wide, round, charcoal-grey, floppy hat upon his head, the style of which Theo had never seen before. The hat looked like it was from the royal court of a medieval fairy tale. The old man walked in a regal fashion, with the fingers of his left hand tucked into the side pocket of his coat.

Intrigued, Theo focused upon and read the elderly man's resonance. There were no physical desires, no negative emotions and no mental disturbance at all. The old man was steadfast and completely balanced: confident, contented and self-assured, with the same compassion and love for humanity, society and existence that Theo now displayed.

Theo's heart leapt into his throat, his eyes widened.

He detected a resonance, the calibre, the purity of which he had never seen before. Theo had to take his time to process and correctly identify the qualities of the old man and the state of his true nature, such was its rareness. The elderly man possessed a knowingness, the attainment of a certain kind of knowledge, sacred, resulting in realisation and an acquired truly unshakeable awareness, connection to and trust in… his ideal of God above.

The elderly man noticed Theo staring at him with an expression of perplexed surprise. He tipped his hat with the handle of his walking stick as he strode past in long steady steps. The old man walked south and then turned east heading for the Strömbron Bridge. Theo was instantly spellbound, transfixed by the old man. His curiosity compelled him to follow.

Exiting the bridge, the old man turned right and approached the ferry terminal in front of the Grand Hôtel Stockholm. With timing perfect, the old man boarded the waiting ferry. Theo ran to catch up, purchased a ticket and leapt aboard just in time before the ferry cast off. The old man did notice an exasperated Theo quickly make himself inconspicuous and disappear out of sight once the ferry entered the open waterway.

The ferry made a couple of quick 'drop-off hop-on' stops before reaching Gröna Lund. Theo spied the old man preparing to disembark. Once he saw the old man safe on dry land, Theo merged in behind a large family group and was the last to disembark the ferry. Suspicious, the old man kept an eye out for him.

Gröna Lund is Stockholm's premier entertainment precinct. The theme park provides a multitude of rides, themed cafes, bars, beer gardens and an array of theatres, circus shows and music houses, with a huge array of colourful eccentric entertainers and performers. The old man entered the vast theme park. Theo followed, mingling amongst patrons as best he could.

The old man maintained a steady pace and entered an alley of sideshow game stalls all offering a chance to win a fluffy toy. Following fifteen paces behind, Theo saw the old man duck into and disappear between two stalls. Theo reached and peered into the narrow passage. It was empty. He ducked in, searched behind the stall on each side and popped back out. The old man was nowhere to be seen. At a loss, he looked up and down the alleyway.

Theo was devastated and extremely disappointed that he had lost track of the old man. His distress showed visibly on his face. He looked back into the narrow passageway, one last time. The old man had managed to evade him and was gone.

"Damn! I lost him," Theo muttered indignantly. Resigned, he gave up.

TAP! TAP! Theo felt on the back of his left shoulder.

Startled, Theo spun around. The old man stood before him with the bone handle of his walking stick raised casually shoulder high. Theo, with a stunned mullet expression, stared at the calm, composed face of the old man, unable to utter a word.

"Are you following me?" the old man asked in a soft steadfast voice.

Theo knew denial would only make him look a fool.

"Yes… I am," he said simply.

"Why? Why are you following me?"

"Because…," he began with a long thoughtful pause, "…I think you can help me. Actually, I'm quite certain you CAN help me."

"How? How do you think I can help you?"

"This might sound a bit…" he began and thought better to just say it straight, "…because I can see it in you," he said matter-of-factly.

"See it in me? What can you see in me?"

"I don't know how you would describe it. I've never seen this in anyone else before. It's like, you are devoid of all base human emotions and possess a higher state of being. It's like you possess a higher state of awareness, or maybe an expanded state of consciousness," he said.

"Really?" the old man replied a little intrigued. "You can actually see this?"

"Well, it's more like a sensation. I can read a person's core emotional resonance, which forms an image in my mind of what that person is really like under their skin," he explained.

"If you can do this, then, why would you need my help."

"Because… I'm not sure what's happening to me. I don't know how this is happening, or why?" he confessed. "And when I saw you…

when I read you… I knew you might have gone through something similar and be able to tell me what's going on."

"Ooh, right, I see!" the old man mused with a wry, flat smile. "What's your name?"

"Theo…. Themore… or just, Theo," he said nervously.

"Leif! My name is Leif," he paused momentarily. "Come with me!" he said flatly.

Leif stepped around in front of Theo and using the bone handle, motioned for him to follow.

Leif led Theo southeast out of the theme park, to a small group of five-storey, red-roof-tiled stone buildings each separated by a small lane. Leif entered the longest building on the right, which turned out to be a dormitory for the actors and performers guild. Walking through the entry foyer, Leif waved a greeting to the receptionist and led the way straight through an open archway and into the lounge bar.

The ceiling of the expansive room was dimly lit with elaborately decorated light shades which hung down from the high timber beams. The antique bar depicted an elaborately carved tragic Shakespearian scene across the front wooden panel. A huge mirror ran the height and length of the back panel behind the bar, divided by three levels of glass shelving. An impressive collection of spirit and liqueur bottles of all colours and shapes were on display, intermingled with a glorious collection of old retired puppets. Many a puppet also hung down from the ceiling over the bar, laughing at and patronising the patrons below.

Rugs of theatrical and circus scenes covered the polished wooden floor, as did tapestries on the walls. A dozen lush lounge sweats were strewn intermittently throughout the large chamber. A half dozen private booths were positioned along the far wall at both ends of the bar. Other than the romantic couple who had positioned themselves comfortably in one booth, the lounge bar was completely vacant. Leif approached the bar and turned to Theo.

"What would you like to drink?"

"Uhm, how about a double shot of Punsch, slightly chilled, since it's quite a warm day," he replied with a thin smile.

"Very well!" Leif said straight-faced.

The bartender heard the order. Leif simply held up two fingers to double it.

With drinks in hand, Leif led Theo over to a pair of wide, very comfortable leather-bound tub chairs, angled in towards each other. A circular side table was positioned between the adjoining arm of each chair. On approach, Leif motioned for Theo to take the left chair.

"This place is amazing," he commented looking at all the impressive décor. "Are you like... a member?" he asked.

"So, you want my help!" Leif said, ignoring the question. "What do you think I can do?"

"I'm quite hopeful you might know what's happening to me," he replied. "Can you help me? I just don't know where to go, or where to begin," he said, looking into his glass.

"Well, start at the beginning," Leif offered. "Tell me everything that has happened to you. Tell me the complete truth... and... don't dare leave anything out."

Theo nodded and began his tale. He told of the sequence of dreams and the events that followed each one, over the past six and a half years. He explained everything thoroughly in detail and did not leave anything out until finally falling silent when complete.

They both sipped their drinks in quiet contemplation.

"You're right!" Leif said breaking the silence. "You won't find any answers from a pastor, your mother or father, or any of your friends."

Leif sat back against the tub chair, rested his arms on either side and stretched out his legs. A crooked smile broke his expressionless face for the first time whilst he hummed... once.

"So, can you help me?"

"I can only tell you what I know."

Leif paused long enough to build tension and force Theo to be patient and listen intently.

"You've gone through a process of transformation, Theo," he began. "Let's move through the boring bits quickly, shall we. You've contemplated the existence of a high power. So, let's just say there is a God. By natural extension God has created you, your very own soul, eternal, which survives the death of the physical body. Do you think you only live one life? How ridiculously preposterous!" he yelled clicking his fingers in front of Theo.

"Now, the other problem is that there's very little in the way of explanation detailing what the soul really is, its true nature, where it goes, what's really on the other side and what actually happens there, right?" he articulated. "Are you with me?"

Theo nodded in the affirmative.

"You must take a broader view and consider that the soul actually lives more than one life and that the process of reincarnation is, in reality, a fact."

"Yes, ok!"

"Then your entire perspective shifts to a new paradigm, whereby you reorient the way you live your life towards the progression of the soul... and not the progression of just one life. And in so doing, you set yourself apart."

"Yes, yes, that's exactly how it feels," he responded on cue.

"Now we get to the good stuff," he paused. "Your total being, your consciousness, is composed of three components which are all connected. The higher self of your spirit remains permanently connected to your monad in the high heavens. The ego of your soul lives and exists on the other side of physical reality, in the next dimension. Your personality is an extension of your soul."

"When you incarnate into a physical body, it's only your personality which at first occupies the physical body. The soul only begins to make its presence known and felt during one's late teens and early twenties. And if the call is heeded, then that person may go through a process of transformation which will culminate in the soul becoming infused with the personality, within the physical body," he explained and paused.

"I believe in your case, you have received an undeniable calling by your soul and literally been forced through the most intensive process of transformation I have ever heard of. For most people, this process can take a great many years, or even lifetimes, for any significant progression to occur. You seem to have managed a leap forward in the minimum amount of time; under seven years wasn't it! And a soul is never given any more than it can handle, which leads me to believe that your soul was already quite advanced."

"How do you know all this?" he enquired a little mystified.

"Because I'm familiar with the process of transformation," Leif replied with little fanfare. "The first stage you went through was the process of calcination. You burnt away the dross of physical attachments. The second stage you experienced was dissolution, whereby you learnt to dissolve and let go of your negative emotions. The third stage you passed through was separation. Within the space of your own mind, you separated yourself from, and defeated the illusion of, your lower self. And once all the earthly materium had been cast out, you were then left with only your core essence, allowing the soul to proceed forthwith to absorb the personality and merge with the physical body, in the operation of conjunction. This is what happened to you when you were taking leave in the mountains. You now stand in the light with a soul-infused personality."

"Is that chemistry you are...," he began to question.

"Alchemy!" Leif instantly corrected. "It's alchemy... like me, of the 'old' ways."

"You... you're an alchemist?" he asked with wide-eyed incredulity.

Leif glanced back at Theo, expressionless. He displayed no intention of repeating himself.

"Now then... you still have the work of completing the remaining operations of fermentation, distillation and coagulation. You may research all this in your own good time. Although, I will say that a person cannot progress more than two operations in one lifetime, and certainly not without the guidance of a master. I surmise that your soul, apart from being advanced, was also well progressed on the path of transformation and merely had to catch up on the first two operations during this, your current incarnation."

"Well, that's all I can tell you about what's happening to you," Leif concluded.

"I cannot tell you why this is happening? You are still young... and obviously... the answer has yet to reveal itself. I dare say you have a very important purpose to fulfil sometime in the near future. Be patient. The world has a funny way of working... and before long... you will soon know the answer to that," he counselled and fell silent.

Theo was leaning back in his chair looking up at the ceiling deep in thought. He soon realised Leif was looking at him.

"Thank you. Thank you very much," he said gratefully. "You don't know how much this means to me. You've been tremendous and helped put my mind at ease."

"I do have one warning for you, Theo, which I trust you already appreciate," Leif said sternly. "Never use your ability for personal gain, or you will risk losing it altogether... or worse still... you could suffer a far greater consequence," he prophesised, hauntingly.

Waning Crescent

Feeling jubilant and buoyant, Theo left the lounge bar with business card in hand reading, 'The Poor Puppeteer'. Upon bidding farewell, he was instructed to leave a message and contact number at the bar if he wished to meet again. Leif did not seem open to making a new friendship. Instinctively, the old man knew trouble when he saw it.

Theo made his way back through the fairgrounds of Gröna Lund.

"What a strange fellow," he muttered. "I didn't learn a thing about the old man, other than he's an 'old alchemist' and that he hangs out at that bar. He's probably the owner. Ooh, wait, no, he's more like… the patriarch of that guild. I can certainly imagine Leif performing in a theatre," he grinned with a chuckle.

Theo checked his watch – 1:28 pm. Famished, he bought a small pizza from a vendor and walked back to the ferry terminal. He hopped on the next ferry planning a return to the terminal in front of the Grand Hôtel Stockholm. He thought it best to visit his parents to inform them of his new unemployed status and to say hello since his return.

Disembarking across the ferry's gangway, a tall broad-shouldered man rudely bumped Theo out of the way, as he hurriedly pushed through the line. He was six foot two, robust in build and lightly tanned, with wavy dark-brown hair cut in line with his collar. He wore a wide, black-brimmed hat, gold-rimmed sunglasses, a heavy bejewelled gold watch, shining black shoes and a very expensive navy-blue suit covered with an open long black overcoat. He carried a brief-case chained to the wrist.

Looking completely out of place, Theo could not help but notice him boarding the ferry at the previous stop, appearing agitated and constantly checking the time.

Where's your limo? Broken down, has it? He mused.

Feeling a little aggrieved, Theo casually read the man's resonance. Nothing! Bemused, he checked again, this time focusing avidly with intent. Still nothing! No matter how hard he tried he simply could not pick up an emotional reading, as though he were completely dead inside. Baffled, intrigued, he decided to follow the man from a respectful distance.

The executive walked into the Grand Hôtel Stockholm and straight up to reception. Feigning a tourist Theo followed and inconspicuously inspected a brochure nearby. He could barely hear the man speak and only managed to pick up on a few words.

"Erik Andersson," he announced upon arrival to the counter. "I'm here… meeting… arrived… ready… important… now…."

The nervous receptionist immediately directed Erik to the reserved conference room.

Erik nodded acknowledgement, turned, walked down a corridor on the left and disappeared behind a set of double doors. Theo dared not follow. Instead, he walked into the hotel's lobby café, bought himself a cappuccino and pastry and sat in a corner to watch the exit.

"Erik Andersson, hey!" he whispered. "That's the most common name you could have in Sweden. It's like 'John Smith' in America," he chuckled.

With a second empty cappuccino on the table, the stone-faced Erik finally re-emerged, walking briskly across the lobby and out through the front entrance of the hotel. Theo waited until he passed through the door before proceeding to follow. Erik's figure was easy to track.

From the hotel, Erik cut across the southern portion of the Kungsträdgården Park. He walked around behind St Jacobs Church and into Jakobsgatan, heading west. After two blocks he turned north and entered a long, inverse, triangular-shaped court adjacent to Brunkebergstorg.

Erik stopped momentarily in the middle of the open-paved court. He suddenly raised his left hand to scratch an itch behind the left ear, reacting in like manner to an insect bite. Theo paused fifteen paces directly behind Erik's left shoulder. The sun was high in the west. Erik brushed back his hair to tinker with his ear. For a fleeting moment the sunlight reflected brightly from something tiny and very shiny behind his left ear. The sharp, unmistakeable reflection caught Theo right in the eye. Theo could not see a ring or any jewellery on his hand.

Satisfied and at ease, Erik allowed his hand to fall by his side and resumed his brisk walk. He crossed the street and walked straight into the headquarters of the Sveriges Riksbank, the Central Bank of Sweden, the oldest central bank and third oldest bank in the world.

Theo stayed outside, a little bewildered and uncertain what to do. He was unsure if he should enter the building. He knew he should not follow Erik too closely and attract attention. He waited for three minutes before walking through the front entrance. He stood, searched for a moment, turned and walked straight back out. Erik was nowhere to be seen. Theo knew he was out of place. A security guard was immediately glaring at him suspiciously.

Theo returned to sit upon the stonework surrounding a fountain in the open court and pondered on what to do next. He had little choice but to wait.

"Why doesn't Erik have an emotional signature?" he pondered quietly. "Everyone has an emotional signature. You can't be... human... otherwise."

He gasped. His eyes widened. His mind raced, considering the possibilities.

"And what caused that reflection behind his ear. That was weird, right?" he muttered, before an idea struct. "An implant!" he exclaimed under his breath "It's an implant... a brain implant. It has to be, right? That would explain everything," he paused.

"Oh... my... God! If that's true... then who... no, what is Erik?" he gulped.

Theo checked his watch. He knew the bank would close at 3 pm, in ten minutes.

The bank soon closed. Theo waited. Half an hour, one hour, then two hours ticked by. He was on the verge of giving up when he heard the familiar sound of a brisk walk behind him. He knew the sound of those shoes. Already leaning forward, he peered around his left shoulder to see Erik walk past his seated position heading south. He must have used a side exit.

Theo feigned a yawn and stretched as he rose to his feet and casually turned to pursue. He followed Erik onto the Norrbro to cross Riksplan, continuing around to the other side of the Royal Palace and entered the small inner city island district of Gamla Stan from the north.

Erik soon turned left down a narrow street. Trailing far, far behind, Theo had to run to catch up. Spying round the corner, he just saw Erik turn right two blocks down, heading west. He moved quickly, jogging quietly and turned the next corner. Erik walked into a very condensed area of narrow lanes between tall and rather aged stone buildings.

Theo did his best to keep out of sight and only moved when he lost sight of Erik. Suddenly, Erik stopped and turned to confirm he was alone, before he ducked into a small heavily shaded alley with no other way out. He walked a few metres and stood in front of a heavy arched, locked wooden door with oversized wrought iron hinges. Theo crept up to the corner wall of the alley and dared not peek around.

Erik retrieved his mobile phone from his inside jacket pocket, dialled and waited to be connected.

"Good morning," he said in a flat brisk tone.

Good morning! Theo thought. *Where in the world is it morning right now? America?*

"Everything is on schedule," Erik reported. "We have majority interest. We now control the EU. You may proceed to buy the rest. Report when you have secured the US. Yes... move to the next phase and secure the communist block. Soon... we will control the entire system."

Erik promptly hung up and returned the phone to his jacket pocket. He was about to unlock the door, but stood still for a while, in thought, processing. Suddenly, with a change of mind, he turned and walked out of the alley so quickly, he bumped right into Theo.

"What the hell!" Erik gasped startled.

Erik reacted swiftly, reaching out with his left arm to grab a handful of Theo's collar as he tried to duck away from the wall. Erik recognised him.

"Are you following me?"

"What? No!" he replied feigning innocence.

He pulled back and dropped low trying to break Erik's grip of his shirt.

"Yes, you are! I remember seeing you earlier this afternoon."

Erik tightened his grip, restricting Theo's movement with ease. He leaned forward and took a good long look at Theo's face.

"What is your name?"

"Let go! You're hurting me!" he yelled.

"Tell me… what is your name? Who are you with?"

"What! I have no idea what you're talking about. Let me go," he screamed.

Theo brought his right clenched fist down hard on Erik's left wrist. The first blow did not break his grip. The second one did, and Erik let go.

Theo fell back. He scrambled to his feet and backed away as Erik simply watched. Theo spun and ran back down the lane. He turned the corner and disappeared. He ran through a twisting maze of lanes and back streets until he felt it safe to finally return home.

New Moon

Arriving home Theo recited the entire encounter with Erik to Axel while pacing between kitchen and lounge, and giving the coffee machine a workout.

"What do you think he meant by, 'control the EU'?" Theo asked.

"He had a meeting at the Grand Hôtel Stockholm and then the Sveriges Riksbank?"

"Yeah!"

"They can only be buying... stocks, right!"

"Yeah. The global economy is only just starting to recover from the GFC. Stocks are still low, at discount prices."

"They'll target banks and financial institutions, the ones that have survived."

"If you secure control over the monetary and financial system, you control everything else," Theo pondered. "But who... who would want to do this?"

"To 'OWN' the world?"

"Yeah!"

"Well! You can't do it through war anymore, now that everyone has nukes," Axel commented. "You have to own it from the top down... you know, you know how it works... and use the power of interest to acquire everything else below."

They sat in silence for a long while, simulating exactly how a takeover would play out.

"You said he had an implant! Do you think he's a human controlled by a brain implant?"

"I'm not so sure. He had no resonance, no feeling, at all. He was like... empty, dead, inside."

"Do you think he's an... android?"

"Maybe! But who could build something so... human like?"

"I don't know! Maybe… he's not… human at all," Axel pondered.

They both stared at each other, a shudder of dread ran down their spines in unison.

"Someone… or something… is taking over the planet!" Theo whispered in conclusion.

A wave of weariness suddenly overwhelmed him. Theo climbed the stairs to his room. He had a long, hot shower and collapsed into bed. He was too tired to visit his parents. Absolutely, tomorrow. It had been a really long day. He promptly fell asleep.

Deep in the dream state, Theo detected a pressure being applied to his consciousness. The source unknown, external, foreign, was a force being applied from the outside upon the bubble of his awareness, the bubble of his dream. The point of pressure was trying to penetrate his mind, through his mind's eye, the eye of his imagination, trying to force entry into his mind. It felt like a blunt instrument, pressure building and pressing upon his mind with aggressive, malicious intent.

His survival instinct quickly rose to resist. From the depths of his subconscious, the alarm bells rang sounding, 'danger, danger!' which echoed through his mind.

How? How do I resist? his mind protested.

Wake up! Wake up! resounded the answer with urgency. *Wake UP! Now! NOW!*

With warning heeded, Theo mustered the power of his now fully evolved, soul-infused will to resist, to defend himself and began the urge to wake up from deep sleep. His will drove to awaken his body. He could feel his will pushing, forcing his body to respond, again and again and again, with increasing increments of determination.

Wake up… Wake UP… WAKE UP! the command resounded loudly.

Open your eyes… open your EYES… Open Your EYES! his will surged with exertion.

He groaned out loudly. His body twisting sideways awkwardly.

Suddenly, Theo forced his eyes open. Lying across his left side, he stared directly into the adjacent corner of his room. With eyes wide open, he saw the vision of his dream, superimposed over the image of the corner of his bedroom.

His first realisation was that his eyes were really open. He felt the rise, the resurfacing, of his waking consciousness... where... the pressure of the penetrating sensation upon his mind, suddenly receded. His orientation, however, was still in a state of confusion.

Theo saw two overlaid images in his vision. Which was real and which was dream? They both seemed to move, his mind spinning. He tried hard to focus his eyes, but on what? It was impossible, his vision swimming. The dream began to fade, the corner of his room slowly solidified. Steadily, the dream vision receded, and Theo was finally left staring at the one remaining image, that of his bedroom's corner wall. The confusion dissipated and he knew exactly where he was. He was now completely awake.

The entire phenomenal experience had lasted for roughly three minutes.

Theo slowly rose into a sitting position, holding his head with his right hand. He was stunned, shocked and bemused. He instantly recalled the experience, replaying it clearly through his mind, thereby committing the entire sequence to memory.

"Wha... what the hell was that?" he muttered. "Something... just attacked me... tried to penetrate my mind... while asleep!"

Realisation and understanding solidified as to what had just transpired.

He glanced at the clock – 3:17 am. Still utterly shaken, he slowly climbed out of bed and walked to the bathroom basin to wash his face.

"What was that?" he asked of his reflection.

Theo was completely perplexed by the experience. He had never read or heard of anything like this. He thought of telling Axel and dispelled it immediately. His parents most certainly would not believe him. What about Leif? Maybe even he would have trouble with this one. In fact, Theo realised that if he told anyone of this experience, they would surely think him mad and out of his mind.

"How ironic!" he mused.

Theo decided to keep this, whatever it was, to himself.

A little after 3 am, the night after next, the exact same psychological attack happened again. Armed by the previous experience, his conscience instantly recognised the repeating threat upon his mind and rang the warning bells immediately.

This time, Theo mustered the power of his will, opened his eyes and forced himself awake in half the time. He sat bolt upright in bed, with gritty resolve.

"Who are you?" he called out in muffled tone.

He spoke more forcefully, projecting out through his mind, rather than with his voice. He felt whoever it was, would hear. Of course, there was no reply.

He experienced no further attack. With the exponential improvement following the success of his second defence, any further attempt to break his mind would only force Theo to become stronger and more powerful.

Because the experience was so real, it could never be dismissed. Theo was left to ponder, to contemplate, upon all potential perpetrators, and how he could even find a way to determine their true identity.

Was it Erik? It had to be. Erik was able to identify me. I'm a threat to them now, they to me. Yet Erik is only an agent, a pawn. So, who… or what… is behind Erik?

Are they human?

Are they of spirit, demonic?

Or are they… alien?

Lightning

Lightning

Lightning

1

Cold Murder

Sunday 2nd July 1854

The two oxen grunt, snort and blow hard as they both labour to pull the wagon to the top of the small grassy knoll, with horse in tow. Barrin gently pulls on the reins to halt, giving them time to catch their breath and recover. The glow of the predawn light begins to push the long shimmering shadows out of the vale below. A wisp of black smoke catches his sharp eye.

Arriving from the southeast, he peers out overlooking the southern bank of Crane Creek which runs along the lower foothills on the western side of Sonoma Mountain, now in the distance off his right shoulder. He is roughly nine miles north of Petaluma and ten miles southeast of Santa Rosa, in northwest California.

The sun breaches the horizon. Light rays bloom behind the mountains and instantly disperse the deep purple from the cloudless sky.

The thin line of smoke rises a few yards off the ground, wriggles and is captured by the soft morning breeze. His eyes follow the smoke to its source, a camp beside the creek, a half mile ahead, down the hill. He snaps the reins across the rump of both oxen.

After half an hour, Barrin pulls his wagon up adjacent and close to an embankment and looks down upon the strewn camp, in front of an almost dry creek bed. There is only a trickle of water. The smoke did not originate from a campfire, instead from the burnt-out wagons.

On the furthest edge of the camp, the blackened remains of two wagons lay with the undercarriage of their bellies on the ground, their wheels reduced to ash and blackened splinters. The bodies of four oxen lay dead along the dry creek bed, shot behind the ear. The entire contents from the wagons lay strewn across the ground. The horses taken.

Around the blackened campfire lay four bodies. Two men dead beneath their blanket, shot while sleeping beside the fire. A third man managed to jump to his feet, gun drawn and was shot dead in a valiant attempt to defend himself. He had fallen backwards over the campfire, his legs now burnt black and filling the air with the scent of cooked flesh.

A woman lay face down over the top of her blanket. She wore a simple double-layered full-length skirt over boots and a thick linen long-sleeved shirt beneath a tightly buttoned lady's waistcoat. She had managed to crawl a couple of feet but then stopped. There was blood on the blanket beside her hip, indicating she had been shot in the stomach.

Barrin stood up and looked around. He inspected the shrubs, small trees and tall grass that grew beside the creek. There was no one. He applied the brake to secure the wagon and jumped down to the ground. Gingerly, he walked down the embankment towards the camp.

He walked around the outer edge of the camp to survey the soft sand. The imprints clearly told the story of what happened during the night.

Five horses had quietly ridden in from the western end of the dry creek bed. The soft sand muffled their approach. They attacked by surprise two hours after midnight. The camp did not stand a chance. He walked around the wagons and moved in closer to the campfire.

"Five men!" he muttered. "Four with boots and one soft shoe, moccasins. Four bandits and a native, here to rob and kill pioneers, looking for gold."

Barrin checked the bodies of the two men wrapped in their blankets. He rolled their rigid bodies over. He pulled the half-burnt body of the third man clear of the spent campfire and laid him beside the other two. There were no guns. All their revolvers and ammunition had been taken. He then walked over to check on the woman's body.

He crouched down to turn her over and found that her body was not as frozen as the men's. She had been shot once in the stomach. The waistcoat helped to prevent a massive loss of blood. In her right hand she held a small four-shot pistol, forcing her assailants to shoot her first. A massive bruise had appeared on the right side of her face which was covered in sand. They had knocked her out with the butt of a rifle.

He used the edge of the blanket to dust the sand away revealing a very pretty, youthful face. He touched her cheek with the back of his hand. It was warm. He placed his index finger across her top lip and felt the faint warm breath of air exhaled through her nose.

"Holy crap, she's alive!" he exclaimed.

He hastily gathered a few pieces of strewn clothing, rolled them into a ball for a pillow and found a half-full waterskin before returning. He placed the pillow under her head to make her more comfortable. With a piece of wet cloth, he wiped her face and forehead.

He wet a second piece of cloth and squeezed water over her lips. He pushed gently on her chin and waited for the water to enter her mouth and trickle down her throat. He repeated this a second time. He held the back of her head up with his left hand.

"Hi there, wake up! You're safe now. Wake up, it's ok. Wake up!" he whispered softly.

A few long moments passed by. Suddenly, meekly and very weak, she opened her eyes and looked up at Barrin with large brown eyes. She moaned in deep pain and then coughed as the water began to sooth her dry, burning throat.

"Here, drink some more water," he said gently.

He squeezed some more water from the wet cloth onto her lips. After a few moments, he poured a couple of sips from the waterskin. She closed her eyes and opened them again. She managed a few more sips of water. Barrin paused to give her time to rest and recover. She stared up at him, fear in her eyes. A tear rolled back into her left ear.

"Hi, can you talk? My name is Barrin," he said softly. "You've been ambushed and robbed. I'm sorry to say all your companions have died. Can you tell me your name?"

She closed her eyes and opened them once more and strained to speak.

"Mary... Gillespie. I'm with my husband Jonathon, his brother, and his...,"

She paused and coughed violently. Blood trickled from the corner of her mouth.

Barrin wiped away the blood and offered her another sip of water.

"...friend. We were heading back south," she gulped. "They came in the middle of the night. Four, maybe five," she paused. "There was one man, a brute... dressed in black... big hat... black hair and a big moustache. You couldn't miss him."

Mary closed her eyes. Barrin administered another sip of water.

"They were looking for gold... the goldfields are all but finished now, you see. They thought we had gold," she coughed violently.

Another thin trail of blood trickled down from the left corner of her mouth across her cheek. Her head rolled a little to the left.

"Tell the sheriff... tell the sheriff what happened... tell them to..."

Mary stared vacantly past Barrin into the sky... and died.

He placed his hand lightly upon her chest and when he was sure there was no heartbeat, he laid her head down and stood up. He surveyed the campsite once more.

Barrin returned to his wagon to retrieve a small spade. He dug four shallow graves at the base of the embankment. Keeping them in their clothes, he wrapped each body in a blanket and placed one in each grave and covered them over with sand. He found and retrieved stones from the creek to place over each grave and stood back satisfied an hour before high noon.

"Well, that's all I can do. The wolves will probably dig 'em up," he mumbled.

He looked over at the dead oxen.

"Maybe I can give 'em a diversion."

He walked over to the oxen and withdrew a long, sharp, curved dagger from a sheath behind his belt. He sliced open the bloated bellies of all four animals. Their entrails spilled out onto the sand. He carved a few prime cuts, salted them and wrapped them in a linen cloth, for himself. He washed his blade and arms in the creek water and turned towards his wagon.

It was mid-afternoon when Barrin finally left the camp sight to continue northward. As he sat in the seat, gathered and slapped the reins to move the wagon forward, he glanced across his right into the distance. High up on a faraway hill, four Indians sat upon their horses watching him from afar. The early morning smoke trail had also piqued their curiosity.

Barrin travelled a further four miles north before stopping to make camp for the night. He found a thick grove of trees with a small clearing on one side. He parked his wagon and made camp in the clearing. Finding some stones, he made a very small campfire and cooked himself a meal from a cut of oxen meat, with bread and cheese from his stores.

As the campfire burned down to glowing coals, he arranged a bed of sand beside the fire and threw a blanket over the top to make it appear as though a body lay there asleep. With a second navy-blue blanket and musket rifle in hand, he nestled in between the roots at the base of the largest tree only a few yards away from the campfire. A row of thick shrubs blocked the way behind him. He lay close to his two oxen who were tethered to the neighbouring tree. They would sound the alarm if anything spooked them.

Well camouflaged, he had a clear view of the camp. The coals burnt out permitting the darkness to set in. All was quiet and he fell asleep.

2

A Saint of Roses

As was customary, Barrin would wake in the predawn darkness an hour before the first rays of light appeared behind the horizon. He lay there for a long while listening. The birds leapt to the highest branches to cheer the imminent arrival of their beloved golden orb. He enjoyed the sound of the cool predawn breeze beginning to stir in excited anticipation the new day. It was at this moment he always felt most at peace.

Satisfied he was completely alone and just as he saw the first ray of light break through the night sky, he rose slowly from his burrow. He moved quickly and broke camp efficiently and was on his way within a quarter of an hour, continuing northward.

Allowing his oxen to take a gentle pace, Barrin took most of the day to travel the remaining six miles to Santa Rosa. He did pull up under the shade of a red spruce tree for an hour during the middle of the day to rest and water his two oxen. It was three o'clock in the afternoon when he entered the southern outskirts of town.

Originally a small Mexican outpost, Santa Rosa had grown through the gold rush and the influx of settlers into quite a bustling borough. The town boasted two dozen large buildings of business and trade, several saloons and brothels, a couple of general stores, the sheriff's jail, two hotels, a doctor and surgery, several blacksmiths, a tanner, barns of livestock and feed, and a caretaker for the dead. A sprawl of small houses and cottages appeared around the larger buildings and spanned out to the outer limits of town.

Barrin drove his slow wagon down the main street and stopped outside what looked like a well-established general store, with a stable and quarters built behind the main building. He applied the brake to secure the wagon and dismounted. He climbed the three steps, walked across the porch and entered the store. A small doorbell rang.

He looked around to find himself the only customer in the store. Behind the counter stood a tall woman with thick shoulders and arms, a light-brown complexion and a mass of thick wavy black hair. She had a round voluptuous face with thick eyebrows, nose and lips, wore a full-length black and red dress, and watched him through large dark-brown eyes. A thin vase of three red roses was positioned upon the middle of the counter, a ruse to placate aggression.

"Good afternoon, madam!" he greeted loudly.

He stepped around a row of shelves stacked with stock and approached the counter.

"My name is Barrin Cade Balthasar," he proudly announced.

"Well, hello… Barrin!" she replied in a thick Mexican accent.

She ran a discerning eye over his appearance. Barrin was twenty-eight years old, five foot six inches tall, with a lean agile muscular disposition, making him appear a little smaller than the average person. With darker than normal olive skin and a clean and youthful face, he gave the impression of being somewhat innocent. He had short-cut, messy, light-brown hair, a thin face, eyebrows, nose and lips, and intense hazel eyes. Yet he carried himself in a confident self-assured manner, displaying no sign of malice.

Barrin dressed in a manner between that of a Mexican and a cowboy. He wore rancher's boots, the tough leather hides of a horseman, and a long-sleeved cotton shirt with a bandana tied around his neck. He threw a Mexican poncho over to cover and hide the top half of his body and topped it with a smaller-sized sombrero hat, adapted and shaped to his taste.

He holstered two, long-barrelled, six-shot pistols, one on each hip. The handle of the pistol on the left hip, was facing forward in reverse. Both holsters were affixed to a fully loaded bullet belt around the waist. The belt housed two small throwing knives, one tucked in behind each hip, and a long curved, sheathed knife tucked in behind the middle of his back.

"I'm Marrinella," she replied with a broad smile. "Welcome to my general store."

She waved her left arm in a wide arc to present her well-stocked store to Barrin. He looked around at the store impressed with the variety of goods on display.

"Your name's unusual," she noted. "I've not heard of a Balthasar before. Where're you from?"

"I started out from Oakland, east across the bay from San Francisco. I headed northeast around Mount Diablo and took the Kirker Pass between Walnut Creek and Pittsburgh, and then headed east to Stockton," he explained, cheerily recounting his trek. "I followed the San Joaquin River, crossed the Sacramento River and stayed west of the Sonoma Mountains. I began a month ago... the start of June," he beamed with delight.

"No, no! I mean... your skin! It's brown not red, and you ain't Mexican or Spanish. So, where're you from... originally?"

"Oh, right!" he said, pausing.

Barrin looked down to inspect the skin tone on the back of his hand with solemn expression.

"I don't rightly know where I was born. Somewhere between Greece and Persia. My parents were merchants, traders and travelled... a lot. I think I might be Sumerian... or maybe Persian. I can't seem to remember which."

"Well, I'm sorry to say, I'm not sure where that is," Marrinella confessed.

"I grew up mostly in Cairo, Egypt."

"Ooh, I've heard of that place."

"When I was thirteen, my father sent me to school in London for five years, to learn geography, history and mathematics. I think he wanted me to grow the family business into shipping throughout the British Empire."

"And how did you manage to get to San Francisco?"

"Well, after school I returned to Cairo, to work for my father. A few years ago, I heard about America. I saw pictures. I dreamed to see America. Three years ago, I bought passage on a British ship to see this new colony of Hong Kong, via the Cape of Good Hope and India. Then I travelled to an amazing place called Japan, stayed there for two years and even met the emperor. Anyway, I finally found a Russian trade ship bound for San Francisco and that is how I landed in America."

"Wow, sounds like one amazing adventure. And so young!" Marrinella exclaimed. "There's some people round here who've not travelled more than ten miles outta town."

"Well, I was wondering if you can help me," he said with a pause. "I'm looking to restock some provisions… and… lodging for a night."

"Yes, of course I can provide any provisions you need and a stable at the back as well. However, lodgings and supper you'll find at the saloon across the street."

"I prefer to avoid the saloon. I seem to attract unkind attention on account some folks tend to think I'm a native Indian when drunk. I would prefer a nice quiet place to rest."

"Ok, then. There's a small workers' cottage behind the stable. I have a couple of helpers who normally stay there, but they've gone home for a few days. It's the 4th of July tomorrow, you see. You can stay there for a night," she explained.

"I'm very grateful. Thank you."

"I live up top with my old man. He can't do much anymore. Bring your wagon around back and stable your horse and oxen. I'll bring you supper once I close the store."

"That sounds perfect," he replied graciously.

Barrin proceeded to quickly collect the provisions that he needed: salt, sugar, coffee, flour; bread, a few jars of pickled vegetables, a couple of rolls of dried sausage meat, a generous cut of cheese; an assortment of grain to refill his grain bins on the wagon, feed for his animals; soap, a new cotton shirt, socks; lengths of leather straps for the wagon, rope, a roll of thick linen material; and a small tin of boiled lollies. He paid for everything in American dollars.

"That's quite a haul you have there," she said. "So, what do you do… for a dollar?"

"Hmm… let's see. How can I describe it. I kind of… help people," he chuckled.

"How so?"

"Well… most of the time, the people I help don't even know they need it. I generally run into a person who is in a bit of a mess… or a crisis… and I just… help 'em out," he shrugged.

"Are you a lawman… like a sheriff?"

"No, no, I'm not a sheriff. Sometimes though, someone will be having a tough time, so I help make things right... if you know what I mean?"

"Ummm, well... not really," she replied a little confused.

"It's different every time... for each person," he paused. "It's complicated!" he said rolling his eyes and waving it away with his left hand. "Well, thank you once again, Marrinella. I'll load all these things onto my wagon and bring it round the back."

"Yes, yes... it's been a pleasure," she said checking her timepiece. "It's almost time to close the store. I'll bring you supper in an hour or so, once you've settled in."

Barrin gathered his goods and loaded them aboard his wagon at the front of the store. Sitting relaxed against the wall on the porch in front of a saloon across the street and three buildings further down, a small group of men amused themselves watching him work.

Remaining on foot, Barrin walked to the front of his wagon, took hold of the reins and guided his oxen to turn the wagon around. The full circle of the turn was right in front of the saloon. He glanced over the head of his oxen and, with a sharp eye, took note of the group loitering upon the deck all peering his way.

He walked his wagon back and then down the southern lane beside the general store and around to the rear of the building. He stopped to inspect the layout.

The general store was a two-storey building, with the shop at ground level and living quarters above on the first floor. Adjoining the rear of the store was a row of four stables facing the workers' cottage across a courtyard. The stables were separated in half by a walkway leading to the rear door of the main building. There was also a small, enclosed animal pen at the furthest end of the courtyard. The courtyard was shaded by a Mexican-style pergola.

Barrin brought the wagon around behind and parked it alongside the north-facing wall of the cottage. He locked the wheels in place. His wagon was just a few feet short of being in front of the animal pen. This made it easy to remove the yoke, untether and pen his oxen. He made sure they both had some of his special feed mix, hay and water.

Each night, before leaving his oxen, Barrin would stand in front of each one and run the palm of his right hand slowly down the middle of their face to the tip of their nose and then caress their ears for a minute or so. They had become very accustomed to this kindness, were completely at ease and never displayed any resistance.

He now tended to his horse tied to the rear of the wagon. He filled a bucket with water and using a heavy cloth, washed him down from nose to ankles. He scraped the water off with a thick leather strap. His young palomino stallion stood perfectly still and enjoyed a long rub under the cheekbone to end the ritual. He led his horse into the fourth stable with feed and water waiting. He pushed the bolt home to secure the stable door and turned for the cottage.

The sun dipped below the horizon and dusk was fast approaching.

As Barrin strode across the courtyard, four men appeared from the southern laneway and fanned out loosely in a straight line.

"Well, who might yer be, taking hospitality of our lovely Marrinella?" asked a big, burly, rough-looking man, in a deep menacing manner.

Barrin slowed his gait right down without flinching, continuing his walk across the courtyard in slow motion. He took stock of each man from the saloon.

The one speaking, their leader, was wearing a wide black-brimmed hat, a black full-length jacket over a soiled white shirt, thick black leather pants and boots, and a pistol holstered on his right hip with a mostly empty bullet belt. He had thick black, wavy hair, stubble and a large, thick black moustache.

The man to his left was tall, thin and gaunt looking. He wore a nice pair of shiny tan boots, loose-fitting brown pants cut an inch too short, a long-sleeved off-white shirt, waistcoat and a smallish cowboy hat. He also wore a six-shot pistol holstered on the right hip with bullet belt. He displayed a long thin sheathed knife tucked into the front of his gun belt, which also doubled as his favourite cheese knife.

The man to his right was of medium height, chubby and overweight, but solid and strong. He wore a white baggy long-sleeved shirt and baggy brown pants made of thick stonewashed linen. He appeared to be the miner he was. He wore a six-shot pistol on his right hip with no bullet belt and preferred to hold a loaded musket, on account of being too slow on the draw.

The man lurking further back in the shadows was a Pomo Indian. He wore the native loin-cloth over a pair of baggy deerskin pants, held in place by a thick leather strap and had donned a pair of Indian-style moccasins. He wore a leather open-cut double-lined sleeveless shirt stitched around the edges, with three buttons down the front. He wore several beaded necklaces, an eagle feather in his braided hair and sported scars across arms and shoulders. A pistol was tucked into his front belt and two sheathed knives behind his back. Spare bullets were kept in a small leather pouch attached to the right-hand side of his belt, given he was left handed.

Suddenly, a bright golden light appeared and illuminated the interior of the wagon. The light splashed across the wall of the cottage and across the northern portion of the courtyard. A fifth man had snuck in around back, climbed into the wagon, found a small chest behind the front driver's seat, picked the lock and carefully pushed open the lid.

"Wahoo!" he squealed with delight.

Barrin moved with lightning speed. He turned swiftly and ran the few paces to his wagon. He leapt up the side rail, onto the driver's seat and stooped through the front opening of the canopy. He stepped over the front seat and chest into the interior and landed a forceful kick right in the middle of the intruder's chest, while his eyes were gleaming in the glow of golden light. The intruder flew back through the air and landed on his back upon the rear edge of the wagon. His legs swung up in the air and over his shoulders as he fell out of the wagon, landing awkwardly on his belly across the ground.

Barrin hastily closed the chest and locked the latch once more. The golden light which illuminated the interior vanished, returning the wagon to darkness.

The Mexican leapt to his feet and ran back around the cottage to appear beside his boss.

"Gold, gold... he has a chest of gold!" he yelled.

Barrin turned and swiftly reappeared to stand on the step, the foot rest, in front of the driver's seat of his wagon. With a steely poised expression, he stared directly at the Mexican.

The Mexican was dressed in a loose-fitting pair of thick black trousers, black riding boots and a baggy, long-sleeved, open-cut white shirt, now sporting a patch of dirt on its front. He wore a six-shot pistol on his right hip with a half empty bullet belt. A second pistol was tucked into his belt in front of his belly. In his left hand, he held his large Mexican sombrero hat which had fallen off his head behind the wagon, revealing short messy, black hair slick with sweat, and a thick black moustache across his top lip.

"Gold… there's a chest full of gold in that wagon!" the Mexican announced once more.

The big one in black nodded, pushed the Mexican away and stepped forward glaring at Barrin. The other men followed the lead and fanned out in a semi-circle across the courtyard.

Barrin jumped down from the wagon, walked forward three paces and stood facing the group with a very relaxed posture. With cold sharp eyes he now calmly glared back at the big man in black. Fifteen yards separated Barrin from the five men.

"Yer have gold… a chest of gold, I hear," the big one spat. "How did… a scrawny little man like yer get yer hands on a chest of gold?" he said. "The gold in those, there mountains are all but gone now. Did yer steal it?"

"It's not gold!" Barrin stated flatly.

"It looks like gold. It smells like gold. So, it must be gold. I think yer a LIAR," he snarled loudly. "Yer just wanna keep it all for yerself, don't yer!"

"It's not gold," Barrin calmly reaffirmed.

"If it's not gold, what is it then, huh?"

"It's not gold. You can't sell it and it's not for you."

"Well, I'll be the judge of that. Why don't yer just go on back there, get that chest, bring it down here and open it, so we can all see if yer telling the truth."

"I can't do that."

"Well maybe we oughta just do it for yer, then," the big one said taking a step forward.

Suddenly, just at that moment, Marrinella walked out of the main building, along the path between the stables and appeared on the edge of the courtyard. She instantly froze, holding a tray with a plate of supper and orange juice, realising she had just walked into a standoff.

"Jack Beuford… stop this at ONCE!" she decreed.

Everyone, except Barrin, turned at once to stare at Marrinella.

"What do you think you're doing? Causing trouble, are you?" she scolded. "Where's your hospitality? Barrin's my guest and there'll be no fightin' here on my premises tonight."

"Barrin? What kinda name is Barrin?" Jack asked, casting a snarly look at Barrin.

"He's... exotic... from a faraway land. You wouldn't know, anyhow," she said. "Tomorrow's the 4th of July. Why aren't y'all over at the saloon having a drink to celebrate?"

Turning his gaze from Barrin, Jack looked once more at Marrinella, his intent wavering.

"Jack! It's suppertime," Marrinella continued. "Why don't you take your tall Frenchman Louis Reitt, and chubby Galvin Cooper over to the saloon for a feed. Galvin looks like he's starving. He hasn't stopped looking at my tray this whole time. Peirdro Martino, I'm disappointed in you. Where's your woman? You should be at home looking after your woman. And George Gomatchu Littlegrass! Why are you hanging out with this bunch of trouble? Don't you have a family? Why aren't you back with your Pomo tribe, looking after your family? Don't you have a woman either?" she scolded. "Men who don't have a woman are always making mischief. Isn't that right, Jack?"

"Guess yer might have something there... ma'am," Jack confirmed, unable to fault her logic.

He decided against killing someone with a respected lady of town as witness.

"Come on, boys... let's go get us some dinner then," Jack said.

Jack took a step back, half turned to Marrinella and tipped his hat.

"A'right then... enjoy your evening with... Barrin. Good night, m'lady."

"Good night, Jack."

Marrinella offered Jack a slight nod of the head in gratitude and a curtsy. Jack turned on his heel and walked down the lane with a jovial swag, leading his men back to the saloon.

Once they were gone, Barrin turned to Marrinella as she approached with tray in hand.

"Thanks for your help. I certainly didn't wish to cause any trouble."

"Oh, that's alright. Those boys are up to no good. They've been hangin' around town for a couple of months now and only seem to be looking for trouble. I bet they'll be back. Here's your supper," she said, handing Barrin the tray.

"Thank you," he said, famished. "Smells wonderful."

Marrinella half turned, but before going back inside she asked, "So, what was it they wanted? I thought I heard them talk about gold?"

"I have no gold," he affirmed immediately. "That Mexican was snooping around my wagon. He found a small chest which has been in my family for generations. It's a small heirloom that's very valuable to me. It has no value other than that."

"Intriguing! I'm sure, like you, it has an interesting story. Well, good night, Barrin."

"Good night, ma'am," he replied.

Barrin watched Marrinella walk through the stables and into the main building. He sat on the porch of the cottage, ate his supper and left the tray on the floor in front of the door. He returned to his wagon and waited. He waited until a full hour after all the lights were put out in the main building. There was light enough beneath the half moon.

An hour before dawn, in the pitch black of night, Jack and his men silently crept up to the front door of the cottage. Turning the unlocked latch, they burst in, lighting up the two-room cottage with a kerosene lantern. They stripped the two low-set cots.

"Empty… it's empty," Galvin announced.

"The wagon's gone, and so are his two oxen and horse," George reported.

The Pomo Indian followed the tracks northward down the back lane and returned to the front of the cottage a short time later, where Jack was waiting.

"He left four, maybe five hours ago. He didn't sleep here. He'll camp somewhere out there," George waved into the northern sky with his left hand.

"Smart lad! He packed up and left as quiet as a squirrel," Jack said scornfully. "Anyone carrying that much gold would know we'd be back. Let 'im have his head start. We'll ride out at first light and catch 'im in the hills. Better out there than here in town, anyhow."

The gang dowsed the lantern and peeled away into the darkness to collect their horses.

3

A Horse's Arse

For two days Barrin steered his wagon northward, setting a solid pace. He would make camp just as the last rays of light sank into the west, always among a thicket of trees and shrubs. He would rise and be on his way again two hours before sunup. During the middle of the day, he would rest his two oxen under shade and give them feed and water.

Then he would saddle his horse and backtrack a mile or two in a wide sweep, which he repeated once he made camp for the night. He found the gang in hot pursuit each time he rode out. He observed them for a while from the edge of a hill or from under the shadow of a distant tree. He did not give them an opportunity to set an ambush.

During the mid-afternoon of the third day, beneath a clear hot blue sky, some twenty-three miles north of Santa Rosa, Barrin led his wagon out onto a large dry basin of hard earth, sand, stone and rock. There was only a sparse covering of ankle-high shrubs and spinifex. He judged the basin to be about four miles in distance and slowed his wagon to a gentle walk. He did not want to tire or overheat his oxen. He also wanted to give his pursuers time to catch up, as he aimed for a line of trees at the opposite end.

With less than half a mile to go before reaching the tree line, the gang rode out from those very trees directly in front of him. They had ridden around his right flank, reached the tree line and cut back left to be directly in his path. Jack decided it was to their advantage to intercept Barrin on clear open ground, with greater numbers and the tree line at their back.

The gang rode out in a V formation. Jack led, with Galvin and Peirdro behind his right shoulder, and Louis and George Littlegrass behind his left shoulder. Galvin, Louis and George Littlegrass each had their loaded musket rifles at the ready, with the butts resting atop their thighs and barrels pointed into the air. They slowed to a canter and stopped fifteen yards in front of Barrin in a small cloud of dust.

"Well, well, who do we have here? We meet again, Mr Barrin!" Jack announced.

Barrin gently pulled on the reins to halt his wagon and pressed his foot on the brake. He tied the reins loosely through the metal loop in front of his seat and slowly stood up. His feet were wide apart and slightly offset to give himself the best balance.

"And so… here we are!" Barrin concurred. "What do you want… Jack?" he shouted.

"Yer know very well what we want! We want a share of that fine gold yer have stashed in yer wagon. There's no lady to save yer this time," he chuckled, mockingly. "So… how about yer just hand it over… like a good fella," he said, scowling at Barrin.

"You're a horse's arse Jack!" Barrin fired back. "You should've stayed a miner. Better still, you would find life much more rewarding mating with a fat sow in a filthy pig pen, than murdering good folk in their blankets before sunrise."

Jack, stunned by the insult was, for a moment, lost for words. Barrin continued his taunt.

"You're a yellow belly snake, Jack. You're a fool, leading your band of idiots out here into the open. Jackarse. Yes… jackarse! That's what you are, Jack. A JACKARSE," Barrin yelled.

Jack's temper fired. He instantly lost complete control of rational thought. With his right hand he reached down to draw his pistol as fast as he could.

At that very moment the golden specks in Barrin's eyes flared and began to glow with a subtle hue. The olive skin all over Barrin's body also began to glow with a very subtle, almost imperceptible golden hue. And in that instant Barrin drew with lightning speed.

With his right hand, Barrin drew the pistol from his hip and, in the same moment, with his left, drew a pistol out from his right ribcage beneath the poncho. As Jack's hand reached the handle of his pistol, Barrin fired two shots in quick succession. The first bullet took Jack's thumb off clean at the first major knuckle. The second bullet took his index finger clean at the second knuckle, as the finger was being extended towards the trigger.

Barrin extended his left arm straight out in front, with pistol in a horizontal position. Moving in an arc from right to left in a straight line, he released three shots in quick succession. Each bullet hit the trigger and metal casing of the musket rifles of George Littlegrass, Louis and Galvin, ricocheting with high-pitched metallic sounds. The tips of Louis and Galvin's right index fingers were nicked. George did not have his finger near the trigger.

Peirdro moved to draw the pistol tucked in behind his front belt. As his hand reached for the handle and with index finger extended, a fourth bullet hit him at the base of the finger, and smashed into the metal of the pistol. Both Jack and Peirdro screamed out in agony.

The sound of gunfire, ricochets and screams startled their horses. Galvin's horse jolted forward. Not holding the reins properly, he rolled backwards off the horse and tumbled onto the ground. Louis' horse lurched to the left and almost flipped him out of the saddle. He was forced to drop his musket and grab hold of the horse's mane and neck to fight for control, while the horse bolted for the trees with Louis clinging onto its right side.

Jack's horse reared. With his wounded right hand jammed into his belly, he gripped the reins hard with his left, squeezed hard with his legs and managed to stay on. The horse, not happy with the rough treatment, tried to buck but Jack yelled and kicked into the ribs forcing the horse into a gallop after Louis. Peirdro looked down at his mangled hand with tears of pain in his eyes. He turned and followed Jack, with only the thought of self-preservation.

Galvin scrabbled to his feet. He drew his pistol while running towards a large rock only a few paces away. As Galvin stepped forward with his right foot, Barrin fired from his left pistol. The bullet smashed Galvin's big toe as he brought his foot to ground. He completely stumbled, falling hard and flat across the front of his body, hitting his forehead on a flat stone, knocking him out cold.

Lastly, with extended right arm, Barrin aimed his pistol directly at the head of George Littlegrass. After dropping the musket, he managed to keep his horse calm and under control and did not reach for another weapon. He simply half raised both hands in surrender.

Barrin flicked the barrel of his pistol in the direction of Jack. George slowly gathered the reins, turned and cantered off after Jack. The subtle glow behind Barrin's eyes and around his skin subsided. The gunfight was all over in the space of seven seconds.

Barrin holstered his weapons, grabbed the reins, released the brake and jolted the wagon forward. He aimed for the tree line half a mile further west. As his wagon approached the first row of trees, he retreated and lay low, out of sight behind the driver's seat inside the canopy. He simply allowed his oxen to find their way through the bush. Feeling safe after a couple of hundred yards, he reemerged to steer the wagon northward once more.

On an outcrop of rock far off in the distance to the east, Barrin had noticed a group of four Indians sitting upon their horses, watching the events unfold down below. They were the same group of Indians he had spotted near the camp of murdered pioneers.

George rounded up Galvin's runaway horse and returned to revive him with a splash of water over his head. The gang made camp in a gully a short distance inside the tree line from where they had emerged to intercept Barrin. Dusk was approaching. Jack, Peirdro and Galvin were each tending to their wounds beside the campfire.

"Aargh!" Jack grimaced in pain.

He seared the end of his thumb and finger with the red-hot side blade of his knife pulled from the fire and wrapped his hand in a strip of linen cloth.

"He shot me thumb and finger off... dammit," he grimaced once more. "He gotcha in the finger too... Peirdro!"

Jack stared at Peirdro's hand while he seared his own wound in grief.

"And he gotcha in the toe."

Jack turned to gaze at the wreckage of Galvin's exposed right foot.

"Have yer ever seen anyone shoot like that?" Jack exclaimed. "I've never seen anyone shoot like that before!" he answered. "Do yer think it was pure dumb luck?"

"Nah! I think he hit every target he meant to," Louis replied. "Look at my rifle."

He held his rifle up for everyone to see.

"He shot the trigger out. And he did the same to Galvin's and George's rifles too. No one's that lucky!" Louis said and paused. "And there was something funny about his eyes. Did you see his eyes?"

All the men nodded, except for George Littlegrass.

"Yeah… they glowed… like the wild eyes of a creature in the night. He wasn't afraid either. In fact, he seemed possessed… of a spirit… a spirit of fire. I haven't seen anything like this before, but this… Barrin, is no ordinary man."

"Well, maybe," Jack said. "Did anyone get a shot off?"

Jack looked around at all his men.

"Anyone? No one!"

No affirmation was forthcoming.

"Then, one thing is for sure, we're up against a bona fide gunfighter. We can't go up against 'im head on and face to face like that again."

"You sure you wanna go after this guy. I reckon he coulda killed us all if he wanted to," Galvin protested.

"Well, maybe he shoulda, but he didn't, did he. And he's still got all that gold!… We have nothin'… nothin'! We gotta find a way to trap 'im and then we can get that gold. What do we have after toiling in those mountains for all this time… nothin'. We have nothin' to show for it," Jack scolded Galvin and his men.

"And he called me a jackarse. Nobody calls me that. So, the way I see it, we don't have a choice but to get that gold. We'll just follow 'im and see where he goes. Sooner or later, he'll make a mistake and we can trap 'im and kill 'im," Jack asserted. "Right, get some rest. We'll ride out at first light."

4

A Storm Approaches

For ten days Barrin continued to travel north-northwest and covered another hundred miles. He kept the mountains on his right and the hills, creeks, plains and the coastline to his left, through the hot July sun. Every night he made camp in a thicket of trees and small shrubs. He cooked his meals during the middle of the day and did not light a campfire at night. At dusk he would ride his horse to backtrack the approach to his camp.

On several occasions, Barrin and George Littlegrass watched each other from afar, before Barrin turned and rode back to his wagon. George Littlegrass was riding on point, ahead of Jack's gang to track Barrin's progress. He reported to Jack that Barrin was well aware he was being hunted.

Jack knew he could not mount a surprise attack on Barrin while he was in camp, where the thicket itself was used as a defensive barrier. Jack was quite sure Barrin would be hidden, and his camp rigged to be a trap. So, they continued their pursuit and waited, patiently.

The following morning a huge mass of dark cloud started building up over the ocean far to the west. The temperature dropped and a strong westerly gust picked up and quickly grew with intensity. A massive violent storm was approaching.

Barrin steered closer to the mountains looking for a place to shelter his animals and wagon. He hurriedly followed a creek northward, upstream, which turned eastward and opened out onto a small plateau. At the furthest end of the small plateau was a shallow rocky cliff face, rising in height from left to right. The source of the creek flowed from a small waterfall at the lower end of the cliff face.

The right-hand side of the cliff curved around into a hook shape and abruptly disappeared into the sheer granite rock of the mountain that the plateau butted up against. The gully within the hook of the shallow cliff would provide ample shelter for his wagon and animals.

Along the middle length of the cliff face, Barrin found a cave with a high narrow inverted V-shaped entrance. Strewn along the creek and around the small plateau were rusting panes, shovels, picks and other mining equipment, long abandoned. The creek proved to be barren of gold.

He steered the wagon up close to the entrance, stepped on the brake and tethered the reins. He whistled. No response. Tentatively he walked inside to inspect the cave.

The floor of the cave was in the shape of a J, turning left by roughly forty degrees after ten yards from the entrance and curved around by another four yards. The main interior of the cave was shaped like a teardrop, a round chamber with a narrow, high-pointed ceiling. The middle of the rock floor was scarred black by fire, where the miners had drilled a chimney through the highest point of the ceiling. The cave was also littered with discarded miner's equipment: rotting rope, knapsacks, cups, plates tobacco tins and other personal items. He decided the cave and plateau would be the perfect shelter from the storm.

Barrin moved his wagon a little further to the right, in line with the highest portion of the cliff face. The wagon was protected by the westerly wind. He locked the brake in place and secured it. He brought his oxen around behind and tied them to the back of the wagon with his horse inside a roped corral, using the wagon as a further windbreak. He rubbed their cheeks to ease their nervous tension and hoped the tethers would be strong enough to prevent them running away in panic from any lightning.

He secured the front and rear flap to the wagon's canopy and tied everything down with all the rope he had on board. He gathered as many twigs and fallen branches as possible from around the gully and started a small campfire inside the cave. He waited outside for the initial smoke to clear through the chimney until he had a nice pile of glowing red-hot coals, before he brought his blanket and kit into the cave to prepare his evening supper.

A foreboding darkness loomed late in the afternoon. Preceded by a howling wind and volley of lightning the storm broke. The rain fell thick and hard, at almost a thirty degree angle. The wind was a tempest of gusts and swirls. The lightning cracked loud with flashes of bright, white light. The oxen and horse cowered gratefully behind their barricade of wagon.

Standing just inside the entrance to the cave, Barrin watched and listened to the storm unleash its fury. He glanced out now and then to check that the wagon remained secure and the animals had settled down to calmly wait out the storm. Satisfied, he returned to the cave and sat on a rock behind his mound of hot coals, tending to his supper and brew of hot tea.

An hour after the storm broke, the sun finally set, pitching the creek, the stony plateau with its small gully and surrounding forest along the mountainside into a howling, wet darkness. The occasional flash of light cast instant ghoulish shadows across the entrance to the cave. The storm settled in for a long night.

Holding the reins as tightly as he could, George Littlegrass led Jack and his men in single file along the same trail Barrin used, to make their way upstream beside the creek. The gang arrived and stood on the edge of the plateau. They fanned out on either side of Jack and could all see the faint glow emanate from the cave.

The occasional flash of lightning lit up the oxen, horse and wagon a short distance to the right of the cave. The gang quietly peeled back into the forest below the lip of the plateau. They tethered their horses to a couple of small trees. Jack pulled his musket out from its sheath beside the saddle of his horse.

"Peirdro, give Galvin your rifle. He's too slow with a pistol," he commanded.

As Peirdro handed Galvin his musket, Jack continued.

"Now Peirdro… go round the back of that wagon and get inside. See if yer can find that chest of gold. We'll stand behind that line of trees just in front of the wagon and watch the cave."

Peirdro nodded and crept along the line of trees on approach to the front of the wagon. He quietly crept around to the rear of the wagon and checked to make sure all four men were ready and watching his back. He unsheathed his dagger and sliced a vertical cut into the fabric covering the entrance into the wagon. Squeezing through the slender opening, he crawled inside. He waited for flashes of lightning to proceed.

A row of two upright barrels were positioned against the left panel, followed by a long bench seat under which was stored wooden crates. A low row of wooden cabinets ran along the right-hand panel, each with a liftable lid, which contained food stores and supplies. Rolled up bedding was tied across the top of these cabinets. A newly fashioned wooden box was recently installed behind the driver's seat which served the dual purpose of being a step and was secured with a padlock. A roll of two blankets was tied to the top of this small box.

Peirdro cut loose the roll of blankets, picked the padlock and opened the lid. Inside was the chest he had opened some two weeks earlier. The chest was antique. It was made of a very dark, hard red wood. All the edges and corners were set in ornately fashioned cast iron joinery. There were cast iron handles on both sides of the chest, held in place by cast iron bolts drilled through the entire width of the thick wooden panel. The chest contained a built-in lockable latch, now blocked by the outer box.

Crouching forward, Peirdro squeezed his hands into the narrow space and grasped the handle on each side of the chest. He lifted. The chest did not budge. He ran his hand around the perimeter of the chest inside the box to check for obstructions. There were none. He set a stronger lifting position and with increasing applications of pressure tried to lift the chest out of the wooden box. The chest would not budge. He clasped both hands around the handle on the right and tried to lift just one end of the chest. It did not move. He gave up and decided to leave the wagon and report back to Jack.

"Boss… I found the chest. But it won't move. I can't lift the chest at all. Maybe he bolted it to the wagon," he quietly whispered to Jack.

"What! What yer mean yer can't lift the chest?" Jack exclaimed in frustration. "Watch the cave," he barked to the other men in a hushed tone.

Peirdro led Jack down the obscured side of the wagon. Jack inspected the planking beneath the driver's seat. He ran his hand along the under-belly and could not detect any hole or bolt. Satisfied, he quietly slipped into the wagon and stood over the open box with the exposed chest inside. He bent down, grabbed hold of both handles and lifted. His face turned red with exertion. He tried everything Peirdro had tried. It was futile. The chest simply would not budge.

Jack turned to glare at Peirdro, who simply shrugged his shoulders. They were both at a loss. Jack stepped down from the wagon, his red face swelling with rage. He returned to the trees.

"If we break that box, we'll give ourselves up," Jack whispered to his men. "Right now, we have the advantage of surprise. Get yourselves ready. We're going to storm that cave and get that bastard," he announced and continued. "Peirdro, light a cigar and take a stick of dynamite. Climb up there… above the entrance to the cave. If we come out and he follows… light the fuse and throw it at his feet… ok."

"Why don't we just throw the dynamite into the cave?" Galvin asked.

"Because I wanna shoot this son of a bitch myself. I wanna make 'im pay," Jack snarled. "Besides, we dunno what's inside that cave or where it goes. If we blow it, how do yer know if he's dead? We'd have to dig it out to be sure. Nah! I say we just rush 'im and shoot 'im dead. He won't be expectin' us in this storm now, will 'e? Right, let's go."

Jack gave Peirdro a nudge and beckoned him to go around behind the wagon and animals and climb the cliff face on the right-hand side of the cave. Leaving the cover of the trees, Jack crouched stealthily along the front of the wagon, followed closely by his men in single file, until they were only a few paces from the entrance.

When Peirdro was high enough, Jack took a long quiet breath to steady his nerves and raised his left hand in a fist. He briefly turned his head to his men and nodded. They all nodded, ready, in return.

"Ok… NOW!" Jack ordered in a whispered yell.

With musket aimed forward at the waist and the middle finger of his right hand upon the trigger, Jack rushed into the cave, closely followed by Louis, Galvin and George Littlegrass.

5

Whose Trap Is It?

Barrin was sitting on his rock behind the glowing mound of coals facing the entrance of the cave. He had removed his poncho, folded it neatly and placed it on the blanket behind the rock he sat upon. He was wearing a hand-crafted light-brown, waistcoat made of softened Sika deer leather, over a light-blue, long-sleeved, collared cotton shirt.

A soft leather holster was sewn into the front right-hand panel of the waistcoat, which held a short-barrelled six-shot pistol, angled to be easily retrieved by the left hand. Three small Japanese crafted throwing knives were held in sheaths sewn into the front left panel of the waistcoat, to be easily retrieved by the right hand.

Jack rushed through the narrow entrance into the cave. He saw Barrin illuminated behind the campfire. They locked eyes. Jack aimed the barrel of his musket at Barrin's chest and fired.

The golden flecks in Barrin's eyes lit up. His body began to glow, surrounded with a very subtle iridescent golden hue. He simply raised his left arm to block the musket ball. The ball ripped through the blue cotton midway along his forearm… and hit metal. A sharp ricochet resounded through the cave as the ball bounced past his left shoulder and smashed into the back wall of the cave.

Barrin kicked back extending both legs. As he dived backwards through the air, he drew his right pistol from the hip as his legs straightened out. With the barrel already aimed at Jack, he fired almost instantaneously in the same motion. With left arm already bent across his chest, he drew the pistol from his waistcoat, in mid-flight.

Jack's body weight leaned forward on his extended right leg bracing against the recoil of the musket. The bullet hit him square on the kneecap. In the motion of moving forward with his left leg off the ground, his right leg buckled under him. His legs crumpled as he fell forward and to his right.

Right behind Jack's left shoulder, Louis had his musket raised, aimed and fired at Barrin's chest at the exact same time he fired his second shot. Again, Barrin blocked the ball from Louis' musket with his left arm guard which ricocheted into the ceiling. While Jack was falling, Barrin's second bullet hit the base of his exposed middle, trigger finger.

Jack screamed in double agony. The barrel of his musket slammed into the ground, his body crashed and rolled over the top of the musket. He hit the ground hard with arms and legs in a mangled mess. Barrin landed on his back comfortably upon his folded poncho and blanket, with head raised and left arm extended straight out with pistol aimed at Louis.

Louis dropped the musket rifle whilst taking a forward step to the left of Jack's crumpling body. He drew and began to raise his pistols, one in each hand, bringing them up to aim at Barrin. Barrin fired first. The bullet blew the top loop of his right ear off.

Jerking his head in pain, Louis winced and fired his right pistol. The bullet was short and hit the ground just in front Barrin's toes. Barrin fired twice more. The second bullet clipped Louis' inner elbow joint of his left arm. He dropped the gun. The third bullet grazed, deeply, the inside of his left thigh above the knee and continued on to hit rock. Louis crashed heavily into the wall of the cave, fell forward and rolled over himself in an awkward and ungainly shambles of lanky limbs.

Galvin appeared directly behind the fallen Jack. His levelled musket was aimed at Barrin's head, whilst he lay flat on his back on the ground. Barrin swung his left arm back a few degrees and fired. The bullet hit the underside of the musket, forcing the barrel to pitch up high. Barrin fired once more.

The bullet hit Galvin square on the left knee cap. Being the forward leg carrying the momentum of Galvin's excessive body weight, it instantly crumpled. His right foot dragged along the ground as he began to fall. Galvin tripped and fell over Jack's body. The musket left his hands as the ground approached fast. He fell hard across his front and smashed his forehead into the floor of the cave, knocking him out cold.

An opened small bag of white powder suddenly burst over the campfire obscuring Barrin's view. A tomahawk appeared spinning in the air through the gap between Louis and Galvin. With his left hand, George Littlegrass threw the tomahawk as hard as he could at Barrin's belly. Then with two knives drawn, one in each hand, he moved as fast as he could and leapt through the powder screen in hot pursuit of his tomahawk.

Barrin had only a split second to focus and with the last remaining bullet in his left pistol, he fired. The bullet hit the tomahawk at the top of the handle as it spun in mid-air, splitting the weapon in half. The axe head and handle fell to the ground.

George Littlegrass screamed a war cry as he traversed through the air towards Barrin. There was no time to aim and shoot. Barrin immediately dropped both guns. He just managed to grab the tip of the handle of one small throwing knife from his waistcoat with his right hand.

George Littlegrass landed on top of Barrin's body, stabbing down hard with the blade in his right hand, aiming for Barrin's heart. Barrin raised his left forearm to block the blow, the sound of metal-on-metal singing through the cave. Barrin stabbed upwards with his dagger. The razor sharp, one-inch blade bit deeply into the hamstring under George's left leg. He grunted in pain but did not scream.

Barrin immediately kicked up with his left leg, kneeing George in the middle of the back, forcing him to stumble forward over the top of Barrin's head. George tried to stab Barrin in the neck with his left blade but missed. Barrin was too nimble and slid down and out through George's legs, withdrawing the dagger from his thigh. Barrin swiftly flipped his body onto his feet in a crouching position behind George and drew a second dagger with his left hand.

George had to roll forward over his right shoulder to quickly find his feet and spun around to face Barrin. Not hesitating, he lunged forward trying to stab Barrin in the throat. Barrin simply stepped back and plunged a dagger into the top of George's extended left hand and let go. George stepped forward slashing wildly with his right hand across Barrin's face and found a dagger plunged into the top of his right hand. He dropped both knives and fell to his knees, staring at the small handle protruding from each hand. He looked up at Barrin, beaten.

Barrin stepped back away from George. He drew the pistol on his left hip with his right hand and quickly surveyed the scene to make sure no one was holding a weapon. He picked up his dropped pistols and returned them to his waistcoat and right hip holsters. He dropped a couple of small logs on the campfire to raise more light by flame.

George pulled the daggers out and dropped them to the floor. With the flick of his barrel, Barrin told George to move back over towards Jack. He complied with a severe limp. Barrin stood casually behind the campfire to address the gang with pointed pistol.

"I see you idiots fell for my trap… again!" he said denouncing the gang. "You guys have been following me ever since Santa Rosa. George here… has even seen me watching you. So, what makes you think I wouldn't be ready for you guys… eh?"

Jack rolled onto his side and then into a sitting position. He pushed his right hand into his stomach and clasped his knee with his left, grimacing in pain. Louis began to unravel himself, clasping his left elbow across his body with his right hand and climbed to his feet. With shaking hands George Littlegrass sat on his haunches and strapped his cut leg tightly with his bandana. Galvin was still out cold, prostrate in front of Jack.

"Who are yer?" Jack asked. "Yer shoot like no one I've ever seen. Why didn't yer simply kill us?" he enquired.

"Unlike you Jack, I'm not a murderer," Barrin answered simply. "Don't you realise Jack, when you kill and take the life of another, you open your heart to darkness. I cannot allow that to happen. I cannot become like you Jack… consumed with evil-doing. But I am compelled to defend myself from… a bunch of buffoons like you guys," he said and paused. "I'm giving you an opportunity, Jack. Stop this madness! Find something more meaningful, more rewarding to do, than lead your men into disaster. Continuing with this madness will only get you killed, Jack. You know this, right?"

"Yer arm? What's on yer arm?" Jack asked.

Barrin looked down at his left forearm and smiled wryly. He loosened the button on the cuff and peeled back the sleeve.

"It's an iron and brass arm guard, from wrist to elbow."

Barrin tapped the barrel of his pistol upon the metal, twice.

"And look at yer waistcoat. Who does that? Are yer bounty hunter, or somethin'?"

"No Jack. I help people… usually from the likes of you."

"So, a marshall? A lawman?" Jack suggested.

"Not quite but close enough, Jack. If it helps, think of me as more of a… guardian… or in your case, an angel of mercy," Barrin said with a mischievous grin.

George Littlegrass climbed to his feet and took a step towards his dropped knives.

"Uh, uh!" Barrin said, shaking his head from side to side. "Wake him up and get him on his feet. You all leave your weapons on the ground," he warned. "Now, for the last time, Jack. I don't have any gold. So, gather your men and go back to Santa Rosa."

"But, that chest in yer wagon? If it's not gold, then what is it?"

"That's none of your business, Jack. But rest assured, it's not gold. So put the question out of your mind. And I hope for your sake, Jack, that we don't have the pleasure of ever meeting again. Now, get your men up and leave my camp," he barked.

Barrin waved his pistol menacingly at Jack's head.

Gingerly, George hobbled over to Galvin, turned him over and with a few gentle slaps to the cheek, managed to revive him. George pulled Galvin to his feet and whilst supporting each other, they hobbled past Jack and Louis and out through the cave entrance back into the driving rain. Louis climbed to his feet and quickly followed. Jack was the last to leave. He limped backwards out of the cave, maintaining eye contact with Barrin.

Barrin followed and watched the gang leave the cave at a casual distance. He stopped just inside the entrance and leaned back against the wall making himself a slim target. He knew that the Mexican was missing. The gang walked towards the furthest tree line.

Crouching, Peirdro remained perched on a rocky ledge fifteen feet above the floor of the cave entrance, wondering what was happening. When everyone limped out, he knew the answer and made himself ready. Once well clear of the entrance, Jack looked up and gave the signal.

Peirdro puffed on his short cigar, brought the stick of dynamite out from under his poncho and lit the fuse under his wide sombrero. He half stood and leaned out over the edge to see the cave entrance below. He extended his left hand to drop the stick and nervously shuffled his front foot forward involuntarily. His foot slipped on wet rock.

In a screaming panic, with arm extended holding the stick of dynamite, Peirdro hit the ground hard. The bone in his wrist snapped instantly. His left arm folded under his body. The heavy thump winded him into silence. Three... two... one... BOOM!

Killed instantly, the explosion blew a massive cavity through Peirdro's chest, diaphragm and stomach. His head, shoulders, right arm and legs remained intact. Jack and the gang dived to the ground. Barrin stepped back into the cave and looked away.

As the driving rain began to wash away the blood, Jack climbed to his feet grimacing in pain. Disgusted and disappointed, he turned and hobbled back through the trees to find his horse. Jack, Louis and Galvin mounted their horses. In single file, they allowed their steers to slowly find sure footing down the mountain track, to safety.

George Littlegrass took some cotton strips and medicine from a saddle pouch. He walked to the water's edge and sat down on a rock beside the stream. He washed his hands, legs and the wound under his thigh. He pushed the herbal mulch into the wound and strapped it tightly. He did the same to both hands as well.

Once complete he laid back against the rock allowing the rain to fall across his face and body. He closed his eyes, perplexed about his defeat to Barrin. Almost ten minutes elapsed. Jack and the others had long since left. Finally, he sat up, climbed to his feet and turned. Just in front of him stood four Pomo Indians.

With a long, sharp knife in hand, the lead Indian quickly and determinedly stepped forward the few paces up to George. He thrust the knife deep into George's stomach, twisted the blade and raked it sideways. He withdrew the knife. George fell to his knees. He did not cry out. The Indian stepped around behind George, grabbed the thick knot of his hair to pull his head back and slit his throat. As George died, the Indian scalped the knot of hair he was holding and held it up high into the air. The lead Indian let out a series of cries and howls, swiftly mimicked by the other three. George's dead body was pushed into the now fast-flowing stream. The four Pomo gathered George's horse and melted back into the night.

Further downstream, Jack, Louis and Galvin spun in their saddles on hearing Indian war cries. A cold shiver ran through their spines and their pace immediately quickened a notch.

Barrin conducted a quick search through the nearby tree line and checked on his wagon and animals before returning to the cave, when he heard the Indian war cries just below the lip of the plateau. He threw a fresh stump of wood on the campfire.

He collected and cleaned his two daggers and returned them to his waistcoat. He gathered the broken tomahawk, the two knives, dropped pistols and muskets. He removed the bullets and threw them all into the fire. He threw his poncho back on, collected his folded blanket and left the cave. He climbed in through the back of his now partially flooded wagon. He tidied up the few spilt items and put away the blanket he held.

Curious, Barrin lifted the wooden lid on the box containing his chest. He bent down, clasped a hand around the handle, one on either side and lifted the chest effortlessly out of the small wooden box. He unlocked the latch and lifted the lid by only two inches.

A brilliant golden light escaped through the opening and illuminated the interior of the wagon. Barrin peered through the opening. Inside was a perfectly round golden orb, the size of a large cannon ball, sitting comfortably within its perfect mould within the chest. Satisfied all was well, Barrin closed and locked the chest, returned it to the small box and locked the outer padlock. Wrapped in his blanket, he squeezed himself between a barrel and the bench and went to sleep within the darkness of the wagon.

The storm finally began to clear around lunchtime the following day. Vultures, crows and other birds were gathering upon the plateau, eyeing what little there was left of Peirdro. Barrin could not bring himself to gather all the pieces for a proper burial on a difficult rocky mountainside and decided to leave him where he lay.

He tethered his oxen and steered his wagon slowly down the mountain track. He saw George's body stuck beneath some fallen logs a couple of hundred yards downstream. Once clear of the mountain he resumed his north-northwest heading.

6

The Pipe of Peace

Late in the afternoon on the following day, Barrin guided his wagon to the top of an embankment which looked out across a coarse sandy beach. The flat sandbank was thirty yards in length and reached a calm shallow pond inside the curved bend of a point bar. A small but fast-moving river flowed around the northern end of the point and continued to snake down towards the southwest.

Barrin decided to make camp early, on the sandbank below and within the curve of the embankment. This was the first time in a few weeks that he made camp in the open.

He brought his wagon around to the southwestern side of his camp, set the brake and untethered his two oxen. He rounded up a few stones to build the border for a campfire. He gathered enough wood along the riverbank and nearby shrubs and trees to last the night.

He found a long thin straight branch. He cut one end and spliced a sharp hooked bard with a length of string between each tip. Standing on a rock which jutted out into the pond, Barrin easily speared four trout for supper. He gutted, scaled and washed them right there upon the rock. He found a nice long flat stone, carried it to his camp and placed it in the middle of his campfire. He arranged some wood around the stone and lit the fire.

He led his two oxen down to the pond for water and let them wade in for a bath. When they returned to the camp, he fed them some grain and fodder and tied them loosely to the back of the wagon. He did the same for his horse. His animals calmly settled in for a restful night.

The campfire had reduced to a nice layer of red-hot coals. He set a small camp pot on the coals and dropped quite a few quartered potatoes into the boiling water. He then placed all four trout on the hot stone to cook. Dusk had set in and the last light was disappearing fast.

From the wagon, Barrin withdrew a long pipe and filled it with some fine tobacco from a large square tin. He lit the pipe and purposefully blew big clouds of smoke up into the air above. Coupled with the smell of cooking trout, the tobacco smoke was picked up by the light breeze and drifted eastward into the nearby hills.

It did not take long for the first Pomo Indian to appear on the embankment overlooking the camp. Facing him, Barrin rose to his feet and offered a wave with the pipe in his right hand. He raised his left hand and jiggled the tobacco tin, inviting the Pomo to join him.

The Pomo Indian calmly walked down the embankment and sat on a washed-up tree branch Barrin had set aside for them to the left of his stone. Barrin handed the Pomo his tobacco tin. The Pomo drew out a small pipe with a long slim stem, placed a knot of tobacco in the bulb and lit the pipe with a burning twig. He took a couple of puffs from his pipe, sat down and proceeded to study Barrin.

"I see you, Lightning," the Pomo greeted in his native tongue, followed by a weary, reluctant smile. "I'm Greycloud… on account of my dark, reflective disposition."

"I see you, Greycloud. Welcome to my camp," Barrin replied in fluent Pomo.

Greycloud immediately sat upright. His eyes sprang wide open in shock.

"How do you know our tongue?" he asked.

"I have many talents," Barrin responded. "I'm naturally gifted with many tongues," Barrin said and offered a mischievous grin.

Still bemused, Greycloud began to relax.

"Well… you're the strangest person I've ever seen. You appear and do everything like the settlers… yet you're NOT one of them."

"No, I'm not," Barrin replied. "I'm from a faraway land, across the great ocean to the west. It is a land of hot dry earth and endless, unforgiving deserts. In the old days I think they called it Persia," he said.

"I see," Greycloud reflected briefly. "I don't know of this place."

Greycloud sat in silence, drawing on his pipe and nodded his approval. He issued a bird call. Within seconds, three more Pomo Indians appeared over the embankment and cantered down into the camp. In order of rank, they each offered their greeting.

"I see you, Lightning," said the first. "I'm Chelan," said the oldest.

"I see you, Lightning. I'm Howling Wind," said the chubbiest.

"I see you, Lightning. I'm Running Fox," said the smallest of them all.

They sat beside Greycloud in order, whose native dress displayed more beads and feathers than his peers. The tobacco tin was rapidly passed along.

"Lightning, eh! How did I earn this name?" he asked.

"You are the shooter of fingers and toes, before anyone can even put their hand on a gun," Greycloud replied, with a wry smile.

He raised his right hand with thumb and index finger folded in, mimicking having lost both fingers. All three laughed and giggled merrily and proceeded to fill the air with expertly crafted rings of tobacco smoke.

Barrin checked on the fire and turned the fish over on the stone. When ready, he shared his meal of trout, potatoes, bread and cheese. To conclude the feast the tobacco tin was passed around once more.

"So, Greycloud…" Barrin began. "Two days ago, I… encountered one of your tribe. I believe his name is… was… George Littlegrass. Do you know of him?"

"Yes," Greycloud replied flatly.

"Did you kill George Littlegrass?"

"Yes!" Greycloud said simply with no change in his expression.

"Is that why you've been following me all this time?"

"We follow George Littlegrass and his band of outlaws. It's they who have followed you," he said. "Now that we have punished George Littlegrass for his crime, we return to our tribal camp, in the mountains, to the north."

"What was the crime of George Littlegrass?"

"As a child, Littlegrass would hide in the grass with his little sister and watch the tribe. That's why he is called Littlegrass. As he grew up, he took a liking to the tobacco pipe. His sister was married to the eldest son of the chief. Late one night after too much smoke, Littlegrass killed the chief's son in a fit of jealously. Secretly, he was in love with his sister and became twisted by his own unnatural desire. He fled the tribe and joined this band of outlaws who have murdered both settlers and several Miwok, in the south. Our chief offered us the honour to bring back his scalp. We have fulfilled our duty and will now return home."

"A tragic tale indeed," Barrin reflected.

"Yes, it is."

Greycloud soon rose to his feet.

"It's time. We humbly thank you for the meal, tobacco and hospitality," he said gratefully.

Each Pomo stood and offered Barrin their gratitude in turn and began to file out of the camp towards the embankment. Greycloud turned to Barrin.

"I should tell you… the black-haired one… he sits alone in his camp close to the fire with his whiskey. He's one day's ride behind you. He broods and is consumed by his demons. The tall skinny one and the clumsy fat one have left and gone back south."

"I gave him a warning. But I fear he's not yet learnt his lesson," Barrin replied.

"Yes, I think you're right. His heart is filled with sickness, with Wetiko, and he means more trouble. Farewell, Lightning and go in peace," Greycloud said and waved goodbye.

"Go in peace, Greycloud," Barrin replied and waved goodbye.

The group of four climbed up and over the embankment and disappeared into the darkness.

Barrin tidied up the camp and settled down for the evening. At 4 am in the morning, he broke camp and steered his wagon once more north-northwest, setting a brisk pace.

7

Eureka, Just in Time!

At dusk on Friday evening, 28th July 1854, Barrin finally entered the outskirts of the coastal town of Eureka. The small frontier outpost community with a seaport serviced the northern limits of the gold rush, as well as the fur and forestry trades. The town was also home to the newly established Fort Humboldt, its purpose to maintain a sense of law and order throughout the very rough region and to protect the civilians from harassment by the local native Indian tribes.

Barrin steered his wagon towards Pine Hill and around to its eastern flank, a mile and a half southeast of Eureka. He found a small circular grove surrounded by a thick brush of trees, which obscured his wagon from the view of the trail he had just used. Barrin parked his wagon out of sight and made camp. He aligned his wagon alongside the thickest treed part of the grove and dug a shallow hole into the earth for a small campfire which was also concealed by the wagon, so that the flames could not be seen from the trail. His well-hidden camp was on the opposite side of the hill from Pine Hill Saloon.

Late on Saturday afternoon 29th July 1854, just before dusk, Barrin left his camp and walked along a path around the summit of the hill and headed on down to Pine Hill Saloon. Standing at the front, he surveyed the building.

The saloon was a two-storey, square building levelled into the gentle slope of the hill, which sat atop a set of thick stumps dug and hammered into the ground on the lower side. The back right corner of the building was cut into the hillside. Five steps led to the entrance and through a set of double swinging doors located at the front left corner of the building.

A wide veranda ran along the front and left side of the building, boarded with a thick handrail and posts at regular intervals to support the overhanging roof. A row of six large windows ran along the front wall to the right of the entrance. The external latrines were at the back at the end of the veranda on the left. The roof was a high, wide and steeply inverted V shape and overhung the entire building by a few feet to account for the heavy rains and snow. A row of half a dozen small cottages nestled into the trees on the opposite side of the road behind Barrin. He slowly and purposefully climbed each step and entered the saloon.

The doors swung closed behind him on squeaking dry, rusted springs. In the dim smoky haze, he saw a wide and spacious L-shaped bar in front of him.

The front half of the saloon was wide, spacious and open from floor to ceiling for the two levels of the building. The short length of the bar ran adjacent to the left-hand wall of the building, and four small booths ran along the inside of that wall. In the corner at the end of the booths and bar, a spiral staircase led up to the second level.

A narrow balcony ran along the wall, overlooking the bar, which provided access to four doors of four individually numbered rooms, receding into the top back half of the building. A door behind the middle of the bar led into the lower back half of the building, housing the kitchen, stores, office and private quarters of the saloon's owner. A rear exit led out into a small courtyard.

The main gallery of the saloon consisted of half a dozen small round tables in the open area, some with two chairs, some with three. Larger round tables, each with four chairs, were placed near each window, with two along the short wall at the furthest end. They were used mostly for cards and other such games. An upright piano was set dead in the middle of the front wall, with a set of three windows on either side.

The feature wall above the piano and windows was adorned with the trophy heads of hunted native animals, including buffalo, stag elk, coyote and cougar. The saloon was lit with shaded lights between each window, three behind the bar and two more on the wall above the booths. The bar was three foot short of the wall at both ends and blocked by a bolt action, thick wooden waist-high, swinging gate on rusty old hinges. The whole place looked rough, its clientele consisting of fur traders, mountain men, loggers and miners.

The bar was manned by a huge round bull of a man with a full orange-brown beard and shaggy mane of hair, wearing a dark burgundy kit. Nearby, on his left, stood an older, tall woman sporting a thin scar on her top lip, in a tight-fitting, amber-coloured dress which amplified her full bust and lush arrangement of chocolate-brown hair. Barrin approached.

"What can I getcha?" asked the barman, in a deep gruff logger's voice.

"Whiskey and a beer!" Barrin barked.

Barrin looked around, while the barman prepared his order. A younger mistress was playing a tune at the piano. On a large table to her right, three elderly miners were playing cards and exchanging chips with each other. A couple of solitary travellers, each sipping their drink of contemplation, sat alone at their respective tables. A young man was propositioning a girl inside one booth, while in the darkest booth a tired old miner was eating his supper.

A well-groomed man in his early thirties lay slumped over a table by the furthest wall. He was dressed in a full-length navy-blue coat. His slouch hat had fallen from his head onto the table in front of several empty tumblers. The man's right temple rested upon the back of his right hand, as the right side of his body rested against and was supported by the table.

The barman placed both drinks on the bar and Barrin nodded his thanks with two silver dollars. He shot the whiskey, left the empty tumbler on bar and grabbed hold of his beer.

"Looks like he's had enough for one night!" Barrin motioned at the unconscious man.

"Yeah… when he wakes, he'll stumble back to the fort," the barman commented.

"Oh, he's Union Cavalry, then?" Barrin asked, making conversation.

"Yeah… I'd say so," the barman replied. "Bin comin' 'ere on a Saturday for a month or so now I reckon. Gets dressed in civvies and sneaks out for a bit of a bender… if you know what I mean. Life in the army must be rather boring round 'ere, I guess."

"I bet it would be," Barrin agreed.

"He drinks until he passes out, then gets up and leaves an hour or so later. Keeps to himself and doesn't say much to anyone."

"Right! I'll leave him in peace then."

Barrin carried his beer over to the far wall and sat at the vacant table beside the one with the slouched, drunken man. He positioned his chair with the wall to his back, his beer and left arm resting on the table and the drunken slouch a little behind his right shoulder. He took up a relaxed demeanour and enjoyed the piano music while sipping his beer.

Three-quarters of an hour ticked by. The old miner eating his supper had left. The young man and girl had gone up to room two. Several of the loners had left to be replaced with a couple more. Two groups of four men had each taken up residence at one of the large tables either side of the piano for a night of cards, drink and gambling.

Suddenly, a Mexican entered the saloon. He stood in the shadow while the swinging doors closed behind him. He wore black boots with spurs attached, baggy black pants and a blue alpaca poncho over a white shirt, but no hat to cover his mop of black hair. His hands were rough and scarred from mining. His luck was down, since all the gold was taken and the rivers now ran dry. He walked to the bar and ordered a double whiskey. He shot half the tumbler and turned to survey the gallery, the noise and atmosphere rising with the smoke. His gaze fixated upon the slouching man in the far corner. He gulped the rest of his whiskey and slammed the tumbler down on the bar. He leaned forward a step to take a better look and… recognised him.

"It… it's… Grant!" he exclaimed, with thick accent.

The Mexican was suddenly struck by the emotional memory of grief and pain and of his vow for vengeance. A strong bolt of adrenalin shot through his body. Without any further thought of where he was and what he was doing, he drew a pistol out from beneath his poncho.

"Grant!" he yelled. "You killed my brother, back in Mexico. For that, you DIE!"

The Mexican fired the first shot.

At the loud utterance of his name, Captain Ulysses S. Grant woke up and sat bolt upright, startled and confused in his drunken haze.

Barrin's sharp eyes were on the Mexican when he first walked in. The subtle aura around his body instantly began to glow the moment the Mexican went for his pistol. Barrin pushed back his chair, rose to his feet and drew his right hip pistol all in the same motion.

The Mexican did not even notice Barrin, his focus completely fixated upon Ulysses.

With right arm half extended in front of his chest, Barrin fired a split second after the Mexican's shot. Moving upwards and to the right, Barrin's bullet hit the Mexican's bullet in the centre of its undercarriage a few yards in front of and directly in line with Ulysses' throat. The Mexican's bullet deflected high into the wall above Ulysses.

The Mexican fired a second shot. Now standing with arm fully extended, Barrin fired a split second after the Mexican. His bullet hit the Mexican's bullet a little left of the front centre of the cartridge, a few yards in front of the Mexican, jamming and fusing both cartridges into one and causing them to fall to the ground, spinning in the middle of the floor between them.

On hearing gunfire, Ulysses drove with his legs to stand up and fumbled with his long coat, his hands feebly trying to locate his pistol. Whilst in motion, halfway to standing, his torso leaning forward over the edge of the table, Barrin quickly stepped back two paces and drove his right shoulder into the middle of Ulysses' back.

The Mexican fired his third shot.

Ulysses' body was pummelled forward. He fell through the right edge of the table to the ground. The table flipped over the top of his body, pinning him down and protecting him at the same time. The chairs scattered in all directions.

Barrin kept eyes on the Mexican continuously. Whilst bracing for the shoulder charge, Barrin raised his left arm in front of his own chest, which now stood in place of Ulysses, in a semi-crouched position. Swiping his forearm forward, the bullet hit the metal guard and ricocheted skyward with a high-pitched ringing echo.

Barrin swiftly moved his pistol forward beneath his left forearm and fired all in the same motion as the block. The bullet hit the front trigger guard of the Mexican's gun, whiplashing the gun out of his right hand.

At that very moment, Jack burst through the double swinging doors, brandishing a wide-barrelled blunderbuss, fully loaded with small shot balls and powder. Hearing the gunfire, he knew this was his only opportunity to ambush Barrin during the ensuing melee.

With a heavy limp in his right leg, Jack rushed forward to get a clear shot at Barrin. He held the blunderbuss straight out from the waist. Seeing Jack appear from behind the Mexican, Barrin lunged forward over the flipped table and dived for the small gap at the end of the bar. The Mexican did not notice Jack.

In the same moment and wincing from the pain in his right hand, the Mexican drew a long knife in his left and lurched forward, eyes only for Ulysses in his blinding mad rage.

"Dodge this!" Jack screamed at Barrin.

Filled with vile vengeance, Jack fired whilst Barrin was leaping mid-air to his left.

The Mexican moved forward into the partial field of fire of the blunderbuss at point blank range. The muzzle had followed Barrin's dive. Half of the shot ripped through the Mexican's lower right side, under his rib cage and into a kidney, shredding flesh.

The force hurled the Mexican forward and spun him to his left, smashing his body into the front of the bar. He ricocheted and fell onto his back screaming in pain and writhing on the floor, while reaching for his lower right back. The rest of the shot sprayed into the flipped table and the far wall.

Barrin's dive was across the line of the Mexican. He smashed into the waist-high side gate ripping the bolt from its hinge. He dropped his gun when he hit the ground in a half-broken roll through the splintered wood of the panel. Barrin quickly and smoothly rose to his feet, with left shoulder facing Jack.

Jack was both shocked and bewildered at his miss. He saw Barrin rise to his feet from behind the end of the bar. He immediately dropped the blunderbuss and drew the pistol from his front belt with his left hand. Jack fumbled with the pistol in his offhand, his panic rising from his stomach with each passing second.

From the inside lower back portion of his waistcoat, Barrin drew a small, five-pointed throwing star with the right thumb of his hand. The waistcoat and fitted weapons were a hand-crafted gift from the Japanese emperor, for… services rendered.

Held between thumb and curled index finger and with a small quick step of the left foot, Barrin raised his right arm and expertly threw the star in a smooth forceful throwing action.

The star hit Jack vertically across the left eye socket. One point of the star penetrated the eyeball. The adjacent points cut into the flesh but stopped at the bone both above and below the perforated eyeball. Jack dropped his pistol, reeled back and screamed in pain. He fell to his knees and brought both hands up to remove the intrusive obstruction and shield his damaged eye. Barrin's subtle glow subsided.

The whole engagement lasted ten seconds.

The piano had stopped playing. Everyone in the saloon looked on in stunned silence. Barrin promptly retrieved his gun from the floor and drew the pistol out from under his poncho with his left hand. He stepped back around from behind the bar and avoided the Mexican, who was still squirming and writhing in pain and slowly losing consciousness. A pool of blood was spreading out from under his body. Everyone watched Barrin loosely holding both pistols. He had everyone in his field of view.

"Keep calm, everyone… it's all over now. There's no need for any more killing."

Barrin scanned the gallery and quickly assessed each person in the saloon. No one made a single movement. They all correctly assessed that he was highly skilled and absolutely lethal. Barron slowly turned to the barman, who stood frozen having watched it all unfold.

"Sorry for the commotion. I'm just here for him," he said.

Barrin indicated with a tilt of his head towards Ulysses, only just now managing to extricate himself from beneath the flipped table. Satisfied no one posed a threat, Barrin holstered his right pistol. From the inside of his waistcoat, he drew a small pouch of silver dollars and lobbed it at the barman, who promptly caught the pouch in his right hand.

"Are we good?" Barrin asked.

The barman tested the weight of the pouch in his hand. He nodded in confirmation and his disgruntled expression immediately reverted to one of hospitality. He smiled as the pouch promptly disappeared. The clientele collectively emitted a sigh of relief and began to relax.

On his knees whilst holding his damaged eye, Jack looked down at the blood-stained throwing star in his right hand. He held it up… higher as he spoke, for everyone to see.

"Wha'… what da' hell is this!" he exclaimed. "I've never seen anything like this before. Has anyone ever seen anything like this before?"

Barrin quickly and smoothly walked over to Jack. He bent forward and picked up the blunderbuss. He returned the left-held pistol to its holster under his poncho.

"What kind of rifle is this? Some kinda bird-shootin' shotgun?" he mocked.

He bent forward a little closer to Jack.

"The last time we met, I gave you a warning Jack. What happened? Why didn't you do the same as the others? Just couldn't let it go, could you, Jack?"

"Yeah… yer're right, I couldn't," he said with a wry defeated smirk. "I knew yer wouldn't kill me Barrin. I knew yer couldn't do it."

"Well, know this, Jack. If I ever see you again, I'll take the other eye," he said followed by a brief pause. "Do you understand? Say it… say it so I know you understand."

"Yeah, I understand."

"Say it… repeat what I said," Barrin pressed firmly.

Jack looked up at Barrin with bitter hatred.

"Yeah… I understand! If we meet, yer'll take me other eye… and I'll be blind!"

Satisfied, Barrin stood up straight. With a quick spearlike action, he smashed the butt of the blunderbuss across Jack's forehead just above his eyebrows snapping his head back. Jack was knocked out cold. His body fell back over his bent legs.

Barrin leaned the blunderbuss up against the bar. He brought his foot down hard upon the rifle, snapping it where wood joined metal just behind the hammer. Barrin then bent down to retrieve the throwing star from Jack's open right palm. He wiped the blood on Jack's shirt and returned it to its pocket, inside the back of his waistcoat.

He turned to face the barman and the patrons of the saloon once more.

"Both these men are criminals… bent on killing," he pronounced. "This one was trying to shoot me and that one was trying to shoot the captain over there. I simply acted in self-defence… understood?" he paused long enough, "So, no need for a lawman to get involved. Besides, he…" Barrin gestured towards Jack, "…is the one who just shot that one."

Everyone now looked down at the misfortune of the Mexican.

"We don't like having lawmen round here," the barman replied. "I'll take care of it."

"Right then… I'll be on my way and leave you folks in peace."

Barrin walked back to where Ulysses had managed to get himself into a sitting position. He gathered Ulysses' stranded hat and placed it on his head. Bending forward and with both hands, Barrin grabbed the front lapel of Ulysses' coat and pulled him to his feet. Barrin tucked his shoulder under the captain's left arm and began to march Ulysses out of the saloon, in a somewhat jagged line.

Barrin nodded farewell to the bartender who returned the acknowledgement in kind.

Barrin walked Ulysses out through the swinging doors and down the five steps to leave Pine Hill Saloon. Barrin located Ulysses' horse and managed to get him mounted. He then turned and led the horse along the path towards the summit of Pine Hill. He waited a few moments behind a line of trees to make sure no one dared to follow. Satisfied, he turned for his camp.

8

The Spirit of Liberty

Shortly after Barrin and Ulysses staggered out of the saloon, the Mexican let out his last breath and died. His body went limp, his open eyes fell vacant.

As soon as he died a dark subtle shadow left the body of the Mexican. No one in the gallery possessed the eyes to notice, let alone see the shadow. The dark spirit slowly floated up into the air and through the roof of the saloon. It paused high over the building surrounded by the treetops gently swaying back and forth in the light evening breeze. The spirit stopped and began to search… for an escape.

At that very moment inside the wagon, the padlock suddenly snapped open and fell out of its metal ring. The lid to both the box and the chest inside flung open. A brilliant golden light flooded and illuminated the interior of the wagon. The spirit of the orb shot out through the quarter circle gap, out of the wagon and flew up into the treetops above. The glowing spirit dashed with incredible speed towards Pine Hill Saloon. The wagon returned to darkness.

Within three short seconds, the subtle golden green semi-transparent spirit of the orb appeared before the dark spirit suspended high in the treetops above the roof of the saloon. Both spirits manifested bodies of equal size and width.

The spirit of the orb's body formed the appearance of an ancient Greek god, an older, very muscular man dressed in a long sublime royal toga, with a thick head of greying hair waving back in the breeze and a long wise beard whose ends separated into writhing tentacles.

The dark spirit formed the appearance of a ghostly black spectre, its head, arms and body wrapped in a long thick black hooded cloak. Two dark purple-red eyes illuminated the inside of the hood, and a very subtle, deep crimson border highlighted its black beating heart. The torn and tattered tail of the cloak fluttered in the breeze.

The golden flecks in Barrin's eyes suddenly glowed with a bright brilliance. He turned and looked back high above the saloon. Through the trees he could see the spirit of the orb confronting the dark spectre. He turned away and doubled his pace to his wagon.

Both apparition's glared at each other for a few moments.

"You have failed once more, Spectre," the spirit said in a deep ornate and commanding tone.

Only the dark spectre possessed the ears to hear.

"It's but a small victory, Emerald," the spectre replied in a slow, rasping, husky voice of pure evil.

"The General lives and he will fulfil his destiny," Emerald pressed on.

"There's another, you know. He's the leader of your cause and I will take him."

"No, you will not. He will be protected until his task is done," Emerald countered. "Little by little we shall force the light into the hearts and minds of this world. Soon the sickness, the Wetiko of slavery – as our brethren like to call it – will be at an end, and the light of liberty will forge this nation into a new unity and become a beacon of hope. Your hold over this world will weaken a little more."

"A noble sentiment indeed, Emerald. But you place too great a faith in man," Spectre said in a nonchalant manner. "If one form of slavery is to end, it will be replaced by another. Where men seek power for themselves, there I will be. All I need do is whisper in their ear… and their desire will do my work. It's all so very easy."

"Soon… your feasting off the suffering of man will be at an end. The forces within man will finally be balanced and you will perish," Emerald replied with clear conviction.

Spectre raised his voice into an antagonised rage.

"Man inflicts suffering on his fellow man. They cry for it, they yearn for it. They even think that suffering somehow defines them. They will forever be caught up in these illusions, no matter what you say or do. Bah! I tire of your prostrations, Emerald."

Spectre turned and glided into the night, heading for the nearest body of still black water.

"Until we meet again, Emerald!"

Spectre slammed silently into and through the black stillness of a nearby pond and was gone, having crossed back into the underworld.

Emerald watched, then turned and swiftly flew through the treetops back towards the wagon.

Barrin had already arrived at the camp with Ulysses prostrate forward over the neck of his horse. He helped Ulysses down from his horse and laid him on his back on a blanket next to the dead coals of the campfire. Barrin gave him water to drink and gently pushed a cushion behind his head. Ulysses was conscious, yet dazed and confused whilst looking up at the starry sky above, his head spinning hard from the booze. Barrin melted back into the tree line at the edge of camp.

Emerald arrived and changed his appearance into a mighty fine gallant General of the Union Army and stood twice as tall as a normal man looking down upon Ulysses from the end of his feet. Emerald slowly added density, colour and light to his form allowing Ulysses to see him.

A glowing green, semi-transparent apparition of a mighty Union General stood over Ulysses.

"Whoa!" Ulysses gasped.

His wide unbelieving eyes now saw the vision, his mind swimming in wonder.

"Who are you?" he asked instinctively.

"You can call me... Emerald."

"Umm. Ok... E... Emerald," Ulysses stuttered.

"We have brought you here to give you a very important message," Emerald began.

"A message... important," Ulysses repeated, still not believing in his eyes.

"Resign your post here at Fort Humboldt at once. There is nothing for you here. This place will be the death of you. Leave this frontier and head back east," Emerald paused. "Do you understand?"

"Resign... go back east," Ulysses repeated.

"In a few years the nation will become divided. A great duty will be bestowed upon you to lead the armies of the north. And you must fight, Ulysses... you must fight when it is necessary to do so," Emerald paused. "Do you understand, General Ulysses S. Grant?"

"In a few years... lead an army... and fight," he repeated.

Ulysses rolled his eyes back to look up at the sky and then closed them, as the vision and the head spin became overwhelming.

"Lead an army… and fight," he mumbled.

He did not wish to open his eyes again and fell asleep upon the blanket. Barrin reappeared from the tree line.

"Take him to Fort Humboldt in the darkness before dawn and tell the guard at the gate to leave him in the paymaster's office."

Barrin nodded in acknowledgement. Emerald dissolved his current form and swiftly returned to the comfort of the orb. The lid of the chest slammed shut as the golden light disappeared within. Barrin's eyes returned to normal. He climbed into the wagon, closed the lid of the small box and secured the padlock.

Two hours before dawn, Barrin roused Ulysses from his coma and pushed him onto his horse once more. He then walked the horse and slumbering rider the mile and a half to the gates of Fort Humboldt. He raised his arms thirty yards from the gate as the first rays of the new day appeared behind the horizon.

"Guard! Guard! Are you there?" he calmly called out.

"Who goes there?" the guard replied, with musket at the ready.

"I have Captain Ulysses S. Grant here. He left the fort without a pass, and I found him on a bender at a saloon over the ridge there. May I approach?" Barrin asked.

"Yeah… but make it slow."

Barrin approached slowly and stood before the guard.

"Take a look," he said.

The guard walked around the horse and inspected its rider.

"It's Captain Grant!" He exclaimed. "He looks like hell."

"Yes, he does!"

Barrin handed the reins over to the guard.

"Here, take his horse. It would be best if you lay Captain Grant down in the paymaster's office and tie his horse at the front. Do you think you can do that?"

"Umm… yeah. I guess so."

"Very well, then. I bid you a good day."

Barrin tipped his hat with a slight bow, turned and briskly walked away.

The guard did as he was asked. A short time later Captain Ulysses S. Grant was found passed out asleep on the floor of the paymaster's office, in dishevelled civilian clothes and reeking of booze. The commander, Lieutenant Colonel Robert C. Buckanan was summoned and Ulysses was confined to his quarters for twenty-four hours. He was ordered to appear for a disciplinary hearing before the commander at nine o'clock the following morning.

Captain Grant stood before Lieutenant Colonel Buckanan upon commencement of the hearing. He could not excuse his conduct of leaving Fort Humboldt and going on a bender. He explained that the dull life in the fort, on the frontier, was not the place for him. He almost mentioned that he saw an apparition of an emerald, green General and checked himself just in time; Ulysses realised how this would make him appear as though he had lost his mind in front of his commanding officer. He decided never to speak of that incident.

Captain Ulysses S. Grant resigned his commission in the Union Army on the morning of Monday 31st July 1854. He gathered his few personal belongings and prepared to travel back east, home to his family in the state of Ohio.

Barrin also broke camp that same morning and set his plan to trek back south and then east across the California trail, destination Baltimore, Maryland.

He had plenty of time to spare.

9

One Long Night in Baltimore

Friday 22nd February 1861

Deep into the cold of night one hour before midnight, Cipriano Ferrandini emerged from a side entrance to Barnum's Hotel, well past curfew. He left his barber shop located in the basement of the hotel. Dressed in a full-length black coat, Cipriano headed south for three blocks, entered a small lane and ducked into the rear entrance of a three-storey terrace house.

A few minutes later Cipriano reemerged into the lane, accompanied by two more gentlemen, all dressed in black. One was taller and broader through the shoulder than Cipriano and the other about the same height but much wider in girth. In single file behind Cipriano, the group made their way through the shadows of side lanes and back streets, on approach to President Street Station. They all held a loaded long rifle musket.

Barrin followed a close thirty paces behind. He was completely covered in tight-fitting dark-blue clothing. His soft sole slippers were strapped around his calf and shins. His gloves only permitted the tips of his fingers to show through. His neck, head and face were completely covered by the Shozoku mask, only allowing his eye sockets and the small bridge of his nose to be visible. A light, smaller musket rifle was strapped to his back. He carried a pistol on each hip, covered, several throwing knives and a very sharp twelve-inch Katana blade.

Three blocks from the station, the group emerged from a side lane and walked under cover of shadow along the front veranda of a long row of business houses and shops. Barrin skipped ahead down a back lane and turned into the street ahead of the group. He lay in wait behind the corner of the building as the group crept closer. The veranda ended with three steps leading down to the wide street. They were now just two blocks from the station.

Cipriano approached the end of the veranda. He extended his right foot to step down onto the first step. Standing in darkness a few paces back, against the side wall of the building, Barrin raised his extended right arm with pistol in hand. His wrist, hand and pistol were wrapped, twice, with a dark damp towel, with only the tip of the barrel protruding. He fired. A very muffled pop sounded through the side street.

The bullet hit the heel of Cipriano's right boot just as it was about to land on the first step. The heel was shot away. Cipriano's right ankle twisted outwards as he placed his full weight down through his right leg. The right ankle buckled. The right knee caved inwards. Cipriano twisted and fell across the right side of his body. His right hip landed in the pit in front of the bottom step, his right shoulder slammed hard upon the ground and the right side of his head slapped the roadway. Cipriano screamed out in shock and pain and rolled onto his back, dazed, with his legs straddled over the three steps. The musket flew out of his hands and landed in the middle of the street ahead.

The other two quickly leapt to his aid. They looked into the side street. No one was there. With one person on each shoulder, Cipriano was lifted to his feet and carried back up the three steps and sat down against a wall under the cover of shadow. The fallen musket was promptly retrieved.

It took a couple of minutes for the dizziness to subside, while groaning and grimacing in pain. Cipriano finally climbed to his feet. He found no bones were broken, but his swelling right ankle was badly sprained, his right hip and shoulder badly bruised and he was severely concussed.

Cipriano could not go on. He persuaded the other two to proceed with the mission. He turned and hobbled back towards the terrace house, using his musket as a walking stick.

The taller man now led the way by half a dozen paces. They crossed the street and entered the shadowed veranda of the next row of buildings. As soon as both men had crossed the street Barrin dashed to the corner of the building behind them.

The man with a wide girth crept along the front entrance of the first shop. He was wearing an unbuttoned shallow jacket which ended in line with his belt. With silent efficient speed, Barrin climbed the three steps of the veranda and slipped right up behind him.

With his left hand, Barrin grabbed and pulled the belt above his left buttock up and back. With his right hand he slipped the Katan blade faced in reverse, between flesh and his belt and trousers. In one quick motion, Barrin sliced through the belt and trousers right down to the back of the knee. He began to turn. In a crouched position, Barrin drove up and forward with his left shoulder, into the man's left rib cage.

The force of Barrin's drive forced him to stumble the two yards to the edge of the veranda and out over the three steps below. He landed hard on his right shoulder blade in a puddle of cold muddy water, with belt and trousers flailing around his shins. His musket was flung out over his head. He squealed in agony.

The tall one turned and drew his pistol in response to the commotion. Barrin vanished. There was no one behind him on the veranda. He stepped up to the edge of the veranda in front of the shop entrance. He looked down at his companion, who in noisy painful complaint had rolled onto his stomach and then onto his knees, to present his wide wet backside to full view. He gathered his tattered trousers around his waist in a feeble attempt to protect his dignity and climbed to his feet.

"Screw this," he said, no longer concerned about remaining in stealth. "We've been compromised. Look, someone has sliced my belt and trousers and knocked me off the veranda," he said, displaying the evidence.

"I'm sure whoever it is, could've stuck his blade under my ribs and killed me. It's over, I'm leaving. Cipriano will just have to wait for another opportunity."

And with a staunch, defiant expression, he collected his musket and trudged off in quick steps back in the direction of the terrace house.

The tall man stared at his companion leaving. He then turned and glared down the street towards the train station. Alone, he judged that he was now at a severe disadvantage, under threat by a mystery assassin and that the chances of successfully completing their master plan was now next to zero. All motivation evaporated. He calmly holstered his pistol and followed the other two back to the terrace house.

Having foiled the gang of three, Barrin made his way around to the opposite side of President Street Station. He waited under the cover of darkness between two parked rail freight cars. He knew all too well that Spectre would not rely on a band of buffoons.

On the station platform, two heavily armed guards patrolled the eastern end while two more patrolled the furthest western end. An hour following the stroke of midnight, a train with three carriages arrived from the northern city of Harrisburg and pulled up a hundred yards short of the eastern side of the platform.

All three carriages were dimly lit and the blind for every window was drawn down. The front door of the middle carriage opened. Two heavily armed men stepped out of the carriage and filed down the steep set of stairs to the ground. They fanned out around the carriage and inspected the surrounding area. The all clear was given.

After a few moments, a tall thin man, wearing a straight-brimmed hat, wrapped in a thick navy-blue blanket stepped through the door and descended the narrow stairs. He had high cheekbones, dark sunken eyes, a large thick well-defined nose and a thin beard running down both sides of his face, along his jawline and ending across the front of his chin.

Two more armed men emerged from the carriage and followed. All four guards surrounded their charge and used their bodies to shield him. The troupe quickly shuffled forward ahead of the locomotive. Thirty yards ahead a four-horse team had been hooked up to a single railway carriage. The front two guards filed into the carriage, followed by the tall man, and then the final two guards. The last guard quietly gave the order for the driver to proceed, before closing the carriage door behind him.

A Baltimore city ordinance prohibited a locomotive to travel through the downtown portion of the city during curfew. The only way the president-elect could circumvent the ordinance and secretly pass through Baltimore, a Confederate municipality, was via a horse-drawn rail carriage.

The carriage pulled forward slowly and proceeded at the pace of a brisk walk. Heading west, the carriage passed quietly through the station, then turned north to skirt around the northern boundary of the harbour and through the downtown precinct, before turning west again towards the Camden Yards. Barrin followed at a discreet distance on the northern side of the railway track for the duration of the two-mile journey to Camden Street Station, on the corner of South Howard St. and West Camden St.

The horse-drawn carriage stopped thirty yards short of the eastern side of the platform. The connecting three-carriage locomotive was parked alongside the platform ready for departure.

Barrin continued north silently through the railyards and hooked back around from the northwest side of the station. He positioned himself between two parked rail stock cars with a clear side-on view of the waiting locomotive. The platform was dimly lit with only three lanterns hanging on support beams. The rail line, rail yards and adjoining cattle yards were all in pitch-black darkness.

Once again, the first two guards opened the carriage door, descended to the ground and hurriedly scouted the area. The tall thin man appeared, descended the carriage and stood behind the first two guards. The second pair of guards were quick to follow. In formation, the group briskly walked the thirty yards to the back of the third carriage.

The first two guards climbed the narrow stairs, opened the door to the carriage and went inside. The tall thin man stepped up onto the landing in front of the open carriage door and stopped for a brief moment. His face and torso were illuminated by the light emitted through the open carriage door. He looked back at the horse-drawn carriage, as though to make a mental note and commit the event to memory.

From the northeast recesses of the rail yards, beyond the horse-drawn carriage, a shot rang out. A split second later, a second shot rang out, followed by a resounding high-pitched ricochet. The crack of a single spark lit the air, five yards in front of the tall man's left shoulder.

"Get him inside and shut that door!" Pinkerton yelled from within the carriage.

The two guards behind leapt up the stairs and shoved the tall man into the carriage and slammed the door closed. Orders were yelled through the interior of the carriages. With boilers hot, the locomotive lurched into action, rapidly pulling the three-car train out of the station and was quickly on its way to Washington DC.

The subtle glow in Barrin's eyes and body subsided as he lowered the hot smoking musket.

Chickamauga Chill

Chickamauga Chill

Chickamauga Chill

Monday 1st January 1900

A little after midday, the sun managed to break through and appeared from behind a blanket of clouds on this cold winter's day. Old man Robert Randolph seized the opportunity. Having just finished lunch and tired of being cooped up for days in the house, he craved some sun and exercise.

He put on his boots, scarf, gloves and long coat. He grabbed the wide flat shovel, walked out and began to clear the overnight snow and ice from the stone-paved walkway. Starting from the three stairs below the porch, he dug his way towards the front gate. Long retired, Robert and his wife Penelope lived in a cottage in the small community of Frenchtown, New Jersey, on the east bank of the Delaware River, sixty-seven miles west of New York City.

Three doors down, young Harvey Lewis also took advantage of the opportunity and decided to visit a friend. He walked out of his house, closed the front gate behind him and trudged down the footpath through the shin-deep snow.

"Good afternoon, Mr Randolph. Happy New Year!" Harvey exclaimed.

"Happy New Year to you too, Harvey."

Robert stopped to lean against the long handle of the shovel, almost done with his chore.

"Isn't it an auspicious occasion? Not only is it a new year, but a new century as well. My, my... if only I could have my youth back. It would be quite something to live through the next one hundred years. You know... I feel a great many changes are ahead of us," he said and paused. "Well, you might be a bit young to appreciate my meaning. Anyhow... so, what plans have you for the afternoon?"

"I'm just going over to visit my friend. He lives just over there, down the road a bit."

Robert sported a long thick pure white beard and a full shaggy head of pure white hair, which made him look like a spooky old ghost. As the sunlight shone through brightly, Robert's hair and beard glistened with a sheen of shining silver. Harvey noticed.

"Your hair and beard, Mr Randolph, seem to be shining in the sun. It looks more like… silver… than white!"

"Yes… well… actually, it is silver now that you mention it."

"I don't think I've ever seen that before. Is that natural?" Harvey asked.

"I'm not entirely sure. I'd hazard a guess that no, it's probably not a natural thing at all."

Robert rested an elbow across the top of his spade handle and displayed a wry smirk.

"Well… then how did you get silver hair, Mr Randolph?"

"Let's see now… I might have caught the Chickamauga Chill," Robert teased.

"Chickamauga Chill? What's that?" Harvey enquired, suddenly intrigued.

"It's difficult to say. It's like a cold but is not really a cold. It's like a curse but is not really a curse either. It might be an affliction but again, it's not really an affliction. It's like ALL these things but not any one of them. That's all I can say about that," Robert said, amused.

"That sounds confusing. I've no idea what you're talking about," Harvey said disappointed.

Robert paused for a moment to consider.

"The only way to explain what the Chickamauga Chill is, is to tell you how it began. It's a bit of a scary story, you see… and… I'm not sure if you would like to hear such a story!" he said evaluating Harvey.

"I'm seventeen! I can handle a scary story," he replied with confidence.

"Well, we shall see, won't we. This story really did happen, you know."

Robert grabbed his beard and puffed it up as proof.

"Remember… silver hair," he said in a gruff voice.

"Right, yes… of course, how can I forget?"

"Ok then," Robert said letting go of his beard.

He grabbed hold of his shovel and quickly dug a thin path to the gate and loosened the latch.

"Let's go into the kitchen. I've got the pot belly stove going and it'll be nice and warm. Penny can prepare a nice hot cuppa' cocoa and a slice of warm apple pie."

"Sounds great," Harvey replied, temporarily forgetting about his friend.

Robert led the way into the cottage and through into the kitchen. Jackets remained hooked upon a circular hanging stand near the front door beside a low rack for boots.

A small rectangular kitchen table was nestled into a padded L-shaped bench seat built into one corner of the warm kitchen. A chair was positioned at one short and one long length of the exposed table. Robert indicated for Harvey to slide into the shorter bench seat at the head of the table. Robert shuffled into the middle of the bench seat along its length. Penelope walked in from the sitting room, she also used as a sewing room.

"Good afternoon, Mrs Randolph, and Happy New Year," Harvey greeted.

"Hello Harvey. Happy New Year to you too. This is a nice surprise. We don't have many visitors these days," she said.

"Would you be a dear and make us both a hot cuppa cocoa and cut a thick slice of that lovely apple pie you made this morning?" Robert asked his wife.

"Mr Randolph is going to tell me a story about the Chickamauga Chill," Harvey reported excitedly.

"Ooh, right," Penelope replied, giving Robert a discerning look.

"Now Harvey, there's no need to be shooting off with your bottom lip like that and telling everyone what we're doing. Now that we're going to be friends, please call me Bobby. You can call my lovely wife Penny. And let's do away with the Mr and Mrs!"

"Ok, no problems... Mr Rand... um... Bobby."

Penny began preparing the cocoa and apple pie.

"Now, Harvey, are you particularly religious?" Bobby asked.

"I go to church on Sundays. But... I'd say I'm no more or less religious than anyone else."

"I see," he said and paused for a moment. "Well, do you know... what the problem is with religion?" he did not stop for an answer. "There's no real mention or teaching on how a prophet really becomes a prophet, or what it takes to become one. In the same manner, there's no real teaching on the true nature of things, the underlying forces within man, within nature and of the true reality in which we live," he paused and then continued.

"For me to tell this story, you'll have to broaden your perspective on what you think you know of the world we live in and of the forces behind the natural world. Do you understand?"

"I think so," Harvey said, still with a lingering element of doubt.

"I see you're not quite sure of my meaning. Well then, do you believe in demons, Harvey?"

Bobby left a long pause for Harvey to consider the question.

"I… I'm not sure. Nobody has ever asked me such a question before," he stammered.

"Just for a moment let's say, that demons are real. And by this, what I really mean is that we should call them by their proper name… 'a fear demon'!" Bobby paused for effect. "Now, how do you propose a fear demon is made… or created?"

"I have absolutely no idea," Harvey answered mystified.

"Well, they certainly can't create themselves now, can they?" Bobby exclaimed loudly and a little scarily. "As you should well understand, only God has the power of creation. But… I'm going to tell you how a fear demon is made," he said and then leant forward a little closer and continued in a loudish whisper.

"A fear demon is created when man goes to war, Harvey, from the Wetiko of war," he said. "You see… all those prophets knew of and understood this and told us how best to live and behave towards each other. And most of all, they told us of the things we should never do. But does man listen? Does he heed thy warning? Of course NOT!" Bobby paused once more and sat back up against the bench. "Man prefers to listen to the whispers of his own desires and wars continue to persist, more and more terrible each time."

"Now… I've not told this story in many a year. Actually, I can't remember if I've ever told anyone this tale… except Penny, of course. I always felt that all the people I've met would not have the head for such a story. But it's a new century and times are a-changing. And so, once I've told you this story, you must be very discerning about who you do and do not repeat this story to. Do you think you can do that?"

"Yes, I must keep it a secret and only tell someone that I trust."

"You catch on quick," Bobby said with an approving grin. "And if you were to err in this, you could bring upon yourself the direst of consequences. Do you accept this burden?"

"Yes… I do," Harvey stated eagerly.

"Right, then! But before we start, I must let you know my first secret," Bobby paused for a long moment. "I am a man of… the Rose and Cross," he said and allowed that to sink in.

"The Rose and Cross?" Harvey repeated, intrigued.

Robert fiddled inside the pocket of his waistcoat, drew out an old brass ring and handed it to Harvey to inspect. Harvey turned the thick solid ring around in his grasp and then studied the flat circular, finely crafted debossed emblem set upon its front. It was a richly layered perfectly round red rose positioned over the middle of an even-length, thin white cross. Each branch of the cross touched the outer edge of the circle of the emblem.

"Wow!" Harvey exclaimed. "It really looks like a red circle inside a white square."

He correctly placed the prominent ring on his right index finger and extended his hand to see.

"Yes, you are indeed perceptive. It's an Order of men and women of the highest calibre. Those who become members are instructed in the true forces within man and nature, and the numerous relationships that exist between them."

Harvey looked a little perplexed. Robert continued.

"Don't worry too much about that. Your comprehension will become clear with the telling of our story."

Penny placed a hot cup of cocoa and slice of apple pie on the table in front of both Harvey and Bobby.

"Thank you, my dear," Bobby said gratefully.

"You're welcome," Penny replied. "Try not to frighten Harvey too much."

She turned and left the kitchen for the sitting room, leaving the door slightly ajar.

"So, where shall we begin?" Bobby pondered, sipping his hot cocoa.

Harvey sipped his cocoa in eager anticipation and picked up his fork.

"It was… late in the afternoon of Thursday 17th September 1863. My two companions Lesley Llewellyn and Christopher Dee… and myself… arrived at the Gordon Lee Mansion at Crawfish Springs, which had become the headquarters of the Union Army."

"We had travelled southwest from Chattanooga and followed some distance behind the Union Army. We rode through Steven's Gap, through Lookout Mountain into McLemore's Cove and turned north at Davis's Cross Roads following West Chickamauga Creek to Pond Spring and then onto Crawford Springs some two miles southwest of Lee and Gordon's Mills."

"As we descended from a small hill on the eastern slope of Missionary Ridge overlooking the main camp of the Union Army, we observed that three divisions were now encamped between Crawford Springs and Lee and Gordon's Mill, on the west side of Chickamauga Creek. Each was under the command of Major Generals James Negley, Thomas Crittenden and Alexander McCook."

"The long ride through the day was hot, dry and tiring. No rain had fallen in the region for over a month. The marching army had churned up the dirt roads and we were covered in a fine layer of dust. We now searched for a place to rest, water for the horses and to clean ourselves up before our evening supper. As dusk fell...".

Thursday 17th September 1863

... ℭhe trio made a small camp along the bank of Crawfish Spring Lake which was a short 200 yards from Gordon Lee Mansion. They unsaddled, fed and watered their horses. A small campfire was lit to cook a light supper. A screen was erected behind which they could each bath using a bucket full of water and a large cloth, and henceforth change their dusty soiled cloths for a fresh set.

Robert 'Bobby' Randolph was thirty-four years old. Naturally tanned, he was six foot three inches tall, broad across the shoulder, with fierce blue eyes and wavy sandy-brown hair. After riding for three consecutive days, he sported thick stubble down both sides of his face, along the jawbone under his chin and displayed the beginnings of a moustache. He was lean and finely muscled as an athlete, having been a boxing champion in his mid-twenties. He now looked splendid in his disguise of clerical garments.

He wore a thick black protective shoulder coat over the top half of his torso, ending at the base of his rib cage, which covered a thick black long-sleeved woollen shirt. A white cross was embroidered into the cuff on each sleeve aligned with the top of each wrist. He wore a black waistcoat, with a silver cross on a long chain neatly woven through each buttonhole and ending with the cross hanging over the front of the left pocket, instead of a gentlemanly timepiece. The dress code was completed with a pair of thick tough black trousers held in place with a black leather belt, black riding boots, a cappello romano upon his head and a pure white silk cravat wrapped around his neck and tucked into his shirt collar.

Lesley Llewellyn was thirty-one years of age. With olive skin she stood at five foot four inches tall, was robust, agile and flexible in her muscular disposition, having grown up whilst training as an acrobat in a travelling circus. She had deep, dark-brown eyes which matched her straight hair that during the day was always pulled back tightly into a small bun. She wore the exact same men's clothing as Robert, to disguise herself as a man and a simple white detachable pastor's collar. The shoulder coat also helped to hide her bust.

Christopher Dee was the youngest at twenty-seven years of age and stood five foot eight inches tall. He was cream-skinned, thin and lean muscled with unnatural agility, being quick on his feet and able to move with speed in close quarters. He was highly intelligent, had short black hair and very unsettling dark lime-green eyes that seemed to pierce into the heart of things. The only facial hair he could grow was a small line of stubble around the back of the jawbone on each side, a small tuft around his chin and a very thin moustache, which all added to his strangeness. He appeared in identical dress to Lesley.

The evening was growing late when all three were dressed and ready. Time had just ticked over to nine o'clock. Walking out of their camp in single file, they made their way towards Gordon Lee Mansion. The small lake was on their left. Fields stretched out to their right, now filled with neat, row after row of orderly white tents glowing in the fiery light of a legion of small campfires, slowly growing dim in the cool night air. At regular intervals around the edge of the massive camp, groups of three or four men were posted to stand guard over the resting army. Scouts hid in the nearby tree line to watch for anything suspicious.

Robert, Lesley and Christopher approached the perimeter guards to Gordon Lee Mansion. It was a grand old red-brick square-shaped southern house, consisting of a raised ground floor and first level. A flight of ten stairs led to the top of the veranda and then onto the oversized front door, set in an even larger, white-painted timber and stained-glass door-frame.

Four massive, perfectly round columns supported the front overhanging roof. There was one column at each front corner and one column standing upon a cubed arrangement of stone bricks, on either side of the staircase. The whole house was lit up like a huge ornament.

There were two long rows of horses, facing each other along the front lawn and separated by the path leading up to the house. They were held by junior officers waiting for their superiors. Robert approached the first lieutenant, the most senior of the four guards.

"Evening, sir," Robert greeted.

"Evening, pastor. State your business," the officer countered bluntly, efficiently.

"We are here for a meeting with Major General William S. Rosecrans."

"General Rosecrans is still in council with a number of other generals and senior officers and is not to be disturbed," the officer reported. "Who might you be then?"

"I'm Robert Randolph. These are my companions Lesley and Christopher. We might wait back over there until the meeting is concluded. Will that be alright?" Robert asked.

"Yeah, sure. Come back when they all leave and I'll enquire of General Rosecrans if he's willing to receive you," the officer said.

"Very good," Robert replied with a slight bow.

He turned and moved twenty-five yards back and to the right of the check-point and waited within view of the guards. During the next ten minutes two couriers passed through the check-point and handed written messages to a senior officer at the front door of the house. A few minutes later a written order was handed back and the messenger left to deliver it.

After a further fifteen minutes, the war council finally ended, in a noisy but efficient commotion of generals and senior officers. Aided by their junior officers, they all mounted their horses and rode out through the front check-point in excited haste towards their respective divisional commands. Once quiet orderliness had returned, Robert approached the check-point once more.

"Evening again, sir. Robert Randolph, Lesley and Christopher here to see General Rosecrans," he said straight to the point this time.

"Right, yes. I'll go and check," the officer replied.

He quickly marched to the front of the house and spoke to the guard posted below the stairs. The guard nodded, glanced their way and disappeared through the front door. Three minutes later he reappeared to issue instructions. The officer promptly returned to the check-point.

"The General will see you now. Follow me."

The officer opened the gate and allowed the trio to pass through. With a brisk march, he led the way to the front door of the house. Chief of Staff Brigadier General James A. Garfield appeared to greet the trio at the front door.

"Follow me please. It's right this way," Garfield directed.

He led them through the front door into the main hallway of the house. Just beyond the first door to the right, through which the war council had been held, the long staircase climbed the right-hand wall to the first level. James knocked twice and opened the first door on the left, the parlour, now converted to an office. He walked in and stepped aside.

"The three clergymen are here to see you, General," Garfield announced.

Major General William S. Rosecrans rose to his feet, behind a large desk strewn with papers and maps. The desk was placed in the front and middle of the wall to the left and partially across the window which looked out to the front of the building. Robert filed into the office followed closely by Lesley and Christopher, who all stood at ease in the middle of the chamber, facing the General.

"Thank you, James. Robert Randolph, my dear friend. It's so good to see you."

General Rosecrans stepped around from behind the desk and quickly moved forward to take Robert's right hand in a warm handshake.

"General, it's such a pleasure to meet with you once again," Robert replied.

Garfield looked rather surprised at the warm greeting.

"Thank you, James, that'll be all!" General Rosecrans instructed.

"Do you all know each other?" Garfield asked.

"Now, one must keep the faith and be on the good side of our Lord. Please close the door behind you, James," the General commanded.

With a brisk nod of acknowledgement, Garfield turned, marched out of the chamber and closed the door behind. A long quiet pause persisted while they listened to the sound of Garfield's boots enter the opposite chamber, close the door and proceed to tidy up after the war council. The General returned to standing behind the desk.

The thick wooden floorboards were covered with an immense, lavishly woven rug. A fireplace was built into the right-hand wall now filled with a beautifully constructed mound of glowing coals. Two identical tall, narrow side entrances with glass-fitted French doors opened out onto a patio which ran along the left-hand side of the building. The window and both French doors were closed, locked and covered with thick drapes. All other chairs were removed when in the presence of the General.

Whilst standing, General Rosecrans slipped his left hand into the inner pocket of his jacket and withdrew a large brass ring. He placed the ring upon his right index finger and held his right arm straight out in front, clenching a fist.

Robert also withdrew a large ring from a hidden pocket and thread it onto his right index finger. Both rings were debossed with the image of a richly layered red rose set across a white cross. Robert extended the fist of his right hand. The emblem of both rings touched.

"May the righteous stay the path to light," the General and Robert recited in unison.

General Rosecrans nodded. Robert stood aside. Lesley approached the desk and repeated the sacred greeting, quickly followed by Christopher. Once the rite of attendance was complete, all rings disappeared and the General took his seat behind the desk.

"Christopher, would you be so kind and fix us all a nightcap?" the General asked.

He casually pointed towards a bookstand behind the entrance door, to the right of the fireplace. Robert and Lesley stood at ease. Christopher made his way over to the bookstand. The books had been boxed and removed. He laid out four tumblers in a row and opened the decanter of fine southern Tennessee whiskey. He brought the open lip of the decanter to his nose and savoured the rich vapour. He then poured a double shot into each glass.

"How was your trip, Robert?" the General asked.

"It was hot and dry, with a heck of a lot of dust. We had no trouble to report and didn't encounter any Confederates," he replied.

"Did you encounter any issue having Lesley travel with you?"

"Lesley went mostly unnoticed, being dressed like a man an' all. All the infantry we passed took one look at us and kept their eyes averted. Maybe, they didn't wish to attract the attention of God upon their meagre souls," he said with a wry smile.

"One captain did notice and asked why we have a woman riding along with us. I said, "Well Captain, sir, when you are dying on the battlefield, whose face would you prefer to be looking at, giving you your last rites? My ugly face! Or that of an angel?""

"And what was his response?"

"He had no rebuke. He simply turned and waved us on. I guess, the imagining was too much to bear and brought back harsh memories," Robert replied.

Christopher handed each person their tumbler and with quiet tribute, everyone took their first sip of the fine whiskey at the same time. After savouring the warm, settling flavour for a few long moments, General Rosecrans broke the brooding silence.

"Well, this is a dastardly business and it's about to get a whole lot more serious. As you know, we are in pursuit of General Braxton Braggs and his Confederate Army. I have received reports he has bolstered his numbers to sixty, or maybe as many as seventy thousand men. Looks like he's going to make a fight of it," he paused for a further sip.

"I have brought all our divisions in closer together. They were too far apart and could not support each other in the event of a major engagement. I judge there could be up to one hundred and thirty thousand men in the field, from both sides," he paused.

"The main body of the Confederate forces are camped just on the other side of Chickamauga Creek, not more than ten miles from here. The chances of engagement are extremely high. Once begun, the battle will escalate very quickly. So, you know what that means!"

"Yeah! The numbers are high enough to form... a demon," Robert confirmed.

"Yes indeed. So, gentlemen... and lady... prepare yourselves. Have any of you borne witness to a fear demon before?" the General asked.

"No. None of us has encountered an actual demon. We've studied the manifestos and understand the basic principles. We've all been trained in etheric vision and general combat tactics," Robert replied.

"Well, I have yet to lay my eyes on one myself. A fear demon formed at Gettysburg. Unfortunately, it was too late when our man found it. The demon was already fully formed and too powerful. Our man died trying to kill it before it managed to escape," he paused.

"So, we'll never know how he tried to fight it. Now you travel in teams of three. Once battle on the field begins, the most important thing is to find its spawning location. The earlier we can do this, the greater our chances will be to destroy it."

310

"What we know is that they need a heat source from which to be born… like a furnace or a stove. They are more active at night and very averse to the sun. It takes some time for their body to form and take shape. And if they escape, they will escape through a clear, still body of fresh black water which acts as a gateway to their plane of existence."

"Once escaped, we can no longer reach them. They will then begin to prey upon the fears of man and eventually, evolve into a spectre. So, as you can imagine, once we've found it, we must contain it and then destroy it before it can cross over. So…" he paused "…are you up for the challenge?"

Robert, Lesley and Christopher all glanced at each other.

"Yes, General," they all said in unison.

"Wonderful!" the General said, finishing his whiskey which was mimicked by the others.

"Now, you all know the one rule above all rules… right?"

"Yes," Christopher spoke for the first time in a raspy voice. "Whatever you do… never allow yourself to be touched by a fear demon."

"Indeed, that is correct. We don't really understand the consequence of what might happen if you are touched by one, suffice it to say that I cannot think of anyone who has survived being touched by a demon."

The General stood up.

"If you do find it, you must contain it, immediately. You know what to do. Get yourself a good amount of salt, bushels of all the herbs you can find and plenty of rose petals soaked in holy water. Very well! I wish you all Godspeed and good hunting."

"Thank you, General," Robert replied.

The trio offered a light bow, turned and walked out of the door and into the hallway. Passing through the front door, they bid Chief of Staff James Garfield good night and left Gordon Lee Mansion for their small camp.

Friday 18th September 1863

The first rays of light loomed across the eastern horizon. The Union Army was already busy. Following a hasty breakfast, the massive camp was efficiently broken down and the men quickly formed their respective divisions. The heavy woodlands opened into wide expansive meadows around a large loop in Chickamauga Creek just north of Lee and Gordon's Mills.

Here the individual brigades of General Crittenden's infantry division formed easily on the edge between woods and meadow along La Fayette Road. Slowly, the front lines began to move forward northeast along the course of Chickamauga Creek. Officers on horseback rode between each brigade issuing orders and carrying messages back to Crittenden.

Through the tree line upon a small rise behind the Union Army, the trio watched the glint of twenty-five thousand rifle tips sparkle before the sunrise, begin to move forward and fan out.

> Negley's and McCook's divisions took up their positions and formed the southern line on Rosecrans's right flank. Crittenden's division formed their lines in front of Rosecrans and pushed forward approaching the west side of Chickamauga Creek around and to the north of Lee and Gordon's Mills. Two further divisions were loosely arranged to the north and northeast of Rosecrans guarding his left flank, while Granger's reserve corps held the road back to Chattanooga.[1]

Chickamauga Creek was a narrow creek and not all that deep, with high and steep banks flooded with thick brush, shrubbery and small trees. The creek was windy and contained many loops as it made its way downstream and northeast from Lee and Gordon's Mills to Dalton's

Ford, Thedford's Ford, Alexander's Bridge, Fowler's Ford and Reed's Bridge, and on to finally connect with the Tennessee River.

The entire region on the east side of Missionary Ridge down to Chickamauga Creek consists of gentle rolling hills of thick woodlands occasionally broken with clear meadows of waving knee-high grasses. The meadows and woods close to Chickamauga Creek managed to retain some greenery, but otherwise had quickly turned a dry brown from the lack of rain.

General Braxton Bragg of the Confederate Army arranged his forces into five divisions and planned to cross Chickamauga Creek from east to west at four crossing points, intending to draw the Union Army out into a fight. Polk's division to the south were entrenched on the east side of Chickamauga Creek opposite Lee and Gordon's Mills and the approach to the Dalton's Ford crossing. Polk found the west bank heavily defended by Crittenden's Union division. Buckner's division approached Thedford's Ford crossing. Walker's division marched on Alexander's Bridge, and Johnson's division with Forrest's mounted cavalry were ordered to take Reed's Bridge to the north.

The first engagement began at 7 am when Johnson's division and Forrest's cavalry encountered cavalry pickets from Colonel Robert Minty's brigade who were ordered to guard the approach to Reed's Bridge. Johnson and Forrest eventually broke Minty's stout resistance and prevented him from destroying the bridge. Minty was pushed back to Jay's Mill by 4 pm in the afternoon, a half mile west of Reed's Bridge.

Meanwhile, Colonel John Wilder's mounted Union infantry brigade, armed with the superior Spencer repeating rifles, held Alexander's Bridge against Walker's Confederate division. Walker was forced to withdraw and move his forces north and a mile downstream to cross Chickamauga Creek at Lambert's Ford at 4:30 pm. As Minty quit the field having been driven from Reed's

Bridge and Jay's Mill, Wilder decided to withdraw to the vicinity of Viniard Farm just east of La Fayette Road to protect his left flank. The Confederate division of Johnson, aided by the arrival of Hood's corps, met up with Walker's division and forced Wilder to withdraw to a new position by nightfall, leaving a large number of Union men scattered along the road behind.

Further south during the afternoon Buckner only managed to push one Confederate brigade across the creek at Thedford's Ford and one at Dalton's Ford. Polk faced the main force of Crittenden across the flat shallow rocky rapids at and north of Lee and Gordon's Mills, and decided not to risk his division at a crossing there.[1]

Earlier in the afternoon, the scattered Union soldiers separated from Minty's brigade and made their way south along Chickamauga Creek below Reed's Bridge. Now behind the Confederate line, they dug themselves into the steep west bank, hiding beneath the thick brush and shrubs.

About forty yards down, another small group of Union soldiers, also separated, found their way to the west bank of the creek and dug themselves in to hide, with the thought of being captured by the Confederates a terrifying prospect.

Several Confederate deserters from Johnson's division had managed to sneak away, just as the battle against Minty for Reed's Bridge began. The weeks of running and evading the Union Army had instilled a sense of gloom and inevitable hopelessness against the north and left them with little stomach to fight. They found their way to the east bank of Chickamauga Creek below Reed's Bridge and dug in beneath the thick foliage.

Each time either a Union or Confederate soldier hiding along the creek bank had an overwhelming thought of fear or terror which sent a shiver down their spine, a small wisp of dark etheric thought matter would leave his body through the top of his head. The wisp would rise above the treetops and plateau about two hundred feet above the ground.

As the battle ensued, whenever a soldier enacted an action accompanied by extreme hatred and violence, especially during a killing blow, a dark wisp would leave his body and rise. When a soldier died in battle accompanied by the realisation and terror of what had happened to him, a wisp of dark ether would leave his body and rise two hundred feet into the air.

With dusk approaching, the shadows of the trees grew longer and longer while more Union soldiers found their way to the west bank of Chickamauga Creek as Minty was driven from Jay's Mill and Wilder from Alexander's Bridge back to Viniard Farm. Chaos and confusion reigned when fighting and retreating in heavy woods. With thick gun smoke and swirling dust in looming shadow, visibility was twenty yards at best.

This meant that if you became separated from your company, navigating your way back to safety was near impossible and extremely dangerous in near darkness. On many occasions during the engagement through sundown, Union soldiers fired upon Union men and Confederate soldiers fired on Confederate men. If stranded, self-preservation was the only priority, rather than face being captured or shot by your own side in the woods.

Fleeing the chaos, lost Union troops found their way to the west bank of Chickamauga Creek, along the winding, looping stretch between Thedford's Ford and Alexander's Bridge. Those who were lucky found holes or small caves in the steep bank of the creek. Checking for snakes and other creatures first, the soldier would then wiggle himself into the narrow burrow feet first, until fully submerged alongside his rifle. Only then could he relax and wait out the cold night ahead.

Further south between Dalton's Ford and Thedford's Ford, many Confederate infantry men slipped into the banks of Chickamauga Creek during the crossing of Polk and Buckner's divisions. Having glimpsed Crittenden's Union division amassing across the creek, these few men did not have the mettle to stand and fight. They also crept into small holes and caves and pockets of undergrowth to hide from the battle. By the time night fell, a thousand Union men and three hundred Confederates had found refuge along the banks of Chickamauga Creek. And all the while, wisps of fear continued to rise in a steady stream.

Earlier during the morning, Robert, Lesley and Christopher were straggling behind Crittenden's division. Word arrived announcing that contact had been made with the enemy a few miles northeast at Reed's Bridge. Robert decided to take leave of this division and accompanied by Lesley and Christopher, they rode north from Lee and Gordon's Mills using the La Fayette Road. They arrived at the Brotherton Road intersection by mid-morning, among a steady stream of wounded soldiers shuffling along Brotherton Road from the front lines at Reed's Bridge and then Jay's Mill. Brotherton Farm, adjacent to the intersection, was quickly converted into a field hospital.

Robert, Lesley and Christopher dismounted and began to conduct their officially designated duty. They administered last rites and prayers to those who had died. For those whom the attending doctor said that their wounds would be fatal, Robert, Lesley and Christopher calmed and comforted the dying soldier. They told the truth, offered a soothing drink or last smoke of a cigarette and shared a peaceful prayer before they slipped away and died.

As the day moved into the afternoon the steady stream of wounded and dying men grew as both Minty and Wilder were forced to withdraw. For those who would live but could no longer fight, due to a broken bone, bullet wound or amputated limb, wagon trains were organised to evacuate the wounded back through McFarland's Gap to the safety of Chattanooga.

The fighting slowed and settled into a tense truce through the night. Robert, Lesley and Christopher washed up using a bucket of fresh water from a nearby well. They ate a meagre supper, collected their horses and took their leave of the field hospital. Riding out of Brotherton Farm, Robert stopped at the intersection and peered up into the darkened south-easterly sky for a long while. He tried to use his altered vision and searched his feelings as he was trained.

"I sense a darkness forming... particularly over there in the southeast along the creek."

Lesley pulled up alongside Robert's right flank, Christopher stopped on his left with an intense stare ahead into the night sky.

"Yes, I sense it too," Lesley confirmed.

"A lot of fear is rising from Chickamauga Creek," Christopher reported.

"When it gets dark, we must search every farm, every barn and mill we can find. If a demon is to form, it will search for a source of heat. It will not be an open flame… nor a place with lots of people and activity," Robert said. "It will be somewhere dark and quiet."

"Well… after today, we should be familiar to most officers and soldiers. Hopefully, we can move unimpeded," Lesley commented.

"Let's hope you're right," Robert said. "No need to check Jay's Mill. The Confederates will have it locked down. Let's work in a circle of the area. We'll search east and then north first before the Confederates push the Union Army further back. We'll backtrack west and then head south. We must find it early and give ourselves the best chance to destroy it," he said. "Ok, let's go."

The trio headed east along Brotherton Road to Brock Farm, which had long since been abandoned. The remainder of Minty's cavalry had set up a temporary command post here, sending out and receiving riders with valuable information and intelligence. The junior officers checked and collated information, before sending riders back west to deliver information to Minty and General Thomas. Robert was warned not to ride further east to Winfrey Farm as this would be flirting very close to the Confederate lines.

They knew everything along Brotherton Road would be far too busy. Robert, Lesley and Christopher turned north to connect with Alexander's Bridge Road and soon searched McDonald Farm. The farm was occupied by a Union brigade guarding the road to Granger. They used small open campfires to cook and for heat.

Their search turned southward back along La Fayette Road. The trio checked on the Snodgrass and Kelly farms, and the Poe and Dyer farms. The Brock and Viniard farms were encamped by an entire Union division. The Union headquarters was now stationed at Widow Glenn, which meant Weathers Farm would not need to be checked.

The trio checked the Osborn farm before arriving at the Scott farm a half mile north of Lee and Gordon's Mills, an hour before midnight. The Scott family were home except for their very young children who had been taken further south to stay with relatives.

Robert sat around the kitchen table enjoying a hot cup of soothing black tea, with Lesley, Christopher and old man Scott. He had a simply drawn scouting map open on the table, relishing the opportunity to talk to a local.

"Every farm we've searched is too busy and occupied by Union officers," Robert said in frustration. "Is there any farm we've missed?"

"There's the old Dalton Mill House not more than a half mile east from here," old man Scott announced. "Just go down Alexander's Road there and you'll see a not too well-used track on the right. Take that track through a thick wood to the bank of the creek. There you'll find the mill. The Daltons keep mostly to themselves. Can't imagine they'd have stayed with Union on one side and Confederate on the other side of the creek."

In unison, Robert, Lesley and Christopher instantly leapt to their feet, bid farewell and promptly left the Scott farm. They rode east along Alexander Road.

Sure enough, a half mile on and just before the road crossed a tributary stream, a narrow track appeared on the right. The track displayed a pair of narrow wagon wheel furrows. Ankle-high grass grew on both sides and along the middle mound between the furrows. Thick shrubbery grew over to partially obscure the track. Robert turned into the track, followed by Lesley and Christopher in single file. They entered the wood.

The wood was thick and dark and seemed strangely quiet beneath the waxing crescent moon. The narrow track followed the stream southeast, curved southward and turned sharply west to loop around a natural protrusion of rock, then south and a little east for the last thirty yards.

The track finally brought Robert, Lesley and Christopher out onto a wide semi-circular clearing on the west bank of the Chickamauga Creek. It had taken twenty minutes to slowly traverse the three hundred yards of hard-to-see woodland track. The first hour past midnight was fast approaching.

The semi-circular clearing was located at the northern end of a long straight south to north flowing length, before the creek conducted a 180° loop back south, around a point bar. Being covered in thick semi-submersed marsh-like vegetation made the point bar a natural barrier to crossing the creek from the eastern side. The water current flowing into the loop was quite strong, making it ideal to turn a mill wheel.

On the edge of the clearing, the trio stood still before a large, very wide, single-storey house, built on low set, thick wooden stumps, dug deep into the ground. A flight of four steps led onto a wide veranda and up to the front door. The front half of the building was a house, whereas the back half was a sawmill.

The entire structure was built from rough-cut timber planking in a large barn-like manner. A steep timber slate roof overhung the veranda and the entire building by two feet. Internally, across the middle of the building, the back half, the sawmill, was a sunken level by seven steps. Naturally the ceiling was high, with thick timber walls on both sides and an open space facing the creek.

The floor was laid with timber beams as thick as a railway sleeper. The platform overhung the creek by a few feet, with a gentle curve down carved at the end, to allow logs that were floated down the creek to be pulled up into the sawmill. The workspace was wide, open and expansive and sat about one and a half yards above the water level of the creek. A medium-sized water wheel was built into the right corner of the platform and partially submerged into the creek, which powered the sawmill's machinery. The wheel was locked with a metal pin.

Outside around the building, there were pens for ox and cattle, a row of three small stables, a hen house, smoke house, latrine and a vegetable patch and herb garden. A charcoal kiln could be seen further back near the edge of the wood. Everything was dark and eerily quiet, broken occasionally by a bang or clatter of window panel, internal door, or loose timber board by the swirl of a gentle gust of wind. They dared not light a fire and attract the attention of a Confederate scout.

"This place is rather dark and creepy," Lesley mused. "There's no one here."

"Looks like a bunch of swamp people live here," Christopher added. "With the Union Army behind us and the Confederates on the other side of the creek, just behind those trees, I'd say the Daltons have packed up and headed south for a few days. See, there're no animals left."

"I think you're right… but let's make sure," Robert said.

They all dismounted and tied their steeds to the veranda's handrail at the front of the house. Robert climbed the stairs followed by Lesley and Christopher. Robert gripped the handle and turned. It was unlocked. He pulled open the front door and stepped inside.

The layout was straightforward. They stood in an open chamber. There was a kitchen with a small pot belly stove, bench, wash tub and pantry on the left. A dining table and chairs were positioned just on the right, with a couch and several armchairs arranged beyond the table, around and against the walls. A wide dark hallway loomed in front of them. Upon a gust, the front door swung open and slammed shut behind them with a bang. They all jumped and looked back at once to breathe a nervous sigh. They slowly crept further inside.

There were three long, narrow bedchambers on the left and three on the right, each with a cot, discoloured straw mattress and small square window. They were all empty and stripped of blankets. Christopher checked the small pot belly stove in the kitchen. It was dead cold.

In the dark hallway, Christopher and Lesley soon filed in behind Robert who stood before the closed door into the mill. The door had a simple wooden handle. Robert reached forward, grabbed the handle and pulled the door open. They stepped through and out onto a narrow balcony which ran along the length of the wall on both the left and right and was protected by a waist-high balustrade. They looked down and across the mill floor below, from atop a narrow, steep seven-step staircase with waist-high handle rails on both sides.

A long bench was built up against the inner wall below the balcony on both sides of the stairs, strewn with broken tools in need of repair, or new ones still being crafted. There were saddles, harnesses, bridles, parts of wagons and tools for farming and lumbering along the right-hand wall on both sides of a tall, narrow door which led out into the yard. A long table with a circular saw stood on the inner-right front portion of the platform alongside the housing holding the water wheel in place. Suspended machinery used to handle heavy logs also hung idle over the table saw. Planks of cut timber lay upon the floor in the corner to the right of the table saw.

Two identical rows of four large wooden support beams ran parallel along the width of the building. The first row ran parallel with and a few feet beyond the balustrade. The beams were evenly spaced with two on either side of the stairwell. The second row stood about three yards inside the open end of the platform. Thick high struts connected each neighbouring beam and supported both the ceiling and the hanging machinery. The high-pointed ceiling angled down by 40° over the left and right wall and the end of the platform.

Christopher stepped down the flight of steps onto the main deck. The middle of the platform was open and clear. He turned to his left and stepped forward a few paces to approach the left-hand wall. Robert and Lesley's eyes followed him. In the dim light they had all seen it.

Christopher continued until he was within arm's reach of the furnace. It was a small makeshift design used to craft and repair the tools used within the mill. The furnace was the equivalent of a tall, oversized pot belly stove set inside a multi-layered brick housing, with a brick chimney rising up through the ceiling. A large iron door with thick hinges on one side and lever handle on the other, allowed access into the pit of the furnace. A wooden drum of water sat to the left, between the furnace and a nearby waist-high anvil. A drum of charcoal sat to the right of the furnace. There were air vents built into the base of the brickwork.

Christopher leant forward and placed his hand on the under-belly of the furnace.

"It's still warm!" he announced. "They must've left earlier in the day."

He reached forward with his left hand and took hold of the lever handle. He pressed down and opened the door. It was completely black inside. He grabbed an iron poking fork and shoved the tip into the pit. He moved the top layer aside to reveal the dull red-orange glow of hot coals.

"Lesley, look at this," he called out.

Lesley quickly moved down the stairs to appear beside Christopher. She stared into the belly of the furnace. Robert followed and stood a half dozen paces behind them both.

"Listen... do you hear that?" Christopher asked.

They all stood still to listen and slowly gazed up into the blackness of the ceiling.

"It sounds like... moths... the wings of a thousand moths," Lesley replied.

"Yes, it does," Christopher agreed. "Watch this."

Christopher turned to face Lesley, reached into his knapsack and withdrew a small bottle.

"This is holy water infused with rose petals."

Christopher removed the cork stopper and poured a little of the water into the cup of his right hand. He slowly reached back with his right arm and with a swift forward motion threw the liquid high into the air, into the cavity of the ceiling. They all watched intently. The spray of droplets hit something invisible in the blackness, hissed and instantly evaporated into tiny puffs of steam. Lesley gasped and turned.

"Robert!" she exclaimed. "I think we've found it."

"Yes, and we've found the heat source," Christopher added. "Watch!"

Everyone took three paces back. Christopher threw a second spray of holy rose water into the air above the furnace. A pyrotechnic display of steam sparks briefly filled the air.

"We've found the spawn point. We've found the demon… and very early. It's yet to form a body," Christopher proclaimed.

"Yes… indeed," Robert agreed. "This is it, we've found it!"

"The furnace is still warm. If we extinguish the heat source, maybe we can prevent the demon from forming," Christopher suggested.

"Water… let's get a bucket of water," Robert replied urgently, following the logic.

Lesley spotted an old, dented mug on the bench. She grabbed it and plunged it into the tub of water beside the anvil. She tossed the water through the open door into the belly of the furnace. The water hissed, boiled and bubbled with noisy violence and evaporated. The water had no effect but seemed to bring the furnace to life. Small, sharp, dark purple-blue flames erupted and flickered between the coals. The door to the furnace slammed shut. Christopher reached forward, touched the handle and immediately pulled away.

"Whoa," he exclaimed. "It's burning hot. The whole furnace is burning hot. I think we may have roused the demon. I'm not sure we can stop it now."

Lesley threw a second mug of water over the top of the furnace. A plume of spluttering steam erupted and floated upwards. They took a few paces back and stood clear of the furnace.

A glint of moonlight reflected off the rising steam and momentarily illuminated the area. They all managed to see the subtle dark opaque outline of a large body forming around the furnace. The outline of a large round abdomen appeared around the belly of the furnace. Its torso reached up and began to form around the chimney stack.

The demon was in a sitting position. The outline of two thick legs, bent at the knees began to form across the front of its abdomen. Two thick arms of medium length appeared, just reaching but not touching the floor, with rounded knobs for elbows and thick round mittens for hands. A large round head sat upon a short stump of a neck. The hair atop its head waved and flickered with black flame. The steam dissipated.

Trained in the use of etheric vision they all managed to continue seeing the demon once the outline was established. They saw the fluttering wisps of fear being absorbed and begin to fill its form, as the demon sat dormant.

"Whoa... are you both seeing this?" Robert asked.

"Uh-huh," Christopher replied while staring agape at the apparition.

"Yeah... I can see it," Lesley confirmed. "Its body... is huge!"

"Yes, it is! Right, then," Robert said.

He grabbed both Christopher and Lesley by the shoulder to gain their attention.

"Christopher... Lesley... do not allow yourself to be afraid. Remember, we are dealing with a fear demon. You must control your emotions. If you give in to fear, it will consume you. So, let's focus on how we are going to destroy this thing. Do you understand?"

"Yes... no fear here," Christopher assured.

"What's the plan?" Lesley asked, distracting herself with action.

"Good!" Robert replied satisfied. "Let's get out of here."

He led the way out of the mill house and into the front courtyard.

"What did General Rosecrans say? The priority was containing the demon and to stop it from finding still fresh water. Salt... we need lots of salt. And herbs... bundles of herbs. Let's get back to Lee and Gordon's Mills and find the supply wagons. Nothing will happen while the demon's body is still forming. Let's go."

Once mounted and keeping their head down, they swiftly made their way along the track back to Alexander Road. They kicked their horses into a gallop and arrived at Lee and Gordon's Mills just on 4 am. They immediately began to search for the location of the Union Army supply wagons.

Saturday 19ᵗʰ September 1863

All the brigade cooks were well at work preparing breakfast at the newly formed camps around Bloody Pond, Widow Glenn and Weathers farms when the trio arrived. Robert commandeered eight sacks of salt from the supply wagon, lashed two over the rump of his and Christopher's horses and commandeered a mule to carry everything else. Christopher and Lesley ransacked all the lavender, jasmine, sage and thyme they could find from the wagons and stripped every bushel from the local herb gardens in the area. While scoffing down breakfast they discussed the plan.

"The salt and herbs can only contain the demon, but for how long? What are we going to use to destroy it?" Christopher pondered. "The holy rose water didn't do anything but evaporate. We need something stronger than holy rose water."

"Yes… you're right," Robert replied. "But what… can we use?"

"Don't churches use holy oils for anointing and other ceremonies? An oil would be far more potent than water," Lesley chimed in with a suggestion.

"Yes… anointing oils. Great! Well… the closest church is McAfee's Church about five miles north along La Fayette Road," Robert said pondering the logistics. "Lesley… ride to the church and find some anointing oils. And while you're there, grab anything else you think might be useful. We won't have time to make a second trip. Christopher and I will secure the perimeter of Dalton Mill with the salt and herbs. Keep to the west, avoid any fighting and get back as quickly as you can. Ok, let's go."

"Right… see you soon. God willing… I'll return before the midday meal," she said.

Lesley rode out of camp towards La Fayette Road at a steady gait.

Before leaving the camp, Robert prepared a message for General Rosecrans, which read:

Contact with the enemy at Dalton Mill, a half mile east of Lee and Gordon's Mills. Initiating confinement strategy. Will report at sundown.

Robert signed and added a quickly drawn emblem of a cross through a circle. He sealed the envelope with a wax stamp and ordered a junior staff courier to deliver the message.

During the night Rosecrans moved Thomas's division forward in a wide arc directly west of Jay's Mill to the north of Crittenden's position. A brigade of Granger reserves was brought down from the north and tasked with destroying Reed's Bridge. Rosecrans relocated the Union headquarters to the single-storey timber cabin at Widow Glen.

The Confederate divisions of Polk and Buckner crossed Chickamauga Creek using Dalton's Ford and Thedford's Ford and linked with Hood and Walker to form a wide arcing line from Dalton's Ford on the southern end to Jay's Mill on the northern end. Forrest's cavalry was positioned further north on the Union left flank.

With the onset of daybreak, a the brigade of Granger reserves moved forward in their attempt to destroy Reed's Bridge. They encountered Forrest's 1st Georgia Cavalry near Jay's Mill. The Union brigade fell back to Thomas's northern line on the La Fayette Road. Thomas ordered three brigades forward under Croxton to destroy Reed's Bridge. Forrest dismounted his troops and dug in to form a defensive line to halt Croxton. Forrest was soon reinforced by a Confederate brigade from Walker's division under Colonel Wilson who hit Croxton's right flank roughly at 9 am, to begin the battle in earnest.

The divisions on both sides came together and engaged like a closing zipper, in a straight line about a half mile east of the La Fayette Road from the McDonald Farm down to the Scott farm on Brotherton Road, then back westward to the Brotherton Farm itself and again down the southern portion of the La Fayette Road to the Scott Farm about a half mile north of Lee and Gordon's Mills. By early afternoon three to four divisions from both sides were fully engaged in heavy woodland fighting, pushing each other back and forth along this line. From both sides, as many as seventy thousand men would engage in battle at some point throughout the more than twelve hours of fighting which took place during the day.

The fighting extended into the night and finally came to rest around 9 pm. The line essentially ran the length of the Lafayette road from the McDonald Farm at the northern end to the Viniard Farm at the southern end. Both sides were so close to each other that no fires were allowed to be lit and reveal their respective positions. With the night-time temperature approaching zero hundreds of wounded soldiers, on both sides, were left unattended in the field and died, either from their wounds or from exposure. Both sides suffered as many as ten thousand casualties, dead or wounded, in the day's battle.[1]

All the while, the rage, the hatred and the terror, of those who felt fear, or faced death in battle, all emitted a steady stream of dark wisps. They rose above the woods and followed the path to the Dalton Mill to coagulate into the black etheric body of the fear demon.

By the time Robert and Christopher returned to the Dalton Mill, the sun had cleared the horizon and was racing into the sky. It was a little after 7 am. They unsaddled the sacks of salt and bundles of herbs.

"Right... lets lay a row of salt around the outside of the mill house and a row just inside the main walls. Let's make as many small bundles of herbs as we can and strap a bundle to every door and window. Strap a thick bundle onto some long wooden poles so we can carry and burn them if we need to," Robert instructed.

"Do you think any of this is going to work?" Christopher asked.

"What did Rosecrans say... it will search for still fresh water. It won't go near salt or flowing water to cross over. Salt is corrosive to most things and neutralises others. So, we know the demon doesn't like salt and will try to avoid it," he said and paused.

"The herb? I'm not sure. They have healing and medicinal properties. Even if we burn them, the aromatic smoke might be offensive to the demon. Anything is worth a try, right? Make sure you mix a little of every herb in every bundle. We won't have time to work out which herb will work better than the others," he said. "We just need to keep the demon inside the mill for as long as possible."

"Wow... I can't believe this is our first fear demon. Even during training, I wasn't sure if they were real. Now I've seen one with my own eyes? It's bigger than I expected," Christopher mused excitedly.

"Yes... I didn't anticipate how big it would be. Now we can see how it forms, which might help us figure out a way to destroy it," Robert pondered. "Let's hope we can do it in time, since no one has ever lived to tell the tale of how to destroy a fear demon."

"Well... you certainly know how to kill the moment," Christopher retorted with a dour face.

"Let's get to work," Robert said, ripping himself out of a deep dark thought.

They could not work in clerical garments and replaced them with trousers and loose-fitting long-sleeved, white-collared shirts.

They dug a shallow, straight, one-inch-wide furrow, one foot from the outer three walls of the mill house. They filled the shallow burrow with salt to a small, pointed heap. They poured the same amount of salt one foot inside and along the three perimeter walls of the building. They doubled up and spread the salt out across the open edge of the platform. They lashed together and nailed small bundles of herbs to both sides of every door and window. Bundles were hung down from the rafters to cover the open platform. They cut six, ten-foot wooden poles and lashed a bunch of herbs to one end, which could be carried, lit and waved back and forth. They would each have two.

During the day it was far more difficult to see the outline of the fear demon. The pot belly stove shimmered with heat. Both Robert and Christopher refrained from approaching. They knew the demon was still there in its slumber and would not want to move or expose itself to direct sunlight.

"Do you think it's asleep?" Christopher asked when working across the platform.

"More like a state of dormant hypnosis, I'd imagine," Robert replied.

"If we removed the roof, do you think direct sunlight would kill it?" Christopher pondered.

"I'm not so sure if that would work," Robert replied and thought about it for a while.

"Consider what it's made of... the dark etheric thought matter of thousands upon thousands of soldiers killing each other. Ether is a form of matter between two worlds and not wholly physical. Look closely. If anything, sunlight just changes its state from one of being more soluble to one more like a vapour... just like water from ice to steam. See how much more translucent it is. It's like a thick, suspended, invisible vapour. It can't cross over in this state or be destroyed either. We can only destroy the demon once it takes a more physical form. But how... how are we going to destroy it?" the question began to weigh on Robert.

"Yes... I see what you mean," Christopher replied taking a closer look at the suspended outline of the demon. "How *are* we going to destroy this thing?" he whispered.

For the final task, Robert and Christopher dug four firepits into the ground, each fifteen yards from the walls of the building. Two pits were at the front and one each was positioned on both the north and south-facing walls of the mill. Each firepit was filled with a pyramid of wood ready to be lit after nightfall. A stack of timber and bucket of coals was positioned beside each pit. The firepits would only be lit if the demon became active and tried to escape.

By midday, Robert and Christopher had completed their preparations. Their shirts were covered in grime, dust and sweat. They could hear the battle raging to the north, especially when the breeze stood still.

"Well... we've done all we can for now. It's time for lunch," Robert announced, answering his stomach's protest.

After washing and back in clerical dress, they sat upon the top stair of the veranda and ate a simple meal of bread, cheese and pickled vegetables. Lesley suddenly appeared. She rode into the courtyard, dismounted and tied her horse to a rail in seamless efficiency.

"Afternoon, Robert, Christopher," she greeted in both an aggravated and excited manner.

"Lesley!" Robert replied. "Thank God you made it back. I was beginning to worry. How did you do? Did you have any trouble?"

She untied a knapsack from the back of her saddle and approached the stairs to the veranda.

"It's all-out war along La Fayette Road," she reported. "I had to ride further west close to Pigeon Mountain, which took me a lot longer on the way back."

Robert and Christopher stood up. Lesley climbed the stairs and followed the other two into the house. She continued as they walked in and congregated around the dining table.

"Only a very old pastor remained at the church. I told him I had a crisis… that I needed everything holy to save the souls of men. He did take a little convincing, but he opened the church's secret vault and gave me what I needed. I'll show you," she beamed with a smile. "I'm famished, by the way. Did you just have lunch?"

"Yes, we did," Robert replied.

Christopher quickly dashed out to fetch a portion of bread, cheese, pickled vegetables and a large pitcher of water for Lesley. Robert provided a quick update regarding their preparations while Lesley washed using a fresh bucket of water in the kitchen area.

Christopher soon returned. Lesley drank a healthy swig and dug into her rations.

"Show us what you've found at McAfee's Church?" Robert asked growing impatient.

"Yes… absolutely," Lesley replied with one bulging cheek.

She stood, opened the knapsack on the table and carefully drew out each item.

"I found a flask of anointing oil. Just as you asked for."

"Very good," Robert replied happily.

"I also found a canister of frankincense resin and one of myrrh resin… and two thuribles. You mix the two resins and burn them like incense within the chamber and carry the thurible on a chain."

"They might help contain the demon inside the mill," Christopher commented.

"I also took these: a half dozen wooden rosary beads with a cross; a flask of holy red wine, which I think is just fortified port; a one foot high brass cross; and a small ceremonial cup, which I believe is actually made of gold," she said and paused. "The pastor was very reluctant to give up the cup. I felt it was important... and you did say to grab everything I could. Well... that's it," she said and stood back from the display.

"Well done," Robert congratulated. "Now... what are we to make of all these things?"

They all stared blankly at the dining table. No one could think. Lesley broke the silence.

"Maybe we ought to get some rest. I'm exhausted and you two look like your eyes are about to pop out of your heads. We haven't slept in almost two days. Let's get some shut eye. It's going to be a long night ahead and we'll need our wits if we are to beat this monster."

Robert nodded in agreement. Christopher threw a blanket over the table. They each picked a bedchamber and instantly collapsed into an exhausted slumber through the afternoon. Five hours drifted by. Exactly at sundown, Robert jolted awake first. He roused the other two. They ate a light supper, washed beside the creek and readied themselves for the night ahead.

Returning to the kitchen, Robert looked at all the holy items on the dining table.

"Divide the anointing oil into three smaller flasks. Take two rosary beads each, although... I'm not sure what help they'll be. You two prepare and take one thurible each," he said and paused. "I'll take the lead and engage the demon first. You two stand back a few paces and be at the ready to ward it off if we need to retreat and buy more time. I don't know if any of these things will work... but... we must try everything we have. Ok... let's get ready."

The sun and last vestiges of light disappeared below the western horizon, replaced by the illumination of the near first quarter moon. In the deepest pit at the front, they lit a very small fire making sure the flame was obscured from view.

At 7 pm, Robert, Lesley and Christopher congregated in the dark hallway. Robert opened the door, walked down the stairs and stood ten paces in front of the demon. Lesley and Christopher stood well apart at the base of the stairs. The round, robust body of the demon had evolved and formed into a more solidified black mass around the furnace, shrinking in size by a foot during the process. It was now quite visible. The iron metal of the furnace was now glowing a dark orange-red within the gloom of the mill.

The demon's wide gaping mouth opened and closed. It began to stir. A small wave of purple-blue flame and dark energy exploded and radiated out from its body in all directions. The force knocked Robert off his feet and back into the middle of the platform. The explosion singed black the stone of the furnace, wood panelling and flooring that its body touched. The demon's eyes suddenly opened and glowed with the same intense colour as the furnace. The demon was born, conscious and alive.

Grimacing with determination, the demon exerted an immense effort to stand. It ripped the iron furnace out from its stone housing, which now became the belly of its body. Loose stone from the furnace and chimney fell to the floor behind the demon as it slowly climbed to its feet, on one large round stumpy leg at a time. The demon stood at an immense fourteen and a quarter feet tall. It had a thick round head and neck, a fat round abdomen twice the thickness of the now suspended hot glowing iron furnace and thick round arms and fingers.

The demon glared down at Robert as he recovered from the explosion and slowly climbed to his feet. The demon took one, then two slow deep-muffled thudded steps towards Robert. It leant forward and extended its right arm with the intention of grabbing him. Robert darted to his left between the wall behind and the anvil.

Robert withdrew the small flask of anointing oil from his jacket pocket and pulled the cork stopper. He poured half into the open cup of his right hand as the demon turned towards him and took another step forward. He flung the oil at the demon. The oil flew up and passed straight through the demon's body and landed on the floor beyond. Nothing happened. The demon took a further step towards Robert. He pulled out a set of rosary beads and doused it with some of the anointing oil and flung it at the demon. It also travelled straight through its body and landed on the floor behind. The demon took another step.

"Light those herb poles," Robert yelled.

Christopher ran back up the stairs and out through the front door. He dropped the thurible beside the lit firepit. He grabbed three herb poles and quickly lit the bundle of herbs strapped to the end of each pole and ran back into the mill.

In the meantime, Lesley dashed forward and stood beside Robert who was now pushed back against the lower wall of the balcony. She held one thurible and began to swing it around in a wide circle on the chain. The fanned herbal resin burned hotter and built a wall of incense to shield them both. The smoke had more of an effect. The demon stopped moving forward and reeled back a step, as though in reaction to a pungent odour. It did not wish to be tainted by the vapour's cleansing properties.

Robert and Lesley escaped the corner they were trapped in and slipped past the demon back towards the stairs. Christopher appeared and almost tripped down the stairs. He handed over one pole each. They blew out the flames and a thick plume of herbal smoke rose before them as they quickly turned to face the demon.

The demon had taken steps towards the middle of the platform and then moved in towards the stairs. They waved their smoking herb poles up at the demon's head. The stronger, more potent herbal incense forced the demon to reel back once more, taking offence to the stench.

"We've nothing left! Let's get out of here," Robert commanded.

With the demon distracted behind the wall of smoke, they all climbed the stairs and ran out through the front door into the courtyard. They gathered loosely behind the firepit at the ready to light all the other firepits and watched the front of the building. They waited for a long while catching their breaths, until satisfied that the demon had not pursued them.

"Wow, that was close," Robert sighed.

"Yeah... too close," Lesley agreed.

"Did you see that?" Christopher exclaimed. "The demon exploded and came alive! I've never seen anything like that before."

"Yes, we all saw it... and felt it," Robert said. "It felt like... I don't know... like nothing I've ever felt before."

"It felt like an all-consuming evil... it radiates, resonates the pure emotion of fear itself," Christopher muttered. "The closer you are, the stronger it becomes. We cannot be exposed to the demon for too long."

"That thing almost touched you. The oils and beads didn't work. Thank God the incense did something... otherwise we wouldn't have survived," Lesley said.

"Yes… the herbal incense repelled it. But that's all the herbs can do," Robert said. "The anointing oil! Why didn't the oil work?"

Robert brought out the flask and poured what little was left into his hand. He felt its texture. He brought it to his nose and sniffed it.

"Actually, this is familiar," he said.

He then tasted the oil on the tip of his tongue. He recognised what it was.

"Huh!" he exclaimed with a wry smile. "Olive oil! It is just olive oil. No wonder it didn't work. The church just uses olive oil for anointing. A simple truth we should've realised. Discard the oil… it's useless," Robert stated flatly.

Lesley and Christopher discarded their flasks beside the firepit. Robert wiped his hands clean.

"So, what now?" Christopher asked. "We don't have anything we can use to destroy the demon. What are we going to do?"

"We need more time… to figure this out," Robert replied. "For now, it's big and slow and confined to the ground. Let's hope the salt and herbs can contain it within the mill."

"Even though its alive, I don't think its fully formed and ready to cross over just yet." Christopher pointed out.

"Did you see how it pulled out that iron furnace. Well… with a furnace for a belly, it won't be able to move through walls," Lesley added. "When it discards the furnace, that's when it'll be ready to cross over."

"Yes… and we don't have much time," Robert said, pausing to ponder the dilemma.

"The General! I must report to General Rosecrans and inform him of our progress and what we have discovered of the demon. Maybe he can help figure out a plan. Do you have any other ideas?" Robert asked.

Lesley and Christopher both shook their heads in the negative.

"Right, then. I'll ride out immediately and seek council with the General. You two keep that fire burning. Check the perimeter and make sure there's no breach in the salt and herbs. Keep a vigil on that demon and don't engage it under any circumstance. I'll return as soon as I can"

Robert mounted and sped off along the track into the woods.

Not knowing where the position of the front line was, he travelled a little south and then west scouting forward through the cover of the woods cautiously at first, until he found the Union front line. He rode west to avoid La Fayette Road and turned north to arrive at the low set timber house of Widow Glen a little after 10 pm.

The same perimeter guards recognised Robert and marched him up to see Chief of Staff Brigadier General James A. Garfield, who was stationed outside the front of the cabin.

"Good evening, General Garfield. I have an urgent report for General Rosecrans."

"Very well. If you hand it to me, I'll be sure to pass it on to General Rosecrans. Currently, he is in a meeting with command reviewing the latest reports and positions from each brigade."

"The report I wish to convey is not written down. It's vital I deliver my report in person and receive the General's immediate counsel in return. And time is of the utmost urgency, General Garfield," Robert replied with direct sternness.

General Garfield gave Robert a disapproving glance with a protracted pause.

"I assure you the General is expecting me. If you were to delay any further you would only court the wrath of the General," Robert warned.

"Very well! I'll inform the General of your arrival," Garfield stated flatly.

Garfield climbed the steps, knocked twice, opened the door and stepped inside. The moment the message was delivered everyone was immediately dismissed and ordered to wait outside. In a surprised hurry, Garfield, followed by all the senior commanders, filed out of the cabin.

"Robert, get in here!" General Rosecrans bellowed loudly. "And close the door behind you."

Robert entered the sparsely lit, sparsely furnished chamber of the house and closed the door.

"You have news?" General Rosecrans asked impatiently. "You found it!"

"Yes General, we've found the fear demon and very early as well. It's located at the Dalton Mill in a secluded wood on the west bank of Chickamauga Creek, a half mile northeast of Lee and Gordon's Mills," Robert reported.

"Aaah, well done!"

"The demon has coagulated around an old iron furnace in the mill house. It has formed a body and is now alive, as of three hours ago. As you advised, we prepared a containment perimeter, which appears to be working. Strangely, it carries the furnace as its belly and is bound to the ground for now," he said and paused.

"Lesley retrieved anointing oil from McAfee's Church. It proved ineffective. Turns out it's just olive oil. And holy rose water just evaporates into steam. Currently, we don't have a plan on how to destroy it. We believe the demon is approaching a transition where, once fully formed and self-sufficient, it will cross over."

"I see," the General replied in deep thought. "The demon will continue to absorb dark ether from the battle and grow in power and density for as long as possible. When the battle ceases and there is nothing left to absorb, the demon will drop the furnace and cross over."

"Unfortunately, we are in a tough, desperate fight. The Confederates are making a go of it and both sides have suffered heavy casualties. The battle is very much at the brink. It will be decided one way or the other, tomorrow."

"So, the demon may linger for one more day, until the fighting subsides," Robert calculated.

"Yes, if it's still there by daybreak," the General agreed.

"And it won't be able to cross over during the day and will have to wait until nightfall."

"I've been giving a great deal of consideration on how to defeat one of these things. Let me show you something from my personal wagon. I'll be right back."

General Rosecrans jumped to his feet and hustled out of the cabin. Everyone watched, bemused. He skirted around the side of the house to his personal wagon and soon returned with a small rectangular locked chest weighing around fifteen pounds. He gently placed the chest in the middle of the table atop all the maps, messages and orders. He opened the chest and allowed the lid to fall back at 100°, which was held in place by a thin leather strap on both sides.

The main cavity of the chest was divided horizontally into three rows of five compartments, each filled with a single jar or canister of one substance or another. From a leather sleeve under the lid of the chest, the General withdrew a well-used handbook and placed it on the table between himself and the chest.

"Well Robert, what do we know about the makings of a fear demon?"

"That's simple enough. It's made of the very thing that it is… fear. Or more specifically, the fear, hatred and suffering of man in the act of war."

"Yes, but in the simplest of terms, what is it?" the General pressed.

"Darkness… it's darkness."

"Yes, it is. And what is the eternal counter to darkness?"

"Light!"

"Yes… light. Now for the grand prize… what is light?"

"Hmm… I'm not sure what you're getting at. Light comes from the sun… and in religious terms, it represents purity and enlightenment of the soul."

"Yes, that is true… but… not quite the answer I was looking for," the General said and paused as he looked up through the ceiling. "I once heard light described as… the fire of a chemical wedding," he said and turned to Robert with a wry grin. "In other words, Robert, light is the product of a chemical reaction," he said and quickly turned back to the chest.

"Luckily for me, being a General allows one a few privileges. In conjunction with a few new inventions, the military has been experimenting with and testing new types of munitions since the advent of the war. We have found some substances which can create a light flash and a light burn at very high temperatures."

General Rosecrans reached forward and withdrew a medium-sized glass jar from the open chest and placed it on the table in front of Robert. The clear glass jar had a metal screw on lid, was filled with water and had a lump of red material sitting at the base. He opened the handbook, turned to the relevant page and read from the notes written there.

"This is yellow phosphorus suspended in water," he began. "It looks red when it has been exposed to sunlight and the outer layer oxidises into a reddish colour. This substance is extremely dangerous and can only be handled safely in water. If it is exposed to air at normal room temperature it will ignite with oxygen and cause a brilliant white light, a high temperature burn and highly toxic fumes," he said and briefly looked up from the page. "I think we can use this as a weapon against the demon."

General Rosecrans reached forward and removed a second jar from the chest and placed it on the desk next to the first. Both jars looked identical except the second jar contained a white powder. Rosecrans turned the page.

"This is called… magnesium powder. It's being used to produce a flash with this invention… um…photography! I had my photograph taken last month… truly incredible!" he paused to reflect. "Anyway, you can ignite it with a naked flame. It will burn at a very high temperature and produce an extremely intense light. It also reacts with water to produce a very toxic fume. So, if it gets out of control, don't use water to try and extinguish it, just let it burn out."

General Rosecrans closed the handbook, returned it to the table and turned to face Robert.

"We need to separate these substances into smaller amounts that can be used against the demon. The phosphorus must always remain in water until used. The magnesium powder must never contact water. Do you understand?"

"Yes, yes. Loud and clear," Robert replied a little mesmerised.

"This is all I can procure, which is why I've kept hold of them until now. You'll need to use something to cut and separate each substance without using your hands. They are volatile. One mistake and you'll burn your fingers off," the General warned.

"I'll search the supply wagons and find something I can use."

"Report back when you're done. I'll hold onto these substances until your return."

Robert promptly left the cabin. General Rosecrans kept the small chest between his feet beneath the table and resumed the war council. Robert searched all the stores and military blacksmiths. He returned within the hour with eighteen small glass ointment jars sealed with a cork stopper, a brass four-slot shot mould, brass tweezers, a block of paraffin wax, one very sharp skinning knife and three pairs of leather riding gloves.

"Do you have everything you need?" General Rosecrans asked.

"Yes, I believe so," Robert replied.

"What's your plan? How are you going to weaponise these two substances?"

"Well… we cannot risk being within arm's reach of the demon. So, we must create a throwable projectile for each substance.

The phosphorus will be cut into small pieces and placed in each water-filled jar. The magnesium will be set inside small round wax balls using the shot mould," Robert explained.

"Very good! Looks like we have a plan," the General stated with a wry smile. "Ok, let's get a move along. Show me the way to Dalton Mill."

"You… you want me to take you to Dalton Mill?" Robert asked not believing his ears.

"Yes, of course. I've never seen one of these things. I need to know what we are dealing with first hand," the General countered.

"Very well! We need to return as quickly as possible. I worry how Lesley and Christopher are faring," Robert said with urgency.

Suddenly, couriers arrived with conflicting reports concerning the deployment of brigades under the command of Thomas Wood, James Negley and Alexander McCook. The depleted forces of Negley had not yet been relieved. Wood and reserve brigades were in the wrong position. Rosecrans was forced to inspect these brigades to resolve the confusion and ensure there was no breach in the lines, and that the defensive positions were fortified with log breastworks.

After an hour's delay, General Rosecrans, a small entourage of six junior officer aides and Robert finally left Widow Glen and rode out for Lee and Gordon's Mills. Dropping all but two junior officers, Rosecrans allowed Robert to lead the way through the wood to Dalton Mill, arriving well after midnight.

"Robert… General Rosecrans!" Christopher exclaimed in shock. "Thank God you've returned. We've been rather worried. You've been gone for over four hours."

"Yes… I know. I'm sorry about that," Robert replied and shot Rosecrans a sharp glance.

He dismounted and tied the horse to the rail, following by Rosecrans and the two officers.

"We have a plan," Robert announced. "What of the demon?"

"We can hear movement. We're not sure if it's trying to find a way out, but it's still contained inside the mill. We've just been keeping watch on the perimeter," Christopher reported.

"Right! Let's go into the kitchen. I have something to show you," Robert stated.

Everyone followed Robert into the house except the two officers who were assigned to guard the horses and instructed that under no circumstances were they to enter the building. General Rosecrans placed the phosphorus and magnesium powder canisters on the dining table and explained how they work to Lesley and Christopher.

Utilising the skinning knife, tweezers and riding gloves, Robert cut small pieces of phosphorus in a drum of water in the kitchen. Whilst submerged he managed to divide the stone and drop one piece into every glass jar and affix the cork stopper.

Outside, Christopher poured heated paraffin wax along both the top and bottom arms of the shot mould and allowed it to cool. He carefully scooped and poured a small amount of magnesium powder into each cavity of the lower arm. While the wax was just warm enough, he pressed the two arms of the mould together, to produce four magnesium wax bombs. He used all the powder to make eighteen shot balls.

Robert, Lesley and Christopher were allocated six phosphorous bombs and shot balls each.

They collected as many buckets and drums as they could find, filled them with water and positioned them around the building, to extinguish a potential fire caused when using the ordnances. The pit fires were already loaded with wood. Everyone was ready.

Robert and Christopher each gathered one herb pole and lit the end. General Rosecrans held an old military style oil lamp by the large circular handle. Robert led the procession of Rosecrans, Lesley and Christopher into the dark hallway. Except for Rosecrans, they all held a phosphorus bomb.

The house was dark and quiet as Robert pulled open the door and silently walked through into the mill. Everyone followed and spilled out along the narrow balcony. The dark shape of the demon was clearly visible as it stood, resting in the middle of the platform staring out at the low, moderately flowing creek. The demon had shrunk by another foot whilst it continued to solidify in density. It was unnaturally warm inside the mill.

Standing beside Robert and on seeing the fear demon for the very first time, General Rosecrans let out a small exclamation of stunned surprise at the size and form of the fiend. Being unfamiliar with and unprepared to withstand the demon's resonance, the General fought to control his emotions, and caught his breath.

On detecting the General's fear, the demon promptly turned to face the group standing along the balcony. The demon immediately began to raise its arms and took a step forward. Being further evolved the demon was able to move more freely.

Robert raced down the stairs, strode forward two paces on the platform and threw the phosphorous bomb at the suspended glowing furnace inside the demon's abdomen. The glass shattered, the water fell to the floor and the small piece of phosphorus burst into a hot intense ball of burning white light. The demon reeled back on its feet in pain.

General Rosecrans followed Robert and stood at the base of the stairs. Robert glanced back and saw the disturbed expression on his face.

"Stand back General and keep out of harm's way," Robert yelled. "Yes, it's a bit of a shock at first… but get a grip on your emotions!"

Everyone watched the phosphorus burn a small tubular hole straight down through the demon's abdomen towards the floor and fizz out. The demon's fury had now been evoked. It emitted a scream, or growl, of such low and deep vibrational resonance that it was barely audible, like a distant thunder. Yet, everyone felt it.

It worked. Robert, followed by Christopher, both discarded their smoking herb poles. Lesley and Christopher descended the stairs and stood either side of General Rosecrans.

"Lesley, stay with me," Robert commanded as he moved around to the demon's right. "Christopher, go round the other side and get in behind the demon," he yelled.

Christopher immediately began to move around to the demon's left, as it recovered, turned and began to peruse Robert. Robert and Lesley quickly moved behind the anvil, stopped and together, they both threw a phosphorous bomb at the furnace.

The thin glass shattered, the phosphorus ignited and two parallel funnels burnt down through the front of the demon's abdomen. Behind the demon, Christopher removed the stopper from his glass bomb and poured the water and phosphorus out into his gloved right hand. Just as the phosphorous began to fuse, he immediately threw the small stone up at the demon's head.

The phosphorus ignited in mid-air, bursting into a white-hot ball and plunged deep into the back of the demon's head. The phosphorous burned a deep gash down through the demon's head, neck and back. The demon reeled back and forth in agony from multiple burns.

The demon reached out in angry desperation for Robert's head. He was a little too far away, its reach short. Robert easily stepped back to avoid the extended grasp.

Robert darted forward and slipped past the demon along the wall where the furnace used to live. Lesley moved back towards the stairs. The demon turned to follow Robert, saw Christopher and turned towards him with fury in its eyes.

The demon suddenly realised it was fighting on three fronts and clearly understood it lacked the speed and agility required to defend itself.

The demon noticed the stack of six smallish logs to the left of the table saw, each roughly between six and seven inches in width. The demon moved as quickly as it could towards the stack. Everyone watched the demon bend forward, wrap its plump hands and short arms around the top log and lift it with ease. The demon lifted the log up over its shoulders and then lowered the log down through its body and held it in place through the middle of its chest above the furnace. The twenty-five-foot log extended out evenly through both the front and back of the demon's chest. Everyone stared at the demon in astonishment.

Once the log was in place, the demon turned and rushed forward towards Christopher, aiming to crush his head with the cut end of the log. Christopher immediately retreated to the wall, ducked and dived to his left towards the internal balcony. The log slammed into the wall hard and cracked two of the vertical panels. The demon took one step back, realigned the log once more for Christopher's head and rushed forward.

Christopher quickly rose to his feet and dived to his left just in time. The log rammed the wall below the balcony and smashed a hole through the panel. The demon struggled to pull the log free while Christopher made his escape up the stairs.

Two wax balls hit the demon in the middle of its back, one each thrown by Robert and Lesley, who stood side by side behind the demon in the middle of the platform. The furnace quickly melted the wax and the magnesium powder ignited into a small explosive flash of intense white burning light and heat. The dark etheric plasm was stripped from the demon's body in a sphere surrounding the ignition point. Once the powder burned out, the dark etheric matter of the demon's body would slowly begin to fill the void and repair its wound.

The demon reeled backwards by two steps in agony. It turned, fixated its gaze on Robert and used the weight of the log to rush forward. Robert dived and rolled to his left and stood on the edge of the platform, beside the stack of logs above the creek. Lesley easily skipped out of the way towards the stairs. The demon rushed past, slowed and glanced towards Robert.

The demon backtracked towards the open edge of the platform and began to turn its body clockwise. Robert ducked beneath the front of the spinning log and quickly moved behind the support beam near the table saw, as the demon continued with its spin. The rear end of the log thumped against the beam stopping the demon's rotation so that it now faced Lesley and Rosecrans.

The demon rushed forward aiming for Lesley. Rosecrans ran to his right. Lesley nimbly leapt up and over the balustrade as the log smashed into the wall beneath her feet. The demon pulled the log free and in reverse, rushed backwards for Robert's chest. Robert dodged behind the beam and ran around to his left as the log crashed into the table saw. The demon turned to follow Robert's trajectory and rushed forward once more.

As the demon pursued Robert, Christopher moved closer across the balcony and threw two wax balls. One penetrated the top left shoulder of the demon and the other sank into the lower left chest area. Both exploded simultaneously and blew out a large gaping hole. The demon instantly halted its rush forward, reeled back on its haunches and issued a deep bellow of excruciating pain, momentarily paralysed in shock.

Robert, Rosecrans, Lesley and Christopher all saw the demon's black beating heart through the open cavity in its chest. It was a solid black pumping mass with a deep crimson purple-red glowing border around the organ.

The demon's body began to quickly fill the void and repair the wound to protect its heart. Once it had recovered, the demon fixated its furious gaze once more on Robert as he stood in the right corner of the platform below the balcony. He held a wax ball at the ready to throw.

At that very moment three Confederate infantrymen burst through the hallway door into the mill. Having been separated from their brigade, they were lost in the nearby woods and had heard the commotion. The two junior Union officers thought it prudent to move the horses and remain out of sight and fortified inside the stables.

The lead Confederate stood at the top of the stairs. One infantryman appeared on his left and the other on his right. Rosecrans who stood on the platform below and to their right, raised his lantern above his shoulder to identify the intruders.

"You're a Union General!" the lead Confederate exclaimed, surprised. "What are y'all doing here? What's going on?" he asked holding his musket forward and ready at the hip.

"Oh my... lost Confederates," the General proclaimed. "You boys shouldn't be here. You're all in grave danger and must leave this instance."

The General's warning only sparked the infantryman's curiosity.

"Why? What's going on?" he repeated. "Stand aside, General... let me see."

The lead Confederate began to descend the stairs and brandished his musket menacingly at the General forcing him to stand aside.

"You're placing yourself in grave danger," the General warned once more. "Oh... very well, see for yourself."

General Rosecrans withdrew into the corner towards Robert as the Confederate stepped off the stairs and out onto the platform. The other two appeared beside their leader in quick time.

The lead Confederate suddenly noticed the glowing furnace and log, hanging in mid-air over the middle of the platform. The other two quickly noticed the same phenomena. They were all stunned into muted silence... unable to comprehend what they were seeing. Doubt entered their minds. The General's warning suddenly seemed pertinent when they realised their mistake of walking straight into danger.

A pang of fear shot up their spines, their hearts skipped a beat and their lungs gasped for air. The demon immediately detected their resonance, turned and rushed forward. The log hammered the Confederate closest to Rosecrans, square on the chest. He was lifted from the ground, slammed back into the wall beside the staircase and crushed instantly.

Watching the log move forward and crush his companion, the lead Confederate became consumed with uncontrolled terror. The demon stepped back two paces and reached forward to push its black right hand and arm straight through the chest of the infantryman. The lead Confederate laid his head back, glared up at the ceiling and with wide open eyes, screamed a long high-pitched, blood-curdling scream. His heart spasmed out of control. All colour left his body. His skin and hair immediately turned an ash white. Out of breath, he fell forward, flat and hard on the ground... dead.

The last standing Confederate lost all cognitive ability, dropped his musket and stood stuck in his shoes completely confused. He released his bladder and wet his pants, whilst he watched his companion turn white and fall. His heart filled with terror, he simply could not move.

The fear demon stepped back and, for a moment, mused with satisfaction over the death of the infantrymen, as though it had just eaten a meal of his soul. The demon looked up at the last remaining Confederate and began to turn in his direction.

General Rosecrans placed the oil lamp down on the floor and drove forward with his legs. Robert, Lesley and Christopher all threw a wax ball. Rosecrans ducked under the log and outstretched right hand and hit the infantryman under the rib cage with his right shoulder and lifted him off the ground. The three wax balls exploded. The demon reeled back in shock.

Rosecrans turned and lunged for the stairs, grabbed the handrail with his left hand and pulled himself up as he drove with each leg upon each step. The demon's torso recoiled to swing forward. It took one step forward with right foot and reached out with a backhand swipe of its right hand.

The demon's hand hit and moved through the top of the infantryman's back as he hung over Rosecrans's shoulder and ever so lightly touched the tip of Rosecrans's right elbow. The infantryman screamed, convulsed, turned ash white and died.

General Rosecrans climbed to the top of the stairs, took three paces forward and crashed through the hallway door. The Confederate's body was flung forward in a dishevelled heap. Rosecrans lay on his stomach, in a confused daze, gulping for air from his exertion. The hallway door swung closed and caught on his right ankle.

"Get to the General," Robert yelled.

Robert threw another wax ball which sank into the left side of the demon's thick neck. He grabbed the oil lamp and climbed up and over the balustrade onto the balcony whilst Lesley and Christopher both followed suit and threw a wax ball. The consecutive explosions rocked the demon, with plasm stripped from neck, shoulder and hip.

Lesley pushed through the hallway door first and held it open for Christopher and Robert to run through. Robert handed her the oil lamp before helping Christopher lift the General up by the arms. She glanced back at the demon, seeing it repair and recover before closing the door.

"He's been struck. Take the General to the firepit!" Robert said.

Robert and Christopher burst through the front door of the house and shuffled down the stairs. They gently laid the General down on his back beside the firepit. Robert threw several fresh logs into the pit. The two officers suddenly appeared from the stables and were immediately ordered to fetch a blanket and water. The General mumbled something.

Robert sat the General up and gave him some water to drink. He removed the General's jacket and inspected his upper torso. He found a strange dark singed burn mark on the back of the General's right elbow. The General was conscious but developing a cold feverish sweat.

"Yes, he's been touched. It's only slight," Robert confirmed. "Wash the wound with salt water. Crush those herbs into a paste, apply it to the wound and strap it with a bandage. Prepare a warm herbal tea and make him drink it… all. Then wrap him in a blanket."

The two officers did not quite understand what was happening but went to work as instructed.

"I can't think of anything else to do," Robert muttered. "Let's hope he'll recover by sunrise."

"Maybe direct sunlight might help," Christopher added.

Robert glanced up at Christopher to consider the possibility.

"We still have at least three hours until sunrise," Robert said. "You two go and conduct a perimeter check and report back on the status of that demon."

They both returned within ten minutes. General Rosecrans was stable and resting.

"The salt perimeter is intact. The demon is contained within the mill," Lesley reported.

"The demon dropped the log and still holds the furnace. It's slowly walking around in a circle," Christopher added.

"I think it's hurting... and agitated. The demon knows it's vulnerable. It's only a matter of time before it finds a way out," Robert mused. "We hit it pretty hard in there, didn't we?"

"Yes, yes, we did," Christopher agreed.

"The phosphorous bombs and wax balls worked well," Robert said. "They do a hell of a lot of damage, don't they?"

"Yes, they certainly do," Christopher affirmed.

"Did you see how its dark tissue fills in and repairs each wound?" Lesley pointed out.

"Yes, it can repair rather quickly. So, I'm not sure if these bombs can kill it," Robert said. "And I think we've used about half our stock of ordnances."

"Did you see... the demon had a black heart! Did you see it?" Christopher asked.

Robert and Lesley nodded in confirmation. Christopher stepped out in front of them both.

"If it has a heart... then... we can kill it!" he said emphatically.

"Yes, of course, but how?" Robert pondered.

"We need something that can pierce... its black heart," Christopher continued along a train of thought. "Something which is pure... something incorruptible... like... GOLD!"

Christopher stared at Robert who scowled back in return. They seemed to read each other's thoughts.

"A spear of gold!" Lesley replied intuitively, staring at them both.

Robert dashed up the stairs and into the house. He quickly returned and held out the solid gold cup between the three of them. The cup glowed in the light from the firepit.

"At first light, ride to Chattanooga and forge one gold-tipped spear," Robert said and handed the cup to Christopher. "They have foundries there. And return as soon as it's done."

"Make sure you bring back some leather straps and flax seed oil," Lesley added. "I have an idea," she said with a mischievous grin.

"Yes... absolutely," Christopher replied, instantly understanding what she had in mind.

Christopher took hold of the cup, wrapped it in a cloth, tucked it into a knapsack and tied it to the saddle of his horse. Robert returned his attention to the General.

"How's General Rosecrans?" he asked of the two officers.

"He's stable, groggy and has a fever," one replied.

"Make him drink some herbal tea every half hour. We'll have to wait it out till sunrise."

As soon as the light of the rising sun shone across General Rosecrans' body, he woke up and regained consciousness. The fever subsided. He was still very much shaken but was able to speak and think cognitively.

"General... we must get you up and on a horse. You have to return to your command," Robert explained.

General Rosecrans nodded, climbed to his feet and fixed his jacket and appearance.

"Did we get it?" the General asked.

"Not yet. But we have a new plan. We'll kill it soon enough," Robert assured him.

"You must get it before it can cross over... you know that right?" the General affirmed. "Oh, my head! I'm not sure if it hurts, but it's... it's hard to think."

Robert turned to the two officers.

"Get him mounted and out of here. It's far too dangerous for the General to remain here with the Confederates so close. Christopher, make sure they make it back to Widow Glen."

The two officers helped the General mount and prepared to depart.

"When it's safe to do so, wash the General down with salted water. Change that dressing with a fresh herb patch and keep him drinking herbal tea," Robert instructed. "Hopefully, the General will function normally after a couple of hours' rest."

Christopher, General Rosecrans and the two officers rode out through the woods, turned and rode straight and hard for Lee and Gordon's Mills. Once behind Union lines and with full entourage they soon arrived at Widow Glen. Chief of Staff Brigadier General James A. Garfield was ordered to accompany Christopher to Chattanooga to ensure their secret mission would be accomplished without delay.

Sunday 20th September 1863

General Braxton Bragg reorganised his army into two wings along the front line. The command of the right wing was given to Polk, which absorbed Hill's and Walker's corps and Cheatham's division. The command of the left was given to Lieutenant General James Longstreet who had arrived by train from Virginia during the night with reinforcements, and incorporated Hood's and Buckner's corps and Hindman's division.

The battle began late at 9:30 am on the Union's left flank by two separate divisions of Hill's corps of the Confederate right wing, with the plan to progress leftward down the line and push the Union Army southward and away from the escape route to Chattanooga. The Confederate lines met heavy resistance, with attack and counterattack creating heavy casualties on both sides.

Due to poor communication, Rosecrans thought there was a break in the Union lines where there was not and issued a poorly scribed order to Woods in the Union centre to move to his left to fill the apparent breach. Receiving the order at 11 am Woods obeyed and moved his command northward, which actually did create a gap in the centre of the Union line, just as Stewart's division of Longstreet's wing advanced and attacked Brannan's Union division to the right of Wood as he was marching northward as ordered. Longstreet finally got organised and attacked the Union centre with three divisions in a narrow but deep formation just after 11 am, directly at the point in the Union line just vacated by Wood.

With little resistance, the Confederate forces easily broke through the line, inflicting a heavy toll on the Union brigades on both the left and right of the breach resulting in a devastating route of the Union Army in the centre and southern flanks. The Union headquarters at Widow Glen was directly west of the breach and quickly fled north through McFarland's Gap, back to Chattanooga. What remained of the Union centre and left assembled while making a fighting retreat, taking a stand beginning at 1 pm at Horseshoe Ridge near Snodgrass Farm, using the natural geography to set up a strong defensive position. The Union position was soon bolstered by Granger's reserve corps from the north near McAfee's Church.

The defensive action at Horseshoe Ridge halted the Union route, giving enough time for the majority of the Union Army to escape through McFarland's Gap and regroup to defend the city of Chattanooga. After sustained attacks by the Confederate forces upon Horseshoe Ridge, the Union Army finally retreated and the fighting ended a little after 6 pm. Even though the Confederates had won the battle of Chickamauga, they had failed to destroy the Union Army, where the casualties sustained by the Confederates weakened their ability to maintain a sustained effort.[1]

Christopher burst out through the woods and rode into the courtyard of Dalton Mill. His horse was blowing hard, hot and wet with sweat. It was now early in the evening. The setting sun was not long touching the western horizon. Robert ran out from the house and down the stairs to greet him. Lesley was close behind. Christopher dismounted and tied his horse beside a drum of water.

"Christopher, thank God! How did you go?" Robert asked impatiently.

"Yes… I have it!" he exclaimed.

Christopher withdrew a long thin bound bundle from the underside of the saddle. He gently placed the bundle down on the ground, untied the leather straps and unrolled the navy-blue Union blanket. Robert and Lesley stared down at one gold spear set on a long straight six-foot, dark-chocolate, oak wood shaft.

"Wow… fantastic!" Robert exclaimed.

They all marvelled at the clean, simple elegance of the weapon.

"Did you get some rest while you were in Chattanooga?" Robert asked.

"Yes, I did. I was exhausted once I found a blacksmith who could forge the spear. I slept most of the morning and rode out after the midday meal, as soon as the spear was ready."

"Yes, so did we after you departed. The demon has been in its hypnotic state all day," Robert said. "What took you so long to ride back?"

"The Union lines were breached and the army almost routed if it weren't for a defensive stand at Horseshoe Ridge. I had to ride southwest around Missionary Mountain and through Steven's Gap. I turned northeast through McLemore's Cove and rode past Spring Pond to reach Lee and Gordon's Mills. Luckily, I didn't encounter any Confederates. The battle is all but over. General Rosecrans is beaten and will withdraw all his Union corps to defend Chattanooga by nightfall."

"How is the General?" Robert enquired.

"He was groggy when I left him at Widow Glen," Christopher reported. "Otherwise, I can only hope he managed to recover."

"Right! If the battle is all but over, then we don't have much time. The demon will try and cross over as soon as it can. Let's get ready. We go in as soon as the sun goes down."

"I also found some leather straps and flax seed oil," Christopher announced.

He walked around his horse and untied a knapsack. He handed it to Lesley.

They walked up the stairs and into the house a few minutes prior to 7 pm. The sun had set. Only one firepit was lit. They divided the remaining ordnances between them. Lesley held the military oil lamp. She wrapped strips of leather around the tip of the spear and soaked it in flax seed oil. Robert carried the spear. When everyone was ready, he lit the spear head.

Holding the lantern high, Lesley pulled open the hallway door. Robert walked through and stood at the top of the staircase. Christopher appeared on his right. Lesley walked through, allowed the door to close and turned left. She found an exposed nail on the wall behind her and hung the lamp upon the hook.

Below them the demon was sitting in the middle of the platform. The demon had shrunk by another foot and was practically a solid mass of blackness. The last rays of light withdrew from the sky. The demon suddenly rose to its feet and dropped the iron furnace, which crashed to the floor and instantly turned a cold ash white. The demon began to levitate two feet off the ground and turned to face its assailants.

"It's ready to cross over. This is our last chance. Come on, time to die!" Robert yelled.

Robert dashed forward down the stairs and onto the platform, followed closely by Christopher. Robert split left, Christopher right. Lesley descended the stairs and stepped forward, taking the centre. She threw a phosphorous bomb at the demon's chest. The small glass jar fell through the demon, landed and shattered on the floor. The water dissipated and the phosphorus ignited below the demon's feet. The demon watched as the phosphorus stone burned a hole into the dry wood which caught alight.

"No furnace! Empty the jar into your glove and throw the phosphorus," Christopher yelled.

Leslie quickly tipped the next glass jar into her gloved right hand and threw the stone just as it began to ignite. The lit stone hit the demon square in the middle of the chest and burnt a funnel straight down.

The demon winced and surged rapidly towards Lesley. She quickly followed with a second stone, which hit the demon in the belly. The demon leaned forward and swung across its burning belly with its left arm. Lesley dropped to the ground on her front, beneath the swinging arm and rolled to her left towards Robert.

Robert threw a wax ball with his right hand. The wax ball hit the demon high on its right hip but did not explode. Without the furnace there was not enough heat. The wax casing did begin to melt from the demon's body heat, leaving a lump of magnesium suspended momentarily before the powder began to slowly disperse in a downward trajectory.

The demon raised its right hand and moved towards Lesley. Robert lunged forward and stabbed the demon in the hip with the flaming spear. The magnesium exploded. The demon groaned in pain and fury and immediately turned towards Robert. He had to wrench the pole to free the spear and stepped back behind the anvil. He found himself dangerously cornered. Lesley, safe, leapt to her feet and dashed up the stairs and along the balcony towards Robert.

Christopher quickly moved up behind the demon and knelt on one knee. He set two glass phosphorous bombs on the platform. He opened and removed the lid of each. He held a wax ball in the right hand using his lower three fingers. He grabbed a jar with thumb and index finger and tipped it into his left. He dropped the empty jar, which smashed on the floor and gently pressed the wax ball against the wet phosphorous stone without breaking the seal. He immediately stood and tossed the bomb at the demon and then knelt to prepare the second.

The phosphorous ignited in mid-air. The magnesium exploded one inch from the demon's left shoulder inflicting a severe wound. The phosphorous stone continued to burn a funnel down the demon's back. The demon reeled in agony and within a few seconds was struck in the same location by a second bomb. Christopher could see the left edge of the demon's black heart.

Enraged, the demon spun around clockwise and lurched forward with unexpected speed and determination. The demon swung out with its right arm in a backhand slapping motion as it turned and lunged forward. Christopher needed to be close enough to hit the demon with the bomb before the phosphorus ignited… he was too close.

Christopher turned to his right and tried to fall away to the ground beneath the swinging arm. The very tip of the demon's right index finger grazed Christopher from his left temple, along the side of his head, across the top and to the back of his left ear. It was a thin, straight two-and-a-half-inch graze.

Christopher fell to the floor stunned and reeling in pain and confusion. Instinctively, he knew he was in danger and had the presence of mind to roll his body over twice, away from the demon and brought his left hand up to protect his left temple. He tried to climb to his feet, stumbled and fell over his right shoulder slamming his body into the pile of logs beside the table saw.

The demon watched momentarily and moved forward towards Christopher eager for the kill. The small fire in the middle of the platform was now well developed and growing.

In unison, Robert and Lesley emptied a jar and threw a phosphorus stone. Robert had to lean the spear against the anvil. One stone hit the demon in the mid-lower back, just above the hip. The second stone hit the demon high in the back of the head, causing it immense distress. The demon turned to face Lesley once more. Its eyes red with fury, its gaping mouth groaning with frustration as it saw her trapped on the balcony.

"Use all your wax balls and hit it in the chest... now!" Robert yelled as he grabbed the spear.

The demon lunged forward for Lesley. She threw all three of her remaining wax bombs. Robert ran forward to intercept the demon and threw his last wax bomb. All four wax balls sank into the demon's body across the top of its chest. The wax began to melt.

Robert stabbed the demon in the right hip and stepped back to avoid the feeble swinging arm. He moved directly in front of the demon, lunged forward and stabbed up and high at the demon's chest. The first powder ball exploded causing a chain reaction of three more explosions, blowing a huge gaping cavity across the demon's chest.

The demon swayed back on its haunches in agony, its head and arms flailing. The top half of its heart was exposed. Robert thrust high and forward with the spear. The flamed golden tip hit its mark, piercing directly through the middle of the demon's heart.

The demon's eyes flung wide open, its mouth agape as though gulping for air and stood still, suspended in time for a long moment. Robert tried to pull the spear out. It was stuck fast, as it began to turn an ash white from the tip down through the shaft. He held on for a second too long and was forced to let go.

In its death throes, the demon fixed its gaze upon Robert as its body began to fall forward. The demon swiped across its body with its left hand as Robert let go of the spear. Off balance, he stumbled and involuntarily threw his arms up, as he began to fall back.

The demon struck Robert across his right elbow. He fell onto his back and immediately rolled out of the way. The demon fell forward onto the spear. The spear drove right through the demon's body, fell to the ground and turned completely ash white. The demon crashed onto the platform and instantly vanished in a cloud of very fine ash white mist. A dark imprint of the demon's body was left upon the wooden surface of the platform where it fell.

The demon was dead. All seemed still and quiet except for the subtle sound of burning wood. The fire had burnt a small hole through the platform. Flame quickly spread across the underside. Thick smoke began to rise through the timbers.

Robert clutched his right elbow against his body with his left hand. Lesley jumped down to help him up onto his feet. He hunched forward in agony.

"Robert, we must get out of here. The place is going to burn," she said urgently.

"I'm ok. I can manage," Robert affirmed with a nod. "Where's Christopher? Go help Christopher. Get him out!"

Robert staggered up the flight of stairs and stood back against the open hallway door. Lesley turned and dashed left around the demon's imprint and expanding fire and found Chirstopher's body face down beside the pile of logs near the front open edge of the platform.

Lesley knelt and rolled Christopher onto his back. He was alive but heavily concussed. She grabbed him by the lapels into a sitting position. She crouched down and jammed her shoulder under his right arm and lifted him to his feet with all her strength. He continued to protect his temple. His eyes were closed. She adjusted her stance to hold his body weight.

Lesley walked Christopher the other way around the platform and guided him up the stairs. She walked him through the door, the hallway and out through the front door. Robert let the hallway door close and followed close behind. Lesley gently guided Christopher to lie down on the furthest side of the firepit from the house and quickly wrapped him in a blanket.

Lesley stood beside Robert facing the mill house. Robert thread his right arm through an open gap in his waistcoat, using it as a sling. He held the silver cross in his left hand and whispered a prayer repeatedly. They watched the flames grab hold of the mill house and develop into a massive inferno. Lesley turned to speak to Robert and was stunned.

"Robert!" She exclaimed. "You... you've turned white... I mean... all your hair... is white."

Robert removed his last glass jar from a pocket, turned it upside down and looked at his reflection. He was also stunned. All his hair had turned a silvery white.

"The demon... struck me across the arm as it died," he muttered. "I can't explain it. It's like an overwhelming darkness fills you. It's as though I can just hear the fear and screams of the dead upon a distant wind," he said and looked up at Lesley. "I can't allow myself to surrender to fear. I'll say my prayer over and over... until the whispers subside."

Suddenly, Robert turned and looked down at Christopher.

"Christopher! You've been struck!" he exclaimed and knelt beside him. "Christopher! Are you awake?"

"Um... yeah," Christopher replied in a whispered groan.

"Here... let me have a look," Robert said.

Robert gently pushed Christopher's hand away from his temple.

A thin black burn mark ran along the side of his head across the top of his left ear. His hair was singed on both sides of the burn. Tiny black capillaries spanned outwards from the scar.

"It seems you've got a nasty burn Christopher," Robert said. "Can you open your eyes?"

Christopher slowly opened his eyes and looked up at Robert.

"Oh God!" Robert exclaimed, bringing his left hand up to his mouth in shock.

"What... what is it?" Christopher asked.

"Your eyes! Well... both irises are still the same intense green. But... your left eyeball... is no longer white, Christopher. Your... your left eyeball... has turned black," Robert explained. "That's not a good look at all. Can you see out of your left eye?"

"It's blurred... and... I can't seem to focus on anything," Christopher replied.

"All right... we can't do any more here. We need to get out of here fast. That fire will attract Confederates for sure," Robert said and stood up. "Lesley, can you strap Christopher's eye and get him to his feet ready to leave. I'll fetch the horses."

Within five minutes all three were mounted. They walked through the woods to remain hidden and avoided Lee and Gordon's Mills. They rode southwest to Spring Pond, around Missionary Mountain and into the safety of Chattanooga right on sunrise...

Monday 1ˢᵗ January 1900

"… And that's how we destroyed the fear demon," Bobby concluded. "Wow, that was an amazing story," Harvey remarked.

"In the years to follow the whole area around Dalton Mill earned an unruly reputation. Sometimes, a person would be caught out at night without proper cover, late in September when the temperature falls to zero, catch a sudden chill and die, no matter what remedy was tried. All the locals were baffled. They gave it a name and called it… the Chickamauga Chill," Bobby said with a mischievous chuckle.

"What happened to Dalton Mill?"

"It burnt to the ground and was never rebuilt. I heard the Daltons moved back south."

"What happened to General Rosecrans?"

"He was traumatised after the encounter with the demon and suffered psychologically. He could no longer hold his command. In time… he did recover, entered politics and became a member of congress for California," Bobby recalled.

"And Lesley?" Harvey continued.

"Lesley went on to bigger and better things. With the knowledge we gained from the battle with the demon, she trained new recruits and developed new tools we could use against them. She soon took over the role of commander in the field from General Rosecrans for the Rose and Cross. She eventually retired and only passed away a few years ago," Bobby said sadly.

"And how about… Christopher Dee?" Harvey wondered.

"Well… as you can imagine, he was a changed man… never the same after that encounter. Once he recovered, he said… he could see what no man had any business being able to see. I believe he inherited the ability to see as a demon does… through his left eye… although I could not imagine what that would be like," Bobby said and paused in thought.

"Christopher became reclusive, withdrawn from society and disappeared. Some rumours say he entered a monastery and lived out the rest of his life in quiet prayer and meditation. Some say he went into the mountains and lived out his days as a hermit. Others say he lived among the Cherokee and other Indian tribes. The darkest ones say that, in the end, he turned into a demon himself."

"He called on me once and I met him on a train to New York City. It was… spring, the end of April 1888. He wore a wide-brimmed hat and a patch over his left eye during the day and seemed a little agitated, erratic. He said… he'd found the trail of something that should not exist and was tracking it to New York City. He soon bought passage on a ship bound for London. The last I saw of him was waving farewell on the docks. In truth, I believe he became a hunter."

"A hunter of what?"

"Only Chistopher could tell you."

They sat in silence through a long reflective pause.

"And… what about you, Bobby?" Harvey asked.

"Me? Well… I travelled for a bit. Um… a lot actually. I travelled all around the world… Europe, the Middle East… Persia, and all through Asia," Bobby said.

"Why?"

"Knowledge, Harvey. To gain knowledge. I sort out all the ancient texts and scriptures. As it turns out the fear demon is not just an American phenomenon, you know. Anyway… eventually, I took up a post lecturing history at several universities in Boston. Funnily enough I was called Count Randolph, due to my silver hair. I met my lovely wife Penelope in Boston and after many a year, eventually retired here in Frenchtown."

"Were you still involved with the Order?" Harvey enquired.

"Yes… I guess you could say that. I built and stocked our library and naturally, was the chief record-keeper and historian," Bobby explained.

"Oh, right! Yes… I imagine every Order needs one of those."

"Enough about me. What about you, Harvey? On such an auspicious day as the first day of a new century, what do you have planned for your future?"

"Oh, I don't know… I'm not quite sure yet," Harvey confessed.

"Well… the interesting thing about the study of history, is that you kind of get a glimpse into the future. You see, the majority of men are quite obedient and compliant. Many of those who rule, particularly in other countries, tend to feel it's their birthright to do so and become impervious to being accountable. And with the emergence of oil and new mechanised technologies, I feel there will be terrible conflicts in the years ahead. Maybe Harvey… you could consider doing something to help counter such a possibility!" Bobby teased.

"Like what?" Harvey wondered.

"Well, now… how do you feel about becoming a man of the Rose and Cross?"

---

[1] A concise adapted summation of the *Battle of Chickamauga*, https://en.wikipedia.org/wiki/Battle_of_Chickamauga. Accessed: 23 October 2024

The Desolate

The Desolate

The Desolate

I

Hamil'phython'aul (Hamil-fy-thin-all) sat comfortably, alone, upon a flat rock a few feet above and away from the water's edge, at the foot of an immensely high cliff. He savoured the peace and quiet. This was his favourite spot and no one else knew of the dangerous, thin hidden trail down the cliff face to an alcove bordered by a shallow shoal of flat wet rock between the sea and the cliff. Hamil liked to spend time here to think and reflect and to find respite from the noise and the hustle and bustle of the city of Sal'Saġev built into the canyon on the other side of the cliff. It was mid-morning. He stared out over the open ocean waters to the horizon deep in thought.

Hamil was tall for his kind, standing at five foot eight inches in height. His body was thick and heavily built weighing in at one hundred and thirty kilos. His skin was thick, smooth and of a light pale-orange complexion, with no pores or body hair. He displayed a long thick head of black hair, which laid back across his head and down to end just above the shoulders. Each strand of hair was four times the diameter of a human hair, ending with pointed pencil tips and did not grow or need to be cut.

His hair was a cooling mechanism for his body which allowed heat to accumulate and dissipate into the atmosphere. During physical exertion, when body heat began to build, the strands would begin to glow with a very dark maroon-red, to discharge excess heat.

With heavy build and thick, smooth skin, Hamil's facial features were larger and rounder than that of a human. He had a wider mouth with thick, yet flat lips in a deeper hue of orange and a full set of straight white teeth with molars in the back of the mouth and a thick, wide tongue. His nose was wide with large round nostrils, but flatter down across the bridge. He had a strong, thick, round jawline, high pronounced cheekbones and large, wide ears which laid back against his head.

Hamil's two eyes were also large, wide and round, like a marsupial's eyes. The eyes were covered by a fine translucent metallic, orange-tinted membrane over each eyeball, to protect them from the harsh light of their strong orange sun. Both eyeballs were a light pastel purple in hue, the large round iris a dark hazel purple-blue in colour, and the central pupil a near purple-black. He had thick-skinned eyelids with a row of very fine, black eyelashes.

Hamil's heavy body possessed thick well-muscled arms, torso and legs. In addition to an internal skeleton, his body was built with a partial exoskeleton around his chest and abdomen consisting of four pairs of interlinked and overlapping skin-covered bone plates, extending from beneath his chest and nipples, down and around his torso to end just above the hip.

The plates could expand to open a small gap between each row to allow for the quick expulsion of heated air from his lungs and close again to protect the organs. His large wide hands consisted of one thumb and three thick, round fingers, as did his feet, with one big toe and three consecutively smaller thick, round toes, all in line.

In human terms these beings would be named *homo brevis fortis*, meaning a short strong man. Commonly they are called the Orraman, simply because they are the orange-skinned people from the planet Orragon.

Today was an auspicious day. Hamil was in town, on the very day he received word that a flagship, interstellar spacecraft was returning to dock at Sal'Saġev's main port for scheduled maintenance. Growing restless with excited anticipation, he loved to watch the spacecraft enter the planet's atmosphere and fly down slowly towards the city. He was an engineer after all and possessed an intense interest in and appreciation for their technology.

The immense cliff face extended out and gently curved around far on Hamil's left. The huge pair of hangar doors were already open. The docking port and maintenance hangars were built into the cliff and went deep underground. He did not have to wait too long, only about twenty minutes, before he spotted the small speck of the ship, high in the sky.

The ship slowly floated down towards the docking station. Hamil knew that the craft's main engine, the photon drive located at the front of the ship, remained idle, as it could only be engaged once in space and was clear of any planet or moon. The ship had already engaged the anti-gravity drives under each wing and the electro-magnetic ion particle propulsion system at the back of the ship to propel the craft down and forward when docking.

The ship consisted of two main features. The wide, thick hull was a tube, with round blunt nose and tail. The top and base of the tube was a flattened curve, making the hull look like an oval shape on its side. The wings extended out on both sides of the hull, giving the craft the appearance of a perfect circle from the top view. The ship was huge, larger than an aircraft carrier, and housed a crew of two thousand personnel.

Located in the nose, was the first component of the photon drive, a large flat circular cylinder containing liquid dark matter, which had a dual purpose.

The first was to absorb light photons directly from the sun. Here, the ship would move closer to the sun, activate the drive which would spin slowly in reverse to absorb photons, convert them to liquid light and then fill and store this fuel, by charging the banks of crystal batteries located inside both wings of the ship. Once fully charged, the ship would glow with the light waves of the colour spectrum of the photons being stored and was ready to commence space travel, its second purpose.

Once in space, two meta-alloy electro-magnetically charged circular arms, would disconnect from the outer circumference of both wings. They were connected to the circular cylinder at the front of the ship and one at the rear. Together, both arms formed a complete circle and would begin to spin in a clockwise motion creating a perfect sphere around the entire ship.

The photon drive consisted of a copper-coiled core axle tube which ran through the entire middle length of the ship from the front to the rear cylinder. Housed inside the length of the tube, the axle was composed of heart-shaped disc magnets, where each interlocking magnet was perpendicular, positioned at 90°, when linked to the one in front and behind. The axle would spin in an anti-clockwise rotation and at the same velocity as the outer circular arms.

Once the speed of the ship, the spin of the axle and the outer arms reached a critical velocity, two electro-magnetic waves were created within the sphere of the ship, at a specific, secretly held frequency. One wave was created by the outer arms and moved inwards. The second wave was created by the axle, was half the wavelength of the first and moved outwards. The perpendicular intersection of the two waves within the sphere rendered physical matter to zero gravity, thus becoming weightless and essentially transforming the mass of the ship and its contents into an etheric state.

The space in space is composed of plasma. The liquid dark matter contained in the front disc would also act as a focal point from which a force field of energy, the size and shape of the ship's sphere, was projected out in front of the ship. The plasma contained within the field would then be extracted by the liquid dark matter and through the electro-magnetic tube of the photon drive to create a vacuum. This engineered fold in space-time in front of the ship, proportionate to the length of the ship itself, would cause the ship to be pulled into that space and thus propel the craft forward.

As the ratio of the spin increased, so too would the extraction of plasma, the force of the pull and velocity of the ship increase. In effect, the entire ship would mimic the properties of a photon of light travelling through space.

In this mode of travel the ship cannot turn. Being only able to travel in a straight line the ship must travel precisely in the direction towards its destination. At the very point the ship exceeds the speed of light, it enters hyperspace and jumps forward in space. Very complex algorithms measure time inside the ship in terms of seconds and milliseconds relative to physical distance travelled, and reduce speed to just below the speed of light to exit hyperspace at or near the predetermined destination. In those few seconds, the ship has entered and dropped out of an interconnecting plane between the third and fourth dimensions. The ship could jump forward one, ten or one hundred light years in space, in seconds.

Hamil dropped out of his momentary daydream of interstellar space travel. He watched the ship descend to a few hundred feet above sea level and hover directly in front of the main hangar door. He could hear a constant deep humming sound from the anti-gravity drives and could faintly feel the electro-magnetic energy being emitted across his cheeks and forearms.

Most of the crew had already been sent on leave. Only the essential flight crew required to dock the ship remained. The ship continued to hover for a few minutes while receiving clearance codes and docking instructions. The ship proceeded forward slowly through the huge bay doors and entered the hangar. Three pairs of thick shock absorbing legs emerged beneath the length of the hull, at the front, middle and rear and took the weight of the ship as it landed on the platform and immediately powered down.

The huge hangar doors began to close. Hamil sighed with the pleasure of the experience. He sat back staring out over the dark waters of the purple ocean before him and imagined what it would be like to travel to other worlds and systems. He had never been blessed with the privilege of experiencing interstellar space travel.

The second of five planets in this solar system, Orragon is slightly larger compared to Earth and has an orbit marginally closer to its orange sun, which is three per cent larger than Earth's yellow sun. The clockwise rotation of Planet Orragon's axis is tilted by 82° to the left of its horizontal orbital plane. It spins on its left side compared to Earth. The planet orbits its sun in a clockwise rotation around this horizontal orbital plane.

The first planet is one-third closer in distance between Orragon and the sun. The third planet is a half distance between Orragon and the sun, further out. Two giant gas planets orbit the outer limits of the solar system on a vertical orbit. The two gas giants orbit their sun directly opposite each other, on identical but slightly different orbits, without touching.

Thus, the poles for Orragon are at the eastern and western ends of the planet. The planet's rock is a deep orange-brown, the surface a pale sun-bleached orange. The oceans are purple due to a unique blend of a dissolved, purple-coloured potassium salt mineral.

Two huge land masses make up the northern and southern hemispheres which are separated by ocean waters. Sal'Saġev is located on the lower southwest coast of the northern hemisphere. There is no land mass at either pole. The planet has no stationary ice, due to the higher-than-normal median temperatures emitted by a larger sun. And because of higher median temperatures, the planet does not generate cloud cover like Earth, but a short, intense precipitation of condensation rotating around the surface of the planet as it transitions from day to night. One moon of a darker-coloured rock orbits Orragon in the same manner as that of Earth. Reflecting orange light, it appears as a permanent dark blood-orange moon.

The cycles on Orragon are a little shorter compared to Earth and manage to fit nicely into multiples of eight. One day consists of thirty-two hours of forty minutes each, allowing for the day's activities to be divided into four quarters of sleep, education or training, work and recreation. There are eight days in a week and eight months of forty-four days in one year. Thus, Orragon would orbit its sun in precisely three hundred and fifty-two days. There are basically only two seasons throughout the year: hot and cool.

The middle of the day was fast approaching with the heat of the sun. Hamil knew it was time to return to the shelter of the city. He stood up, stretched and turned to his left. He looked up, focused his attention and walked back across the shoal of flat rock to the start of the narrow track. Taking due care, he began to slowly climb the narrow path up the face of the cliff. To assist his balance, he used hidden handholds that he himself had chipped out from beneath many a rock ledge.

After forty feet, the path turned sharply at 180° and continued further on up the cliff, this time at a steeper gradient. The path cut back and forth every forty to fifty feet. Hamil climbed the cliff face until he reached the opening of a small cave two hundred feet above sea level. He squeezed through the narrow entrance and followed the tunnel which continued to ascend at a gentle gradient in a north-easterly direction for roughly half a kilometre.

Finally, the tunnel expelled Hamil through a tall, narrow and partially obscured opening between two rock boulders. He stood on a small flat circular rock at the southwestern point of a canyon which was carved out of the immensely high and wide plateau of rock that ran deep inland from the curved bay of cliffs. He gazed up at the immensely high rock walls as the canyon widened and stretched far into the northeast. A long narrow still body of water ran along the bottom of the canyon, where the overflow once trickled into the cave, down through the fissure of the tunnel and fell away over the cliff in a thin waterfall.

Hamil walked briskly along the northern bank of the still, black water lake into the expanding canyon, until he reached the outskirts of the city. Sal'Saġev, as was the case for all of Orragon's cities, was built into the walls of a long, immense canyon. A long protective dome was built over the top of the canyon to protect the city from the harsh light and the heat. Outwardly curved, lightweight and super strong reinforced support beams were anchored into both walls of the canyon. The roof was fitted with lightweight highly absorbent tinted acrylic solar panels, which provided the city with a consistent supply of electricity.

All the buildings were built along the cliff face on both sides of the canyon and deep into the rock. The population effectively lived underground as the planet's surface would regularly exceed 55 °C and become too hot during the day to sustain a comfortable existence.

Sal'Saġev housed two hundred and fifty thousand inhabitants, one of Orragon's largest. The city, as did all cities, produced its own food. Wide expansive balconies grew fruit, vegetables and herbs. Long fruit-bearing vines hung down from the higher levels, as well as from long curved trusses which stretched across the lower portions of the canyon. Most of the plant life had very dark green leaves and red stems. The inside of the city looked like an oasis garden.

Dark chambers were used to grow fungi and mushrooms and hydroponic chambers grew the more delicate, vitamin and mineral rich salad-style plants. From time to time, ships which could fly, sail and submerge went out to hunt some of the deep-sea creatures for their only protein-based food source. All their clothing was made from the coarse thread of a vine similar in texture to hemp.

Stretching out from the canyon along the surface of the plateau, a vast network of water-catching inverted umbrellas was drilled into the rock. They would pop out of their tubes at dusk and open to collect the daily water precipitation and funnel the water through thin pipes into large collection tanks and overflow into the lake at the bottom of the canyon. The water was used for drinking, bathing and irrigation. All waste, both biological and manufactured, was recycled in one way or another. Farming on the planet's surface was impossible.

Hamil climbed several sets of stairs along the pathway into the city. He used the public tube network of small cylindrical, electric rail-like carriages to make his way back to the boarding house he had been staying at for the past couple of days. He entered the dining hall just in time to be served lunch, before returning to his room.

After changing into his mining company uniform, Hamil left the boarding house and made his way across the canyon to the commercial sector. He climbed the network of stairs and used his ID pass to enter the building which housed the head office of the mining company for whom he worked. He rode the lift to the rooftop bar called The Loft.

He walked over to a row of booths which lined the outer perimeter of a balcony where patrons could look through the glass partition down over the tiered city far below. He spotted his managing director seated in the middle booth of a row of seven, well-padded, semi-circular booths and round table. Being mid-afternoon the bar served only a couple of patrons.

Jothril'ker'baliss, on seeing Hamil approach, rose from his seat to greet him.

"Hamil!" Jothril exclaimed. "How are you, my old friend?" he asked.

Jothril raised his right arm with a 90° angle at the elbow. Hamil took the last two steps towards Jothril and also raised his right arm with a 90° kink at the elbow. Their hands came together in the customary loud hard slap. They locked thumbs and grasped each other's hand in a very physical double shake.

"I'm well, Jothril," Hamil replied, with a broad grin and released his grip.

"I have good news for you," Jothril stated.

He guided Hamil to take the left-hand side of the booth and then returned to his seat on the right. The view was spectacular. The barman delivered a double shot of a very strong red spirit and a pint of a dark amber beer. They clicked tumblers twice in their traditional toast and shot the red liquid with a grimace and quickly chased it with a sip of beer.

Jothril was a lot older than Hamil, shorter and nurturing an expanding girth, causing the bone plates around his abdomen to soften and stretch outwards. His hair was fading to grey and he wore business attire with company logo and a pair of round black spectacles.

"Your quarterly delivery of iridium has exceeded your quota. Everyone is pleased," Jothril reported.

"I'm glad to hear it," Hamil replied.

"Your salary and a healthy bonus have been paid into your account," he confirmed. "And... as an act of good faith, the company is willing to offer you a new contract... a further three-year commission, with a ten per cent increase... as long as you can maintain the quota," he announced, followed by a long pause to allow Hamil time to consider the proposal. "Are you happy to continue for another three years?"

"That's very generous," Hamil replied. "Yes, I think I have another three years in me."

"What about, Crystal? Will she be happy to live... out there, for another three years?"

"You know she will support me in anything I do," Hamil affirmed. "Anyhow... after three more years, I'll qualify for the fifteen-year long service package. I can move to the city and do something different. It would even be enough to retire."

"You... retire?" Jothril mocked with a brief chuckle. "What about the kids? Will they be able to handle another three years?"

"Anthil, my eldest boy, is almost eighteen now. He has one more year of school left. Next year, I'll send him back here to start his tertiary education. He can find some work and make new friends in his own age group," he said, staring into the amber liquid. "My daughter Nessyl will struggle the most. She's fifteen and craves some friends of her own other than her two brothers," he said, pausing for a moment. "And then there's Leethil. He's thirteen and starting to grow up. The other two make fun of him a lot... but... he's quite independent and comfortable being by himself. I think he'll be fine for the time being."

"Very well!"

Jothril leant over and withdrew a thin, hand-sized electronic tablet communication device, from a shoulder-strapped soft leather briefcase on the seat beside him and handed it to Hamil.

"Here's the latest mobile communicator for you. Your profile has already been set up with all the same passwords and security features. You'll find your new contract, your payment summaries and the list of supplies you've ordered in the data files," he stated. "Run through the tutorial program... it's quite straightforward."

"Thanks," Hamil said casually, as he reached across the table and took hold of the device.

"All the supplies have been loaded onto your land transport. Everything should be ready for you to head back out," Jothril confirmed.

"Great! Great," Hamil replied. "I'll check everything this afternoon. I'm already packed. I'll start out a couple of hours before dawn… and get a good head start while the air is cool."

"Fantastic!" Jothril exclaimed. "Are there any other concerns to address?"

"Nope. Not that I can think of."

"The drilling rig? Is it in good working order?"

"I keep up with maintenance… and… it's a robust, strong and durable rig. There are no problems to report."

"Excellent. Well… I guess that wraps things up," Jothril announced jovially.

They chatted for a while longer until their beers ran empty. They stood and shook hands.

"Take care and look after yourself… ok!" Jothril stated with concern. "I don't know how you do it. Such a harsh and desolate place… out there… in the desert."

"You get used to it after a while," Hamil replied. "We'll be fine. See you next quarter," he said and turned to leave the bar.

Hamil went down to the depot to check that all the supplies ordered were present and loaded on his vehicle. He conducted a thorough check of his freight truck. He could not risk a break down… out there. He returned to his quarters, ate dinner and lay down to rest, right on dusk.

II

Hamil woke up, bathed, dressed and left his quarters three hours before sunrise. He made his way over to the mining company's loading and unloading dock and depot. The freight truck was the equivalent of a four-trailer, long-haul road train.

The driver's cabin was high and took four vertical steps to climb up and open the door. Inside the cabin were two large, comfortable, well-suspended bucket seats... one for the driver and the other for a passenger. The front of the vehicle had a round, smooth and shiny, pointed nose extending forward out from below the windscreen.

Behind the cabin was a large, chilled compartment which stored the food supplies for the next quarter. Four long trailers were connected to the truck, end to end with each other, using one very large horizontal cylindrical hinge. The first trailer was loaded with maintenance equipment, the second, third and fourth remained empty. The cabin and each trailer had been manufactured using a heat-resistant, highly reflective, silver-purple alloy and were domed with flat sides and underbelly, making the entire vehicle aerodynamic in design.

While parked and inactive, the front cabin and each trailer would rest upon one large hydraulic cylindrical stilt, extended by three feet from a housing compartment located in the middle of the undercarriage of each compartment. The engine was located beneath the driver's seat and extended into the nose of the vehicle. The battery cells were located along the undercarriage of every compartment.

The road was made of small round, heat-resistant glass-like crystals, each encasing a metal component with a dodecahedron shape of twelve hexagonal faces. Large numbers of these crystals are immersed into a gently heated thick acrylic liquid, poured and cast into long, thick rectangular frames. Once set, the semi-translucent panels are locked together, end to end, when they are laid down to form the road.

As the road is often covered by the drifting sands of the desert, it can be detected by radar and pulled up and relocated at any time by automated machinery. The road repulses the electro-magnetic energy field of the vehicle suspended above it.

Hamil climbed into the driver's seat and pressed the button to close and seal the door. He started the engine, which emitted a soft, high-pitched electric humming sound. He activated the electro-magnetic suspension field beneath the full length of the road train. The entire vehicle lifted a few inches off the ground. The suspension stilts retracted into their compartments.

He confirmed the preprogramed destination and route to be taken using the computerised dashboard and display. He conducted a preliminary check to confirm the radar and navigation systems were active and online. He switched on the forward lights, indicating he was ready to leave Sal'Sagev. He engaged the magnetic drive. Gently, the vehicle was propelled forward by the alternation of positive and negative magnetic polarisations along the undercarriage.

Moving smoothly with no friction or resistance, Hamil left the depot and drove through a long tunnel. At regular intervals, he would pass wide intersections of interconnecting tubes on both sides. The tunnel began to rise to an elevation of 8° where, after four kilometres, he passed through an open gateway out of the tunnel and was now travelling in the open, high on the plateau, well north and beyond the city limits.

Once clear of the tunnel, Hamil changed the gear ratio as he steadily pushed the throttle forward. The road train soon reached a cruise speed of two hundred kilometres per forty-minute hour. He headed north for the first two hours to descend from the plateau before turning northeast into the heart of the Northern Hemisphere. His was the only sanctioned vehicle using this route today.

The blazing light of the rising sun filled the landscape from the northern horizon. The desert was stark. No plant or animal life could be seen. A mist of fine sun-bleached orange-white sand blew across the flat desert bedrock. Occasionally, the sunlight reflected a metallic rainbow of colours from the exposed glass crystals in the road ahead. From time to time, deep crevassed, wild mountains of rock would appear in the distance on both sides, as the road train travelled smoothly and quickly across the barren land. The sun began to climb.

The radar housed in the front nose cone would send out a signal every five seconds. On the GPS tracking display inside the cabin, this would sound as a dull ping marking his location from the central dot on the screen. No object had been detected in a wide frontal radius since leaving the city. Thus, no alarm had sounded and the road ahead remained clear.

Hamil allowed the computer and navigation system to control the vehicle which would not deviate from the magnetic field over the road. He turned on some quiet music to help prevent himself from falling asleep inside the cooled cabin. As he stared out over the vast desert, his mind began to wonder. Every time he traversed this landscape, his heart was filled with a heavy sadness.

Planet Orragon had not always been so devoid of life as it was now. In fact, the environment was vastly different just a short three hundred years earlier, before the collapse… before the planet's future was altered forever.

Orragon once hosted vast forests of tall, thick, red-trunked trees with immense dark, green-leafed canopies. The trees soaked up vast amounts of water, which slowed evaporation into the atmosphere, making the air far more humid and temperate and prone to more precipitation. The forest floor was covered with smaller trees, shrubs and ferns, building a diverse array of plant life, which in turn sustained a large diverse insect and animal population. Communities once lived and thrived on the planet's surface. However, this eco system was fragile, the balance of which could be and was easily disturbed.

The Orraman progressed along a straight trajectory of scientific technological advancement. They evolved out of being particularly religious or spiritual. During their early development they quickly understood that a false belief was a trap for the mind and a hindrance to the progression of their civilisation. Their religion became the science of technology, which drove them to gain a scientific understanding of the nature of consciousness, their metaphysical constitution and the principles behind the building blocks of physical reality and the physical universe. Eventually, this led to the discovery of how space and interstellar space travel could be conquered.

The population grew to a height of three billion people. The agricultural needs of a high population in conjunction with the process of technological advancement steadily depleted the planet's natural resources. Little by little, deforestation whittled away at the planet's eco system until it reached a critical point where not enough moisture was being evaporated into the atmosphere and the level of precipitation fell drastically.

The average mean temperature suddenly spiked and shot up, wiping out the vast majority of the planet's insect life whose responsibility it was to pollinate and distribute new seed and spores. The consequences were a complete collapse of over eighty per cent of both the planet's plant kingdom, and subsequently, the animal kingdom which depended upon it. Fire took care of the rest. Today, only one per cent of the planet's plant and animal life have managed to survive, by adapting and evolving to become highly predacious.

This catastrophe had a devastating effect on the Orraman population. Food and water became scarce. The increased temperature caused an explosion in bacterial and viral infections. The planet's surface became inhospitable. Starvation, disease, civil conflict and war among the forty or so nations, decimated the population down to around ninety million people, who were forced to go underground to survive. Two billion, nine hundred million Orraman perished over a twenty-five-year period, three hundred years earlier.

The next one hundred years were spent adjusting to the new planetary conditions and building a civilisation that managed to sustain a return to some kind of normal life. No war has been fought between the Orraman in the years that followed to the present day.

Population growth was now strictly controlled. Permission to begin a family was only granted to replace a person who had passed away. No more than three children were allowed per family. Children born illegally were allowed to live, whereas the parents were arrested and forcibly and permanently sterilised. The planet simply could not sustain a population of more than one hundred million people. Maintaining the fragile balance for survival required very strict governance.

The forty nations collapsed and were abolished. They were replaced by a simple system of elected city state mayors, who formed and took one ministerial seat, with one voting right, in a governing council. There was one council each for the northern and southern hemispheres. Each council elected a chairman from their ranks to serve for a single period of four years. This created a two-council system to debate, vote and decide on major planetary and other worldly affairs. There were now roughly four hundred and fifty self-sustaining city states built into deep canyons, gorges and crevasses mostly along the coastal regions of Orragon.

Hamil dropped out of his daydream of what was. A couple of hours had elapsed. The desert heat was building towards the middle of the day. He could no longer see the horizon, which was obscured behind rolling waves of deadly heat across the desert.

Feeling hungry, he opened the door to the chiller behind his left shoulder and withdrew a pre-made lunch pack and a one litre bottle of light fruit-flavoured water. He took his time to eat the spiced vegetable stew and tuna-like fishcakes. There was nowhere else to be. He had travelled two thousand kilometres in the ten hours since setting out on his journey. There was still five hours to go before he would reach O'san'damis.

Deep in the desert, the tiny old service town of O'san'damis was cut out of and buried deep beneath an outcrop of rock, between and protected by two small hills. The town began as an opal and gem mine, until the cluster of veins were exhausted and the environment made it far too difficult to survive. Its name loosely translates to 'death by sand', on account of the thousands of abandoned mine shafts in the area now filled with fine sun-bleached sand that would instantly swallow you, the moment you stepped on one.

The huge orange sun was low on the southern horizon when Hamil finally reached O'san'damis. He slowed the road train down to first gear on approach to the tight cluster of five dwellings between the shadow of the two looming hills.

Each dwelling consisted of a strong metal-framed patio bolted together and drilled into the ground. They were designed to protect the heavy steel door cut into the curved shallow wall of rock that would lead down to the underground chambers of each dwelling. The framework of every patio was encrusted in a thick layer of pale white-orange salt crystals, with minute fused vertical stalagmites extending out from the metal beams in the direction of the wind.

The largest dwelling was a six-room hotel and diner for travellers. One dwelling belonged to the current operator. One was a general supplies store. Two dwellings were reserved as the self-contained quarters for any staff personnel who were willing to live and work out here. The final dwelling was a long, deep twin garage with workshop below. Every dwelling was connected by a tunnelled passageway.

Hamil had already made a reservation and called ahead a few minutes before his imminent arrival. The heavy steel garage roller door was raised and open. Hamil eased the road train slowly into the garage and parked in the allotted space. He engaged the stilts and powered down. He locked and secured the control console and withdrew the small, encrypted security panel and tucked it into the inside pocket of his company jacket. He opened the door and jumped down from the driver's cabin, carrying an overnight knapsack. The door slowly closed and locked automatically. As soon as he hit the ground and turned, he saw his old friend at the control panel on the far wall, lowering the roller door.

"Marik'foss'reth!" Hamil yelled out. "Great to see you," he said with joy.

"Hamil'phython'aul, you old dog," Marik exclaimed in return.

"How are you?"

"Bloody great… now that I have an old friend to talk to."

Hamil bound over towards Marik and greeted him with a hard-slap handshake.

"How was the trip back out?" Marik asked.

"Boring, uneventful. Nothing lives… so nothing to see," Hamil replied. "Are you lonely? Did you miss me?" he asked with a jovial chuckle.

"Of course," Marik replied without remorse. "No one comes out here. And it's just me and that grumpy old bastard of a cook out the back. All he does is whinge… all day long… gets on my nerves, he does."

They turned and began to walk towards the passage which would lead into the hotel.

"Although, two guys turned up mid-morning in a small sand buggy with those soft, wide rubber tyres, each wanting a room for the night," he reported. "Check it out."

Marik casually pointed at the small low-set, two-door buggy parked in reverse in the dark recess on the right-hand side of the garage.

"Right!" Hamil acknowledged, pausing for a moment's inspection. "Visitors! What a strange phenomenon!" he joked. "What are they doing all the way out here?"

"They didn't really say. Maybe they're prospecting. Nothin' out here but sand 'n rock," Marik said with a knowing smile. "Anyway, let's get a drink. I'm sure you're parched."

"Now you're talking. I'm dying from this heat," Hamil replied.

Marik led the way through the passage to reception... and handed Hamil the key to his usual suite, which he pocketed. They then walked through a low archway to the bar in the dining hall. Carved out of rock, all the chambers were wide, round and low with a dome-shaped ceiling and a dimly lit, shaded light in the centre of each dome.

Marik was two inches taller than Hamil and quite lean and underweight, in part due to a meagre diet in a harsh environment. He was very intelligent, quick-witted and wore casual black trousers, a baggy pale-orange collared shirt and rectangular, black-rimmed glasses.

Hamil pulled up a stool in front of the bar. Marik poured them both a pint of a cold clear golden-coloured beer. They clicked glasses and savoured the first long pleasurable swig. They settled in to discuss all the things going on in each other's lives, the news of what was happening in Sal'Saġev and the latest on council politics.

Two hours evaporated as did two more pints, before the plump face of the grumpy old cook appeared precisely at 8 pm to ask what Marik and Hamil would like for dinner. They made a selection from the three-item menu and returned to their banter concerning new technology.

Within a few minutes the other two guests made their way into the diner. They nodded their greeting and chose a table along a wall opposite and furthest from the bar. The two men were big, heavy, well-muscled and looked rough, as they were dressed in thick black clothing and boots. They were certainly not miners.

After waiting two minutes for the men to get comfortable, Marik left the sanctuary of the bar and walked over to take their orders. Marik returned to relay the dinner orders to the cook and began to pour two of the same beers.

"Do you know those guys?" Marik asked.

"Never seen 'em before in my life," Hamil replied.

"Well... they seem to have an interest in you," Marik warned. "They keep glancing your way for some reason."

He collected the round tray and walked over to deliver the two beers. Hamil half turned and watched Marik try to entice a conversation to no avail. They had an unsavoury air about them and did not display any pleasantness in their facial expression. One man had a pair of fresh, deep scratch marks on his right forearm. Marik returned to his stool behind the bar and Hamil turned back to his beer.

"They look like they're up to no good," Hamil whispered.

"Yeah… they're up to something," Marik agreed. "Looks like we had better keep our wits about us tonight," he cautioned.

"Indeed! I'll be up early and gone before dawn," he advised.

All the meals were soon served at the same time. The grumpy cook promptly cleaned and closed the kitchen and disappeared to his quarters. The meals were consumed in relative silence. The two guests finished their dinner and beer ahead of Marik and Hamil. They both rose from the table and nodded their version of an appreciation to Marik and left the dining hall. Marik replied with a brief right-handed wave goodnight.

Marik and Hamil shared one more beer and chattered for a further hour before Hamil's weary eyes said it was time to retire. Hamil walked to his room, locked and secured the door and had a quick shower. He called his wife Crystal to let her know where he was and to confirm everything was safe and well at the drilling rig, before falling asleep.

Hamil woke up two hours before sunrise. He repacked his overnight bag, unlocked the door and slipped into the corridor. The motion sensors switched on the lights as he made his way past reception to drop the key into a secure box and walked through the passageway into the garage. It was quiet and the predawn was cool, calm and clear.

There was no road from O'san'damis to the drilling rig, which was a further two hundred kilometres a few degrees to the right of direct north. Hamil lowered the hydraulic axles at the front and rear of the driver's carriage and for each trailer. The large, wide rubber tyres folded out and inflated at the same time. He withdrew the stilts.

Travel across the rugged desert of broken rock and sand could only be maintained at a safe thirty kilometres per hour with a permissible tilt between front carriage and trailer of no more than 15°. The navigation system and radar would plot the most ideal course ahead.

When ready, Hamil walked over to the far wall and pressed the button to open the roller door. He engaged the engine and switched the magnetic polarisation to now turn the drive shaft and reversed the road train out of the garage. He returned to the wall, pressed the button and ducked under the descending roller door. Back in the driver's seat, he selected the coordinates for home. The road train slowly turned and drove out of O'san'damis, around the high hill on the left and into the first emerging glow of the northerly sunrise.

After six uneventful hours, the road train finally reached the lip of a crater and stopped. It was 13 am, one hour past mid-morning. Hamil had been travelling along a rising gradient of 2° for the past fourteen kilometres. He now looked out across an immensely long and wide crater with a mostly level base.

He reached for and peered through a set of binoculars and caught a glimpse of a tiny speck of a reflection in the distance, a few kilometres inside the western wall of the basin. It was the drilling rig, now only a short twenty kilometres away. The excitement to see his family welled up through his stomach.

Hamil carefully turned the road train around and drove some distance back down the rising plateau. He veered to the west, slowed and turned into the centre of a large open cut, V-shaped ravine which punctured a hole through the wall of the crater. Slowly, he traversed the many rock obstacles through the ravine and accelerated along the floor of the basin once he was clear and headed directly for home.

The base of the drilling rig was seventy metres square. The pyramid-shaped building reached ten stories in height with a round domed apex. The outer shell was covered by a thick, heat-resistant, lightweight, dark-purple-tinted acrylic glass with a highly reflective surface. Thin solar panels were built into the glass which ran vertically down the entire length of the structure and supplied the rig with power.

A twenty metre cubed structure was built into each corner of the pyramid, like the keep of a castle. Each keep housed a large electric motor in the top half which powered a pair of giant steel feet inside the lower half.

The size of each foot was eight metres wide and fourteen metres long. When in motion, the outer foot in each keep would take the weight and lift the entire rig two metres off the ground. The inner foot in each keep would move forward into position and hold the weight while each outer foot could then step forward in unison. Although slow, the entire drilling rig was a mobile structure.

An internal platform covered the ground, except for the circular drilling hole in the centre surrounded by a protective two-metre high gated partition. The long drill boring machine was built into the apex of the pyramid and suspended directly over the drilling hole. The living quarters and control room were housed at the front half of the complex from floors four to seven, above the main front door and garage. The back half housed the power supply infrastructure, the rock waste storage bins and ore processing unit, the tooling and maintenance workshop, spare parts storage bay and all the associated machinery for the mining operation. The entire automated rig could be controlled and operated by one person.

The drilling rig was designed to mine iridium, the second densest and most corrosive resistance metal on the periodic table, with a melting point of 2,446 °C. The highly valued ore is a very hard, brittle, silvery-white metal of the platinum family and perfect for use in the manufacture of meta-alloys for their spacecraft and heat-resistant electrical components.

Although rare on Earth, it is quite abundant on Orragon. Iridium forms in clusters, between one and a half to four kilometres below the surface. A low frequency emitter is used to detect the iridium clusters. The drilling rig positions itself directly over the top of a cluster, drills down to scoop out the ore and backfills the hole with the crushed rock waste.

The dark pyramidal structure grew larger and more distinct before Hamil's eyes. The anticipation to see his family grew stronger as he drew closer to the drilling rig. He drove in towards the front of the complex. There were two large garage roller doors beside the right-hand keep. He slowed the road train down to second gear and then first, with only one hundred metres to go. The right-hand roller door had already been raised.

Nessyl and Leethil were standing outside the front door and watched him turn the vehicle around in a wide arc. Nessyl was quite tall for her age, thin, soft and smooth of skin and innocent in face. Leethil, one foot shorter, was a little wider in body than Nessyl, but still lean in build. He also had soft skin and the natural enthusiasm and excitement of an adolescent.

Hamil slowly and carefully reversed the truck back into the garage beneath the iridium ore loading machine and powered down. He grabbed his overnight backpack, stepped down onto the platform, closed the cabin door and walked out of the garage back around to the front door. Nessyl ran up to her adoring father to greet him. Hamil bent down, wrapped his left arm around her and lifted her off the ground. He gave her a long warm kiss on the right cheek and received a firm hug in response. The garage door began to close and locked into place. Anthil opened the front door for Crystal as they both appeared through the doorway.

Hamil returned Nessyl to the ground, ruffled Leethil's hair and then bent down to give him a warm hug. He walked up and gave Anthil a firm slap on the back and squeezed his shoulder. Anthil had grown to be just three inches shorter than Hamil and was filling out fast. Being more of an intellectual, he would not attain the same body mass as his father.

Hamil turned to Crystal who smiled back, relieved he had arrived home safely. He gave her a long, loving, unashamed kiss upon the lips. She stood almost as tall as Hamil, but was certainly not as broad.

"Hello family!" Hamil exclaimed. "So good to be back! I missed you all terribly. Come on, I brought a present for everyone," he said, to an excited squeal from Nessyl.

III

The family chatted excitedly as they walked through and beyond the front door and into the open space of the ground floor platform. They meandered towards the staircase on the left wall, which led up to level four, the first floor of the living quarters. A similar, second staircase also climbed the opposite wall behind the garage.

As the excited family huddle moved further inside, the importance of promptly closing and securing the door properly slipped all their attention. The door was closing, although slowly, gently, of its own accord by the inbuilt hydraulic door damper.

Suddenly, a large alpha male wild rockhound appeared, slipped through the open gap and stopped to stand just inside the doorway. The rockhound just ran across the barren basin floor from the nearest, western edge of the crater as Hamil arrived and parked the road train.

Through its glowing red-orange squinting eyes, the rockhound quickly sized up the family. It growled a deep, menacing gurgling growl and charged hard for Hamil. Three more hounds appeared behind the alpha male, an adult female and one juvenile male and female, which formed the pack, each a little smaller in size. The door finally closed and locked into place.

The wild rockhound is one of Orragon's most ferocious and dangerous predators. The dog-like beast stands just above the knee and is normally found in their natural habitat in the deep crags and ravines of the remotest rock mountains. The animal has a long, thick snout with a ridged top bone to protect its round nose. They have a wide, thick, powerful muscular jaw. One large canine tooth protrudes from each side of the top and bottom front corners of the mouth, followed by a further canine tooth half in size. Four sharp incisors followed by three bone-crunching molars, complete each row of teeth.

The thick-skinned hound has a wide muscular and powerful neck, shoulder, chest and two front legs. A thick tuft of hair, starting between the eyes, runs back over to end at the base of the shoulder blades and acts to cool the dog's body. One thick, round, one-inch bone spike protrudes through the skin from the first five vertebrae along its back. The hindquarters are slender, lean and agile, with a thick medium-length tail. Each thickly padded paw has one thick, sharply pointed middle claw with a smaller claw on each side. The purple-black eyes are protected by a red-orange membrane. The long triangular pointed ears sit behind the eyes above the jawline and are folded back along the top of the head and neck.

Nessyl was skipping along excitedly and turned to walk backwards as Hamil was recapping his trip to the big city. She saw the alpha dog slip through the front door. She screamed a high-pitched scream of terror as the rockhound bound forward. Reacting to Nessyl's alarm, Hamil immediately turned his head to see the rockhound race towards him.

Hamil spun around and stepped forward placing himself between the hound and his family. Already holding the straps in his right hand, he pulled the backpack down and away from his shoulder. The rockhound lunged forward and leapt up to bite Hamil around the hip. He swung the backpack as hard as he could and struck the hound directly across the left shoulder while its front paws were trying to claw him through the air. Several items smashed inside the backpack. The rockhound was hurtled across the ground on its right side. Everyone had spun around and now faced the pack. The other three rockhounds looked on in a moment of stunned uncertainty.

Hamil half turned and spoke quickly but firmly to Crystal, "Get the kids up the stairs! Crystal! Now! Go upstairs!"

He nudged her with the back of his left elbow which knocked her out of her momentary unbelieving gaze of shock. Crystal immediately turned and with outstretched arms she literally mustered the kids towards the stairs. The three children also turned. They clearly understood the danger and needed no directive to run for the stairs. Crystal was right behind.

The alpha male flayed frantically across the smooth surface of the platform with its claws and fought to regain its feet. The senior female rockhound leapt forward to attack Hamil. The two juvenile hounds diverted and charged towards Crystal and the kids.

Yelling, screaming and panting profusely in mutual panic, the three children made it to the stairs and bound straight up as fast as their legs could go. Crystal made it to the stairs and leapt up two steps at a time until she reached the first small landing.

The two hounds managed to catch up with her and were snapping at her ankles as she climbed the stairs. On the small landing she abruptly turned to face the two dogs who were side by side right behind her. She kicked out with her right foot and missed.

The senior female lunged at Hamil a little too early and snapped at air. He swung the backpack across the front of the dog's snout. Using the backpack's momentum, he swung it back to dissuade the animal from lunging at him again. The hound snapped at the bag and missed. He moved towards the rockhound's left flank and swung the bag over his head.

The alpha male slowed its leg movements and finally managed to find its feet. The rockhound rejoined the female and began to circle around towards Hamil's right, trying to outflank and manoeuvre behind him.

Crystal grabbed both sides of the railing and used her arms to block the stairs. She halted the progress of the rockhounds and gave the children a few precious moments of time to escape. The two hounds growled and bayed their teeth menacingly. Crystal backed up, step by step.

Hamil was forced to circled around to his right to block and push the alpha male back towards the front door a few feet away. The two rockhounds were side by side in front of Hamil and approached slowly, waiting patiently for the next opportunity to attack.

Hamil stole a quick glance across his left shoulder up at the stairs. He saw that the children had only half a flight of stairs to go before they reached the door and safety. Nessyl led the way for Leethil, who was then followed by Anthil. Crystal was further down, on the third stair of the second flight as she faced the two threatening rockhounds.

The hound on Crystal's left lunged forward and snapped at her foot, at the very moment she stepped back up one more step and withdrew her foot just in time. She instinctively lashed out with her right foot and kicked at the rockhound and swung wide across its snout.

Crystal did not hear Hamil yell, "No! Don't kick at them!"

It was too late.

The second rockhound saw its chance, lunged forward and latched onto Crystal's right back heel as she tried to withdraw her foot. The rockhound bit down hard and all its canine teeth sank deep into the soft tissue to the bone.

Crystal screamed in agony. The rockhound yanked back and down with all its strength. Crystal was violently pulled forward. She lost her footing and balance on her left leg which collapsed under her. She held onto the railings in vain. The male rockhound lurched forward and bit down hard into the exposed calf of Crystal's right leg. Crystal screamed once more. Both rockhounds worked together and pulled hard on her leg.

Nessyl reached the top stair and opened the door, which swung inwards. She stepped through the threshold, held the door open and turned to look down behind her.

Hearing Crystal scream, Leethil stopped, turned and stared down the staircase below. On seeing his mother being attacked by both rockhounds, he screamed in terror; a shrill, high-pitched scream. He threw out his arms and took one step back down the stairs, as tears began to well from his wide, distraught eyes.

Anthil did not turn. He understood clearly what had to be done. He bent forward and drove his right shoulder into the centre of Leethil's chest, knocking him back and winding him a little. He swung his right arm around behind his little brother to catch his fall. He lifted Leethil off his feet and drove forward with all his strength. He climbed the last few stairs and fell through the doorway. Nessyl slammed the door closed and pressed the lock – a push-in-push-out button in the middle of the door handle on the inside of every door. Tears began to well and stream down her face. She placed both hands over her mouth, shut her eyes and sank down to the ground sobbing.

Hamil screamed out Crystal's name in horrified anguish, as he watched her lose her grip on the handrail. The two rockhounds pulled her to the small landing. The hound let go of her right calf and bit down hard on her flailing left hand. Crystal screamed once more in agony.

Hamil took two steps forward in the slim hope he could save Crystal. The senior female blocked his path and growled. The alpha male slipped around behind him. Realisation hit home hard that he could not save Crystal and face all four hounds. The torment almost paralysed him. Both hounds prepared to leap at him in unison.

"Mooove!!!" Hamil grunted under his breath.

Hamil, big, strong and agile, mustered all his rage and anger and charged forward. Both hounds leapt. He used the backpack as a shield and slammed the bag into the open mouth of the female rockhound in mid-air. He drove forward and up with his right knee, hitting the rockhound across her left shoulder as she fell to the ground and kicked her in the stomach as he stomped over the top of the dog with his right foot and continued to ram forward.

The alpha male snapped at thin air as Hamil rushed forward, landed and momentarily lost balance on the smooth surface. The hound scampered after Hamil as he ran towards the workshop, which was built along the back wall, directly opposite the front door.

Crystal's body was dragged down over a few more steps below the landing. The male released her hand, lunged forward and bit down hard upon her neck. The hound crushed her windpipe and snapped the vertebrae in her neck.

Both Anthil and Leethil had scrambled to their feet and watched Crystal die, with arms pressed up against the full-length glass panel beside the doorway. Leethil screamed out in anguish and banged on the glass with tears streaming down his face as they stared down in horror from the observation deck above.

The two rockhounds dragged Crystal's lifeless body down and under the staircase to feed, leaving a trail of dark, plum-coloured blood in their wake.

The alpha rockhound lunged and bit into Hamil's back left calf muscle. He fell forward heavily onto his chest, just three metres short of the workshop door. He immediately rolled onto his back as the female rockhound leapt for his throat. He reached up with his right hand, caught and grabbed the rockhound under the lower jaw around the neck. She struck out with the claws of her left paw just missing Hamil's right eye, and scratched him along his inner right arm. He slammed the heel of his right boot as hard as he could between the eyes of the alpha rockhound, stunning him and forcing him to release its bite. Hamil threw the female rockhound into the body of the male rockhound and frantically scrambled to his feet, as the two hounds fumbled over each other, to do the same.

Hamil limped to the workshop, opened the door, stepped inside and turned to slam the door shut. The alpha male, very close behind, managed to get its head through the doorway. The door slammed into its right shoulder. The rockhound snapped at Hamil's feet, forcing him back. He refrained from kicking out at the rockhound and took two further steps back. He fumbled among the tools atop the work bench to his right and grasped a rubber mallet. The alpha male pushed him to the back wall. He watched the female rockhound walk down the aisle in front of the island workbench which stretched down on his left.

Hamil ran down the isle behind the island work bench towards the closed door into the next adjacent room – the drilling operations office. He did not wish to be cut off from his escape. He reached the door first just as the rockhound lunged to bite his leg. Hamil hit her just below the left ear. The hound yelped in pain and crashed into the front wall of the workshop. Hamil swung a back hand across the snout of the alpha male who was following closely behind. He opened the door, stepped through and slammed it shut.

He stood with his back to the door panting... in shock. He glanced down at the mallet in his shaking right hand and the dark blood oozing from the puncture wounds in his left calf.

Hamil turned and quickly walked to the window. He looked out across the open space of the ground floor. He saw the children, peering back at him from the observation deck and was thankful they made it to safety. He could not see Crystal, only the trail of blood down the stairs. He knew she had sacrificed herself to protect the children. He looked down suddenly overcome with grief and tried to comprehend what had just happened.

He retrieved the medical kit from a cabinet, cleaned his wounds and applied a light pale-purple anti-infection and congealing gel. He placed a dressing over his calf and inner right forearm.

The alpha rockhound left the workshop and briskly walked over to Crystal's body. The senior female followed a few paces behind and noticed the children watching from the observation deck above. She stopped, looked up to her right and saw the now locked door at the top of the staircase. She peered across to her left and noticed the second staircase behind the garage. The door at its summit was… open. She sprang forward and ran for the staircase. She reached the first landing before Anthil saw the hound's approach and realised the danger.

Level four, the lowest level of the family's living quarters, contained the pyramid's control room, which took up the front one-third of the platform. It was accessed through a set of lockable double doors and situated directly above the front door. The remaining two-thirds of the level consisted of a wide open space, where full-length, strengthened, shatterproof acrylic glass panels ran the entire width of the back wall, which allowed full viewing access of the ground floor below.

Floor-to-ceiling support beams dotted the space. A gym and exercise area was located behind the children. A long, padded bench seat ran the length of the back wall. Four single armchairs and two double seat couches and side tables were positioned in the middle area. A small boardroom table, chairs and conference facilities with a drop-down viewing screen were located on the opposite side of the gym.

Anthil took three steps towards the open door on the far side of the floor, looked out through the glass and stopped. He realised that it was already too late. He would not be quick enough to close the door before the rockhound reached the top of the stairs. He turned back.

"Get up… GET UP, quick! A rockhound is coming!" he yelled. "Nessyl! Leethil! MOVE!"

They all ran to the door in the middle of the adjacent wall. Nessyl pressed down on the lever handle to open the door into the stairwell, which would lead them up to the next floor. All three piled through the doorway. The last to enter, Anthil turned and looked back at the rockhound running halfway across the platform towards him. He pushed in the lock and slammed the door shut. They ran, single file, up the split flight of stairs and burst out through the door onto level five. Anthil closed the door behind them and pressed the button.

Containing the family's living quarters, the second floor was smaller in overall space due to the inward incline of the pyramid's outer walls. There was a large, fully equipped open-plan kitchen in the middle, a dining space and lounge on one side, and the media and entertainment area on the other, where the children now stood. The entire level was an open space. The support beams marked the general boundary of each zone.

The diminishing floor space of the third level above housed the bedrooms and bathrooms. The parents' master bedroom, mini lounge and en suite was located on the further side. All the children's bedrooms, each with their own small bathroom, basin, shower and toilet were on the near side. There was a small open common area in the middle against the back wall.

The top, fourth level contained the library and educational facilities for the children. Here, they participated in school lessons via satellite, guided studies and computerised tasks, games and puzzles, with an exceptional view across the landscape.

The rockhound ran right up to the stairwell door and bit down upon the lever handle only to find it locked fast. She let go and sniffed at the base of the door and backtracked to the observation window, where the children had been standing. She distinguished everyone's scent. The rockhound briefly inspected the platform and found no other exit. She trotted back to the open door through which she had entered, sniffed and detected a mix of strong scents leading to and through the nearby closed stairwell door. She bit down on the lever handle. The door opened. She slipped through and raced up the stairs.

Hamil saw the two rockhounds leave the workshop. He quietly opened the door to his office and briskly walked back along the island bench towards the workshop door. He closed and locked the door. He stood back against the door, closed his eyes and emitted a huge sigh of relief. He was still smitten by grief and found it hard to think. He opened his eyes and stared across the workshop.

All the mining tools were big, heavy and blunt. The machinery also big, heavy and slow moving. There were small delicate refined tools used to repair the electronics throughout the complex. He dropped the rubber mallet back atop the workbench and began to search for something he could use as a weapon.

Anthil stood for a moment trying to calm down so he could think. Nessyl and Leethil raced into the kitchen. She opened the fridge door, grabbed a couple of bottles of water and juice, some fruit and the remaining half of a loaf of mushroom bread. She dropped these items into a small bag Leethil was holding open and then grabbed the bag from him when it was full.

Anthil stood back watching, when he intuitively looked over at the stairwell door on the opposite wall and suddenly realised it wasn't locked. He lurched and ran forward. Five paces from the door he stopped and watched with dismay as the lever handle turned down. The door began to open slowly. A snout protruded through the gap. He stood in stunned disbelief as he locked eyes with the rockhound.

Anthil spun around, raised his right arm and began to run.

"Get out. Get out NOW!" he shouted at Nessyl and Leethil, pointing at the stairwell door.

The rockhound pushed the rest of her body through the doorway, gave a menacing growl ending with a sharp, shrill yelp and charged after Anthil.

Quickest to respond, Nessyl bolted past Leethil. She reached the stairwell first, opened and held the door ajar. Leethil was a few feet behind and slowed to watch his brother. Anthil diverted towards the main cooking bench. He grabbed a long thin skillet knife with a sharp pointed tip from the knife rack, as he ran past. The rockhound was a few paces behind.

Anthil ran. He instinctively peered behind and caught a glimpse of the rockhound at the very moment it was in range and leapt up behind him. He suddenly stopped, turned and raised his left arm to protect himself. The rockhound bit down hard through the middle of his forearm. The weight and momentum of the hound's body crashed into the front of Anthil's chest. He thrust the knife forward and up with his right hand using all his strength. They crashed to the ground halfway between the kitchen and the stairwell.

The knife entered the top left portion of the hound's chest to the side of the neck, grazed the collarbone and went deep into flesh. Anthil fell backwards onto his back with the hound on top of him. The rockhound paid no heed to the knife and in a frenzy, ferociously mauled Anthil's left arm. He held onto the knife which sliced two inches further to the right. The rockhound jumped back to maul Anthil's left leg, withdrawing the blade from its flesh. Anthil screamed in agony.

Nessyl watched on in horror as tears began to well. Leethil turned and fell to his knees just three metres in front of Nessyl and screamed a loud, high-pitched wail. Tears welled up and streamed down Leethil's face.

Anthil turned over onto his stomach and looked back at Leethil. He threw the bloodied skillet knife at Leethil, which bounced, rolled and slid to land two feet in front of him.

"GO!" Anthil yelled at Leethil.

He grimaced in pain as the rockhound continued to maul the back of his leg.

"Get out of HERE!" he screamed.

On hearing his yelling, the rockhound leapt forward up onto Anthil's back and clenched her jaws around the back of his neck and bit down hard. The canines sank deep into his neck. The rockhound twisted and bit down harder, until the vertebrae snapped.

Anthil stared at Leethil as his life left his body. Leethil watched helpless as Anthil's body went limp, his eyes dimmed, faded and died. Leethil sobbed and wept inconsolably.

The rockhound caught sight of Leethil and released its grip of Anthil's neck. She stepped over Anthil's body and took a few paces towards Leethil and stumbled. Her left leg buckled and she fell forward landing hard on her left shoulder. She coughed a spray of blood across the floor and struggled to regain her feet. She staggered forward a few more paces, collapsed and died right beside the knife, just three feet in front of Leethil.

A few moments passed as Leethil stared at the corpse of the wild rockhound, who stared right back at him with blank, vacant eyes. His sobbing began to subside. He stood up, walked over and picked up the skillet knife with his right hand. He turned and with a wet face, looked back at Nessyl as she held the stairwell door open.

"Come on," she said, motioning to Leethil. "We have to get up stairs. We'll be safe there."

In silence, Leethil walked through the door, into the stairwell and climbed the flight of stairs. Nessyl locked the stairwell door behind her and followed her little brother. They exited the stairwell into the hallway of the third level and made it into Nessyl's bedroom. She locked the door behind them and placed the bag of supplies on a sidetable. Together, they moved the heavy double bed around to bar the door from being opened.

Finally, they felt safe and collapsed on the bed. Nessyl held Leethil in her arms. He did not say a word. They were both suffering from the shock and grief of what they just witnessed.

A quarter of an hour ticked past. Nessyl had calmed down and Leethil fell asleep. She unravelled herself and threw a blanket over Leethil. She recalled seeing a glimpse of her father running into the workshop. She walked over to the digital panel, which controlled the lighting, air, sound, entertainment and communications. She dialled the workshop.

"Papa? Papa? Are you there?"

"Nessyl! Thank god. Are you alright?" Hamil replied, frantic.

"Yes, yes, I'm alright."

"Where are you?"

"I'm with Leethil. We've locked ourselves in my bedroom," she replied. "But Anthil... Anthil is...," she sobbed. "He... he stabbed one of those... rockhounds," she said, stuttering.

A fresh round of tears began to roll down her cheeks.

"Nessyl! Nessyl! Just stay where you are, ok! Now that I know you're safe, I'll figure something out. Wait there until I come and get you," he instructed. "Those damn rockhounds are prowling around the workshop trying to get in here. Just sit tight!" He assured. "I'll keep in touch every hour, ok!"

"Ok, ok!" Nessyl acknowledged.

She ended the call and stepped into the bathroom to wash her face.

IV

Reaching its zenith, the sun bore down with the full force of its might. Waves of super-heated air rolled across the barren basin. The outer surface of the pyramid became extremely hot and blinding from the highly reflective panels. The tint in the glass darkened. The automated climate control systems monitored and maintained a constant temperature inside.

The rockhounds had now lost their element of surprise. The alpha male and junior female paced around the outside of the workshop. They found a way to climb onto the roof but could not find a way inside. They panted, growled and snapped at each other in frustration as they continued with their search.

Curious, the junior male rockhound followed the scent of the senior female and climbed the stairs behind the garage and walked out onto the observation deck. Nothing there. The hound followed the sent into the stairwell and discovered Anthil and the senior female's dead bodies on the kitchen deck. The rockhound was no longer in any need to feed.

Continuing its search, the rockhound located Nessyl and Leethil's scent around and beyond the stairwell door at the opposite end of the platform. He jumped up and bit down on the handle and found it locked. Turning, he began a thorough scan of the deck to see if he could pick up their scent from a different location or direction.

Hamil was finding it extremely hard to think, to focus. He knew it was up to him. He had to take out the alpha male and the remaining rockhounds, to save Nessyl and Leethil.

He cleared the workbench below the window so he could keep an eye on the rockhounds while he formulated a plan. Following a thorough search, he assembled several items on top of the bench: a medium-sized steel, rock-pick hammer with a rubber-coated handle; a roll of flexible lightweight insulation rubber; two rolls of heavy-duty tape and a pair of heavy-duty scissors to cut them with; a protective hard hat with a chin strap; protective glasses and a pair of chain-mail gloves. He began to cut the rubber into strips which he then taped around his calves, thighs and forearms.

The junior male rockhound found its way back into the open stairwell, climbed the next flight of stairs and walked out into the hallway of the third level. He explored the master bedroom and en suite. Following his snout, he made his way towards the children's bedrooms and soon found the strong scent of Nessyl and Leethil, behind the locked and barred door of her bedroom. He understood the value of silence and was well practised in the art of stalking.

The rockhound quietly walked into the bedroom next door, Leethil's room. He explored the room and soon stood before the narrow-ducted air vent on the back wall, where he detected the strongest scent of Nessyl and Leethil upon the gentle stream of cooled air.

The ducted venting system and electrical works were built into the main weight-bearing structural walls. Covered by a clipped-in front grille, the air vents were just a few inches above the floor, so that the cool air would push the warm air up and out through a special pressure weighted chimney valve at the top of the pyramid.

The rockhound bumped the front grille with its nose and found that it moved ever so slightly. The hound tried to bite the grille but couldn't gain any purchase with its teeth. He clawed at the grille, softly at first and then harder, until its long centre claw punctured a small hole through the grille and then pulled back until the clips popped off. With the grille on the floor, the hound pulled its stuck claw free and peered into the narrow dark air vent.

Crouching down with both fore and hind legs tucked tightly beneath its body, the rockhound crept through the opening and into the air vent. At the intersection he turned left into the main shaft and crept towards the strong scent. After a few minutes he managed to crawl up behind the vent and could see through the grille into Nessyl's room.

The rockhound pressed its forehead up against the grille and pushed, gently at first and then with increasing force. The small rectangular grille popped out and fell to the floor. The hound gingerly extended its head through the gap and peered into the bedroom.

Pushed up against the door, the bed was in front of and a little to the right of the vent. Facing away and covered by a blanket, Nessyl was dozing upon the bed. The narrow open doorway through to the bathroom was on the left-hand wall.

Being as quiet as possible, the rockhound pushed its forelegs out of the vent, stepped onto the floor and then pulled its torso and hind legs out. The hound stood inside the bedroom for a moment, breathed in Nessyl's scent with its snout high and took two steps towards the bed.

Leethil suddenly appeared in the doorway from the bathroom.

He had woken up a few minutes earlier and needed to use the toilet. He had washed his hands and dried the tears from his face using the towel and felt a little better. He returned to find the hound midway between the vent and the bed.

"Nessyl! Nessyl, GET UP!" he yelled.

Nessyl instantly woke up and bolted straight up into a sitting position. With surprised shock and fear she immediately saw the approaching rockhound and gasped loudly.

Now that its stealthy approach was foiled, the rockhound stopped, turned its head to look at Leethil and growled deeply. The hound turned back to look at Nessyl and continued to step forward in her direction.

An overwhelming calmness suddenly fell over Leethil. He took a couple of steps towards the rockhound and growled a menacing taunt at the dog. The hound stopped and turned its head back to snarl at Leethil, as its bottom lip quivered and a long drool of saliva fell to the floor.

Leethil opened and extended his left hand out towards the rockhound, took a further two steps forward and growled once more. The hound turned to glare at Leethil and took two steps to close the gap between them. Leethil moved within arm's reach and stopped. Nessyl watched on in forced horrified silence. She sat upright against the head of the bed with both hands clasped over her mouth, trying not to scream.

The hound suddenly leapt forward at Leethil. Leethil did not flinch or move or withdraw his outstretched arm. The hound bit down hard into the outer portion of Leethil's left hand. The hound's teeth sunk deep into the soft supple flesh. Leethil watched the rockhound bite into his hand. He winced at the pain but did not cry out.

The rockhound looked up into Leethil's eyes. Leethil stared straight back into its eyes completely devoid of fear and remained very still. The hound stopped for a moment perplexed, mesmerised, having never experienced a creature stand and act in this manner before. The warm blood of Leethil's punctured hand began to drip down over the hound's teeth, gums and lip. Three drops fell and splattered onto the floor.

Using all his strength, Leethil suddenly gripped the rockhound's lower jaw with his injured left hand and pulled the hound's head forward. In the same motion he swung his right arm around from behind his back and stabbed the rockhound in its left eye with the tip of the skillet knife. During the standoff, Leethil very slowly drew the knife he had tucked in between the belt and the back of his pants.

In immediate pain, the rockhound clenched its jaw and recoiled back towards its right shoulder. In doing so, the hound tore Leethil's middle and outer finger, including both knuckles from his hand. Blood splattered over the hound's snout. Leethil's left hand recoiled back and into the air, followed by a spray of blood.

Leethil stepped forward, stabbed at the hound and sank the knife two inches deep into its left shoulder. Defensively, the hound lashed up and out with its left paw. The tip of the long thick middle claw caught Leethil on the top of his left cheek and raked straight down his face and neck, to the top of his collarbone, which opened his flesh in a long narrow gash and knocked him backwards onto his buttocks. The hound recoiled backwards and dipped its head down to nurture and protect its now blind left eye.

Leethil did not cry out but simply climbed back to his feet. He immediately pressed forward with his attack, as the rockhound continued to reel at the loss of its eye. He slashed across the front of the hound's snout cutting deep. The hound lashed out with its right paw but missed wide across his chest as Leethil stepped back in time. He slashed forward again, slicing deep above the hound's right elbow while it was a little off balance.

Leethil's body temperature began to rise. His hair began to glow a dark maroon-red from the roots outwards. A deep, calm, focused rage began to consume Leethil. He struck out and slashed the hound once more. He screamed at the hound… this time in pure fury and anger and rushed forward to slash and stab the rockhound again and again.

Suddenly, all Leethil's hair spiked straight up and out in all directions and began to glow with a deep crimson-red leaving only the very tips black. A slight red-orange hue glowed out through his eyes. He screamed at the hound once more. The hound instantly took fright at the sight, turned and tried to look for an escape only to crash into the side of the bed.

Leethil's swinging arm sliced a deep gash along the hound's exposed left flank and returned to slash the back tendon of its left hind leg. The hound slumped to the ground. He stepped up and stood over the rockhound, with one foot on either side its hindquarters. He bent forward and stabbed ferociously at the back of the hound's neck, just above the shoulder blades. After a few attempts the tip of the blade thread between the vertebrae and severed the spinal cord. Now completely paralysed the hound's head dropped to the ground. He placed the tip between the first pair of ribs and plunged the knife deep, to the handle and into the rockhound's heart. The hound coughed a splatter of blood and died.

Panting heavily, Leethil stood up, stepped back one pace and looked down at the dead rockhound. He then looked up at Nessyl. She looked back at him in stunned awe at the sight of her brother. Never in her life had she seen hair spike up and turn red like that. His face and body were completely splattered with blood, as was the floor and the lower left corner of the bed. It all looked like a surreal horror movie.

She crept forward along the bed and looked down at the mutilated carcass of the rockhound, with the handle of the knife protruding from the side of its chest. She felt an overwhelming sense of relief, love and admiration for Leethil… as he had just saved her life.

Leethil's body began to cool. The red colour soon dissipated and his hair returned to normal. He felt faint, staggered and fell back against the wall behind him and sank down into a sitting position upon the floor. He closed his eyes momentarily and opened them again. He was exhausted and had lost a lot of blood.

Nessyl leapt from the bed and ran into the bathroom. She grabbed the medical kit from a cabinet. She found the tube of the light pale-purple gel and squeezed a generous portion around the open wound of his left hand and into the long gash down his face and neck. The congealing action of the gel stopped the bleeding.

She ran into the bathroom, wet a towel and returned to clean around his wounds and face. She removed his shirt and cleaned all the blood from his torso and arms. She applied a dressing over each of his two wounds, helped him to his feet, walked him around to the opposite side of the bed, and laid him down to rest. She threw a blanket over him and gave him some fruit juice to drink. She covered the hound's body with another blanket, affixed the grille back in place and moved the chest at the end of her bed to block the vent.

Nessyl dialled the workshop. Almost an hour had elapsed since she last spoke with Hamil.

"Papa! Papa! Are you there?" she called and waited for a reply.

Hearing the distress in Nessyl's voice, Hamil raced to the wall unit.

"Nessyl! What's wrong?"

"A rockhound! One of those rockhounds managed to get into my bedroom!" she reported. "He came for me, but, Leethil... Leethil stopped it," she said and began to sob a little. "Leethil... Leethil killed it, Papa... he killed the rockhound."

"He did what!?!

"But... but he's hurt, Papa. The hound bit him and clawed him and he's lost a lot of blood. Don't worry... I used the gel, dressed his wounds and... and put him to bed."

"Ooh, Nessyl, you're so brave. You must be strong and look after Leethil, ok!" Hamil said. "How... how did a rockhound get into your room?"

"Through the vent... the air vent," she said twice, to make sure Hamil understood clearly.

"What?" he replied dumbfounded. "I can't believe these wretched animals. They're a lot smarter than anyone could have imagined," he muttered. "Are you safe?"

"Yes... yes. I've blocked the vent," she replied. "What should I do, Papa? Is anyone coming to help us?"

"We only have each other out here, Nessyl. Just look after Leethil. I'll be there soon... ok!" he assured her.

"Ok, Papa," she acknowledged and ended the call.

Hamil briskly walked back to the workbench to finalise his preparations.

"Two rockhounds... only two of those damned animals left. Just kill that alpha male... and it'll all be over. The smaller female won't fight on her own... she'll run," he affirmed and steeled his nerves.

The workshop door flung open. Hamil crossed the threshold and stepped forward back out onto the open platform.

Both of his calves, shins, thighs, forearms and biceps, were encircled with a strip of taped rubber insulation. He wore a pair of thick, metal-capped mining boots, a hard hat, protective eyewear and the pair of chain-mail gloves. He strapped on a neck brace from the medical box, which was trimmed at the top to allow for a little more freedom of movement. He held the pick hammer in his right hand, where the hammer side faced the forehand swing and the pick side the backhand swing. He held an ignited, small mobile, canister-filled propane blow-torch in his left hand.

The alpha rockhound immediately hopped up from the floor near the remains of Crystal's body. The junior female jumped down from the workshop's roof. They soon merged a few feet in front of Hamil. They paced back and forth making half circles while they cautiously evaluated the menacing and completely ridiculous looking figure before them.

Gingerly, with arms stretched out, Hamil took one wide and oversized step forward and then another. He watched both hounds in front of him. He moved clear of the workshop and out into open space. The female rockhound darted around behind. He kept his focus upon the alpha male and lost sight of the female hound.

Picking up his pace, Hamil pressed forward towards the alpha rockhound. Feeling uncertain, the hound was forced to retreat towards the front door. Crossing the middle of the open floor, Hamil could see the faint silhouette of the female hound's reflection upon the inside front panels of the complex. He stopped his advance and waited.

In the reflection, Hamil saw the female rockhound make her attack. She darted in, low and hard, with open jaw. He braced himself. She bit firmly into the rubber around his right calf. Her teeth could not penetrate more than half the width of the insulation. The rockhound shook her head vigorously, ripping at the rubber and continued to maul his leg viciously. He withstood the onslaught and kept his eyes on the alpha male.

The alpha male picked its moment and ran forward. The rockhound darted in towards Hamil's right hand. He swung the pickaxe at the hound's head when in range. The hound simply ducked its head and Hamil missed over the top. The hound caught and bit the back of his right hand as he tried to swing back. Hamil winced at the pain of the pressure being applied. The glove held firm and prevented the teeth from sinking into his flesh.

The rockhound found purchase with its front paws and pulled back as hard as he could on Hamil's arm with a couple of forceful tugs. Hamil's arm was drawn down and forward, forcing him to stagger forward with his left leg. He almost fell, but held his balance and managed to pull back on his right arm. In the same moment he brought the blow-torch forward and burned a three-inch strip across the rockhound's right shoulder.

The rockhound immediately released its grip of Hamil's hand and yelped in pain. The hound frantically bit and clawed at the base of the canister, knocking it out of Hamil's hand and sending the blow-torch spinning a few metres across the floor. The flame went out.

Hamil recovered the use of his right hand and swung again at the male rockhound's head. The hound just managed to duck the hammer and backed away out of reach of Hamil's swinging arm. Still stinging from the flesh wound the hound trotted a few paces around Hamil's left flank, trying to avoid the hammer by going around behind. Hamil turned in like manner to continue facing the hound, with right arm raised at the ready for another strike.

The female rockhound found no success on Hamil's calf. She noticed his right hand raised above and slightly in front of her head. She released his calf and lunged up to bite Hamil's right forearm. The male rockhound seized the opportunity, darted in for the attack and leap up at Hamil's left arm. Hamil thrust his left hand into the open mouth of the male rockhound and closed his grip around its lower jaw, as the hound clamped down on his hand.

Hamil winced in pain, as the rockhound's teeth managed to partially penetrate through the chain mail and into his flesh. Hamil held onto his grip tightly and kept the hound in check. Both rockhound's forelegs remained in the air. Hamil knew if he let them reach the ground, either hound could pull him off balance. He now held the weight of both animals and had to think and act quickly. He had to free his right arm.

Groaning loudly from the exertion, Hamil raised his right arm with all his strength. He lifted the female rockhound clean off the ground and brought her dangling body around to the front of his. In preparation, he shifted his weight across to his left leg and kicked up and out with his right boot. He struck the suspended hound just below the diaphragm where the rib cage begins to separate.

Winded and in pain, the female rockhound let go of her bite, yelped, gasped and coughed. She fell to the ground across her left flank and struggled both for air and to regain her feet. Hamil's arm was now free.

He reset his balance and hardened his grip of the alpha rockhound's lower jaw. Hamil swung the pick hammer as hard as he could into the hound's left shoulder joint. The socket bone surrounding the shoulder ball shattered. The hound squealed in pain. Terror filled its eyes as it desperately shook its head to free itself from Hamil's grip.

Hamil held the hound's jaw firmly and swung the pick hammer once more without remorse. The hammer struck the hound across the top middle of its left ribcage where the ribs join with the spine. Several ribs and a vertebra crumbled. Hamil hammered the same spot a second time and completely crushed the hound's spine. The hound became limp but was still alive. Hamil let go. The hound fell to the floor. Unable to move, the hound glared up at Hamil as he swung the hammer down hard onto the forehead and crushed its skull.

The female rockhound regained her feet just in time to see Hamil kill the alpha male. In that moment, all her courage and fight vanished in an instant. Hamil turned to face her. She whimpered and cowered away from him. He walked forward and pulled the front door open by a couple of feet. The hound saw and smelt the open basin. She immediately dashed through the door and ran out into the open desert. She quickly turned for the sanctuary of the nearest rock walls of the crater and was gone.

Hamil closed and locked the front door into the complex. He turned and leant back against the glass panel. He looked up, closed his eyes and let out of a long sigh, overwhelmed with relief that he had managed to stay on his feet and survive.

Once Hamil regained his composure, he removed his hard hat, safety glasses and gloves and let them drop to the floor. He walked over to the stairs, beneath which lay what was left of Crystal's body. Hamil was horrified at the scene and instantly overcome with immense grief.

He returned to the workshop and withdrew a body bag from the medical box. He gathered Crystal's remaining limbs and bones and placed them into the bag. He sealed the bag, carried it to the operations office inside the workshop and locked the door. He did not wish Nessyl and Leethil to experience any further trauma by seeing the remains of their mother.

Hamil climbed the stairs and walked out onto the kitchen platform. He held a second body bag in hand and soon found Anthil. He crouched down to gather the cold limp body of his son. Hamil gave Anthil a hug and a long kiss goodbye on his forehead, as tears streamed down his cheeks.

He placed Anthil in the body bag and sealed it. Hamil briefly inspected the fatal chest wound of the dead hound nearby. He carried Anthil and pulled the hound by the rear leg back down to ground level. He dropped the rockhound beside the dead alpha male and placed Anthil alongside his mother, in the operations office.

Finally, Hamil knocked on Nessyl's bedroom door.

"Nessyl! Nessyl, it's me. You're safe now. You can open the door," he announced.

"Ok, ok. One minute," Nessyl replied from behind the door.

Hamil heard Nessyl and Leethil jump off and push the bed clear of the door. The lock was released and the door opened. Nessyl stood in the doorway with Leethil right behind her left shoulder. Hamil stepped forward, bent down onto his left knee and hugged her. Nessyl threw her arms around her father and hugged him tightly, in return. He kissed her on the cheek.

After their embrace, Hamil gently pulled Leethil forward and gave him a careful hug as well. He held Leethil at arm's length and inspected his wounds. Hamil stood up, walked over to the dead hound and pulled back the blanket.

"Ooh, man! You really made a mess of this one, didn't you!" Hamil commented with a little remorseless satisfaction at the fate of the rockhound.

Hamil looked back at Leethil with a pang of pride and wonderment. He placed his right boot onto the hound's carcass and withdrew the skillet knife. He held the knife out in his open hand towards Leethil.

"I think this belongs to you now."

Leethil slowly grabbed hold of the knife from his father with his good right hand.

"Come on... let's clean you up," Hamil said.

Hamil sat Leethil upon the table in the common area outside the bedrooms. He removed Leethil's dressings and cleaned the wounds with a strong dark-purple antiseptic similar to Betadine. He stitched the side of Leethil's left hand and the gash down his face and neck. He instructed Leethil to go bathe the rest of his body. Upon his return, Hamil applied a second, generous round of antiseptic, dressed the wounds and gave his son an antibiotic injection.

Hamil prepared a light meal for Leethil and tucked him into his own bed to rest.

Hamil collected the dead rockhound's body from Nessyl's room, carried it down and dropped the carcass beside the other two. He stood back staring down at the hounds, wondering what the heck they were doing all the way out here in the open desert. So uncharacteristic.

Hamil glimpsed a dull flicker of light from behind the alpha male's head. He crouched down and pushed its left ear aside. Hamil found the rounded point of a tiny, semi-transparent, cone-shaped implant protruding from the hound's skull, emitting a dim orange light.

V

"What's that?" Nessyl asked, standing just two feet behind Hamil's right shoulder.

"Whoa… holy cow!" Hamil exclaimed.

Jumping out of his skin, he leapt straight up onto his feet and turned to glare at Nessyl.

"Gee whiz, Nessyl, I just leapt straight into my grave. Don't sneak up on me like that," he scolded. "Especially after what we've just been through."

"I wasn't sneaking," Nessyl professed her innocence. "I followed you all the way from my bedroom. You just weren't paying attention."

"Ok, ok!" Hamil said and returned to look back down at the dead hound. "That's an implant!"

"Well… that's not normal," Nessyl retorted, stating the obvious. "What does that mean?"

Hamil stared out at the open barren basin through the tinted acrylic glass panels.

"It means… this was no accident."

He looked down at the scratch marks on his inner arm and the small puncture wounds on his left hand and remembered the two men he'd seen back at O'san'damis.

"This is set-up," he stated flatly and glared back down at the hounds. "These rockhounds are way out of their territory… extremely unusual. They only ever stay within the protection of their rock mountains. There's no way they would have run across an open basin. There's no food or water anywhere nearby. They would've died out here," he said and paused in thought.

"And they appeared just as I arrived back home. That alone could not possibly be a coincidence. They must have been released nearby. Someone had to release them… and control the alpha male to lead the pack into the drilling rig."

Hamil suddenly turned and raced up the three flights of stairs and ran into the control room on the observation deck. He plunked himself into his large, elevated and very comfortable operations chair. He slid across to the set of security monitors on the far left of the main console. The complex had four, very advanced, high-resolution cameras built into the top dome of the pyramid facing all four directions. Internally, there were several cameras throughout the complex: one over the front entrance; one in the garage; two looking over the main open ground floor; one in the workshop; on the observation deck; and over the kitchen.

First, Hamil checked that the system remained offline and wasn't connected to the satellite. There were no outbound transmissions and, thus, no one was using their security system to spy on the family. The sun was now approaching two hours past midday.

Hamil had arrived at the drilling rig a few minutes prior to 14 am. He programmed the time to start twenty minutes prior to his arrival and replayed the footage of the north, east, west and south cameras through the four screens in front of him. He leaned forward and watched intently. Nessyl stood beside him with an extra pair of eyes to help.

Twelve and a half minutes into watching the footage Nessyl yelled, "There… look! There!"

Her eyes were keen and sharp. She pointed at the monitor displaying the southern view.

Hamil's eyes were getting old and tired. He missed what Nessyl saw, rewound the vision by two minutes and played it forward again at half the speed. He soon saw it. Close to three kilometres south-southwest, a small flying craft flew into the basin and landed in the dispersing wake of dust from Hamil's road train after he drove past two minutes earlier. The craft made a drop and after only forty seconds took off again. The craft flew westward and disappeared just out of sight over the lip of the crater wall.

"Well done, Nessyl. You spotted them."

Hamil looked at her with warm affection and gave her a gentle squeeze of congratulations, on her left shoulder.

"They tried to hide behind the dust," he mused and sat back in his chair thinking. "We're not out of this yet," he stated flatly, staring up at the sky through the thick tinted glass. "If they're still out there, they're probably watching us right now."

Hamil suddenly sat bolt upright in his chair with a realisation.

"If they're to the west on that crater wall watching us... how are they watching us?" he asked, voicing his thoughts and reasoning out loud. "The only way is to use a thermal or infrared imaging device. And during the hottest part of the day, the heat and light reflected from the surface of the drilling rig would render such a device useless... until the sun sets."

Hamil checked the digital timepiece in the console.

"They will be blind for one... maybe two more hours," he calculated.

Hamil spun in his chair to address Nessyl directly. A plan had formed in his mind.

"Nessyl, when the sun begins to set and it gets cooler, some very dangerous men are going to arrive and want to look inside our home. There will be at least two, maybe more. I don't know what they want or why they are doing this, but they are the ones who sent those hounds after us. They won't be able to see us and will think those rockhounds killed us. And if they find us... they'll finish the job. So, we must move quickly... and set a trap for them, ok!"

Nessyl nodded to acknowledge her understanding.

"Right then... let's get to work," Hamil said.

Hamil walked back down to the ground floor platform. He picked up and dumped the three hound carcasses into an empty iridium ore bin in the garage and briskly cleaned the central area of the platform of any sign of rockhound. He left the blood trail down the stairs.

Next, he opened the safety gate and inspected the ground of the new drilling site and then closed it again. While Hamil was away at Sal'Sagev, Crystal had moved the drilling rig a quarter of a kilometre along the iridium vein from the previous borehole.

Hamil checked and prepared the drilling machine before returning to the control room. He powered up and engaged the machine and slowly lowered the circular spinning drill head. He bore a five foot deep perfectly circular hole into the rock. The waste rock was automatically crushed by the internal mechanism of the drill head, sucked and dumped into the large cylindrical waste bin. Hamil returned the drill to its standby position and powered down.

He ran into the workshop, unscrewed and pulled out a small, two-door metal cabinet from its mooring against the wall. He swiped all the contents onto the floor and drilled several venting holes into its side. He lifted the cabinet to the edge of the borehole and allowed the cabinet to fall backwards into the space, with a noisy clank. The two doors slammed shut over the top.

Hamil raced up to the bedrooms and collected a couple of blankets. Returning, he stepped down onto the cabinet, opened the two doors and lined the inside of the cabinet with the blankets. Hamil then retrieved a thermal fire mat from the fire kit and laid it over the top of the cabinet. Watching on, Nessyl understood that she and Leethil were to hide down there inside the cabinet, just below ground level within the bedrock.

Jumping into the small internal crane, Hamil positioned the lift arm over a stack of drilling pipes, which were just wide enough for him to crawl into. He jumped down and hooked the cable to both sides of the pipe. He lifted the pipe and placed it on the floor just in front of the workshop. Using the rest of the roll of insulation rubber, he lined the inside of the pipe equivalent to the height of his body. He raised the pipe and left it suspended just above the workshop roof with one open end facing the front entrance of the complex.

Hamil called Nessyl and Leethil to join him in the control room. Using his security key, handprint and pin code, he opened the armaments cabinet in the back left corner of the room. He reached in and grabbed a rifle and an energy power pack, which he loaded into the butt of the weapon. Leaning the rifle against the wall, he then grabbed a pistol and loaded an energy pack into the handle. He turned and crouched down in front of Nessyl and Leethil.

Similar in shape to those on Earth, the weapons have a thicker insulated barrel and are powered by an energy pack of weaponised liquefied photon energy – liquid light. The barrel, although not entirely hollow, is the chamber which generates and fires a long rounded bolt of super-heated liquid light, the size of a small slender sausage. When the bolt hits its target, it will vaporise the same cubic dimension of physical matter to that of the bolt and convert that matter to energy, in the same manner that fire acts on wood, but in an instant. The colour of the bolts of light are orange, given the source of the power pack's energy.

Hamil briefly explained his plan. He reversed the pistol and placed it into Nessyl's hands.

"Nessyl! Take the pistol. You know how to use it. Those men want to kill us all. I'll try and stop them... but... if I miss or they get me... don't be afraid to use it. When the time comes, you must use the gun without hesitation. Do you understand?" he asked sternly.

"Yes, yes. I understand," Nessyl replied.

She grabbed the pistol without delay and looked at her father with a steely determination.

"Very good," Hamil replied satisfied. "We're almost out of time. Let's get ready."

Hamil powered down the entire complex, except the ventilation system. Without any lights on, the inside of the pyramid was reduced to a darkened eerie silence. The thick tinted glass was very effective. He grabbed the rifle and led Nessyl and Leethil out of the control room and down the stairs to ground level in single file. He helped Nessyl and Leethil climb into the cabinet and gently closed the doors. He pulled the thermal fire mat over the top. He climbed out and closed the safety gate but did not lock it.

He unlocked the front door, walked back to the workshop and climbed up onto the roof. He squeezed into the back of the suspended pipe and thread his way forward until he had a clear view of the front entrance. He pushed up a circular cut-out of insulated rubber with a peephole, to block the front of the pipe. When he was comfortable, he kept still to stop the swaying of the suspended pipe and settled in to wait.

They waited... and waited. Time seemed to slow down. One hour ticked by. Leethil had already fallen asleep. Nessyl listened to her brother's breathing. Each breath seemed to take an eternity. Hamil grew drowsy as his eyelids began to weigh more and more heavily down over his eyes. The middle of the afternoon soon arrived and dripped slowly past. The sun was now well on its way to setting.

The temperature suddenly fell sharply. A short five kilometres to the west, the thermal imaging telescopic camera was finally able to peer into the building. No heat signature could be detected of any person or rockhound. The perpetrators were perplexed, and they deduced there was only one course of action... to investigate.

After a further quarter hour, the two-man buggy raced across the basin floor and pulled up outside the front entrance of the complex. The motor was switched off. One man stepped out from the left-hand side of the buggy and one from the right. They looked uneasily at each other with rifles drawn and approached the front door.

A small flying craft flew in, made one circle around the top of the pyramid and landed beside the buggy. The third man, their leader, descended from the steep rear ramp between a row of two empty cages on the left and a row of two on the right, in the small rear cargo bay.

He removed a thin black cigar from his lips, stopped and spat on the ground. He looked up at the pyramid, returned the cigar to his mouth and walked over to his two companions. He carried his rifle loosely in his right arm with the barrel pointed down to the ground.

All three men were big and heavily built, dressed in black and rough-looking, like outlawed criminals. The driver of the buggy pushed open the front door, stepped inside and held it open. Once his passenger and leader entered, he let go of the handle. They stood still for a moment adjusting to the dimmed darkness before they began to moved forward and fan out from each other by a few paces.

Hamil was alerted by the sound of the flying craft overhead. Through the peephole, he watched the three men arrive and enter the building. He immediately recognised the two who stepped out of the buggy. He gently pushed the rubber cap down, raised his rifle and peered through the scope. He took aim at the one on his left, the passenger with the scratches on his arm. He could not allow the men to walk too much further forward, otherwise he would lose sight of them. He pulled the trigger.

The first shot hit the passenger clean between the eyes, the bolt penetrating skin, bone and brain. He died instantly on his feet. His head swayed back an inch and then he fell forward, slamming into the platform hard across the front of his body.

Startled, the buggy driver ran for the staircase to his left. Hamil fired. The bolt hit him through the right hip bone. The man stumbled and fell hard and awkwardly across his right side. He was well short of the stairs. His rifle slipped from his hands and spun across the floor into a pool of dried congealed blood. He tried to get up. The next shot struck the driver through the right side of his neck. His head dropped forward and he hit the floor... dead.

The leader of the gang did not run. Seeing the orange bolts shoot forth from the front of the suspended drill pipe, he raised his rifle above the hip and fired a series of rapid shots up at the pipe. Two shots went through the front lip of the pipe. One went through the top middle of the pipe just missing Hamil's back by an inch. Several shots missed wide on both sides and one shot hit and severed the front suspension cable.

The front of the pipe instantly dropped down. The middle of the pipe's underbelly crashed into the front edge of the workshop roof. Still connected by cable, the rear of the pipe swung up and forward. The momentum swung the pipe into a horizontal position where Hamil fell out through the front of the pipe and was slammed hard across the front of his arms and chest onto the floor. Severely winded, he dropped the rifle. The pipe swung back and forth over the top of his body and back again to slam into the wall of the workshop.

Hamil rolled onto his back, sat up and turned to face the intruder, nursing both badly bruised elbows and a sore cheek, nose and chin. The leader calmly approached him. The man's rifle was now relaxed and pointing to the ground just short of Hamil's outstretched legs. He kicked Hamil's rifle far out of reach back towards the front door.

"Who are you people?" Hamil asked huskily, recovering his breath. "What do you want?"

"Who am I? ...doesn't really matter... for you," he replied with a deep crackling voice which sounded more like a growl. "What do I want?" he said and paused to looked up into the inner space of the drilling rig and raised his left hand with an open palm. "Well... this drilling rig of course," he said mockingly with a wry smirk.

"Why? The only thing this rig can do is drill for iridium."

"Precisely!" the man countered.

"All this, so you can take over and drill for iridium yourself?" Hamil blurted out a little dumbstruck at what he was hearing.

"Uh huh," the man confirmed.

He took a step closer to Hamil and raised the barrel of his rifle.

"But... who are you going to sell iridium to? There are only two companies on this planet who are sanctioned to buy and process iridium. One for the north and one for the south."

"That's not your concern now, is it?" he said.

The outlaw aimed the point of the barrel at Hamil's chest.

"Time's up!" he announced.

A shot rang out. Startled while looking into his eyes, Hamil jumped out of his skin at the sound expecting to be shot. The outlaw's left eye melted and caved back into the cavity behind his head. A vacant expression crossed his face. The barrel of the rifle dropped back down towards the ground, dangled momentarily in his hand and fell to the floor. He began to fall forward and landed hard across the full front of his body. Hamil swung his legs out of the way as his face and head hit the ground.

Hamil looked up to see Nessyl standing behind the outlaw. Hearing the destruction of the loose pipe she had feared for her father. During the ensuing conversation, she quietly climbed out of the cabinet and the hole, opened the gate and stepped out behind the man who was pointing a rifle at her father. She raised her right arm, aimed the pistol and shot the intruder in the back of the head.

"Nessyl!" Hamil exclaimed, exhilarated. "You shot him. Thank the heavens. I thought I was a dead man for sure," he said with overwhelming relief.

"I knew you were in danger," she replied, "so I knew I had to do it."

"You did great."

Hamil climbed to his feet and calmly walked over to Nessyl. He crouched down, gave her a long warm hug and gently prised the pistol out of her grasp. He tucked the pistol into the back of his belt. He held her at arm's length with a hand on each shoulder.

"If you didn't shoot that man, he would have shot me and then found you as well," he said. "You did exactly what you had to, to save us all."

He gripped her cheeks in his hands and kissed her on the forehead. She acknowledged her father's supportive nurturing with a smile. He knew she would be ok.

Hamil stood and inspected the carnage around him. Nessyl helped Leethil out of the borehole. Hamil locked the front door. He secured all the discarded weapons, removed their power packs and safely stored them inside the workshop's operations office. He raced up to the control room and restored power to the complex.

He returned to find Nessyl and Leethil milling around the dead bodies and sent them to the kitchen to help each other prepare dinner.

"Who are these people?" he muttered.

He searched each body but could not find any identification. All three bodies were soon placed side by side in body bags, a few metres in front of the workshop door.

Hamil decided to search the buggy outside. The only item he found was an old communication device. It was dead, out of power. He walked up the steep rear ramp into the flying craft. He regarded the cages with disdain, made his way into the cockpit and sat in the pilot's seat. He checked each of the side compartments. Nothing but empty packets for thin black cigars.

Tapping his finger on the base of the pilot's seat between his legs, he noticed a small thin drawer under the seat. He gently slid it open and found a brand-new communicator. It was exactly the same model as the one handed to him two days earlier.

"That's strange," he muttered.

He switched it on but did not know the access code.

He tucked the communicator into a pocket and left the flying craft. He walked back into the complex and over to the electronics bench in the workshop. Having maintained the building's electronics for a decade, he was an expert.

He opened and removed the back plate of the device. From his computer he connected several plugs and wires to the tiny motherboard inside the device and ran a codebreaking software program. He soon cracked the access code, gained entry to the device's data drive and began to search through its contents.

The device looked clean. There did not appear to be any incriminating evidence about the three intruders and what their plan was. In fact, the communicator was set up with the exact same configuration as his... albeit... under a different name and access code.

He opened a folder and saw a contract for a drilling rig and territory. He opened the document. He found the price for this contract was twenty per cent less than the price of his new contract. He checked the coordinates and found that the new territory crossed over into half of his own vast territory, excluding the zone he had been mining for the past ten years. He was certainly not aware that he was now sharing his territory. He checked the document to find out who the managing director was that issued the contract. The identification code remained blank.

Hamil decided to log into the mining company's database, so that he could look up the serial number codes of the drilling rig assigned to the contract. The moment he entered his login code into the system, a red alert appeared on the screen informing him that his account was under investigation and had been suspended.

Hamil sat back, aghast. He stood up, paced back and forth a couple of times and quickly jumped back into his seat when he suddenly realised it would be best to disconnect from the satellite feed and shut down the computer. Then he was struck by a moment of clarity.

This was a hostile takeover.

The intruders would arrive to discover Hamil and his family had unfortunately been killed by wild rockhounds. His commission would be quietly removed and the new one inserted in its place. Even though he could not yet find the evidence to reveal the identification of the mole, only one person in the mining company had knowledge of his exact timetable.

Furious, Hamil screamed, clenched his fists and slammed the benchtop.

Hamil removed all the plugs and wires from the communicator and replaced the back plate. He wiped it clean, picked up the rubber mallet and hit the screen with a measured blow, sending a spider web of cracks through the device. He slipped the communicator into a static free bag and sealed it. He put on his jacket, tucked the device into an inside pocket and grabbed a small electronics toolkit before leaving the workshop.

He walked up to the kitchen and shared an early dinner with Nessyl and Leethil.

"Nessyl," he began. "I'm going to confront the man who is responsible for this attack on our family. I'll be away all night. Keep the drilling rig in lockdown until I return in the morning. Do you think you can do that?"

Nessyl nodded in the affirmative.

"And look after your little brother, won't you!"

Immediately after dinner, Hamil parked the buggy in the garage. He walked out of the building and waved up at Nessyl in the control room. She activated lockdown which automatically engaged the security system.

It was right on sunset, 8 pm, when Hamil climbed into the pilot's seat of the flying craft.

He wore heavy-duty gloves and smashed the front panel of the console. He withdrew his electronics toolkit, short-circuited the security, re-looped a couple of select wires and manually started the twin engines, one beneath each V-shaped wing. He checked the fuel cells and instrumentation, before lifting into the air.

Once clear of the drilling rig, Hamil retracted the landing pads. He knew the flying craft used by these criminals would need to be invisible and not possess any tracking devices.

Hamil flew southwest, low over the desert at a near maximum speed of five hundred kilometres per hour. He made a straight line for Sal'Sagev, with the intention of cutting the coastline one hundred kilometres north of the city.

After four and a half hours he reached the coast, flew out over open water and slowed the craft. He turned south, flew just above sea level and tucked in very close to follow the line of cliffs. Approaching the city Hamil slowed right down and hovered a few feet over the water. He hoped that he would be small and well hidden enough to avoid being detected by radar. He most certainly did not wish this trip to Sal'Saġev to be recorded.

Hamil spotted his secret alcove and landed the craft on the small flat outcrop of rock. He disembarked and under a dull moon, climbed his way up the cliff face. He broke into a steady jog through the tunnel, out the cave and into the lower canyon. It was 14 pm at night, with only two hours remaining before midnight when Hamil entered the city.

He wore dark clothing and wrapped a long scarf around his head, neck and mouth against the chilled air. He hopped on and off tunnel trams, ducked through back lanes and made his way up to the affluent part of the city. He kept to the shadows and avoided anyone he saw.

In just over an hour, Hamil stood below the two-storey terrace house owned by the person he was looking for. It was dark, no lights. Nobody was home. He knew the resident lived alone, enjoyed the seedy bars for a spot of gambling and rarely went to bed before midnight.

Hamil peeled back around the corner into the darkness of the narrow, inclining lane beside the house. He was only a few feet away from the gated archway at the front, through which a half-dozen steps led up to the front door. He leant against the wall to watch the pathway just below… and waited.

Hamil did not have to wait long.

A shortish, rather robust man dressed in an extravagant hat and overcoat and carrying a bulging soft leather business briefcase using a shoulder strap, staggered up the pathway. The man stubbed his toe, stumbled and almost fell over. He had consumed a few too many beverages. As he drew adjacent to the intersecting lane and prepared to turn left and reach the sanctuary of his house, Hamil stepped out in front of him from the shadows.

"Jothril!" Hamil said flatly.

"Whoa!" Jothril stammered and swayed back wide-eyed, startled.

It took him a few seconds to recognise who it was.

"Hamil?" he squealed with an expression of shock and surprise he was unable to hide.

"Yes Jothril, it's me," Hamil confirmed, studying every minute detail in Jothril's face.

"Wha... what... are you doing here?" Jothril asked, with a quiver of fear in his voice.

"Something happened to me... to my family... today," Hamil began.

"Wha... what, do you mean?"

"Just as I arrived home, we were attacked by a pack of wild rockhounds. They killed Crystal... and Anthil. We managed to kill three of them. Do you know anything about this?"

"What? No, ooh no. I don't have any idea of what you're talking about."

"Then... three men turned up... with weapons. They wanted to take over the drilling rig. Do you know anything about that?"

Jothril raised his hands and shoulders in an innocent shrug.

"I have no idea... what you think might be going on here... but I have... don't know what you are insinuating!"

"Well, as you can see, they didn't succeed."

Hamil continued to glare directly into Jothril's eyes with intent.

"I searched their vehicles and do you know what I found?" Jothril shook his head. "A communicator just like the one you gave me."

"Anyone can buy one of those from a distributor."

"I hacked the drive and would you believe... I found a contract for a new drilling operation."

Hamil stared at the blank expression coming over Jothril's face.

"So, are you the MD who registered their fictitious operation?"

"What? No... no... I would never do something like that."

"Then why is my account suspended? Why am I under investigation? You're my MD! You should know the answer to that. Is there something wrong with my commission?"

Hamil took one step closer. He was one foot from touching Jothril.

"I... I... don't..." Jothril stammered.

He was unable to think clearly, soberly. Panic began to grow in his mind.

"Let's go inside and take a look at that briefcase you're holding there."

Jothril instinctively clasped his hand over the bag and turned his right shoulder away from Hamil's reach. He looked back at Hamil, his veneer finally cracking.

"So... what was the plan? Deregister my commission due to an unfortunate accident and reinstate a new one! Why go to the trouble?

So… you can skim a twenty per cent commission for yourself?" he whispered into Jothril's ear.

Jothril simply shrugged, twitched an eyebrow and curved his top lip into a snarl.

"I guess your salary is not that great… you're just a desk jockey after all."

"No! And nor is the retirement fund… even when you've given your whole life to the company," Jothril said in a gruff, resentful voice. "It's nowhere near as good as your commission."

They stood there staring at each other for a few long moments.

"So! What now? Are you going to turn me in?" Jothril enquired.

"You destroyed my family. I've lost my beloved wife Crystal and my son Anthil, both of whom I loved dearly," Hamil said calmly. "You don't get to walk away from this."

A long moment passed before clarity entered Jothril's mind.

"Oh, wait, wait! We can make a deal. I'll give you anything you want," Jothril trembled.

Once Hamil knew the truth, he had discreetly drawn the pistol from the belt behind his back and held it, hidden at arm's length beside his right leg.

"There is nothing in this world that you can give me that will alleviate my pain and anguish," Hamil countered flatly, coldly.

Jothril took a step back and thought about running. Futile! He was drunk and overweight.

"You weren't supposed to survive," Jothril resigned.

Hamil brought the pistol out from behind his leg, raised it up in front of his abdomen and pointed the barrel at Jothril's chest. Jothril spotted the pistol and startled, opened his mouth in a vain attempt to…. Hamil fired.

The bolt hit Jothril through the chest and pierced his heart, before he was able to utter another word. The second bolt hit Jothril under the jaw and went straight up into his brain.

"Survive that!" Hamil said with bitter vile.

Jothril's head swayed back, as did his body. A trickle of blood appeared at the corner of his mouth and ran down over his chin. He slumped back against the wall behind him. The weight of the bag pulled his body to his right. He slid to the ground and slumped over the bag… dead, with eyes wide open.

Hamil withdrew the cracked communicator from his jacket and slipped it into the inside pocket of Jothril's overcoat. He stepped back and looked around to see if anyone had been watching. It was dark, quiet and void of any other presence.

Hamil calmly walked back down the pathway. Taking a different route through dark alleys, lanes and tunnels, he soon left the city. He reached the cave entrance at the bottom of the canyon and briefly looked back towards the city, before climbing down to the flying craft. He breathed a huge sigh of relief the moment he plonked himself into the pilot's seat.

He took off and flew northward, low, beside the cliffs. When satisfied he was clear, he gained altitude and turned inland for O'san'damis, at a more relaxed speed.

Hamil woke Marik up bang on 6 am. Marik prepared a warm herbal brew while he listened to Hamil's horrific tale. He had Marik's complete confidence. They had been friends for a very long time and way out here, only had each other to rely on during troubled times. Together, they flew back to the drilling rig, arriving just as the northern horizon began to glow orange.

Nessyl disengaged lockdown and opened the front door. Marik was rather taken aback at the sight of the dead intruders and rockhounds. He climbed into the buggy and reversed it out of the garage. Returning to the pilot's seat of the flying craft, Hamil took off and flew to a distant rocky mountain range three hundred kilometres north. Marik followed in the buggy.

Hamil landed right on the edge of a high ridge which peered straight down into a deep crevasse. He wiped the controls, console and seat clean and programmed the auto pilot to conduct a thruster burn in three minutes time. As he ran out and down the ramp, he poured a highly flammable liquid across the floor of the cargo bay. With its nose dipped downwards, the craft flew forward, crashed into the opposite wall of the crevasse and ignited into a ball of flame. The burning hull fell deep into the darkness below.

Hamil climbed and trotted down the southern slope of the mountain and found Marik waiting for him at a predetermined location. Marik dropped Hamil off at the drilling rig and taking possession of the buggy, drove himself back to O'san'damis. During the course of the week to follow Marik would strip and sand back every panel and reglaze them with a new colour. He reassembled the panels onto the frame in a more aerodynamic configuration and added a few personal touches. The buggy was unrecognisable from its former self.

From the control room, Hamil engaged the drilling machine and bore a one-kilometre hole straight down into the rock. He withdrew the drilling head, walked down to the ground platform and opened the safety gate. One at a time, he dropped the bodies of the three dead men, their weapons, the alpha rockhound's implant and the small pieces of the now crushed drilling pipe in which he had hidden, down the shaft and backfilled it with the rock waste. He cleaned and removed all trace of the three men from the ground platform. He wiped the recorded security vision for the past thirty-two hours and manufactured a fault in the system for an explanation.

Once satisfied, Hamil called in to report the wild rockhound attack on his family and requested a medical unit for Leethil.

The police unit arrived later that evening, recorded all the evidence they could find and took a statement from Hamil, Nessyl and Leethil, detailing the events which had taken place. Leethil spent the following week in hospital recovering from his wounds. Crystal and Anthil's remains were taken for forensic examination, which confirmed their cause of death. This was the first recorded rockhound attack in the open desert for over one hundred years. The authorities and experts were mystified as to how and why this had taken place.

The investigation into Jothril's death revealed an attempt to defraud the mining company of iridium royalties. The person, or persons responsible for Jothril's murder remains unsolved.

Within a couple of months, the three outlaw intruders were listed as missing, having neither accessed their residence, communications or banking, nor responded to governmental checks in that time. The investigation found they were known to Jothril and became suspects in his death. Their whereabouts for questioning could not be ascertained.

Following the rockhound attack, Hamil decided to retire his commission and negotiated a settlement package with the mining company. He relocated to Sal'Sagev with Nessyl and Leethil, to live a quiet, comfortable life and watched them both grow up.

VII

Leethil emerged from the shower with a towel wrapped around his waist and walked through a short tunnel to his locker inside the barracks. He had enlisted in the military, the branch equivalent to the US Navy Seals, and had graduated earlier that afternoon after completing a gruelling two-year training programme designed for off-world deployment.

He did try other fields of endeavour which he found boring and mundane. He was restless, easily agitated and quickly realised he was unsuitable for domestic employment.

Compared to his colleagues Leethil was huge. He stood at five foot nine inches tall, was wide and thick set, weighing just short of one hundred and fifty kilograms of pure agile muscle. He was now twenty-three years of age.

He dressed himself in a strong, thick pair of black and dark-orange military trousers and belt, over which he threw a loose-fitting military tunic of the same colour, which sat comfortably down over the belt to end half way down his thigh. The emblem embroidered on the left breast of his tunic depicted an Orraman's right hand gripping a spear, crossed with a bolt of lightning in front of a full blood-orange moon.

He sat down on the bench behind him, pulled on his thick socks, followed by his black well-padded military boots. He stood and pressed his heels into the base. His boots immediately sealed themselves around his feet and ankles.

He grabbed the towel and made sure his left hand was completely dry. He glared at his maimed left hand with only the index finger and thumb remaining. He caught a glimpse of his reflection in the small mirror affixed to the inside of the locker door. He snarled at the dark, long thin jagged-edge but smooth-skinned scar which ran from the top of his left cheekbone, just below the eye, straight down his face and neck to the collar bone.

With his right hand, Leethil reached into his locker and from a shelf, withdrew an immaculate well-padded glove crafted using an iridium alloy. He gently thread his left hand into the glove. He turned a thin band around the wrist which clicked into place. The glove immediately sealed itself around his hand and wrist. He tested it, where the mechanical middle and outer fingers perfectly mimicked the movement of the index finger.

He clipped a one litre metal bottle of nutrient-rich water onto the front left of his belt. On the front right of his belt he clipped a specially crafted sheath which housed an old but very sharp kitchen skillet knife. He slammed the locker door closed and walked out of the barracks.

A few of his colleagues watched him march past in silence. They revered him both in fear and awe. Leethil topped the entire squad through training by a clear country mile and gained a reputation for being the most determined, ferocious and vicious combatant the academy had seen in very long time. He did not feel inclined to make friends and by and large, just kept quietly to himself.

Leethil's hair did flare straight out with a deep crimson-red… only once… during a training exercise where an accident caused by a fellow cadet almost cost him his life. Everyone in his team were stunned, having themselves never witnessed such a phenomenon.

His commanding officer had seen this phenomenon occur on only one other occasion during his entire career and understood exactly what it was. First triggered by a massive trauma, it had the potential to produce the most dangerous of warriors: calm, fearless and able to focus their rage in such a way that they became a cold, borderline pathological killer… perfect for the military and yet needing to be handled with extreme care.

Leethil made his way through a tunnel and walked out into the wide open underground cavern of the flight hangar. He had been granted permission to requisition an unarmed single-seat flight craft for thirty-two hours. Today was also the tenth anniversary of Crystal and Anthil's death. He had a personal matter to attend to.

He approached and climbed into the cockpit of his assigned aircraft. It was a small thin craft shaped like the head of a spear, with a central tube for the pilot and a single rear thrust engine, a rounded nose and wings folding back at an acute angle. The craft perched on three low skinny legs with round padded feet and housed two small anti-gravity devices, one inside each wing.

Leethil put his helmet on and switched on comms. He strapped himself in, closed the hatch overhead, ran a safety check and primed the anti-gravity devices and main engine. As soon as the control bunker gave him clearance, he lifted off and withdrew the landing gear. He turned 180° and slowly hovered forward, through and out of a small hangar door in the cliff face a few kilometres south of the city of Sal'Sagev.

He flew directly out over the sea until he was in clear space before climbing in altitude. He gently turned the craft to the left and onto a new heading of almost directly east. He opened the thruster and flew the light craft inland at a speed of one thousand kilometres per hour.

After two and a half hours and just on dusk following the evening precipitation which settled the dust, Leethil arrived at a very remote, immense and wild mountain range. He reduced speed and altitude and flew the craft low over the range. He scouted the general layout of a long deep valley of deep ravines and crevasses. He spotted a low flat-topped ridge, with a gently descending slope into the valley from the north.

Leethil flew the craft down and hovered two metres above the ridge's surface. He powered down the thruster and switched the anti-gravity devices into neutral. The craft maintained a stationary hover and emitted only a very mild, low frequency, humming sound. He withdrew the craft's remote control panel out from the front console and opened the hatch. He climbed out over the lip of the craft and let himself drop down to land comfortably, with a heavy thud and a spray of dust around his feet.

Using the remote control he closed the hatch and increased the stationary hover to five metres and turned off the lights, except for a small red, blinking undercarriage safety light. Leethil secured the remote control in a zipped trouser pocket. He looked up at the half blood-orange moon rising into the sky which bathed the land in a dim glowing light.

Adjusting to the feeble light, Leethil walked to the edge of the ridge and peered down into the darkness. He let his head drop back, closed his eyes and breathed the cool evening air in deeply. He listened intently. Several insects emitted their customary clicks and twitches. He could hear the flutter of wings and the trickle of water. And then… there it was… a short high-pitched yelping bark… echoing out from the deep crevasse below.

Leethil opened his eyes and stared forward out into space with a wry smile. He looked down at his glove, opened his hand and closed it again. He punched the closed fist of his glove hard into his right hand. Satisfied, Leethil turned, drew the skillet knife out slowly from its sheath and began a gentle, relaxed jog down the gently sloping stone pathway.

From the very first moment he joined the military, for some strange reason, he wished for a shoulder coat made from the top jaw and skin of a wild alpha male rockhound.

Sovereignty in the School Yard

Sovereignty in the School Yard

Sovereignty in the School Yard

September 2001 – Beginning of the New High School Year

Fletch Braxton rose from his seat and calmly walked down the middle aisle of the auditorium. It was a warm Tuesday morning into the third week of the new school year. He climbed the stairs on the side, walked across and stood behind the lectern placed on the forward middle of the stage. With self-assured confidence, he stretched out his arms and gripped each side of the lectern. With a dour expression, he briefly surveyed the entire year twelve student body gathered before him, who were all eager to hear his nomination speech for the role of senior school captain. As the final speaker of five nominees, he did not begin until he was absolutely sure he held everyone's full attention.

Standing at five foot nine inches tall, Fletch maintained a solid, robust and stocky frame, where his light upper body was supported by the immense strength of his thick hips and thighs. He had medium to dark-brown hair with a hint of ginger, which was trimmed short around both sides and back, and allowed for several tight curls to amass at the top.

Fletch was a naturally gifted and the most accomplished point guard in the school's senior basketball team. Coupled with his charismatic charm, he was very popular among his peers. He was neither foolish nor vain in character and kept true to his nature by clearly expressing his opinion on things, his likes and dislikes, and had an intolerance towards flagrant stupidity or injustice. He was friendly and easy going with no perceivable personal hang-ups, and presented the persona of a determined, intelligent student with a maturity beyond his years. He had a great sense of humour, a warm laugh, enjoyed a cold beer and preferred live music played by a band. Everyone genuinely liked him.

Having just turned eighteen in August, Fletch was the eldest of two brothers, Stephen by four years, and from an immensely wealthy and affluent family. His father, Arthur Robert Braxton and mother, Margaret June Braxton, grew the family merchant shipping and wholesale importation and trade business, as well as managed the extensive landholdings and investments held in agriculture passed down from generation to generation.

In fact, the wealth and lineage of the family could be traced all the way back to Carter Braxton, one of the fifty-five signatories of the United Stated Declaration of Independence of 1776. Fletch understood his long family history very well. He carried himself with a sense of poised self-awareness, knowing that a clear path to power lay before him. And now, beginning to bloom, he had the opportunity to display his most cherished and, in time, feared quality… his unwavering quintessential and ultimately ruthless… American patriotism.

"Class of 2001–2002, good morning!" Fletch began, in a confident, clear voice. "Well… we made it… we made it to our final year. And what a way our last year has begun. Nine days ago America was attacked, violated by the forces of tyranny who wish to destroy the very values our great nation was founded upon."

"I… I… personally cannot understand how this… this transgression could happen. One thing is certain… we as Americans will be changed forever."

"I know we have already offered our prayers and blessings to those who died. Yet, we cannot allow fear and oppression to dictate the course of our year ahead. We must stand firm and continue to be the shining light, a beacon of hope and liberty in the face of adversity."

"So, I say to you, my fellow seniors, that we must forge a bond… a bond which will bring us closer together… a bond where… together we will overcome each and every obstacle and make this… this our last year of school the best yet."

"So! Are you ready? Are you ready to meet this challenge, to test yourself, to find your limit, to exceed your capabilities… and overcome adversity? Do you know what you want to do, what you want to be? Once this year is over… when school is over… you'll all go out there and pit yourself against the world and shine your light in places where hope is needed."

"Now… now is the time to know how you are going to shape your future and the future of America. So, I'll ask again, are you READY!?" He paused for effect.

Fletch changed his voice to a softer tone.

"Now, if you haven't figured it out or you haven't the vaguest clue about your future, I'm here to help you. As your elected senior class captain and as your voice, I will ensure that every fellow student is developing their necessary skills and abilities towards their chosen field. If you're into politics, join the student political club. If you're into the arts join the music and drama club. If you're into sports, take part in any of our school's sporting teams. If you excel academically, enter competitions and get those grades you need for college," he said and paused.

"No one should be left out or excluded. If this is happening to you, let me know and I will work towards helping remove any barriers or resolve whatever it is that is blocking you from where you need to go. Remember, I'm here to help make sure that all our school's resources are available to make you the better person you need to be," he said in a low, serious tone.

"If you are having a hard time or in some kind of trouble… don't drop out. Don't become a liability. Don't become a menace to 'national security'."

Several teachers sitting along the side wall glanced at each other, momentarily amused with what a strange thing he said.

"I'm here to help… the school is here to help… you graduate. And if everyone here today graduates and takes their rightful place out there… your life will be so much better, so much easier… and America will be all the better for it. So, let's just get it done… OK!"

Fletch returned to a booming voice.

"To highlight our accomplishments, I propose that anyone who achieves something in a public domain, no matter what field of endeavour, should be acknowledged on the main noticeboard and in the monthly school magazine."

"We shall continue with our school's charitable tradition. I will help organise several fundraising activities throughout the year, where the proceeds raised will go to UNICEF to help build new schools in Africa, Southeast Asia and the Middle East. We should never take our education for granted, right?"

"And I pledge my unwavering support to all our diverse groups: our black student union; our LGBTQ+ club; our Asian student alliance;

and our multicultural student club. Students from diverse backgrounds now make up twenty per cent of enrolments so, if there's anything you need, I'll be more than happy to help organise and support all the special events you have planned throughout the year ahead."

"So, as I said, no one will be excluded... everyone will find their place... and everyone will graduate," he said and paused. "Now... are you ready? Are you ready to forge our bond together?"

Fletch glared at his audience who stared back at him a little bewildered. He stepped around and in front of the lectern and walked a few steps to the left and then a few to the right while raising both arms as though urging the school body to stand and chant in return...

"Are you ready!? Are you READY!? To forge our bond and make this... the best year ever?"

The majority of the student body stood and clapped yelling... 'Yes, we're ready!' until Fletch was satisfied. He then motioned for the crowd to hush, while they all stood.

"Class of 2001–2002, our bond is 'forged'!" he yelled proudly. "Together we will make this the best year for everyone! Thank you, thank you, and God bless America!"

Fletch jumped down from the stage and calmy walked up the centre aisle towards his seat through monstruous applause. It took a while for the rather perplexed school principal to return some degree of calm to the hall and wrap up proceedings.

****

Three days later on Friday morning, all the votes were in, counted and the result announced. Fletch Braxton won the election by a clear majority of three to one against his nearest rival. He was now the senior school captain of Northside Chestnut Grove Academy.

Northside Chestnut Grove Academy campus is a co-educational private high school of roughly twelve hundred students from grades 9 to 12, located within the very affluent area of Chestnut Hill, ten miles northwest of Philadelphia. Established during the 1860s, the school assimilated a hotel, with rooftop rooms built into the structure of its main building, which now consists of three long, wide multi-level wings positioned in a U-shape. A dark-grey brick and a distinctive bright-red roof tile were used in its construction. The main V-shaped stairs at the front of the building lead up and into a grand cylindrical-shaped entry foyer, topped by a tall, round, red-tiled spire.

The expansive and well-maintained school grounds also house many support buildings, including the main assembly hall (which doubles as the school's theatre and performing arts hall); a separate indoor basketball court; an American football field surrounded by an athletics track; a soccer and baseball field; and many sheltered and cultivated gardens among and between all the buildings. Independent and privately owned squash courts, an Olympic-sized swimming pool, an ice skating rink and country golf club are also located nearby.

On his way to the canteen for lunch, everyone congratulated Fletch on his electoral victory as he walked through the hallway. He received a cascade of handshakes, back pats, salutes and shouts of encouragement. Pleased with the attention, Fletch thanked everyone as modestly as he could. In the cafeteria, he collected a tray, plate, cutlery and received a healthy serving of the day's lunch. He turned and located his friends sitting at their usual round table over by a large window. He sat down on the one available reserved seat.

"Congratulations, Fletch," his best friend Blair Depler said, who sat on his immediate right.

Blair was seventeen and the fourth generation of an Italian family, who had used their expertise in the development of American industrial manufacturing to build wealth. He was of similar height, slimmer in build compared to Fletch, with dark eyes and short black hair.

"Yes, well done," Rayish Prasad concurred from the left-hand seat. "That speech rallied and got everyone very excited," she said.

Rayish was a beautiful slender seventeen-year-old girl, with dark-brown hair and eyes and a light-brown complexion. She was the third generation of a family from India, whose wealth was invested in telecommunications and the development of satellite infrastructure.

"Yes, Fletch! Congratulations! I think you even shocked some of the teachers with that speech," Benson Thomas stated.

Also seventeen, Benson was of African American heritage, six foot four inches tall, lean and agile, with intense black eyes and a short well-kept afro hairstyle, and played shooting guard in the school's senior basketball team alongside Fletch. Although not as wealthy as his colleagues, Benson's family heritage went back at least two hundred years; finding freedom from slavery during the American Civil War, his forebears were the first to enter the legal profession, defending the rights of African Americans and trying to even the playing field through the legislature against immense adversity, often with very little pay.

"Thanks, guys," Fletch replied casually, glancing at each of his friends with a thin content grin on his face. "Yes, that speech did the trick, didn't it? Got me the job... right!"

Fletch arranged his plate, cutlery and drink to his liking and began to eat his lunch.

"Are you doing the same subjects as last year?" Blair asked.

"Yep, sure am," Fletch replied. "English, maths I and II, physics, economics and geography," he reported. "What about you? Are you doing the same?"

"Yeah... English, maths I, history, economics, business studies and physical education," Blair replied.

"Yeah... you're in my history, business and phys-ed classes," Benson confirmed. "I'm also doing legal studies," he said. "Why're you doing so many maths subjects and... geography?" Benson asked Fletch. "Why geography?"

"Well, all good decisions are based on great analysis. And great analysis is based on great mathematics. Everything can be quantified into a mathematical logarithm," Fletch explained. "Even what we're having for lunch right now," he paused. "Geography? Because it's important to learn about the rest of the world... and not to have just a narrow sectarian view of America, don't you think?" he paused. "Since America has become the unrivalled superpower... the challenge now is how to maintain, or even enhance, our dominance to better influence the rest of the world... and to determine where future threats may arise."

"Spoken like a true patriot," Rayish replied with a thin, teasing smile.

"And what are you doing this year, Rayish?" Fletch asked.

"Well... English, maths I and geography... the same as you... biology, business studies and journalism," she replied. "So... judging by your speech... do you have a plan? Do you know what you want to do... once school is over?" Rayish asked Fletch. "No point professing to help others if you don't have a plan yourself, right?"

"I plan to take over from my parents in the family business," Fletch replied nonchalantly.

"Rubbish!" Rayish countered. "Being a CEO doesn't seem like the right fit for you. You're far too calculating for that. Why don't you tell us what you're really planning? That speech was perfect... like you've been preparing it for a long time," she prodded.

Blair and Benson looked on at Fletch, suspiciously perplexed.

"You're rather perceptive, Rayish," Fletch replied. "Taking on my parent's company would be a bore. Blair is more likely the one to take over his parent's business... if not, then politics... right Blair?" he said looking over at Blair.

"Yeah... pretty much," Blair confessed. "There's always the mafia," he joked.

"Waste of time. You're already rich. And who wants to wind up dead in a ditch for a retirement plan," Fletch dashed the idea poetically. "And Benson... will continue in the legal profession. It's in your blood now, right? So, let's see... a Federal Chief Justice?"

"It has crossed my mind," Benson confirmed. "If the NBL doesn't work out."

Fletch turned back to Rayish.

"And you plan to become a journalist... right? An international journalist if possible? Or better still, to run your very own media house!"

"Of course," Rayish replied. "That's not hard to deduce. My family is involved in telecommunications," she paused. "Now that you've worked out all our lives, what about you? You still haven't told us what your plan is," she pressed.

"Well... I think America needs me!" Fletch stated flatly, among groans and grunts and rolling eyes of disbelief. "It's true," he said unflustered. "I... will help America!"

"So, what... you're going into politics?" Benson asked.

"Certainly not the military," Blair confirmed. "You're not military material."

"No, no!" Fletch countered.

"An analyst in the deep, dark basements of the Pentagon," Rayish suggested with a giggle.

"Joke all you like. But I assure you, I'll send the president a message... where he'll have no choice... other than to hire me," he stated with a stoic expression.

"Ok, ok," Benson said with a wavering smile. "How're you going to do that?"

"You'll all just have to wait and see," Fletch replied. "A magician never reveals his magic. A poker player never reveals his best hand... or his bluff... right? Otherwise, the game's up and the power is lost," he said.

They sat in silence for a while eating the last of their lunch before Fletch turned to Rayish.

"Are you planning to do some reporting for the school magazine?"

"I did make an enquiry and asked if I could submit a contribution. However, I was informed that there was nothing available for me to work on," Rayish replied.

"Well, everyone who works on the school magazine is a volunteer. No one gets paid. Every article published is based on merit," Fletch recalled. "So, anyone can submit an article."

"I know," Rayish replied. "But maybe it's not about merit."

"Oh, I see," Fletch realised. "Was it Derrick Hackett, the student editor, you asked?"

"Yes... it was Derrick," Rayish sighed.

"There's our problem right there!"

"So, do you think you can help?" Rayish asked.

"Maybe... maybe!" Fletch pondered. "Let me think about it and see what I can do."

"I don't want any trouble if it's too hard."

"Leave it with me," Fletch replied with a thin, confident grin.

The lunch bell suddenly rang, loudly, causing an instant mad dash to return trays and dishes and a stampede to the next class.

****

Rayish was right. Unbeknown to his family, teachers and peers, Fletch had been planning his ascent to the senior school captaincy for roughly two years now. For as long as he could remember he knew what he wanted to do... what he wanted to become. To him, it felt as though he was born for the job, that secretly... it was his destiny.

Family life for Fletch was stable. He lived in a mansion on a large estate a little over two miles from the school. The family shared breakfast and dinner together, accompanied by the usual small talk around the table. As long as Fletch was achieving high grades, happy and engaged with his friends and not in any trouble, his parents left him to his own devices and attended to their business enterprise.

From his thirteenth birthday onwards, Fletch and his brother to follow became beneficiaries of the extensive family Trust. His father would state, 'Much better to give it to you than pay it out in tax, right?' and... 'Better get used to having money, son... it's a means to get what you want, so learn how to use it... but... don't ever allow money to screw you up.'

The Trust paid Fletch an annual sum of fifty-two thousand US dollars, allocated in weekly instalments. From the time his benefit began he quietly managed to amass a substantial war chest which could afford him certain capabilities.

Over the past two years, through family, business, as well as independent connections, Fletch covertly gathered a wealth of information on the school principal, deputy principal and all thirty-five teachers, including the principal's receptionist. He obtained their home address and phone number; car and registration; place and date of birth; identity and nationality of their parents; their qualifications and employment history; last two income tax returns; what assets they owned; their most recent travels; and criminal convictions, if there were any to be uncovered. Some of the information gathered was offered freely, as a favour, but most of it was paid for in cash, no questions asked. Fletch painstakingly cross-checked every reference, every fact, in his compilation of each person's file. He also managed to acquire the names and addresses of the entire student body.

Moving into the first week of October, Fletch now took a keen interest in Derrick Hackett.

Derrick was quite tall and lean with fair skin and pale blue eyes. He had sandy hair tinged with orange. As student editor, he was responsible for producing the monthly, twelve-page school magazine. He was also the self-appointed official school photographer and developed all his photographs using the school's darkroom. He preferred the camera and hoped to become a world class sports and landscape photographer.

Derrick had four journalists under his guidance, one female and three male students, all friends from a similar background. It would appear that Derrick was not so accepting of students from an alternative diverse culture.

Fletch observed Derrick from afar and made casual discreet enquiries of students who knew him but were not close friends. Derrick was an above average student, doing well in English, journalism and physical education but only just managing to pass maths I and history. He was, however, struggling in chemistry, which he thought would help in the art of developing photographs, but found the subject far more difficult than initially anticipated.

And because he was struggling to understand the theory, Derrick became somewhat disruptive in class, which brought upon him the ire of his chemistry teacher, Mr Martin (Chini) Chinnery. Chini had to continually reprimand Derrick and was forced to move him to an isolated desk at the front-right corner of the room, reserved to correct such disobedient students. Naturally, through this evolving conflict, Derrick developed a severe dislike for Chini, which was felt and reciprocated by the teacher.

Midway through the third week of October, Derrick's best friend and most favoured student journalist found a yellow, unmarked envelope in his locker. He turned around to see if anyone was looking or acting suspiciously. He discreetly opened the envelope and inspected its contents. Comprehension of the value of the information provided quickly dawned on him, where he immediately closed the envelope and sought Derrick's counsel.

On Thursday the 1st of November, the new edition of the monthly school magazine was released for distribution into the student population. Somehow, this edition bypassed the head of the school's media and arts programme, Ms Eleanor Dixon's sign-off. The front page led with a highly inflammatory exposé…

'TEACHER BUSTED IN FRAUD'

The published article displayed proof that exposed Chini for using a fraudulent Master of Education degree as his qualification to be appointed as the school's chemistry teacher three years earlier. Chini, now in his late twenties, did in fact begin an education degree at college, but dropped out halfway through. For several years, he had managed to earn a meagre living working for a tutoring firm, before being employed by the school.

The exposé caused an immediate sensation throughout the student body and overwhelming embarrassment for the school. Chini's qualifications were investigated, checked and found to be fake. Chini confessed and was summarily suspended. A temporary replacement was found, but was ill prepared and the class suffered for the rest of the year.

Consequently, Derrick was summoned to the principal, Mr Lindsay Faulkner's office for disciplinary action. Derrick had circumvented procedure and used the school's magazine to expose and crucify Chini without reporting the issue to the school authority and allowing due process to properly investigate and discipline the offending teacher. Derrick was removed as student editor and photographer of the school magazine and placed into afterschool detention for the rest of November.

Nominations were now open for a new editor and photographer for the school magazine.

Fletch encouraged a rather surprised Rayish to submit an application for the role as soon as possible. He said a fresh new perspective was very much in need. She jumped at the chance and submitted a professional application first thing on Monday the 5th of November.

Just as school ended late that Monday afternoon, Fletch's charismatic charm gained him entry into Mr Faulkner's office. He sat casually in the comfortable, cushioned single armchair in front of Mr Faulkner's desk.

"It's a hell of a thing… this episode with Mr Chinnery?" Fletch began.

"Yes, it is." Mr Faulkner replied. "It's a shame HR didn't check his credentials. Otherwise, this situation would never have happened."

"And Derrick… he should have known better," Fletch continued.

"Yes, he should have. I don't know what compelled him to crucify Mr Chinnery like that."

"A couple of his classmates tell me Mr Chinnery moved him to the front desk for being disruptive. I guess he didn't like Mr Chinnery because of it."

"Yes… well… it's a serious offence to misuse a position of responsibility against a member of the faculty, no matter what you're feeling," Mr Faulkner stated.

"Yes, of course. Derrick abused his power," Fletch agreed. "So… I believe the role of student editor is now open?"

"Yes, I've posted it on the noticeboards. Why?" Mr Faulkner asked suspiciously.

"Well, Rayish Prasad has lodged an application... and... I think she would be great for the position," Fletch said, offering his endorsement. "Derrick gave all his mates the journalism roles and blocked her from making a contribution."

"Is she your friend?" Mr Faulkner asked.

"One of many," Fletch replied. "Her family is heavily invested in telecommunications... and she is keen to pursue a career in journalism and media production. And you know me... always happy to help someone out... and make things a little bit easier for them," he paused. "The school doesn't seem to give many opportunities to students from a different background... and I think we could send a positive message if maybe... she could be given an opportunity. Rayish could bring a fresh approach to the school magazine, don't you think? And her family would be very grateful for the opportunity."

"Well... you present a compelling case," Mr Faulkner said. "I'll look at her application and give it some consideration."

Fletch rose to his feet and slowly walked to the door. On the back wall to the left of the exit, he noticed a photograph of Mr Faulkner's graduation from university. Mr Faulkner was dressed in a graduation gown and hat and held his degree while standing in front of and between his mother and father, and younger sister on his left.

"Were you born here or did your family emigrate to America, Mr Faulkner?" Fletch asked.

"My family emigrated to America in 1958 from Austria... when I was just fourteen."

"I see," Fletch said, as he looked closer at the photograph. "Then, you know what it's like when you arrive from another country... how hard it can be to win an opportunity?"

"Yes, I do," Mr Faulkner responded in kind.

Fletch turned from the photograph on the wall to face Mr Faulkner.

"Are both your parents Austrian? I thought Faulkner might be a German name?" Fletch asked casually.

"My grandfather was German. My mother and father are both Austrian," Mr Faulkner said.

He lied. He just lied… about his parents. Fletch thought to himself. *Why? Maybe… he doesn't want to make a big deal about it… and avoid any attention.*

Fletch already knew that Mr Faulkner's father was German and that his mother was actually from Eastern Ukraine.

"Cool," Fletch commented with a warm smile. "Well… could you check out Rayish's application. If we can make things just a little easier for her that would be awesome."

"I'll look into it," Mr Faulkner assured him.

"Fantastic! Have a great evening, Mr Faulkner," Fletch said, turned and promptly left.

****

On Wednesday morning, Mr Faulkner announced that Rayish Prasad was to become the new student editor of the school magazine. She was delighted and immediately took charge of the facilities and familiarised herself with the process. She appointed a few more reporters, a new photographer and began to compile material for the Christmas issue.

Sharing the same geography class as Derrick, Fletch noticed that he was looking a little withdrawn and dejected at the start of his second week of detention.

On the way out of class, Fletch purposely accidently bumped into Derrick in the hallway.

"Derrick, why so miserable, buddy?" Fletch prompted.

"Argh, this detention is getting to me," Derrick replied.

"It took balls to do what you did… but… it wasn't the right way to go."

"It's not that. Chini deserved it," Derrick said unremorsefully. "I've entered the Philadelphia student sports photographic competition. I've made a great submission and must be there tomorrow afternoon after school to be able to claim the prize, if I win. First prize is ten thousand dollars, to be used to buy equipment and for further training," he explained.

"Oh, right… I see," Fletch replied. "Have you asked to have the afternoon free?"

"Yes, of course," Derrick replied. "But Mr Nelson, has it in for me. He won't let me go, no matter what. Do you think you can speak to the deputy principle on my behalf?"

"I'm not sure," Fletch replied. "He's a tough old buzzard and a stickler for rules."

"Yeah, a real old prick," Derrick assured.

"Would winning this competition help you in a photographic career?" Fletch asked.

"Absolutely! It's the premier student competition in Pennsylvania."

"Ah, right! Well, let me know how it turns out," Fletch yelled and dashed to the next class.

The following afternoon Derrick did win the competition but had to forfeit the prize due to his non-attendance. He was furious and distraught as he reported the outcome to Fletch.

****

Fletch quietly met with Derrick after school at a nearby dinner. He gave Derrick a card for an attorney and instructed him to go and see Douglas Adams and explain what happened. Douglas was Benson Thomas's uncle and a senior partner in the family legal firm. Derrick agreed to do as Fletch suggested, on the provision that Derrick never reveal the nature of their conversation to anyone else.

Enraged, Derrick met with Douglas and explained his story. Douglas agreed to take on the case at no charge, without disclosing the fact that a fee for service had already been paid on Derrick's behalf.

On Monday the 19th of November, three days before Thanksgiving, a lawsuit was submitted to the District Court of Philadelphia on behalf of the plaintiff, Derrick Hackett, challenging Northside Chestnut Grove Academy on two grounds: 1) Their legal right to hold a student on school grounds after the end of school, preventing them from attending outside commitments important to that student's development; and 2) suing the school for damages to compensate Derrick for the loss incurred by the school's action.

A preliminary hearing by the presiding judge agreed with the plaintiff's legal argument and suspended all further use of detention by the school until the legal action was resolved. A court date was set to be held in eight months' time.

In the meantime, Blair Depler joined the student political club.

Throughout November, Benson Thomas and a few friends sold 2002 student diaries to raise funds for the student multicultural club.

November 2001 – Thanksgiving Through to Midwinter Break

The school community returned from Thanksgiving at the end of November, and everything seemed normal except for Mr Geoffrey Becker, Fletch's economics teacher. Mr Becker was quite young at thirty-four years and had been teaching at the school for the past nine years from the moment he left college on completion of a double degree in economics and accounting. He taught senior economics and business studies, which constituted only two subjects per day. The remainder of his time was spent acting as the school's bursar.

Today, Mr Becker displayed rather dark and sunken eyes. His discourse through the economics class was somewhat disjointed and Fletch knew he had a problem. Fletch was well aware that Mr Becker's parents were active in demonstrations against the Vietnam War, liberal in their views and enamoured by the peace and love movement. Their influence would certainly have enticed Mr Becker into smoking cannabis during college, which almost caused him to fail a year before he managed to pull himself together in time to graduate. However, things may have escalated since.

Midway through the first week of December, Fletch knocked on Mr Becker's open office door at the start of the lunch break. All the teachers' offices were located down a long corridor in the same wing, with the principal's office at the end which was diligently guarded by the receptionist who sat behind an enclosed glass partition.

"Hey, Mr Becker, do you have a minute?" Fletch asked.

"Sure Fletch, come in," Mr Becker replied. "How can I help?"

"I have some questions regarding the economics assignment you gave out this morning," Fletch began with his feign.

"Ok. Shoot!"

Standing inside the door to the office Fletch asked several questions seeking clarity on how best to tackle the economics assignment, to which Mr Becker offered appropriate answers without giving away too much.

Mr Becker's office was quite simple, consisting of a generous desk and comfortable office chair, a side table against the wall to his right, a knee-high cabinet along the wall to his left and two plain chairs in front of the desk. A bookshelf stood against the wall behind Mr Becker, with a couple of ornaments on the top shelf, a small collection of economic college texts on the next shelf down and a row of thin folders labelled bank statements; student fees; endorsements and rebates; accounts payable; and leases and other expenses, respectively, on the third shelf. On the wall above the cabinets were pinned a poster each of Madonna, Janet Jackson and Deee-Lite, who were all currently huge in the charts.

"Thanks, Mr Becker," Fletch said, grateful for his advice and made a half turn in preparation to leave. "Say, Mr Becker what music are you into?"

"I like all kinds of music, Fletch. It depends on the situation and the mood," Mr Becker replied. "Why do you ask?"

"Well, judging by those posters, you seem to prefer pop... or club music."

"Oh, right!" Mr Becker conferred, looking up at the posters. "Yeah... I guess they're pretty hot right now. It makes me look like I'm keeping up with the times to you guys," he commented with a grin. "I also like folk and soul music."

Making a calculated assumption, Fletch asked matter-of-factly, "Do you still go clubbing? You might be getting a bit old for that now, Mr Becker," he said with a cheeky smile.

"Huh!" Mr Becker exclaimed with mild surprise. "I guess you're going to find out about that soon enough, right? Well, I don't get out much these days. Only on special occasions, during school breaks, birthdays, weddings, things like that," he said. "But that's nothing to be concerned about. Was there anything else?"

"No, no, all good," Fletch replied, knowing he had overstayed his welcome. "Thanks so much for your help, Mr Becker," he said and turned to leave the office for the cafeteria.

****

On Monday 3rd of December Rayish published a dazzlingly fabulous Christmas edition of the school magazine, which glittered in the bright rich seasonal colours of gold and white, red and green. The artwork reflected a refined, delicate, extremely detailed eye for design. The issue looked like a high-end Christmas greeting card and she included an article describing the way other cultures celebrate the same festival. The quality was far more advanced compared to what Derrick had produced. Rayish's talents gained instant recognition and notoriety among both teachers and students alike.

The political club would meet on the second Wednesday (during term) of each month and gather in the informal setting of the school cafeteria for an hour to an hour and a half, once school had ended for the day. School policy permitted only one political club to make use of limited resources. The school did not wish to split the usually moderate student attendance across party lines and preferred to promote a healthy debate on relevant topics, where both sides of an argument were heard, for the betterment of developing minds. The meetings were officiated by Mr Brian Dwyer, the school's senior English and history teacher.

The person presenting a topic and any speaker would stand in the open space in front of the cafeteria, with the closed shutters of the serving counters, bain-marie and kitchen behind. Republican students, who had a clear majority, sat to the right of the speaker, while Democrats sat to the left. The meeting was regularly attended by around thirty senior students, who were mostly male and from affluent white American backgrounds. There were only a handful of female attendees and students from alternative cultural backgrounds.

Blair's first meeting with the high school political club on Wednesday 12th December was somewhat animated and heated. Most of the discussion surrounded the aftermath of 911, President George W Bush's declaration of a war on terror and Al-Qaeda, and the justification for America's continued intervention to protect its interests in the world's oil supplies. The biggest domestic issue discussed was the blow out of public debt and a debate on the merits of raising taxes against tariffs.

****

Through the third week of December just prior to the short Christmas and New Year's break, the student multicultural club set up several stalls within the cafeteria to sell a variety of traditional Christmas themed deserts. There were Jewish gingerbread sufganiyots and rugelach; Italian cuccidati, struffoli and tiramisu; Greek baklava, melomakarona cookies and revani; Indian gulab jamun, modak and puran poli; small, rolled Caribbean-style pancakes; Chinese custard tarts, chocolate-dipped fortune cookies and green tea ice cream in a waffle cone. The delicious sweets were a huge success and invariably in high demand, with every stall sold out by week's end.

Northside Chestnut Grove Academy closed at the end of the day on Friday 21st December for the Christmas and New Year break and returned on Wednesday 2nd January. Everyone seemed buoyant on the first day back at school for 2002, happily sharing their winter Christmas stories, what gifts they had received and what they did through the holiday. Mr Becker however, seemed a little more… weary and worn-out than usual.

The following morning, on Thursday 3rd January, the *Philadelphia Daily News* tabloid newspaper broke with a sensational story splashed across its front page, leading with the headline…

'PRIVATE HIGH SCHOOL TEACHERS ON LONG WEEKEND BENDER'

The photograph on the front cover was of Mr Becker surrounded by a few of his buddies. He was crouching down in front of a glass coffee table in a booth at one of Philadelphia's premier house and trance night clubs on New Year's Eve, preparing several lines of a rather suspicious white powder with a credit card. Mr Becker looked so out of it and concentrating so hard on the task at hand, he didn't even realise that the photograph had been taken.

A few more pictures appeared on the inside front cover with the story. There was a photograph of how much booze they drank, their semi naked antics on the dance floor and being unceremoniously ejected from the club at 3 am in the morning by the bouncers, at which point, they all looked totally dishevelled and a complete mess. It would be doubtful that they could even remember what happened during the ensuing hangover.

The story detailed the events of this boy's club of private high school teachers, over the long weekend of Saturday, Sunday and Monday, the 29th, 30th and 31st of December: what they did; where they went; the trouble they found themselves in; and the alleged substances they abused. The story finally ended by posing the question, 'Do you wish to pay a premium for your children to be educated by teachers like this?'

The impact of the scandal upon Mr Becker and the school was immediate. Having no inclination to read a tabloid, Mr Becker turned up for work that morning, amid strange looks and quiet whispers as he entered the school and passed dozens of students on the way to his office. Mr Faulkner intercepted Mr Becker outside his office, with a copy of the newspaper in hand and proceeded to have a very serious discussion behind the closed door.

After ten minutes the door opened and a white-faced Mr Becker was immediately sent home, suspended pending a further investigation. Mr Faulkner himself took over Mr Becker's classes for the next two days, while a fill-in teacher was found to cover the classes from the following week onwards.

The police soon arrived at Mr Becker's house to conduct a thorough search of his premises. Luckily, no illegal substances were discovered, where it would seem Mr Becker had the presence of mind to either consume all that he had or get rid of what was left. Unfortunately, Mr Becker's co-conspirators were found to be in possession of illegal substances and subsequently charged.

Late on Friday afternoon, Mr Becker was summoned to the school to attend a meeting with Mr Faulkner, the Chairman of the Parents Association, two members from the State Department of Education and the school's attorney. Mr Becker was asked if he would be willing to submit a blood sample to test for the consumption of illegal drugs, to determine if he was in breach of school policy. Naturally, he refused. The school had no further choice other than to dismiss Mr Becker, effective immediately. He was ordered to clear out all personal effects from his office and to leave the school grounds… never to return. The same fate befell each of his accomplices.

At the end of the tumultuous day, once all the students and teachers had left for the weekend, a quiet calm descended upon the school. Just before 5 pm when the janitors would begin to lock down the school for the night, Fletch casually walked past the open door of Mr Becker's office. The office was clear and vacant. He already knew Mr Faulkner had left with the members of the State Department for a meeting at their city headquarters and that Mrs Dianne Mitchell, the receptionist, had also departed for the weekend.

There was no one around. Fletch slipped into the office, retrieved a folder from the bookshelf behind the desk, dropped it into his bag and then walked out… which took all of fifteen seconds. Amongst the chaos of the preceding events no one would notice the absence of the disappearing folder for… quite some time.

Unbeknown to anyone except the two parties involved, late one night during the middle of December, a certain senior school captain of a prodigious private high school and a local tabloid newspaper journalist had conducted a secret meeting under the cover of darkness in a rundown art deco cinema. The movie was an international film in a foreign language and as such, had a poor attendance. The student handed the reporter an envelope containing information about the person in question, a rather generous 'gift' and some clear verbal instructions, eagerly agreed to by the journalist. It was a scoop and the rest was now history.

****

On Monday the 14th (two weeks late due to the Christmas break), Rayish released the January edition of the school magazine. Maintaining her high standard, the edition was once again a smash hit. Decked out in vibrant neon colours to simulate a party vibe, she skilfully depicted everyone's contributing photograph on how the New Year was celebrated.

Rayish also published a fantastic review of 2001, highlighting the best music and movies for the year and the school's most acclaimed achievements and awkward moments. The results of the fundraising were disclosed, where a generous donation was made to UNICEF. The magazine lifted the mood of the entire school following Mr Becker's scandal.

It was customary for Fletch, Blair, Rayish and Benson to catch up from time to time after school on a Friday afternoon at a nearby milk bar. Friday the 18th January was such an occasion. The group ordered their burgers, fries and milkshakes, and made themselves comfortable in a warm and cosy booth, with soft rock playing in the background.

"How was the political club meeting on Wednesday afternoon?" Fletch asked Blair.

"Rather animated as usual," Blair replied. "Everyone is feeling very pro-nationalistic and patriotic at the moment. The overall thinking on every topic has moved to the right."

"Understandable," Fletch commented. "Retribution for 911 will be motivation enough for a war... and this... so-called war on terror will soon find a target. I see the rhetoric out of Washington is turning back onto Iraq. At least air power over a desert is better than jungle," he said, offering his view on the current situation.

"Well, we didn't quite finish the job in the first Gulf War, did we?" Blair said.

"Do you think the multicultural club should hold off organising any more activities for the time being... until things settle down?" Benson asked Fletch.

"Yes... maybe, maybe," Fletch pondered. "What're you planning?" he asked.

"We were thinking of another food stall for Easter, but I'm not really sure we should do it," Benson replied. "We've already done a food stall... and... Easter is a lot more religious."

"Yes, I think you're right. No need to inflame anyone's sensitivities," Fletch agreed.

"Otherwise, I don't have any ideas," Benson shrugged.

Their order was ready and delivered to their table. Fletch looked up at Benson with an idea.

"How about a dance," he announced.

"What... like a disco?" Benson replied.

"No, no. Like a theatre production," Fletch clarified. "We use the theatre hall and put on a show of six or seven cultural dance shows in full costume... and... we charge a small entry fee," he mused. "Lay low for a couple of months and put it on in April, just before spring break. It's neutral. Attendance is voluntary. So, no one should be offended," he said smiling.

"That's a great idea," Rayish chimed in.

"Yes, we can do that," Benson agreed. "I'll put it to the club and see what they say."

They all paused momentarily to devour their burgers and fries whilst imagining how the theatre production would take shape. Fletch soon sat back with milkshake in hand.

"Great job on the school magazine, Rayish. Everyone is completely blown away with your creative ability. You have more than excelled in the job," he said congratulating her.

Blair and Benson also nodded their agreement and support.

"Thanks, Fletch," Rayish replied gratefully. "I did enlist plenty of help."

"So, what have you got planned for February?" Fletch asked.

"I have a few articles to use, but… I don't have a big theme to run with," she replied looking at Fletch. "You're the ideas man today. Looks like you have something in mind. What is it?"

Fletch leaned forward over the table, closer to the group.

"I have an idea… but… you must all promise not to tell anyone, that it came from ME… ok!" They all nodded. "Do you all PROMISE!" he asked once more.

They all affirmed their oath of silence with a verbal… 'yes, we promise.'

"Rayish, do you want to be a catalyst for change?" Fletch began. "To change something in the school… for the better?"

"Yes… of course," she replied. "That's the whole purpose of journalism, isn't it?"

"Yes, it is," he agreed. Fletch grabbed the lapel of his blazer and pulled it forward. "Do you like the school uniform?" he asked. "It's dark-grey and red! Do you like it?"

"NO!" she replied flatly. "It's hideous."

Both Blair and Benson nodded in agreement.

"So, let's do something about it," Fletch said seeding the idea.

"Do you want me to publish an article attacking the school uniform?" Rayish asked.

"No! That won't get past Ms Dixon now, will it," Fletch countered. "However, what if we write a professional article raising it as an issue. We present a brief history of the school uniform and then ask the question as to why we need to wear one at all," he paused. "Then, once the issue is on the table, the student council can take it up and run with it. And you never know, if we're lucky, we could have the uniform abolished all together," he said, sat back and sipped his milkshake with a mischievous smile.

Everyone sat in stunned silence to consider the proposal for a long moment.

"Perfect. That's a great plan," Blair agreed.

"Let's use the democratic process and get this done," Benson cast his vote.

Rayish looked at every one staring at her.

"Ok, let's do it!" she said, followed by cheers and banging of empty milkshake glasses.

As the group began to climb out from the booth, Blair asked, "Who are you playing tomorrow morning, Fletch?"

"South Philly Baptist High," he replied. "They're second on the table. We're fourth. So, it'll be a tough match. It's a home game if you want to come along."

"Right, see you in the morning."

They walked out of the milk bar, said their goodbyes and parted ways for home.

****

The basketball game was supported by an average turnout of students, teachers, family and friends, from both sides. The extremely competitive game was tough. Fletch was on fire having a blinder with four intercepts and shooting for fifteen points late into the third quarter. Northside Chestnut Grove's power forward fouled the opposing team's man. As the free throw was being taken by South Philly Baptist's power forward, Fletch stood beside their small forward. He was six foot three, lean and agile and of a caramel brown complexion.

"Who's that, bro?" Billy Robinson, the gifted seventeen-year-old asked, pointing up at the stands with a flick of his head.

"Who? The teacher with the short blonde hair?" Fletch clarified.

"Yeah, man."

"That's Ms Dixon. She's our journalism teacher," Fletch confirmed. "Why? Do you fancy her or something?"

"She's fine, man… but she has eyes for you. She's been watching you for the whole game," Billy reported. "Reckon you could do something about that!" he chuckled.

"Really! Nooo… you can't be serious," Fletch replied flicking a glance up at Ms Dixon only to find that indeed, she was watching him closely.

Suddenly, the free throw missed and Billy elbowed Fletch off the ball to catch the rebound.

Through the fourth quarter, Fletch managed a few glances towards Ms Dixon while he was travelling down the court in her direction, sometimes when he held the ball and sometimes without it, and every time, Ms Dixon was watching him. Fletch missed two three-point shots and still Ms Dixon had eyes on him. Perplexing, he thought.

The game was in the balance, down by three points with fifteen seconds to go. Fletch shot a direct bullet pass to his power forward under the basket to score for two points. He had not used such a hard direct pass to his power forward the entire game. The opposing player who brought the ball back into play was looking rather tired and threw a bad first pass in and lobbed the ball a fraction high which allowed Fletch just enough time to dash in and intercept the ball, a play he had been waiting for the whole game. He backed outside the line, faked a three-point throw, to instead shoot a repeat bullet pass to his power forward who had a clear path to dunk the winning basket. The team and school were jubilant in their victorious celebration.

****

Later at home that night Fletch checked the file he had on Ms Dixon. She was twenty-nine years old and would soon turn thirty. She was of medium height and build, with short blonde hair, hazel eyes, a lightly tanned complexion and was a kind and loving person. Everything seemed normal other than the fact that she was not married. Fletch remembered that over the past few years, Ms Dixon managed to acquire a boyfriend from time to time. It did not seem important then, but they were all ambitious young professional men. It would appear that Ms Dixon has a preference for young men… and maybe even boys… who are naturally gifted.

Ms Dixon was also the head of the school's media and arts programmes. Fletch did not have her as a teacher and, thus, there was no casual means with which to interact with her to find out more. They would glance at each other in passing through the crowded corridors between classes, and to and from lunch. Ms Dixon did appear at the basketball team's next home game the following Saturday morning, where, under her watchful eye, Fletch put on another masterful performance. *I wonder what she does on weekends*, Fletch pondered.

Rayish released the February edition of the school magazine bang on Friday morning 1st February, leading into the weekend. At first, Ms Dixon was rather reluctant to sign off on this edition due to the exposé on the school uniform, even though it was professionally written in a light-hearted manner and raised the question with a hint of humour. Rayish, with Benson's support, presented a case which managed to convince Ms Dixon that it was the right thing to do; that in the long term this would greatly benefit the entire school community.

The feature article on the school uniform opened by detailing the history and origin of Northside Chestnut Grove's school uniform and then went on to debate the question of whether the compulsory school uniform would continue to have a place in a modern society. Rayish articulated both the pro and con sides of the debate.

The pro side stated that

'the school uniform is a powerful rite of passage for students, helping to build a sense of identity, oneness and belonging to the school tradition, its symbols and ideology. It fosters equality within the school community and removes the rise of pandering to fashion, brand image, peer pressure and class identity, and provides a safer learning environment for both students and teachers alike.'

The con side countered with

'the school uniform does not produce order, discipline and obedience, but animosity towards authority. High standards of discipline and performance are not synonymous with school uniforms, but a simple exercise in conformity to sterilised uniformity. Students should be able to develop self expression and personal identity to help build esteem, independence and creative thinking. A uniform is a punitive measure meant to limit and deny a student's right to freedom of expression and individuality.'

The article concluded with a parody highlighting the school uniform as an unnecessary bureaucratic legacy inherited from an outdated British tradition and thus called for a review of the regulation. The impact of the article was immediate and managed to get under the skin of the entire student population, bringing the issue to the top of everyone's agenda.

First thing on Monday morning, Mr Faulkner reprimanded Ms Dixon for signing off and allowing such a divisive article to be released into circulation. Letters began arriving from many parents calling for an end to the school uniform. The school student council was unanimous in its sentiment towards the abolishment of the school uniform.

The high school student council comprised one male and one female representative from each secondary grade: freshman (grade 9); sophomore (grade 10); junior (grade 11); and deputy seniors (grade 12), who also hold the secretary and treasurer roles; and of course, the senior school captain, for a total of nine seats.

On Thursday 7th of February, Mr Faulkner, followed by his loyal deputy, old Mr Mike Nelson joined a meeting called by the student council immediately following the end of the school day, in the library's conference room.

Now forty-six years old, Mr Faulkner was a tall, solid and wide-shouldered man, who did not carry a lot of excess body weight. He had thick dark bushy eyebrows over deep-set, wrinkled blue eyes, a thick slightly flat nose and a strong chin. He had one deep wrinkle line on both sides of his face, which began below the cheek bone and ran through the cheek to end at the corner of his mouth, which revealed thin straight lips and very clean white teeth. He had short thinning black hair combed to one side with grey hairs through his short sideburns and temples. Dressed in a simple charcoal-grey suit, Mr Faulkner presented an imposing figure similar in demeanour to a colonel in the army.

The student council were all present and seated and looked quite tentative as Mr Faulkner and Mr Nelson entered the room, closed the door and took their seats around the long oval table.

"Good afternoon, Mr Faulkner, Mr Nelson," Fletch greeted confidently while standing. "Thank you for making the time to meet with us," he said and resumed his seat.

"Hello Fletch, ladies, gentlemen!" Mr Faulkner replied formally, courteously.

"Let's get straight to it, shall we?" Fletch began. "Well, since the article in the school magazine regarding the school uniform was published, a large number of students have approached me and expressed their opinion that the school uniform is no longer needed or wanted by the student body. I have been asked... as their representative... to put forward an official motion through the student council requesting the abolishment of the school uniform."

"Thank you for the submission, Fletch. However, this is not a public school. It's a private school with a long-standing tradition and a high ideal to maintain," Mr Faulkner explained.

"Yes, but are they truly American traditions?" Fletch countered. "Like the article stated, they seem more like British traditions, used to foster obedience and conformity."

"They are universal in their design and intended to benefit the student," Mr Faulkner replied.

"Do they wear a school uniform in European high schools, Mr Faulkner?"

"I'm not quite sure, Fletch."

"Well, I've conducted a little research and other than England, the vast majority of high schools in mainland Europe do not require a school uniform. And there is virtually no difference or impact on discipline or academic performance being reported."

"I see," Mr Faulkner said. "I'll have to look into that myself."

"Have you never gone back to visit Austria? As a school principal you would be able to check out how schools work over there," Fletch said.

"I've never returned to Austria since arriving in America," Mr Faulkner replied flatly.

What!? He just lied. He lied... again. Fletch thought to himself. *He went back for two weeks during the summer break after school last year. He flew in and out of Vienna. Why? Why would he lie about that?*

"Well, as you know, the student body is no longer in favour of continuing to wear a compulsory school uniform. And having spoken with the student council..." Fletch paused to look around at his fellow councillors, "...we would like to propose a trial, where the wearing of the school uniform is no longer mandatory. Of course, we understand that we also don't want students turning up to school in singlets and sandals... so... we would also stipulate what the new required dress code should be," Fletch explained. "And if the trial proves to be a success, then maybe we could consider the abolishment of the uniform altogether," he said and paused for a moment. "Can we put it to a vote?"

Mr Faulkner looked at Fletch and then the student council with a stoic grim expression.

"There will be no vote. There will be no free dress trial. There will be no abolishment of the school uniform. It's not for students to decide on whether the school imposes a uniform or not. It's school policy and school tradition for very good reason... and... it's here to stay," he said flatly. "That's my final word on the matter and the subject is now closed. Good afternoon, people."

Mr Faulkner promptly ended the meeting by standing up and walking out with Mr Nelson.

The following day, Mr Faulkner issued a well-composed notice stating that the school uniform would not be abolished and the reasons why... that it was integral to the school's unity and identity. He went on to state that it was not the place for students to decide on whether a school uniform was compulsory, that the policy was the responsibility of the school board in conjunction with the Department of Education. The movement to abolish the school uniform was now quashed.

At the end of the following week the school closed for the short midwinter break.

February 2002 – Midwinter Break Through to Spring Break

After a one-week break, Northside Chestnut Grove Academy reopened for the return to school on Monday 25th February. All freshman and sophomore students arrived. However, roughly only thirty junior and senior students showed up for class. It was an incredibly surreal sensation having only one or two students sitting in an empty classroom.

Naturally, the junior and senior class teachers were stunned and perplexed. Mr Faulkner quickly realised a non-attendance student protest was afoot. One student in grade 11 showed Mr Faulkner a mail-out he had received at the end of the previous week.

The anonymous, no return address, mailed out envelope appeared to be a corporate department store advertisement, addressed directly to the student at their home address. Inside the envelope was a twenty dollar voucher to the department store named on the front. The first page of the mail-out was a very short and concise letter. It read...

Dear student,

Northside Chestnut Grove Academy has refused to reconsider its policy regarding the wearing of a compulsory school uniform. In fact, the school's authorities have explicitly stated that the student body has no say in the matter whatsoever.

In protest, you are hereby instructed, as a member of the senior high school student body, to boycott school classes for the first three days following the midwinter break. If a free dress day trial is not permitted, further action will proceed. This is your school. Let's make it the best school possible!

Enjoy the voucher.

The second page was a one-page legal document titled – *New School Dress Code*. The document articulated the rules of the new dress code:

> …only a collared shirt or top with full coverage of the chest for both boys and girls (no singlets or T-shirts); long trousers or dresses; no denim jeans, shorts or skirts to be higher than the knee; dress shoes to cover the whole foot, where sports shoes can only be worn for sports. There is to be no excessive jewellery, makeup or visible tattoos. There is to be no vulgar, obscene or offensive language or symbols on any clothing or the display of any gang-related colours or insignia. The intention is for every student to dress as a young professional adult.

The document referenced the 1969 US Supreme Court school dress code ruling as the standard guideline.

Every student who received the mail-out was instructed to sign and date their agreement to the new dress code and submit the form directly to Mrs Mitchell's reception office.

The post office from which the mail-out was sent came out of New York City. Mr Faulkner realised trying to track down the culprit, one of a potential three hundred students, would be extremely difficult. Due to the high standard and quality of the document, Mr Faulkner also sensed the helping hand of a legal professional. Someone was playing a very serious game indeed. He decided not to engage the police and felt an urgency to resolve the matter quickly while the situation was still within his control.

****

The following day, Tuesday, not a single secondary high school student bothered to attend class. As word spread, half the freshman and sophomore students stayed home. A local newspaper reporter rang and rudely demanded an interview. Mr Faulkner called for an immediate emergency meeting with the school board. Once concluded, he then called every member of the school council and asked them to attend a meeting at 10 am the following morning.

"Good morning, Mr Faulkner, Mr Nelson," Fletch greeted and calmly sat down after they had entered the conference room, closed the door and taken their seats.

The entire school council were present, seated and in high anticipation of the meeting.

"Good morning, Fletch," Mr Faulkner replied in a quick businesslike manner. "Thank you all for attending this meeting," he said politely. "In lieu of this mail-out…" (he placed a copy on the table for everyone to see) "…and what has followed with a near ninety-eight per cent compliance by all senior students, the school has decided not to take any further disciplinary action. It is felt that this will only escalate the situation… and distract everyone from their purpose for being here… to learn, in a safe and secure environment," he said and paused to look at Fletch when a sudden thought struck him.

"Did you have anything to do with this, Fletch?" Mr Faulkner asked.

"My only action was to carry out what has been asked of me by the student body and student council, Mr Faulkner," Fletch replied with a serious stoic expression.

"Hmm… right!" Mr Faulkner replied with doubtful suspicion. "I don't know who is responsible for this mail-out. If I ever find out that it's a student at this school, there will be severe consequences. However, I'm not prepared to waste time and resources trying to establish the identity of this person," he paused, for effect and glared at the faces of the students present. Everyone stared right back at him blankly with bated breath. "Anyway… the school board has decided to grant the student council's request for a free dress trial."

Every member of the student council exploded with a cheer and clapped in celebration.

"Settle down. Settle down!" Mr Faulkner yelled over the top. "On the provision that ninety-per cent of the senior student body return their signed agreement, the school board will grant an extended trial period, which will begin on Monday 11th March and continue for the remainder of the school year. I'll make the appropriate announcements once the entire student body has returned to class. Hopefully, we can get back to normal."

"Thank you, Mr Faulkner," Fletch said gratefully. "You won't regret this."

"I hope not," Mr Faulkner replied, stood up and left the conference room with his deputy.

****

The following day, Thursday, all students returned to class and upon hearing the news were joyous and jubilant. A long procession of students filed into and out of Mrs Mitchell's reception office throughout the day, to submit their signed free dress code agreement. The form received an impressive, near one hundred per cent acceptance rate.

Rayish released a smart business-style March edition of the school magazine on Monday 4th March. Apart from his verbal notification to the school, Mr Faulkner included a letter notifying the student body of the imminent free dress trial, an endorsement and affirmation of the dress code, and a warning that any non-compliance of the code would threaten the success of the trial. There were pictures and illustrations of what was and what was not acceptable. The rest of the edition reported on other general school news, sports and academic results and achievements, and a celebration dedicated to the start of spring.

On the following Monday, the entire student body looked splendid, all dressed, essentially, in smart casual wear. They did indeed look like young professional adults and the school spirit soared to new heights, which carried through the rest of spring. Representative school sports teams were naturally still required to wear the sporting uniform and colours when competing against other schools. The school blazer was required for any public academic pursuits, such as interschool spelling, debating and science competitions.

No one would ever find out who was responsible for the mail-out. No one would ever know that Fletch, assisted by Douglas, secretly collated, organised and distributed the mail-out over two days from the legal firm's New York City office during the midwinter break. All material component costs were invoiced and paid for in cash from different vendors and not by Fletch in person.

No one would ever put it together or imagine what was really going on, of what the true objective was, except for... the agent who had been assigned an order, 'to keep a watch'.

On Friday of the first full week of the free dress trail, the troupe gathered once more after school for a catch-up at their favourite milk bar. Once orders were issued to the waitress, they all made themselves comfortable in their usual booth of choice.

"How was the political meeting this month, Blair?" Fletch asked.

"Rowdy, as ever!" Blair replied. "A lot of attention seems to be moving back onto Iraq, sparking a heated debate about the viability of another war in the Middle East," he said. "On a lighter note, we also had the state Republican Senator visit us."

"Really?" Benson exclaimed.

"Yeah... he was great," Blair said. "He presented a talk on the challenges and rewards of a life in politics and how things work in Congress. He was rather impressive."

"Did he inspire you to consider a life in politics?" Fletch asked.

"Maybe!" Blair replied. "There's plenty of time. I don't have to rush into anything just yet."

"Well, doesn't look like things will settle down in the political club anytime soon then," Fletch said. "So, how are things going in the multicultural club, Benson?"

"Pretty good, actually. I have enough people to put on seven dances and permission to use the school hall. But... I'm not sure when we should organise the show," he said.

"Well, spring break starts on the 25th, just prior to the Easter long weekend. There's no way we could organise the show by next week. So, I think probably mid-April would be best," Rayish offered.

"Yes... and then the show could be a great lead-in to our Prom in May," Blair added.

"How about straight after school on Wednesday the 17th of April," Fletch said making the decision for Benson. "I don't think that'll clash with anything else. The political club meets the week before, right?"

"Uh huh!" Blair confirmed.

"Cool... that sounds perfect," Benson agreed. "Let's do it."

"I'll insert a full-page advertisement in the April edition of the school magazine," Rayish suggested.

"Wait!" Fletch said. "I think we should keep this out of the school magazine and hand out flyers during lunch to promote the show."

"Why?" Rayish asked. "Why don't you want to put it in the school magazine?"

"What else do you have for April?" Fletch asked.

"So far, only the cultural dance," Rayish confessed.

"Well… I have something for you," Fletch announced.

Suddenly, their orders were promptly delivered to the table by the waitress. Fletch did not wish to explain his big reveal while everyone had a mouth full of food. He purposefully and patiently waited until they ate their burgers and fries, and for the table to be cleared and wiped, leaving just their half-full milkshake glasses.

"Well… out with it," Rayish prompted, unable to withstand the suspense any longer.

Fletch clenched his right fist and extended his arm out into the middle of the table.

"Before I show you what I have, you must all swear an oath NOT to tell anyone where the information came from," he paused to allow them time to consider the proposition. "It's for the good of America," he assured, at their disbelieving expression. "If any of you tell, you'll never see me again for the rest of your lives. Do you understand?" he said with a deadly serious look in his eyes and waited.

Blair was first to clasp his hand over Fletch's outstretched fist and swore his oath. Benson immediately followed suit. Rayish pondered reluctantly, a little longer.

"Will this get me into trouble?" she asked.

"There's risk in everything… but… let me worry about that," Fletch assured.

Rayish slowly placed her hand on top of the stack and swore her oath.

"Very good!" Fletch exclaimed, satisfied.

They all let go of their grasp and Fletch reached into his bag and withdrew an unsealed yellow A4 envelope. He placed the envelope on the table in front of Rayish.

Rayish picked up the envelope, pulled out a small cleanly bound stack of documents and gently placed the stack upon the envelope on the table before her. She spent a few moments reading the first page, before flipping to the next and examining each page thereafter. Everyone waited patiently. A few minutes passed before she looked up at Fletch.

"This is amazing! Did you write the article? Where did you get the proof?" She said stunned.

"Yes, I had help with the article. So, all you need to do is publish it as is," Fletch instructed. "The proof? Well… I'm not at liberty to tell you where that came from and… it's best that you don't know anyway. And if you get into trouble, just use the letter at the back. It will protect you, ok," he assured.

"What? What is it?" Blair asked finally losing patience.

Rayish handed Blair the documents and envelope to examine, which then went to Benson.

"Ms Dixon won't sign off on this," Rayish pointed out.

"Don't worry about Ms Dixon," Fletch replied. "I have a feeling she's about to get herself into a whole lot of trouble," he predicted. "Just make sure you're ready to release the magazine for April," he instructed.

Rayish nodded. She secured the documents inside the envelope inside her bag. They all sat back in quiet contemplation sipping on the last of their milkshakes. They each began to see Fletch in a new light, seeing in him something they had never before realised.

"Did you have something to do with the 'mail-out'?" Benson asked.

"What, me? No way!" Fletch replied throwing his open hands up to feign his innocence.

"Seeing what I've just seen, I wouldn't put it past you," Rayish commented.

Fletch looked at his watch. "Well, it's time to go. I have a big game in the morning," he said, changing the subject.

"Ah yes, we're in the playoffs," Benson chimed in.

"Who're you playing?" Blair asked.

"Would you believe it's South Philly Baptist High again!" Benson replied. "They were second on the table. We were third. So, we must play them to see who gets into the final."

"Oh, ok," Blair said. "I guess they have home court advantage?"

"Yes, they do," Fletch confirmed.

"It'll be a tough game. They're undefeated at home," Benson said.

"Yes! It'll be the toughest game of the season," Fletch agreed.

They all rose from the table, collected their bags, coats and headed on home.

****

The basketball game was indeed the toughest of the season for both teams. The defence was intense, making baskets difficult and reducing the game to a low scoring match. No team managed to get ahead by any more than five points throughout the game. When Fletch had the ball, South Philly players would stand to block the inside bullet pass to his forwards and force the passing to remain outside the key. When South Philly had the ball, their point guard and small forward Billy would take their time to bring the ball back and dribble for long periods of time to preserve energy and attack with only five seconds remaining on the shot clock. Thus, there were a lot of missed shots with plenty of intensely competitive rebounding.

With ninety seconds remaining in the fourth quarter, South Philly had the ball and were ahead by four points. Their point guard shot the ball for a three-point score to put the game out of reach. He missed. Fletch, Benson and Billy went up for the rebound. Billy accidently elbowed Fletch across the bridge of the nose as Benson grabbed the ball. Blood splashed down Fletch's shirt. A timeout was called with seventy seconds on the clock. On the sideline, Fletch managed to quickly stop the bleeding and changed to a clean, dry shirt and whispered something to Benson.

Chestnut Grove threw the ball in to restart the clock and made their way to Philly's basket. Benson had half an opening at the top of the key, jumped and shot the ball. He missed and Philly grabbed the rebound. Chestnut Grove ran back to defend except for Fletch, who feigned discomfort and lagged behind.

Philly stuck to their tactic of winding the clock down. Their point guard slowed the pace and took his time to bring the ball back into offence. He passed to Billy who dribbled for a couple of seconds more than he should have. Benson lunged forward to tap the ball away from his right hand. Billy stepped backwards and switched the ball to his left hand. As the switch was taking place, Fletch ran and dived onto his stomach. As he slid forward, he reached out his left hand in desperation. Billy bounced the ball right onto Fletch's outstretched hand.

Fletch pulled the ball into his chest, rolled and sat up. Benson sprinted forward. Fletch lobbed the ball high across court, which bounced up for Benson to gather and with a clear path, he slam-dunked the basket. Billy, his point guard and the crowd were stunned, astounded, having never seen such a play in all their lives. With a two-point lead and forty-five seconds remaining on the clock, Philly had to make a score or risk presenting Chestnut Grove with a ten-second opportunity to score a winning basket.

Philly brought the ball back into offence with a little more urgency. Each Chestnut Grove player was applying maximum pressure and giving their opposing man very little room to move. Philly's point guard received a pass, turned and bumped Fletch on the chest with his right shoulder. Fletch stumbled back two paces. Billy dashed into the top of the key. The point guard passed to Billy. Fletch recovered enough to lunge forward, reach out and touch the ball mid-flight with the tip of his right middle finger. The ball deflected straight to Benson who stood right behind Billy.

Fletch sprinted forward. Benson passed to Fletch and sprinted to reach the offensive key in time. Billy ran between Benson and Fletch to intercept the pass. Fletch reached and stopped outside the three-point line. He faked a hard bullet pass to Benson. Billy dived with hands flailing to intercept the pass, instead of trying to block Fletch. Fletch was clear, jumped and threw the shot. The ball went straight threw the hoop for a three-point score. The crowd went silent with seven seconds remaining on the clock.

Billy threw the ball back in. Every Philly player was marked and under immense pressure. They could not move the ball out of their own half before the buzzer sounded. Chestnut Grove won the playoff by one point.

At game's end, Fletch walked over to shake Billy's hand.

"Congratulations man. Sorry about the nose," Billy said.

"Thanks. It's not broken, so don't worry about it," Fletch replied.

"Geez man, you really got me at the end there. Never seen anyone intercept a dribble before."

"Yeah, well… I kinda hate to lose."

"Yeah… same here!" Billy said. "Well, that's us done for the year. Good luck in the final."

Billy turned to walk back over to join his teammates.

"I know losing a playoff is hard… but, what if… I can make it up to you?"

"What do you mean?" Billy asked half turning back.

"I can't talk here. Meet me out front in an hour when y'all cleaned up."

Fletch invited Billy to lunch at a ritzy café and presented him with a rather lucrative proposal.

Throughout the week that followed, Fletch fitted Billy out with several top designer outfits, a professional hair style, a manicure, an expensive watch, some jewelled accessories, a perfect, yet false, identification for a twenty-two-year-old and an American Express credit card. Billy was instructed to frequent a certain hip wine bar for young professionals in the city, that Friday and Saturday night.

****

Right in the middle of spring break on Wednesday 27th March, the *Philadelphia Daily News* tabloid broke with a highly provocative front page story, leading with the headline…

'HIGH SCHOOL TEACHER SHAGS HIGH SCHOOL STUDENT'

The front cover displayed a photograph of Ms Dixon from the side, naked, straddling a young black student with her head angled back, in an expensive looking hotel suite. Several smaller photos with the story displayed across the inside two pages, revealed her undressing the young man, a shot of the student on top of Ms Dixon with her arms and legs around him and one where she was standing naked at the mini bar preparing two drinks.

To protect the student, the story did not reveal his name or face in any photograph and did highlight the fact that he carried a falsified identification. The story detailed the events of their sordid encounter throughout the evening, from the wine bar to a night club and into the hotel suite. The story alluded to the fact Ms Dixon had a fetish for young men, even boys and ended by asking whether such a predator should continue to teach and be a role model in a high school community. No charges would be laid as Ms Dixon had been misled. However, the story was extremely embarrassing for her and for the school.

Ms Dixon did not arrive at work on Monday the 1st of April and took an immediate leave of absence… which would be extended for the remainder of the school year.

Once more, Mr Faulkner was thrust into damage control. He had to search for an immediate replacement to cover Ms Dixon's classes. The entire student body was abuzz with gossip caused by the scandal and speculated on who they thought the blessed student was.

Fletch covertly met with Rayish and asked her to proceed without a sign-off.

Late in the afternoon on this Monday, just before the end of the school day, the April edition of the school magazine was released in time so that all the students could grab a copy before heading home. This made it impossible for the school to block its distribution. The school magazine also broke with a highly inflammatory article leading with the front page headline…

'OUR SCHOOL SOVEREIGNTY IS FOR SALE'

The article revealed in detail all the endorsements and rebates the school worked to obtain. From the highly visible branding of all the vending machines, which only sold soft drinks, chocolate bars and crisps, to the advertisements in the school's basketball stadium and sports facilities, to the placement of company logos on sports team uniforms, to the food and beverage products consumed in the school canteen. All the choices and decisions the school made were based on what kickback it would be able to obtain. As a result, the healthy options and choices which were of greater benefit for the student body were being superseded and circumvented by a monetary interest.

The article published proof, by tabulating all the figures from each and every transaction and just how much money was truly being generated by this activity.

The article pointed out that there was no disclosure about what happened to the money being generated, that there was no auditing or accountability to prevent any corrupt, fraudulent or misuse of the funds. This was the cornerstone on which the article questioned the ethics and morality of such a practice.

Looking at the bigger picture, the article detailed the extent to which the corporate world had infiltrated the school to place and sell their products; and how the corporate world had even managed to influence the school curriculum to influence the developing youth into becoming brand loyal consumers.

In principle, the article stated that the sanctity of the school had been eroded, that it was vitally important that the learning environment and development of society's young minds should be free from external corporate influence to foster a healthy discerning society. The article closed by stating… 'the sovereignty of the school is sacred and should never be a consideration up for sale'.

An immense shockwave rippled throughout the entire school community, from students to parents, from teachers out to the wider community. The sensation the story created was quickly picked up by Philadelphia media outlets and Pennsylvania state media outlets and a couple of the national carriers. In time, the issue would find its way onto the agenda of state and national educational bodies, looking to make changes to limit the widespread practice.

The Department of Education would order an audit of the school's endorsement practice. This revealed evidence that Mr Chinnery had in fact been skimming funds to pay for his drug habit. Furthermore, it was shown that a large proportion of the money was spent on improving teacher facilities. The department now saw this whole endeavour as problematic and were determined to implement appropriate regulations in the years ahead.

****

On Tuesday morning following the release of the school magazine, Mr Faulkner summoned Rayish to his office. He reprimanded her and asked how she managed to obtain the school's financial data on endorsements and rebates. She refused to reveal her source. Mr Faulkner threatened to dismiss her from the student editor's role if she did not comply with his request and reveal her source. Rayish pulled out a letter from her bag and placed it on the desk in front of Mr Faulkner.

The letter was a legal document prepared specifically for Rayish in her current predicament. It stated the First Amendment's protection to the right of the freedom of the press, which in this case, only reported on exactly what was happening within the school without actually incriminating any particular person. The letter stated that Rayish was simply carrying out her duty. The letter went on to cite the Fifth Amendment, where the school could not remove her as the student editor unless the school could prove that she broke school rules or the law and that if the school did so, such an action would be challenged in court.

Rayish also pointed out that the school had not nominated a replacement for Ms Dixon as the authorised signee for the April edition. Frustrated, Mr Faulkner dismissed Rayish back to class. With no qualified person to oversee the student magazine, he decided to shut down the publication for the remainder of the year.

When the lunch bell rang, Mr Faulkner felt drained and exhausted. He closed the door to his office. From the bottom drawer of his desk, he withdrew a half empty bottle of Scotch malt whisky and a single tumbler. He poured a double shot, kicked off his shoes and hung his feet over one corner of the desk as he reclined back in his office chair. He took a long sip of the whisky, laid his head back and closed his eyes. The whisky eased his tension, and he began to relax. He opened his eyes and stared up at the ceiling.

"What a year!" he whispered. "This must be the worst year ever. What's going on with this damned school?" he wondered.

He thought back over everything that had happened during the past half year. A few minutes ticked by while he continued to stare up at the ceiling. Suddenly, a realisation entered his mind. He promptly sat straight up. He dropped the bottle and empty glass back into the drawer and slammed it shut. He hurriedly put his shoes on and scrambled out the door.

Mr Faulkner soon appeared at the cafeteria's entrance and looked around with urgency. He set his eyes on Fletch sitting with Blair, Benson and Rayish, by the window eating their lunch and chatting happily. He watched them intently for a little too long.

"Mr Faulkner is over there watching us," Benson observed.

"He's looking directly at you, Fletch," Rayish said.

Fletch turned slightly to his right, looked back at Mr Faulkner and proceeded to ignore him.

"Do you think he's onto you?" Benson whispered.

"He doesn't have anything. He can't prove anything. All he knows is that we're all friends. Just ignore him," Fletch said quietly and continued to chat, paying no heed to Mr Faulkner.

A few moments later Mr Faulkner turned and left the cafeteria.

Later that afternoon Mr Faulkner was prowling the corridors. He knew which class Fletch was in and moved to block his path as Fletch was making his way to the next class.

"I'm onto you, Mr Fletch Braxton," Mr Faulkner said in a menacing tone.

"What? What do you mean?" Fletch replied in an offended manner.

"I don't know how you've managed it… how you've manipulated this school, but I know it's you!" Mr Faulkner said. "I don't know what your game is… but when I figure it out… when I can prove it, I'm going to expel you from this school."

"I don't know what you're talking about," Fletch replied. "I think you're being completely paranoid and delusional, Mr Faulkner."

Fletch saw no benefit in continuing the conversation and simply, calmly walked around Mr Faulkner and onward to his next class. Mr Faulkner watched him intently as he walked by.

Once classes had ended for the day, Mr Faulkner turned up at the political club meeting on the second Wednesday of the month. He watched Blair intently, suspiciously. However, Blair held no organisational role in the club and was merely an observing participant just like most of the other students there. The debates were heated and passionate as usual.

The following week Mr Faulkner prowled the school hall during the multicultural club's traditional theatre dance show. He kept an intent eye on Benson who was running the event, and Fletch, Blair and Rayish who sat together in the middle of the auditorium in support. Even with all the flyers handed out, the show only received moderate attendance. Once all seven performances were complete, Benson thanked everyone for taking the time to see the show. The performers and students alike all dispersed and headed home without any further incident.

Mr Faulkner's frustration and patience was reaching its limit. Trying to catch Fletch was proving to be a fruitless waste of time and energy. Feeling uncertain, undermined and vulnerable, he decided to rethink his strategy and took the initiative to find a connection and maybe, some evidence. He was not about to be bettered by a year twelve student.

****

Late that Friday night, Fletch received word that the reporter, his contact at the *Philadelphia Daily News*, had been dragged into a city alleyway, assaulted and badly beaten as he left work for the evening. The reporter was now in hospital recovering from his injuries.

Right on midnight, Fletch dressed in dark plain clothing with a hoodie. He left his house and rode his bike across a park, down a few streets and across another park to make sure he was alone. He pulled up at a row of nearby shops and locked his bike at the back in a hidden location. He walked to a busy road and hailed a taxi to the hospital.

He scoped out the entrance from afar before going into reception. There were only two elderly patients dressed in hospital gowns standing near the front door, smoking and sharing some banter. He asked the reception nurse what ward and room number the reporter, apparently now his older brother, was admitted to. She provided the information but said visiting hours were closed and that he could not go up and visit the patient.

Fletch thanked the nurse, moved to buy a drink from a vending machine and spotted the door into the stairwell. He took a seat in the waiting area. Roughly twenty minutes passed until the receptionist finally rose for a quick dash to the amenities. Fletch slipped into the stairwell and quickly made his way up to the ward. He slipped past a couple of non-attentive, sleep-deprived nurses and into the reporter's room.

"Hey Pete... Peter, wake up," Fletch whispered, gently waking him up.

"Fletch! Oh hi, man," he replied groggily, in pain and discomfort.

"Are you ok? What happened?" Fletch asked.

"They're onto you, man," Pete announced.

"Who? Who're you talking about?"

"They found me. They found out I wrote both stories," Pete explained. "They asked me how I knew who to target. Who gave me the information?" He paused. "At first, I gave them a false name. But they knew... they knew it was false. He kept hitting me until I gave him the name they were looking for," Pete admitted, looking up at Fletch remorsefully. "I gave them your name, Fletch. He had a gun... at my temple. He said that if I reported this to the police, they would be back to finish the job."

"Do you know who they are... what they look like?"

"It was a man... a big man as strong as an ox... and... a woman," Pete recalled. "She was in charge... calling the shots. She spoke almost like an American... like she was from somewhere else and had been here for a long time... but... the man... he had a thick accent."

"What... like Mexican... French?" Fletch prompted.

"No, no... thicker... heavier... more like eastern European," Pete corrected.

"And the woman? Describe what she looks like."

Pete described the woman. An image of a photograph popped into Fletch's mind.

"His sister! It's his sister!" Fletch whispered.

"What?" Pete asked. "Whose sister?"

"Never mind, Pete! I have everything I need. Thank you for telling me what happened. Don't worry about reporting it to the police. I'll take care of it. You just stay low and get better, ok," he said reassuringly as he clasped Pete's hand.

Fletch said farewell, slipped out of the room, the hospital and made his way back home. Once Fletch arrived home, he gathered all his files and materials on the school and dumped them in the old brick barbeque at the back of the house. He doused everything in naphtha, zippo lighter fluid, lit a match and burnt the lot to a fine ash powder.

****

Midmorning on Saturday, Northside Chestnut Grove played and lost the basketball final. The best team in the competition boasted three players who stood at or over six foot seven inches tall and would each find their pathway into the NBL. Chestnut Grove could not counter the overhead passing. Furthermore, Fletch was tired, slow, distracted and off his game.

April 2002 – Through to the End of the School Year

On Sunday, Arthur and Margaret Braxton booked the function room for a three-course lunch they had organised with family, friends and business partners at a nearby country golf club. Once a dejected Fletch was finally ready and climbed into the motor car, Arthur drove the family down the long driveway, through the main gate and along the curved road adjacent to the estate. Glancing back through the rear window from the back seat, Fletch noticed a dark-grey sedan pull out from a little used access road three hundred yards from the entrance to the estate and began to follow them. The car maintained a generous, discreet distance as the family drove to the club and continued to drive on once they went through the entrance.

After returning home late in the afternoon, Fletch rummaged around in an old cardboard storage box filled with well-used toys from his childhood. He found what he was looking for... a powerful slingshot with thick rubber bands and a small square leather cup. He dressed in camouflage gear and collected a handful of large palm-sized stones from the garden and jogged off towards the southwestern boundary of the estate.

Using trees, shrubs and tall grass, Fletch crouched and crawled his way closer and closer until he could see the car on the other side of the road. It was reverse parked alongside a row of trees and a half dozen yards back into an access track of an open field. Sitting in the driver's seat was the big burly-looking bloke matching the description of the man who had assaulted Pete. He was sitting there patiently watching the entrance to the Braxton estate.

Using the long grass and shrubs inside the boundary as cover, Fletch lay on his back and used the big toes of his feet as pointers to mark each side of the car. He selected a good-sized, round stone and loaded the leather chamber. He aimed through the middle of his toes and judged the angle of trajectory from experience. He pulled back hard on the sling shot, held it for a second… and let go.

The stone flew forward, rising through the air and then fell… to smash straight through the front passenger's side window. The man jumped in sudden fright. On hearing smashing glass, Fletch quickly let loose a second stone… which slammed into the top left corner of the windscreen, sending an instant spider's web of cracks through the glass.

The man leapt out of the driver's seat and ran to the edge of the road in search of the culprit. Fletch remained still under the shadows of his covering foliage and watched. The man contemplated conducting a search of the grounds on the opposite side of the road. He knew he would risk trespass, police and thought better of it. Knowing his cover was blown, he decided there was no further benefit in maintaining the surveillance. He climbed back into the driver's seat, started the car and quietly drove away.

When Fletch returned to the house, he showered, changed and called Blair, Rayish and Benson to invite them over. He rented the latest blockbuster DVD from the store just before everyone arrived and gathered in the rumpus room around a large round table of pizza.

Once the small talk died down, Fletch began a new conversation on a more serious topic.

"Mr Faulkner! There's something about Mr Faulkner!" he began. "I think he's hiding something." Everyone looked at him a little stunned and bewildered. "In fact, I think he's dangerous… very dangerous," he warned. "So from now on, none of you are to go out on your own. If you wish to go out, always go with your parents or some friends. Don't be alone outside your house… ok… for at least the next couple of weeks."

"Are we in some kind of trouble?" Rayish asked somewhat worried.

"In a way, yes," Fletch replied truthfully. "But not like being in trouble with your parents or with the police. It's a lot more serious than that," he said and paused for everyone to grasp the gravity of what he was saying. "Even though it was never my intention to do so, I think I have inadvertently discovered something about Mr Faulkner. He's not what he seems to be. And I think he feels afraid and threatened and is trying to protect himself."

"What do you mean? What are you talking about?" Benson protested.

"Well, I have a hunch about Mr Faulkner… but… we'll need to find some evidence. And there's only one way to resolve this situation! We'll need to reveal what he truly is. So, here's what we're going to do…" Fletch said and proceeded to unveil his plan.

****

As usual, school returned on Monday to begin the new week. Mr Faulkner continually made his presence felt in the corridors, cafeteria, school hall and sporting facilities, and made things very awkward between himself and Fletch. Mr Faulker looked on Fletch with a growing indignant spite and in return, Fletch looked at Mr Faulkner with utter contempt and regularly gave him a military salute.

Prom night arrived on Saturday the 4th of May. The venue for the lavish event was the school's basketball stadium which was converted into a dance hall.

Benson, dressed in a splendid long-tailed two-piece wool-rich tuxedo, with satin trim and off-white waistcoat, arrived with Rayish, who wore a sparkling full-length red designer dress. Blair arrived with a lovely Italian girl, also a member of the political club and both looked wonderful in tuxedo and elegant black gown, respectively. Fletch arrived alone as he did not wish to be encumbered with a date. He appeared in the same styled tuxedo as both Benson and Blair. They all arrived within a few minutes of 7:30 pm, half an hour after the Prom began.

The Prom was spectacular. The entire year twelve class looked amazing. There was a live band and everyone danced together with their partners and friends throughout the evening. There was plenty of food and fruit punch, party lights, streamers and lots of confetti. The Prom king and queen were announced at ten and the event would soon come to a close half an hour before midnight.

Blair and his partner left the Prom a little early at 11 pm in a taxi heading for an after party. At the same time, Fletch jumped into a cab with Benson and Rayish, while Mr Faulkner watched with relief from afar outside the front of the basketball stadium. However, Fletch asked to be dropped off a couple of hundred yards down the road once the taxi drove out of the school entrance. The taxi took off. He turned, jumped the fence and disappeared into the darkness.

Fletch backtracked along the tree-line of the school's sporting fields and found his pre-stashed sports bag. He quickly shed his tuxedo for a tight-fitting black outfit with gloves, rubber-soled shoes, ski mask and a small kit bag.

Under the shadow of darkness, Fletch made his way to the teacher's wing. All the school's offices and classrooms were locked down. He counted on the alarm being disabled while the Prom was in progress. Fletch withdrew a lock-picking kit from his bag. Having practised on all the locks of his own house, he had the lock of a side door open within a few seconds. He entered the hallway, closed and locked the door behind. He knew he didn't have much time.

Fletch turned into the main corridor which led to Mr Faulkner's office and reception at the end. Dim security lights illuminated the hallway. The glass door into reception was unlocked. Fletch glided through the door and allowed the hydraulic damper to slowly close the door. Mr Faulkner's office door was locked. He picked the lock in a few short moments, slipped inside, closed and locked the door. He grabbed his pencil torch.

Fletch searched Mr Faulkner's office. He checked the desk drawers, inside both filing cabinets and all the wooden built-in cabinets along the wall and behind all the pictures. A metal two-door cupboard stood against the wall behind the desk with a set of three ornamental shelves above. The doors were locked. He tried to move the unit. It was bolted against the wall. He sat for a while to pick the lock and slid the right-hand door open.

Fletch found what he hoped for… a small safe located at the back and beneath the lowest shelf cavity of the cupboard. It was bolted into the wall and floor and had a pin padlock.

Flipping onto his stomach, Fletch withdrew a small fine water mist spray bottle and a small fluorescent black-light torch. He sprayed the pin pad once and brought the black-light torch right up close to the number pad. He looked at the numbers closely from a side angle. The residue of dried skin oil moistened by the water, showed up as a slightly stronger highlight under the black light. The numbers one, four and nine were illuminated.

Fletch tried the following combinations: 149; 194; and 491. None of them worked. He stopped to think for a couple of minutes.

"What could the combination be?" he whispered. "Wait! Could it be that simple?"

He pressed… 1… 9… 4… 4. The lock released and the safe was open.

"His birth year… he used his birth year," Fletch muttered, not believing his luck.

He gently pulled open the door to the safe and looked inside.

The safe had two shelves. The top shelf contained a couple of folders and two passports for Mr Faulkner – one American, the other Austrian – which Fletch thought was a bit dubious. On the bottom shelf, Fletch found a long, shallow, metal box which was locked with a padlock. He drew the box out, placed it on the floor and picked the lock. He flipped the latch and opened the lid to look inside. Fletch's eyes widened in disbelief.

Suddenly, he heard the clear and distinct echo of footsteps cut through the silence. Having overseen the end of the Prom and closure of the basketball arena, Mr Faulkner entered the building, turned into the corridor and marched towards his office with authority.

Fletch didn't panic. He moved with efficient speed. He returned the latch and padlock to secure the metal box and returned it to the bottom shelf of the safe. He closed the safe door and the lock automatically clicked home. He quietly slid the cupboard door closed, engaged the lock and dashed to the office door. Crouching on his knees, he opened the door by just an inch and peered through. Mr Faulkner was more than halfway down the corridor and looking down at his first new mobile phone in his hands.

On his hands and knees Fletch opened the door just enough to slip his body through. He turned and locked the door while pressing in the latch and pulled the door closed. The latch clicked into place. Mr Faulkner's ears were still ringing from the live band. Fletch remained low and crawled in under the reception desk and held his breath.

Mr Faulkner pushed open the glass door and walked straight through reception to his office door. With key ready, he unlocked and opened the door and walked into his office. He turned on the light, closed the door and walked to his desk. He sat in his office chair with a loud, tired thud and sighed with relief. He opened the bottom drawer and withdrew the almost empty bottle and tumbler. He poured a double and kicked off his shoes.

Fletch crept around from under the reception desk and slipped through the glass door just as it slowly closed into place. Brisk but silent, he walked along one side of the corridor until he reached the end and turned the corner for the exit. Once outside, he breathed a sigh of relief and ran into the cover of darkness to collect his sports bag. He made his way through the two miles of back streets and parks until he was safely back home, almost two hours later.

Fletch didn't reveal what he had discovered to Blair, Rayish and Benson. To maintain the utmost secrecy, he dared not tell them what he was planning at the close of Prom, and had deflected all invitations to a post-Prom party. It was imperative Mr Faulkner didn't have any suspicion that his security was about to be and, in fact, had been compromised.

****

Northside Chestnut Grove Academy was in high spirits during the week that followed the Prom. The plan Fletch had unveiled to Blair, Rayish and Benson would now come into play on Wednesday and Thursday, the 8th and 9th May.

At the end of the day's classes on Wednesday, the political club gathered for its monthly meeting in the cafeteria. The usual topics seemed dull and boring. Once Mr Faulkner left, Blair instigated a new topic: the rise of the Asian Tiger economies and the trend for transnational companies to relocate to these countries to take advantage of the low labour costs and how this was eroding the American manufacturing base.

Blair delivered a prepared dissertation with statistics supplied by his parents. The ensuing debate argued the merits of whether the American government should support this trend or implement more nationalist policies to curtail its impact. The debate became heated with nearly all the right-leaning students siding towards a more nationalistic approach.

Following the theatre dance show the multicultural club had gained permission to organise and hold a mini food fete in the school's courtyard during Thursday's lunch break. This was the club's final fundraiser for the school year.

The club set up a few marquee food stalls around the courtyard, which were intermingled with different cultural games and activities which participants could play for a quarter and potentially win a prize. The stalls sold Indian curries, pad Thai noodles, Mie Goreng, pho noodle soup, Chow Mein and Japanese sushi. Benson manned the Caribbean stall which sold bright yellow saltfish ackee, professionally prepared off site and delivered to the fete.

A large proportion of the student body investigated the fete at the onset of lunch and took advantage of some of the offerings. Fletch, Blair and Rayish were inconspicuous while Mr Faulkner prowled the grounds. Satisfied, he soon departed for his office.

Blair popped up and mingled with a group of about twenty seniors, who consisted mostly of the right-leaning students from the political club. The previous day's debate was still fresh and raw in their minds, as they looked on at the fete with some scepticism.

A couple of students peeled away from the main group and walked over to a stall to try a particular offering they had not seen before. Blair remained with the core group.

"What's this?" Blair commented. "This isn't American food!" he said with disdain. "What's happening here? What's America coming too?" he continued to rant. "Is this what we want America to become?"

The group took a couple of steps forward and casually fanned out to give themselves a little more space, yet remained hesitant and uncertain.

"Is this the food you want to eat?" Blair pressed on. "Before long you'll be eating this every day of the week. Is this what you want?" he asked of the group.

Two senior boys broke from the group and walked over to the Indian curry stall. Two more decided to have a look at the Caribbean stall. As they approached, Benson remained guarded with a slight scowl in his expression.

"What do you call this?" the one on Benson's left asked.

"It's saltfish ackee."

"What's that?" the other one asked.

"It's a traditional Jamaican dish made from the ackee fruit and saltfish," Benson explained.

"So, it's not American then?" the first one stated.

"Can any food be called American?" Benson countered.

"Well... this... isn't American!" the second one said pointing down at the dish.

"What's that supposed to mean?" Benson replied. "I don't care what you think… so… just piss off, will you!" Benson retorted, forcefully.

"What? What did you say to me?" the first one asked, exaggerating his offence.

"Get out of my face!" Benson yelled.

He then grabbed the serving spoon with his right hand, scooped up a generous amount of saltfish ackee and flung it at both students harassing him. The hot mixture hit them both square across the chest. They looked down at the mess on the front of their expensive shirts… stunned. They looked up and glared at Benson, smiling mischievously at their misfortune. Their faces turned bright crimson with rage.

Rayish stood beside the Indian curry stall. She reached forward, grabbed a serving spoon and flung curry at the two senior boys. She then screamed… as loudly as she could. The entire fete stopped, stunned, for three seconds… before chaos broke out.

Both offended boys tried to grab Benson, who stepped back from their swinging arms. He pushed and flipped the table, knocking over the two boys in front of him, spilling all the food, utensils and the gas-fired heating plate. As the boys scrambled to get up, one pulled on one leg of the marque snapping the pole, which collapsed the front half of the tent. One corner flap of the marquee tent caught fire. Everyone around the stall scattered.

A similar scuffle ensued at the Indian curry stall. The table was flipped, crashing everything across the floor. Rayish screamed and pelted the two boys with anything at hand. Many of the multicultural students scattered in all directions. Those brave enough stood their ground. Blair sounded the call to arms and rushed forward into the fray. The senior students around him followed the charge and rained destruction down on the remaining stalls… where they became embroiled in the mindless rampage of a full-blown student riot.

Mr Faulkner, with a few teachers in tow, appeared on the edge of the courtyard in distraught shock. They attempted to restore order over the melee and the burning marquee in vain.

Benson peeled back away from his stall and ran with Rayish around to the front of the main building and up the stairs into the entrance foyer. Blair tactfully withdrew from the riot and appeared at the same time. Fletch was already there. He hung up the public phone receiver, ending the call he just made to the police. He then tripped the school's fire alarm.

The response was swift. Within three to four minutes, they could hear a cacophony of sirens roaring towards the school. Three patrol cars followed by two fire trucks screeched to a halt outside the front foyer. A sergeant leading half a dozen officers, raced up the stairs and in through the entrance. They were greeted by Fletch, Blair, Rayish and Benson and a few perplexed school staff who had gathered in the foyer.

Fletch immediately introduced himself and his status as school captain, instantly becoming the sergeant's go-to person. He calmly briefed the sergeant on the situation before Mr Faulkner arrived, in a white-hot temper.

"YOU!" Mr Faulkner seethed, pointing his finger at Fletch. "YOU did this!"

"And… who are you?" the sergeant asked.

"Mr Faulkner… I'm the principal of this school," he replied. "Arrest this student. He and his friends are the ones who have instigated this riot," he commanded.

"Well, this student… Fletch, I believe… is the one who called us," the sergeant said.

"Of course he did… he's the one who planned it all."

"Stand aside, Mr Faulkner."

The sergeant marched everyone out to the courtyard, to see the ruckus firsthand, which now included two panicked teachers dangerously brandishing fire extinguishers around a group of scuffling students. The sergeant issued orders to his officers, who immediately took down and handcuffed four of the biggest students, which effectively brough an instant cessation to the riot. The firemen took possession of the fire extinguishers and had the fire out in seconds. Calm returned to the courtyard.

The police officers rounded up all the students and detained them in the basketball arena, while they recorded everyone's name and began to take statements of what transpired. The fireman cleared the area of any further threat.

"Shall we go to Mr Faulkner's office and clear this mess up," Fletch suggested.

"Yes, perfect!" Mr Faulkner agreed. "I'll explain everything... how they brought this school into disrepute."

"Very well!" the sergeant replied. "You two... with me," he said to two officers.

"Come along, you lot... I'll have you all expelled by the end of the day," Mr Faulkner vowed angrily to Fletch's entourage.

Mr Faulkner turned and led the way through the teacher's wing to his office.

Mr Faulkner permitted the sergeant, one officer and only Fletch into his office. Blair, Rayish, Benson and the second officer remained in reception. Leaning forward behind the desk with his arms outstretched and hands clenched in a fist upon the tabletop, Mr Faulkner looked at Fletch with pure hatred and contempt.

"When I explain to the sergeant what you've done to this school, I'm going to expel you immediately, Fletch," he said angrily.

"I think we all need to calm down a little," the sergeant suggested.

"Yes, I think we all need to take a minute here," Fletch agreed and immediately interjected. "Before Mr Faulkner starts on his raving rant, I have something for you, sergeant," he said.

Fletch opened the lapel to his blazer and withdrew a one-page document from the inside pocket and handed it to the sergeant. Surprised, Mr Faulkner instantly stood up straight.

"Wha... What's this?" Mr Faulkner stammered.

The sergeant calmly took hold of the document, opened it and read the contents. He then handed the document over to his officer to bear witness.

"Well, what is it?" Mr Faulkner asked, becoming rather flabbergasted.

"It's a search warrant," the sergeant stated flatly. "For this office!"

"What!?!" Mr Faulkner exclaimed, going white in the face. "That's impossible! That's not legal! He can't do that?" he shouted.

"Calm down, Mr Faulkner," the sergeant warned and handed the document over for Mr Faulkner to examine. "Well, this is rather unusual, I must say," he said glancing at Fletch a little puzzled. "As you can see, it IS signed and stamped by a judge of the Philadelphia district court. Everything seems to be in perfect order, Mr Faulkner!"

Mr Faulkner stared at the document. He could not read the text. His eyes filled with panic.

"You can't do this. I forbid it," Mr Faulkner said sternly.

The sergeant sensed that something was wrong.

"Please stand aside by the wall over there, Mr Faulkner," he instructed while he slowly brought his right hand up closer to the pistol holstered on his hip.

Mr Faulkner glance down at the sergeant's gun. He moved and stood against the side wall.

The sergeant called in the second officer and instructed them both to search the office, while he maintained a firm, steady gaze upon Mr Faulkner.

The officers searched the desk, the filing cabinets and the built-in cabinets along the opposite wall and didn't find anything unusual. The officers stood in front of the metal cupboard against the back wall. It was locked. Mr Faulkner reluctantly handed over the keys. The officer released the lock and slid the right-hand door open. He soon found the safe.

"What's the pin number, Mr Faulkner?" the sergeant asked.

"I refuse to give it to you until my attorney gets here," Mr Faulkner replied, in a desperate bid to delay proceedings.

"You're only delaying the inevitable," the sergeant said.

"You were born in 1944… weren't you Mr Faulkner?" Fletch asked, suddenly interrupting.

Mr Faulkner turned to Fletch, stunned. "What?"

"The year you were born… was 1944, right?"

Mr Faulkner gawked at him in stunned silence. Fletch turned to the sergeant.

"He was born in 1944, sergeant," he said once more.

"What? Oh, right! Try one, nine, double four," he said to the officer.

The officer nodded, pressed the combination and the lock released. He swung the door open and peered inside the safe. He reached in and drew out the shallow metal box. He climbed to his feet, walked over and placed the box on the desk in front of his sergeant and decided it would be best to hand over Mr Faulkner's set of keys as well. He stepped back.

Using the smallest key, the padlock opened with a snap. The sergeant gently removed the padlock, lifted the latch and opened the lid, which he simply allowed to fall back. He reached into the box and grabbed half a dozen 3.5 inch floppy disc drives. He flipped through the stack reading the label of each one, which denoted the property of either the US Marine Corps, the US Air Force or NASA.

"I believe you'll find Mr Faulkner is planning a trip to Vienna in July," Fletch added.

The sergeant turned to glare at Fletch, half in admiration and half in wonderment.

"Arrest Mr Faulkner, pending a further investigation to ascertain exactly what we have here. Lock him in the squad car and call the FBI immediately," he instructed his officers.

Mr Faulkner looked dejected as he was handcuffed and removed from his office. The FBI soon arrived and took possession of the evidence and custody of Mr Faulkner. The FBI recorded the personal details of Blair, Rayish and Benson, along with their statements, before releasing them after an hour. The interview with Fletch was far more comprehensive. He presented the photo of Mr Faulkner's sister and a detailed description of her burly eastern European accomplice. He was finally released well after school had ended.

Fletch calmly walked out through the side exit of the main building and into the courtyard, which was still a mess from the riot. It was quiet, with just two janitors busy with the clean-up operation. One entire section of shrubs and hedges had been badly singed by the fire.

Fletch passed through the courtyard in silence. He soon reached the back fence of the school's boundary. The gate into the staff car park was open. He intended to walk home through the back streets and parks. Pleased with his accomplishment, a thin smile began to emerge. He was also relieved that he and his friends were now safe once more.

****

Just as Fletch walked through the gate, a large unmarked black sedan suddenly drove down the street and stopped right in front of him. Fletch was startled but held his nerve and stood still. A tall man dressed in a simple black suit, white-collared shirt and long black tie, opened and stepped out from the passenger door. A second man dressed exactly alike, disembarked from the rear right-hand door and moved around to stand behind the vehicle on Fletch's right.

"Mr Fletch Braxton... I presume?" the first man asked.

"Yes!" Fletch replied, hesitant, uncertain.

"I'm Agent Jones," he said and briefly brandished his identity card. "That's Agent Williams," he continued nodding in the direction of the other man. "And that's… Agent driver," he said with a mischievous smirk as he flipped his thumb back in the direction of the driver.

"Ok!" Fletch acknowledged the introductions.

Agent Jones opened the lapel of his jacket and withdrew a one-page document, from the inside pocket. It had been folded perfectly into thirds to fit comfortably into an envelope. He opened the document and briefly allowed Fletch to inspect its written content.

"Mr Fletch Braxton! What I have here is a letter that I believe you, yourself, have prepared. Is that correct?" Agent Jones asked.

"Yes… it does look like it," Fletch replied, as his thin smile quickly returned.

"Well, looking closely at this parchment, Mr Braxton…" Agent Jones began, holding the page up to the fading light, "…it has a watermark. I believe it's the watermark of one Mr Carter Braxton's family coat of arms. Does this mean this parchment is over two hundred years old?" he asked.

"Yes, that's correct," Fletch replied.

"The envelope was sealed with a wax stamp… which I believe also belonged to… Mr Carter Braxton?" Agent Jones said and looked up at Fletch. "Yes?"

"Umm, yes, that's correct," Fletch replied.

"How did you manage to acquire these items?" Agent Jones asked.

"Family heirlooms," Fletch answered simply.

"Right!" Agent Jones said matter-of-factly. "Here is what you wrote…"

'To my director and, by extension, my president

Today, I have been elected as the senior school captain of Northside Chestnut Grove Academy. This feat is by no means an accident or an act of chance.

For as long as I can remember, I have been possessed by only one ambition. It drives me and consumes me like no other. I wish to serve my country in the best and only way I know how. I will stop at nothing until I achieve my goal... to be... in your likeness and become the director of the most powerful institution on the planet.

You may believe I'm being foolish or question my motives, but I assure you that I've never been more serious than I am right now. To prove my conviction, my capacity to serve, please accept what I shall bestow upon Northside Chestnut Grove Academy over the course of the year ahead as my audition, my application:

To infiltrate the Academy's media publication and turn it against the school,

To embroil the Academy in litigation,

To bring disrepute upon its ruling class,

To break down its structure of governance, and

To instigate civil dissension in the general population.

My only purpose is to protect the pillars of our great nation, against the threats of an ever-evolving, uncertain and unforgiving world.

America's most patriotic servant,

Sincerely yours,
Fletch Braxton.'

Agent Jones closed and folded the letter.

"That's quite a letter, Mr Braxton," he said. "And I most certainly have been watching."

He returned the letter to his inside pocket, straightened his jacket and stared at Fletch.

"Whether intentional or not… you have managed to uncover a sleeping spy cell, Mr Braxton. We have been searching for a mole for a quite a few years now. And, in time, I'm sure Mr Faulkner will reveal his whole network. Who would have thought… the principal of an esteemed private high school… would be a spy?" he said and paused. "So, now, what are we going to do with you?" Agent Jones pondered.

"I would've thought that was quite obvious," Fletch replied.

"Yes, but you will have to earn it, Mr Braxton," Agent Jones countered. "Anyway, I believe it has already been decided. It's far better for everyone that… you remain on our side."

"I'm pleased we understand each other, Agent Jones," Fletch said with a broad smile.

"Yes, indeed. I have orders to bring you in for your first… briefing, Mr Braxton. And when you have completed your last few weeks of school, we shall recruit you and begin your initial training within each branch of the military," Agent Jones announced. "Are you ready?"

Agent Jones opened the rear-left passenger door of the motor vehicle and waited a few moments for Fletch to climb in. Agent Jones closed the door and took his own seat as did Agent Williams. The black sedan gently pulled away from the kerb and accelerated down the street.

Following June 2002 – And the End of High School

Derrick Hackett entered a photographic arts school to pursue further studies in his career ambition. The legal action against the school was finally resolved. The school was able to retain its use of detention as a means of punishment. However, the school had to allow the student a means to apply for a leave of absence to attend a prior engagement to which the student was committed and that was important to their development. If the student could demonstrate continual involvement in the activity, the school could not deny or withhold a leave of absence without exceptional cause. The school was required to compensate Derrick for the loss of his first prize winnings.

Rayish received an internship with CNN's New York bureau, to assist with news gathering, special feature programmes, digital and sports projects and the daily operations of broadcasting. She also successfully gained entry into college to study a part-time business and journalism degree. Rayish did compile a commemorative Prom booklet which was published and distributed during the final month of high school using the remaining funds raised by the multicultural club. It was another smash hit.

Benson Thomas won a scholarship to study and complete a degree in law at Harvard University, while playing college basketball. He would pass the bar examination and begin his professional career working under his uncle, in the family law firm.

Blair Depler also won a scholarship to study and complete a degree in political science, also at Harvard University. He would go on to begin his professional career working as a junior analyst and aide for the Republican Senator for Pennsylvania.

Did Fletch Braxton provide some assistance, some influence, with the winning and awarding of these scholarships and posts? Maybe! Probably! One thing was certain, no senior student would ever forget the class of 2001–2002.

Twenty years further on, at the age of thirty-eight, Fletch Braxton was appointed by the President of the United States of America, in gratitude for outstanding service, to become the youngest Director of Operations for the CIA.

Epilogue

Spoiler Alert!

Warning – To read the epilogue first, will ruin the big reveal of each story! Do **NOT** proceed unless you have worked your way through each and every story.

The purpose of this epilogue is to ensure the correct understanding of how the key pieces from each story fit together to create a much larger reality.

Lost Soul, Lost City: Jaxon is the first of nine heroes. He successfully creates his Causal Body just before being drawn to New York City. A prerequisite, the purpose of the Causal Body is twofold: to utilise an alien technology and to perceive an alternate dimension. Jaxon reveals a total of five dimensions: physical, etheric, prime materium, monadic, and godly, which supersedes, overlays and imbues everything below with the mind of God. These dimensions are imagined through the merging of sacred geometry and Qabalistic philosophy. The secret base beneath the Con Edison Hydroelectric Power Station was built by an alien intelligence, to whom the androids belong. After successfully completing his trial, Jaxon gains direct access to the collective field of human consciousness and the power of quantum entanglement... more on that later.

Resonance of the Bison: Zachariah awakens to realise his spiritual connection with the American buffalo, or bison. His mission is to help save the bison from extermination with the aid of a resonating ruby. Although never revealed, the ruby is seeded by the cosmic being of the same name. Three themes are introduced to build the reader's understanding: resonance, the universal energy field, and Wetiko.

The Rose: Arissa and Ellantine are gifted the cuttings for a tree of roses, which acts as a conduit allowing them to commune with the universal energy field. This field is subdivided by the individual resonance and frequency fields of every species of creature in existence. All of nature, including humans, are thus interconnected. Ellantine, the second hero of nine, successfully creates her Causal Body by the time she completes her trek around the world. She can project an emotional resonance towards a targeted creature to induce a required response.

Alienation Games: Theo faces a massive internal conflict, which is the first demonstration of what is required to build a Causal Body – the dissolving of all negative physical, emotional and mental desires. After enduring the dark night of the soul during his trek to the mountains, Theo successfully builds his Causal Body, becoming the third hero of nine. Once he stands in the light, his emotional clairvoyance, which detects the emotional resonance in all humans, fully evolves. He soon discovers someone with a brain implant and a conspiracy to take over the world's financial system. After withstanding a psychic attack, Theo is compelled to find its source.

Lightning: Barrin serves the cosmic being Emerald and is imbued with lightning speed and accuracy, governed by the rule of 'though shalt not kill'. He can understand all human languages. With Emerald's perception of the future, Barrin works to protect the destiny of those who help push darkness out of human civilization, while forces born of darkness try to prevent this from happening. This cosmic battle between light and dark is played out through human history.

Chickamauga Chill: Three members of the Rose and Cross, Robert, Lesley and Christopher arrive on the eve of the civil war battle of Chickamauga. They are entrusted to locate, contain and destroy a fear demon born from the Wetiko of war. The transformation of evil intent into action produces dark etheric energy, which coagulates to create a fear demon and subsequently a spectre. Once struck, Christopher Dee is afflicted with demon sight through his left eye.

The Desolate: Through immense trauma, Leethil transforms into the most feared warrior among the Orraman, who possess brain implant technology and the means for interstellar space travel. The Orraman are covertly invading our planet, where Leethil will soon arrive on Earth.

Sovereignty In the School Yard: On commencement of the novel, Fletch is the director of operations for the CIA, with the resources of the entire US Government at his disposal, and access to its deepest held secrets. He soon discovers a threat not of this world and realises that our planet is ill-equipped or even correctly structured to mount a feasible defence.

To be continued...

www.ingramcontent.com/pod-product-compliance
Lightning Source LLC
Chambersburg PA
CBHW060212030726
47499CB00004B/1010